He escorted Adeline back the way she had come. "I must thank you for saving me. I . . . I do not wish to think about what could have happened. I should never have gone off with him, but he made me think he was actually interested in . . . Suffice it to say, I know better now."

Lord Littleton grinned. "Maximus and I would never allow any harm to come to you."

She glanced down. The Great Dane was at her side, and she ran a hand along his back. "Then I must thank both of you." They had reached the turn before the path opened to the lawn when he stopped. "Is something wrong?"

With one long finger he traced her jaw, causing butterflies to lodge in her chest. Then his lips brushed against hers once, twice, then settled briefly as his fingers stroked her cheek. "I never kissed Lady Dorie."

Adeline had not asked the question. She was not even sure she had thought about it, but if she had, she would have assumed that he had kissed her friend. Was that not what rakes did? "You didn't?"

One corner of his mouth tilted and brought out the dimple. "No."

"You should not kiss me either." Yet her words were not nearly as firm as she wanted them to be. Suddenly, she didn't know what to think. Her mind was so focused on the feeling in her lips, she couldn't think . . .

The MOST ELIGIBLE LORD In LONDON

ELLA QUINN

ZEBRA BOOKS
KENSINGTON PUBLISHING CORP.
www.kensingtonbooks.com

ZEBRA BOOKS are published by

Kensington Publishing Corp.
119 West 40th Street
New York, NY 10018

All Kensington titles, imprints, and distributed lines are available at special quantity discounts for bulk purchases for sales promotion, premiums, fund-raising, educational, or institutional use.

Special book excerpts or customized printings can also be created to fit specific needs. For details, write or phone the office of the Kensington Sales Manager: Attn.: Sales Department. Kensington Publishing Corp., 119 West 40th Street, New York, NY 10018. Phone: 1-800-221-2647.

Zebra and the Z logo Reg. U.S. Pat. & TM Off.

First Printing: April 2020
ISBN-13: 978-1-4201-4967-8
ISBN-10: 1-4201-4967-9

ISBN-13: 978-1-4201-4968-5 (eBook)
ISBN-10: 1-4201-4968-7 (eBook)

10 9 8 7 6 5 4 3 2 1

Printed in the United States of America

Chapter One

Frederick, Lord Littleton—Frits to his mother and grandmother—gave one final twitch to his cravat before allowing his valet to attach his pocket watch and quizzer. "Lord Turley is dining with me this evening."

"I shall inform the cook, my lord."

"You'd better tell my mother as well." Frits took his hat and gloves. "She should arrive at any time now."

"Yes, my lord." Ayles opened the door to the chamber and bowed. "We shall all be glad to have her ladyship in residence."

Frits refrained from answering. After the fine kettle of fish he'd made of things last Season, it wasn't just his staff that would be pleased Mama was in Town. He should be the most eligible gentleman in London, but for his "mistake," as she so delicately put it.

His butler opened the door as he approached. It was time to face the *ton* in the most public forum possible. The Grand Strut.

Nodding to his groom, he took the reins and swung up on his Friesian horse, Apollo. Never had Frits been so uncertain of his reception in the *ton* as he was today.

Fortunately, he wouldn't be alone for long. His friend Gavin, Viscount Turley, had promised to meet him at the Park. Frits's hands grew damp in the gloves. He hadn't been this nervous since his first day at Eton. Still, it was his own damned fault. Hopefully, no one would remember how badly he had behaved last year. And if they did, he would simply have to prove he'd learned his lesson.

Entering the Park through Grosvenor Gate, he almost turned around and went home. But if he lost his nerve now, it would be worse later. Perhaps he'd be lucky, and the matchmaking mamas would ignore his past behavior in favor of all his good points, mainly his bloodline, wealth, and title. And there was a whole new group of young ladies making their come out this year who must be married off. Not that he was going to advertise his hopes of finding a wife this Season. That would be folly.

Blast it all. Why had he decided to look for a wife in the first place? He should have just done what his father and every other Littleton had done for centuries: wait until he had to marry.

Pulling himself together, he rode onto the carriageway. Within a few seconds, he found himself being genially greeted by four matrons in a landau. The tension eased out of his shoulders. Perhaps it wouldn't be as bad as he'd imagined.

"Lord Littleton"—Lady Wall wiggled her fingers at him—"I am glad to find you in Town."

The lady next to her raised interested blue eyes to his, gave him a come-hither look, and said, "I do not believe we have been introduced."

"Oh, my," Lady Wall exclaimed. "It did not occur to me that you did not know his lordship. Allow me to make Lord Littleton known to you. My lord, this is Lady Holloway."

"It is a pleasure to meet you, my lord." Her generous lips rose in a smile.

In the past, he would have immediately returned her look for one of his own and made an arrangement to meet in a more secluded place. But his hunting instinct didn't press him the way it used to. Perhaps that was the reason he'd decided to wed. He bowed. "The pleasure is mine."

Lady Wall indicated the other two matrons in the carriage. "I trust you remember Lady Jersey and Lady Sefton?"

"Naturally." Frits bowed again, and they exchanged greetings. "Ladies, I hope I find you in good health."

"And you, my lord." Lady Sefton inclined her head.

As the landau moved forward, Frits scanned the verge. He saw the one lady he had not wished to see, Lady Dorie Calthorp—daughter of the Marquis of Huntingdon, and his mistake—strolling with four other ladies. He'd behaved badly toward her last Season. Though not on purpose. For too long, he thought they would be a good match. But the more he grew to know her and her strengths and desires for her life, the more he was convinced marrying her would be a horrible mistake. But instead of finding a way to tell her, he'd fled London and returned to Littlewood, his main estate. And now it was too late to attempt to explain his panic. If he'd even had the words.

After taking a breath, he let it out slowly. He might as well get this over with. Frits just hoped she didn't give him the cut direct.

Riding over to the group, he gave her his friendly smile. "Lady Dorie, well-met."

The smile she returned was strained, and her eyes

were hard. "Lord Littleton, I did not know you were in Town."

"I arrived yesterday." If looks could kill, he'd be lying on the ground bleeding. "Have you been in Town long?"

"Long enough." Her words were clipped. She turned to the other ladies and made an elegant gesture toward him. "On the subject of gentlemen who appear eligible and are not, permit me to introduce to you Lord Littleton." Damn and blast it. He fought to maintain his amiable countenance. She was obviously going to do her best to ensure he didn't have an easy time finding a wife. "My lord, Lady Adeline Wivenly, Lady Augusta Vivers, Miss Featherton, and Miss Stern."

He forced a smile and made what he knew was a stylish bow. "Ladies, it is a pleasure to meet you. I hope you enjoy your time in the metropolis." Miss Stern gave him a hard look. Had Lady Dorie already blackened his name to her friend? Lady Augusta was polite but unaffected, as if she did not care one way or the other if she met him. Miss Featherton had narrowed her eyes as if assessing his worth as a human being. That was disconcerting, but it ran in her family. He knew her older brother and sister.

Then there was Lady Adeline. She just stared at him with considering, soft, gray eyes that shone like silver. Curls of gleaming, dark, honey-blond hair framed her face. She was utterly entrancing. Immediately, he wanted to know what she was thinking. As if she realized she should not continue to look at him, she dropped her gaze, and thick, brown lashes fluttered to her cheeks, drawing his attention to her straight, little nose and a light sprinkling of freckles. If only he'd met her in other company. Naturally, he could not help but notice her deep rose lips and the fact that her bottom lip was just a bit plumper than the top one. His gaze dropped lower, and he sucked in a breath. Even her demure spencer couldn't hide the bounty beneath. He could have licked his lips at the thought of her in an evening gown. Here was a lady worth getting to know.

Frits dragged his gaze back to Lady Dorie but was unable to maintain his smile in the face of her displeasure. Not that it mattered. He'd found out what he needed to. She wasn't going to cut him. Although she'd stick a spoke in his wheel if she could. As reluctant as he was to leave Lady Adeline, it was time to depart. "I hope to see you as well, my lady." He glanced at her friends, allowing his gaze to linger longer on Lady Adeline. "I look forward to seeing all of you again."

"I suppose that is unavoidable." Lady Dorie dipped a slight curtsey. Not shallow enough to be insulting, but then again, her manners had always been impeccable. "Good day to you, my lord."

Touching his fingers to his hat, he made his escape as quickly as he could without drawing attention to himself. As he rode around the carriageway, he was greeted warmly by other gentlemen and ladies. Apparently only Lady Dorie was holding his behavior against him. Then again, it had affected her the most. Hopefully, she would find another gentleman and if not forgive him, then forget him.

He was halfway around the Park when Turley arrived. "Littleton, how have you been?"

"Well enough." Together, they turned and proceeded at a walk. "How is your sister?" The former Elizabeth Turley, now the Countess of Harrington, was with her husband in Paris. Frits had developed a *tendre* for her before she married. Not that he'd ever had a chance of gaining her affections. She was deeply in love with her husband. What had drawn him to her more than anything was that she had not been at all susceptible to him. The time they'd spent together had been for the sole purpose of bringing Harrington up to scratch. That she had no reaction to Frits at all had been a new experience for him.

"Thriving." Turley grinned. "She and Harrington now have a little girl. I'm heading over to France when the Season ends. You should join me."

"I keep thinking I will, but once I get back home, I can't seem to leave." In fact, Frits preferred Littlewood to almost anywhere else except a few of his other estates. Which was a bit of a problem when it came to marriage. Most ladies wanted more society than he liked. The endless round of house parties, or visiting Brighton, or even coming to London in autumn had never appealed to him, even though it meant he did not have to go without female companionship for any length of time. One of the most important things his father had told him was never to have liaisons with women near or on his estates. The bored matrons and widows of the *ton* knew the rules; others might not.

His friend chuckled. "I firmly believe that if it wasn't for the occasional vote in the Lords, you wouldn't come to Town at all."

He couldn't help but agree. "I probably would not. Nevertheless, it's time I start my nursery, and this is the best place to do it. I've been to all the local assemblies and did not find a lady I could face over the breakfast table for the rest of my life."

Turley lost his smile. "Did you see Lady Dorie?"

"I did." Frits glanced at his friend. "She greeted me and introduced me to four other young ladies." He pulled a face. "She described me as 'a gentleman who seemed eligible but was not.'" Frits almost wished he hadn't decided to lease the house he used for his indulgences. Yet, if he was serious about finding a wife— and he was—he could not continue to carry on as he had been. That would insult any lady he decided to court.

"Ouch." Turley grimaced. "That's not going to help you."

Frits's thoughts precisely. "I suppose it could have been worse."

Turley began walking his gelding, and Frits did the same. "The good news is that I've been here for a week and have not heard any talk about you and Lady Dorie. I think most of Polite Society has forgotten, if they cared at all. You were fairly circumspect."

He was glad to hear that bit of news. Yet, he hadn't thought of his behavior as prudent. Neither had his mother. "My mother is arriving today. I am to be chaperoned this Season."

Turley shook his head and started to laugh. "It's about time she took you in hand. You raise hopes without even trying."

Frits rolled his eyes to the sky. But he couldn't argue that his friend was wrong. He'd always had problems with ladies thinking he cared more than he did. That was one of the reasons he did not often attend entertainments where he might be introduced to young ladies. Last Season was the first time in years he'd done so, and look what happened. If only he hadn't lost his nerve about telling Lady Dorie what he'd decided. He truly did hope she would soon find a gentleman who could make her happy. She was a fine woman, even if she wasn't for him.

He had to get over this guilt he was feeling. Maybe

he should find a way to help her. On second thought, that probably was not a good idea.

"Lord Turley and Lord Littleton," Lady Bellamny hailed them, and Frits repressed a shudder. The lady was a terror. And she was accompanied by Mrs. Drummond-Burrell, another dragon. "I shall send you cards to my ball." She lifted her lorgnette to her eyes. "And expect to see you there."

"Yes, my lady."

"Yes, my lady." They'd answered at the same time, sounding like schoolboys.

She motioned for her driver to move on before they even had a chance to acknowledge the other woman.

"Devil of a lady," Turley said admiringly. "She scares me to death."

"I think she scares all unwed gentlemen of marriageable age to death." She was always more than willing to help snare a man in the parson's mousetrap.

As they came to the gate leading onto Park Lane, Turley said, "After that, I'd like a drink. I'm going to Brooks's. Would you like to join me?"

"I might as well." Frits had braved most of the ladies. Now it was time to discover if the gentlemen were as willing to accept him as their wives were.

As they rode out of the Park, a familiar-looking, bright-green landau was making its way in. He trotted up to greet her. "Mama, when did you arrive?"

"Frits, you look like you survived your first foray into Polite Society." His mother smiled. "Shortly after you left. I decided to take a look around while my maid was unpacking. There is no time like the present to see and hear what has been going on." She inclined her head to Turley. "It's good to see you, Gavin. I expect to hear all about your sister at dinner this evening." She fluttered her fingers at them. "I shall see you later."

"She is entirely too cheerful," Frits said, more to himself than his friend. When she'd informed him that she would be in Town with him this Season, she'd refused to answer his questions about what exactly she was going to do.

"Well, at least she'll keep you from making a muck of it around the marriageable ladies." Turley chuckled. "You need to keep in mind that being wed is for life, not a night or two."

"I am well aware of that. It's not like I planned to get myself into so much trouble." Frits glared at his friend. It was so much easier when his only interest in a woman was slaking his lust and hers.

"It will take me about half an hour to change," Turley said.

"I'll see you at Brooks's in just under an hour." Frits saluted his friend as he rode toward Grosvenor Square.

Maybe he should just go home again. Then the image of a pair of intelligent, silvery gray eyes formed in his brain. On the other hand, perhaps he'd stay and see what happened. There was just something about Lady Adeline—beyond her lips and breasts—that made him want to know her better. The one difficulty was that she was a friend of Lady Dorie's, and that wouldn't help him at all.

Chapter Two

Adeline almost gasped at Dorie's comment about Lord Littleton. Only by giving him the cut direct could she have insulted him more. He must have done something horrible to her.

Yet, despite her friend's obvious dislike of the man, Adeline could not help but notice Lord Littleton as he rode away. He sat his horse as if he'd been born riding. And that horse. She had seen pictures of Friesians before, but had never seen a real one. She would have loved to have been able to at least stroke the magnificent animal. If not for watching the horse trot toward them, she would have failed to notice how Lord Littleton's broad shoulders flexed under the well-fitting jacket, and his muscular legs incased in the tight pantaloons were works of art. When he had gazed at her, a lock of his curling black hair had fallen forward, making her want to touch it. And as their eyes met, his emerald ones seemed to warm, making her feel as if she was the only lady, the only person, he could see. Then a dimple appeared on his left cheek. It was a shame he was ineligible; he really was the most handsome man she had ever seen.

"What makes him ineligible?" Georgie asked more bluntly than Adeline ever would have put it.

Adeline glanced at Dorie, waiting to hear the answer.

"He has no desire to marry." Her tone was sharp and bitter. "But he will make a lady think she is his sun, moon, and stars."

In other words, a rake.

Adeline bit down on her lip. Dorie was probably not the only lady he had led on. Adeline knew all about rakes: men who merely played with a lady's heart and did not care how badly he hurt her. Her brother Wivenly had been one, and he'd broken a lot of hearts. At least, that is what she had gathered from over-hearing parts of her parents' conversations. He had even offered to ruin a lady and not marry her.

As far as she was concerned, they did not make good husbands. Not that her brother would stray. He was devoted to his wife, but he certainly was not a comfort-able man. She was sure that came from being a rake and having his way for far too long.

Adeline was not exactly certain what she wanted, but she knew she did not wish for a life like her mother's. She might not know everything she wanted in a gentleman, but she knew what she did not want, and a rake was at the top of the list, followed by ex-cesses in drinking, gambling, wenching, club atten-dance, and politics. She wished for a gentleman who did not pull-cuffs with her every time she turned around, but could enjoy a quiet evening and remain in the country most of the year. Unlike her mother, she would spend time with her children. And she would have a dog—in the house. Something that she had *never* been allowed to have.

That Lord Littleton was a rake was more than a bit disappointing. He *was* very handsome. Adeline men-tally crossed him off her list of none. In any event, it would have been too much to hope that she would meet her true love on her first stroll in the Park.

Ah, well, she sighed to herself. There would be other fish in the sea.

Another gentleman rode up and was introduced as Lord Turley. He was good-looking as well, though his fair, blond looks were not nearly as compelling as Lord Littleton's black hair and emerald-green eyes. But most rakes were handsome and interesting. That was the only way they got away with breaking hearts. Lord Turley was much safer, but Georgie seemed interested in him, and Adeline did not wish to run afoul of her new friend. She was fortunate to have found four ladies she got on so well with in such a short time. She let out a soft sigh. At least she knew which gentleman she would avoid.

The talk turned to Almack's and balls, particularly Augusta's come out ball, which would be the first to be held. Adeline's was not until a few weeks later. They also discussed ways to protect each other from unwanted attention from gentlemen.

Apparently Lord Littleton was not the only rake in Town. "We could even think up some scenarios to help each other," she suggested. "Augusta, can you arrange for us to come to Rothwell House so that we can learn where everything is?"

"Of course," Augusta agreed, but appeared con-fused. "How will that aid us when we will not know the other houses?"

"We will practice slipping away to be found." Not that Adeline thought she had anything to worry about. She was passably pretty, but not beautiful like her friends were.

"Like the game Sardines," Augusta said. Adeline had

never heard of the game. Fortunately, her friend saw their confused expressions and explained, "In Sardines, one person hides and the others find her. It is played in Spain."

"Sardines it is." Henrietta laughed.

It did sound like fun. Adeline looked forward to learning how to help her friends avoid rakes.

"Will you attend Almack's this week?" Augusta's forehead had furrowed. She really wasn't looking forward to going.

"I'll be there with Dotty and Merton." Henrietta used a reassuring tone. "It will be interesting. Think of it as an experiment."

"I suppose I could do that." Augusta did not sound convinced.

"Interesting is one way to put it," Georgie muttered. "I hear that the refreshments leave much to be desired. My mother, brother, and sister will escort me."

"Caro and Huntley are bringing me." Dorie's nose wrinkled. "Supper consists of thinly sliced stale bread and butter, weak tea, and orgeat."

It appeared as if all of them were being accompanied by their brothers or sisters. Adeline had wanted her mother to attend with her for the first time, but Mama had a political event she was helping to host. If Adeline heard another word about politics she was going to—to—well, she would have to think of something that was not too painful as she would no doubt be unable to avoid that topic. The Lords was in session, and most peers were involved in government.

"I will be there with my brother and sister-in-law. Wively complained about going, but Eugénie said he could remain home if he wished, and she would dance with whom she pleased." Remembering the look of pure outrage on his face, Adeline had to giggle. "She says it in such a way that makes one think she doesn't care one way or the other, but my brother hates whenever another gentleman stands up with her. So, he will escort us." Not that he would be much help when it came to knowing who was eligible and who was not. It was most depressing. How was she supposed to know who to encourage and who to discourage? Well, that was what friends were for. Especially Dorie. This was her second Season, and that gave her a great deal of knowledge Adeline and the others did not have.

As they strolled farther, Georgie fell in beside Adeline. "You look blue-deviled," Georgie said. "Did you not wish to come to Town?"

It occurred to Adeline that no one had actually *asked* if she wanted to come out this year. She had turned eighteen last autumn, and none of the gentlemen in her home county had interested her. Ergo, she had to make her come out at some point, so this Season was as good as any. "Coming to Town is fine. London seems interesting. The problem is that I have no idea how to go about looking for a husband."

Her friend laughed lightly. "I do not think any of us do. From what I have gathered, even Dorie does not know. My sister, Meg, took over three years to decide on a husband. She had a couple of bad experiences. If one thinks about it for too long, it's enough to put one off the whole thing."

That made Adeline feel somewhat better. Not that she wanted another lady to have had a hard time, but at least she was not the only one who felt at a loss. "We practice all sorts of things: manners, dancing, musical instruments, languages, and a host of other subjects. Then we arrive here and are told that gentlemen do not wish a lady to be intelligent. But my elder brother and my father married rational ladies. It is very confusing."

Georgie's brows came together as she frowned. "Did your family tell you that? Mine told me that if a gentleman did not want an intelligent female, he could look somewhere else for a wife."

Adeline had to think about that. "No. Not my family, so much as other ladies with whom I have spoken. My mother is so busy with her political events, she has not paid much attention to my come out at all."

"I do not know if that is good or bad," Georgie mused. "Sometimes I feel as if I would like everyone in my family to spend less time thinking about me." She grinned. "Fortunately, I only have my mother and grandmother. My older sister has been busy setting her husband's family to rights."

Adeline wondered what that meant, but decided she would find out at some point. "My sister-in-law has promised help, but she was raised in the Danish West Indies and has not spent much time in Town."

"That must have been interesting. Do not be concerned. It will work out." Georgie linked her arm with Adeline's. "We all have one another now. That will help."

"Yes. You are correct. I should not worry so much." Instead, Adeline would enjoy the company of new friends and take in the beauty of the Park as the leaves began to unfurl. Crocuses were popping up, making bright patterns against the green of the grass. She looked forward to the other spring flowers making a showing. "I shall focus on enjoying my time here. And if I am not married this Season, there is always the next one."

"That is it exactly and how it should be. I feel deeply for the ladies who are being pressured to wed in their first Season." Georgie stopped and peered at the carriageway. "Who is that?"

A gentleman with curling guinea-gold hair riding a bay gelding had stopped and was talking to a lady in a high-perched phaeton. He too was extremely good-looking. Did all the handsome men in England come to Town for the Season? "I have no idea." Although Adeline would like to be introduced. "Perhaps Dorie knows him."

"Dorie?" Georgie raised her voice just enough for their friend, who was walking directly in front of them, to hear and inclined her head in the direction of the newcomer. "Do you know that gentleman?"

"No." Dorie shook her head. "I've not seen him before. He must be new in Town. He is speaking with Lady Riverton. She is my sister-in-law's dead brother's widow. Perhaps he has recently returned from his Grand Tour. She was in Paris until recently, and he does not appear to be in more than his middle twenties."

"I agree," Henrietta commented. "No more than six and twenty, I would say. Well, we can only trust we shall see him at one of the events."

"If he is looking for a wife." Georgie sounded dubious.

Adeline glanced at the man. He was bowing over her ladyship's hand, but there was really nothing in that.

"If he's not, then I do not care to meet him." A line formed between Dorie's brows. She was probably thinking about Lord Littleton. And truly, there was no point in meeting men who were not interested in marriage.

Adeline was still looking at the blond-haired gentleman when he raised his eyes and stared straight at her. She turned her head, but not before she saw his lips tilt slightly. Was it possible she had interested him? That would make two gentlemen—though she could not count the first—in one day who showed an interest in her. Goodness, the Season might not be as bad as she thought it would be. Of course, she must meet more eligible gentlemen. She glanced at the blond man next to Lady Riverton.

As much as Adeline wanted to marry and set up her own household, she had to be certain the gentleman she married met all of her qualifications—such as they were—and that it was a love match.

Crispin, Earl of Anglesey, eldest son of the Marquis of Normanby, held the light gray gaze of one of a bevy of young ladies strolling along the verge. He wondered how long he could keep her looking at him, but the lady next to her caught her attention and the gray-eyed lady turned away.

"I see you are already affecting the just-out-of-the-schoolroom set." The tone of Sarah, the widowed Countess of Riverton was irritable, and he wasn't in the mood for it. Still, for the time being, he needed her.

"I do not know why *you* are put out." He allowed his eyes to drop to hers. "You will not marry me, and my father has demanded I wed this Season or lose my allowance."

"You know very well I shall not wed again." She gave a dramatic shudder. "Once was more than enough. I did my duty, and thanks to my very generous settlements am able to pursue my own pleasures."

Except that she was not thinking of those pleasures at the moment. One of which included him. Crispin decided to change the subject. He always knew when Sarah thought too much about her sons. She became maudlin. She was allowed to see them as much as she wished, but they resided with their grandparents, the Marquis and Marchioness of Broadhurst, and were never brought to Town. Meaning Sarah had to go to the country to visit her children. Not that Crispin blamed her husband for leaving guardianship with his parents. That was the proper thing to do. It just made her less than companionable at times.

He knew one way to cheer her, and him. "Would you like me to stop by this evening?"

"If you wish." As she spoke, she lifted one shoulder in an uncaring shrug. "However, you may not stay the night. I must be more careful here than in Paris."

"Naturally." She wasn't the only one who had to watch herself. He did as well. Any number of people could report his activities to his father. Taking her hand, he kissed the air above the fine kid glove, but as he did, he softly stroked her wrist, and she gave him a seductive look. "Dinner, then dessert?"

"Definitely dessert." He was already picturing her naked and in bed.

Her lips parted in a smile. "I shall see you at eight."

"Until then." Crispin moved on until Mrs. Drummond-Burrell caught his attention. She was a rather homely woman with a long face, riding in a landau with another lady he did not know. Mrs. Drummond-Burrell knew his mother, but, more importantly, she would give him access to Almack's, thus granting him entrée to all the most eligible ladies. And birth was an essential consideration in a wife to his parents, and therefore to him. His wife's bloodlines had to be pure. "Ma'am, it is a pleasure to meet you again."

"Anglesey, I am glad to see you back home again." She held out her hand, and he made his bow. "Your mother wrote to me saying you would be here."

"Paris is lovely but nothing can compare with

England," he lied. He'd still be there if not for his mother's demands.

"Lady Bellamny"—Mrs. Drummond-Burrell glanced at the other lady—"may I make known to you Lord Anglesey?"

The older woman regally inclined her head. "Good day, my lord. I visited your mother before coming to Town."

He'd been wondering how to bring up his search for a wife. As both ladies obviously knew he was in the market, this was his opportunity. "Did she also tell you that I have been told not to show my face until I am betrothed?"

The woman chuckled. "I believe she did mention something to that effect. Clementina, you will have to send Anglesey a voucher for Almack's."

She lifted one thick brow. "Indeed I shall. Are you staying at Normanby House?"

"I am." Along with the servants his mother trusted would keep an eye on Crispin.

"I shall see you on Wednesday." She gave the signal for the carriage to move forward.

"I am honored." He left, making his way past the other carriages. All in all, this had been a productive outing. He was being admitted to Almack's, he'd seen a lady who interested him, and he had a bed partner for this evening.

Making his way out of the Park, Crispin smiled, nodded, and greeted people he had met on the Continent and was introduced to other members of the *ton*. Some of them matrons whose eyes signaled their availability. He had resolved to be on his best behavior— most of the time. It would not do for his parents to get word he was raking about Town. That also meant he couldn't set up a mistress. Even his father—the easier of his parents—had particular ideas about one's conduct when courting a young lady. For the present, he had the lovely Sarah to satisfy any of those needs, but he could not deny other ladies who wished the pleasure of his company. After all, a man could not be expected to ignore his desires. He would simply have to find a set of rooms or a small house for his liaisons. Somewhere his mother's servants could not spy on him.

Chapter Three

On Wednesday evening, Adeline stared at herself in the mirror. The pale yellow gown with her pearl earrings and necklace were well enough, but she wished she could wear brighter colors. "Could we put an emerald-green ribbon in my hair?"

Her maid, Fendall, gave her a critical look before shaking her head. "Perhaps a Pomona green ribbon would look better."

"Anything to brighten me up a bit." Wearing brighter colors was one of the good things about marrying. At least her mother had not insisted she wear white. That would only serve to make her appear ill. But that might be because Mama did not look good in the color either.

Eugénie, Adeline's sister-in-law, knocked on the door and entered wearing a deep purple gown and diamonds. With her rich, chestnut hair and brown eyes, her sister-in-law was one of the most beautiful ladies she had ever seen, and Adeline wished she too was beautiful. "Are you about ready to depart? Will is running a finger between his neck and his cravat. One would think I was taking him to his execution."

Adeline burst out laughing. "He probably thinks you are. I remember Mama complaining that she had

had to drag him there one evening, and he never went again."

"*Tant pis.*" Eugénie shrugged. "He has nothing about which to be concerned. We are not to dance while chaperoning you." Stepping over to the toilet table, she looked at Adeline. "*Tu es très jolie.*"

"But not beautiful." And she never would be.

"Ah, *ma petite.*" Her sister-in-law smiled. "You are beautiful to your family and to the man who will love you." Adeline so wanted that to be true. "Beauty from within is more important than beauty on the outside. Never forget that." Eugénie stepped back as Fendall finished. "*Alors,* we must go before your brother loses his courage." As they made their way down the stairs to the hall where Will was waiting, she said, "I have not been to this place either. It will be the first time for both of us."

Adeline was convinced that even if her sister-in-law had made her come out in London, she would have walked into Almack's and immediately taken control of everyone, including the Patronesses. She, on the other hand, was quite nauseous.

The ride to the Assembly Room was mercifully short, and they arrived at the same time as Georgie and her mother, Lady Featherton. "Come." Georgie linked her arm with Adeline's. "I have been assured that the worst part of this is waiting to be approved to dance the waltz"—Adeline's stomach lurched—"and that the Patronesses will ensure that all the ladies just out will be approved."

"That is reassuring." As much as she tried to make her voice strong, it was thinner than she liked.

"If it makes you feel better, my mother confirmed that Dorie was right. The bread is stale, the lemonade and tea are weak, and the rooms are not opulent." Georgie slid Adeline a glance.

She took a breath and let it out. "Fine. I'll do my best not to be ill."

As it was, they quickly spotted their other friends and joined the circle being formed.

"Are you excited?" Adeline asked Augusta.

"I am . . . curious." She was gazing out at the number of people gathering. There had to be at least two hundred already, and guests were still arriving.

"You look like you are making a study of the mating behavior of an unknown civilization."

Her friend grinned. "I suppose in a way I am. I find many of the *ton*'s mannerisms curious."

"Lords Turley and Littleton are coming toward us," Georgie whispered and glanced at Dorie, who was talking to a worthy-looking gentleman.

Adeline slid a look across the Assembly Room. Drat. Georgie was right. To make it worse, he was even better-looking in evening clothes. *No rakes.* "I have no objection to Lord Turley, but I do not wish to have anything to do with Lord Littleton."

"You cannot refuse to dance with him." Georgie's tone had lowered even more.

"If he even asks me." Perhaps he would not. "He might ask you or Augusta instead."

"I do not think so." She pasted a polite smile on her face and curtseyed. "My lord. Good evening."

Lord Turley bowed. "Miss Featherton, might I ask you for this dance?"

"It would be my pleasure." He held out his arm and she took it, leaving Adeline to face Lord Littleton all by herself.

"My lady"—his voice was low and seductive, just like

a rake's, and his bow was elegant, but it was his deep, meadow-green eyes that held her plain gray ones as they had that afternoon. They still made her feel as if she was the only lady he saw. "Would you do me the honor of being my partner?"

She curtseyed and kept her tone cool. "I would be pleased"—not delighted—"to dance with you, my lord."

Those same eyes that had affected her a moment before now had a cynical cast as he held out his arm. "Thank you, my lady."

At least he seemed to understand that she was not the type of female who would fall into his arms. Not to mention he had hurt her friend's feelings last year and was not on her list of gentlemen to wed.

When they reached the dance floor, she was thankful the set was a country dance that required them to change partners. As he had asked her for this dance, he would not be able to ask her to stand up with him again this evening. A situation that suited her very well. What she did not understand was why her hand began to tingle when it touched his muscular arm. Not only that, but the tingling had spread through her fingers. Much like the electrical current she felt at times when she touched one of the barn cats during the winter. Adeline was positive he had caused it in some way; she just did not know how he could have done it.

As they skipped around the floor, she could not help but be impressed with his lordship's grace. Although she had noticed that many large men—including her brother—were equally agile. No doubt the ability to dance well was part of a rake's required accomplishments. Adeline wondered if there was a list or a guide they all followed. Something entitled *How to Be a Successful Rake*. Perhaps she and her friends could write a pamphlet on ways to recognize and avoid rakes. It would help a lot of ladies avoid falling victim to them.

They came together again and he took her hands. "Have you seen much of London?"

"Only if you consider the shopping areas 'much.'" Adeline had a list of places she wanted to visit before leaving the metropolis.

Lord Littleton grinned, and the dimple made an appearance. It was extremely unfair for men with strong jaws to have a dimple. It made them look much too safe. Something she knew his lordship was not. "Perhaps you will allow me to get up a party and escort you to one of the museums."

Before she could deny that she wished to go anywhere with him, the movement of the reel separated them again. When they came together again he did not mention his plan but turned the subject to the unseasonable cold. "I am concerned for the crops if this weather continues."

That was safe ground. "I cannot fault you for that. I would not wish to see another summer like we had two years ago."

"Indeed." His eyes twinkled at her like polished emeralds. "It would be calamitous."

"I agree." Why was he giving her such a look of approval?

"Tell me, my lady, do you enjoy the theater?" The music ended and he bowed while she curtseyed.

"I have only seen some traveling troupes my father hires to visit our market town. But I have enjoyed their performances."

"I am partial to comedies. Do you like them as well?"

"Oh, yes." They were her favorites. She did not understand how one could enjoy a tragedy nearly as much.

"The troupe last summer performed *A Midsummer's Night Dream*. The presentation was wonderful."

He held out his arm and she lightly placed her fingers on it, not wanting to experience the tingling sensation she'd had when he led her out to dance. Yet even now, sparks were popping.

This could not be good.

It was probably no more than an electrical charge. There was nothing else it *could* be. They were almost to Will and Eugénie; then she would take her hand from his arm and it would all be over.

Frits had stopped to suck in a breath when he spotted Lady Adeline across the room at Almack's. She had been pretty when he'd first met her, but now she was beautiful. He had been right about her bosoms. They were truly splendid. And the candles picked out her hair's golden hue, making it shimmer.

Turley slapped Frits's back, reminding him to walk forward. Yet as he greeted her and asked her to dance, he wondered briefly if he would have been better served by not asking one of Lady Dorie's friends to stand up with him. Neither Lady Adeline's gaze nor her manner had been more than merely polite. In fact, her eyes reminded him of scudding gray clouds before a storm. He was certain that if she could have refused to dance with him, she would have. It might have been unfair of him to ask the lady, but ever since they'd met, he'd wanted to stand up with her. He wanted to touch her even if it was only escorting her to and from the dance floor.

Still, getting to know her was going to be even harder than he'd originally believed. And he had not thought it would be easy in the first place. When he'd mentioned meeting her to his mother, she had pointed out that Lady Adeline might hold his behavior with Lady Dorie against him. He could understand loyalty. It was even possible he might feel the same about a lady who had hurt one of his friends. But how long could Lady Adeline's coolness last? Perhaps the better question was, how long was Frits willing to wait?

During the set, she was all that was well-mannered, but when she looked at him, her smile didn't reach her eyes, and, for the most part, her conversation did not rise above the mundane. He expected that from many young ladies, but not from her. Her intelligence had shone in her eyes before she had shuttered them to him, and he wanted to see it again. Lady Adeline was definitely a challenge, and he did like a good challenge.

Damnation. Was he doing it again? Deciding on a lady before he actually got to know her and what she wanted from life?

Yet he was drawn to her, more than he'd been to Lady Dorie. There was something about Lady Adeline that seemed quieter.

No, that wasn't it. He couldn't think of a word to describe her, but she was different. Yet, until he worked out what she wanted, the only thing he could do was take care that neither of them formed an attachment before he knew if they would suit.

Last year, he'd been dazzled by Lady Dorie's beauty and intelligence and had not thought beyond that. This year, he had to look deeper and move more slowly. The problem was, he did not like being dismissed out of hand. He was too used to not having to work for a lady's attention. Even if his initial thoughts about Lady Adeline were in error, he was determined that she would see him as something other than an object to be ignored.

Frits shook off his wounded pride and went back to reviewing their conversation. When he'd asked about the theater, he'd been happy with her response. He wished he could have spoken to her more, but the damned dance kept taking her away from him. The next time he asked her to dance it would be for a waltz. Perhaps he should have followed his mother's advice and petitioned Lady Jersey to allow him to waltz with Lady Adeline, but he'd done that with Lady Dorie last Season.

Bloody hellhounds.

Was he going to have to try not to repeat anything he'd done last year? That would be impossible. Yet there were only so many options for a gentleman courting a lady . . . Except that now he had his mother in Town. Ergo, getting up a party for the theater would not be difficult, nor would a party to do anything else. He could even ask her to give a ball and a dinner party. As he escorted Lady Adeline back to her brother and sister-in-law, Frits's good mood expanded as he saw his opportunities of contact with her increase. He'd have to speak with his mother about his plans soon.

He bowed to her again. "Thank you for the dance."

"It was my pleasure." Her tone was polite, but again her eyes gave her discontentment away. She really had not wanted to stand up with him. But her hand felt so right on his arm. As if it belonged there.

As soon as he returned her to her family, Frits found Turley. They were strolling back to where Frits's mother was sitting when Mrs. Drummond-Burrell passed by on the arm of a gentleman he'd never seen before. And they were headed toward Lady Adeline.

"Who is that?" Frits scowled at the back of the man.

"Name's Anglesey." Turley had stopped strolling. "I met him last autumn when I visited m'sister in Paris."

"Normanby's eldest?" Frits tried to remember if he knew anything about the man and came up with nothing. He didn't even think he'd seen him in Town before.

Turley nodded. "He's a few years younger than we are. I understand he was schooled at home and then had a Grand Tour."

There was nothing unusual in that for heirs. Frits had been happy he'd been sent to school. He had many more friends and acquaintances than he'd otherwise have. Yet, he *did not* like the look of that fellow. Although it could very well be because he was now bowing to Lady Adeline and she was smiling at him as if he was a gift from Heaven.

Turley chuckled softly. "It appears you have some competition."

They'd see about that. Frits glanced at the other man again. "Do you know anything else about him?"

"No." Turley slowly shook his head. "He was only at one event I attended at the embassy. M'sister might know more." Brows drawn slightly together, his friend glanced at him. "You're doing it again. You jumped into cold water with Lady Dorie prior to considering the ramifications, and you're going to make the same mistake with Lady Adeline. This time you might not be lucky enough to avoid an unwanted marriage."

Frits reached up to rub the back of his neck, but remembered where he was. "I thought about that. I promise to move more slowly, but that doesn't mean I can't find out more about my *competition*." Or the lady.

Turley blew out a breath. "I'll write to Elizabeth to tell her to expect a letter from you."

"Thank you." He really was the best of friends.

"Well"—Turley grinned—"she does owe you a favor for helping bring Harrington around."

"It wasn't that hard to do." Frits had had a good time

getting under Harrington's skin. Frits was happy the couple were still madly in love. He only hoped he could find the same happiness.

He kept his frown to himself as Anglesey escorted Lady Adeline to the floor as the prelude for a waltz was beginning. At first she merely had a polite smile on her lips, and Anglesey was doing all the talking. The only thing Lady Adeline contributed to the conversation was a nod here and there.

Well, that answered Frits's question. Turley had said the fribble had just returned from the Continent. Like many young men who had a Grand Tour, he was probably attempting to impress her with all he'd seen and done. Someone should give the man a hint, but it wouldn't be Frits. As far as he was concerned, his wet-behind-the-ears lordship could bore her to tears while he encouraged her to talk about herself. The more he knew about her, the easier it would be to get her to stop trying to ignore him. But midway through the set, something changed, and soon she was smiling and chatting with the man as if she'd known him all her life.

Hell and damnation!

This was going to be even harder than he'd thought.

Chapter Four

After spending an intimate hour or so at Sarah's house, Crispin and she had arrived separately at Almack's and were now standing at the side of the Assembly Room, where they could see the parties arriving.

"Shall I visit you later this evening?" He was pushing his luck, but an hour hadn't been enough.

She raised one well-arched brow. "I do not remember you being so insatiable in Paris."

In Paris he'd had as many lovers as he wished. "I've missed you."

Her glance slid to the entrance. "Your young lady has arrived."

Crispin wasn't stupid enough to look in the same direction she had. "You have not given me your answer."

"Are you not interested in knowing who she is?" Her tone managed to be arch and sensuous at the same time. He adored sparring with her.

He lowered his mouth to her ear. "I am more interested in seeing to what heights I can bring you tonight."

"Perhaps, but first you must dance to your father's tune or you will find yourself at point nonplus."

"Very well." He heaved a sigh for her benefit. "Tell me about my future wife."

"Her name is Lady Adeline Wively, the daughter of the Earl of Watford. She is eighteen—not quite as young as I had thought—and making her come out this year." He raised a brow, and Sarah's lips curled up. "Her dowry is sufficient for you to ignore your father's threats."

He was not going to ask the amount. If he waited, she would tell him. "She's not beautiful."

Sarah languidly waved her fan. "I wager that her twenty thousand will make her better looking and easier to bed."

He'd never had a problem bedding any woman. His only concern was avoiding the French pox. "Easier to do my duty, you mean. She will never interest me as much as you do."

A pleased smile tilted Sarah's lips.

Mrs. Drummond-Burrell came over to them. "Lady Riverton, how are you enjoying your return to England?"

"It is delightful." Sarah greeted the lady warmly. "Being here brings back memories."

"Good ones, I trust." Mrs. Drummond-Burrell smiled. Then he remembered that the two women had known each other for several years.

"Indeed they are." With one hand, Sarah indicated Crispin. "Lord Anglesey was just asking about Lady Adeline Wively. He appears quite interested in the lady."

A glint appeared in Mrs. Drummond-Burrell's eye. "Come with me, my lord, and I shall recommend you as a suitable partner for the waltz. I am positive that will help your suit."

"You do me a great honor, ma'am." He bowed, then held out his arm. "I need all the help I can get." In fact, he did not expect it to take long to fix the lady's attentions. She was, after all, young, innocent, and not a beauty. She would be glad for his consideration.

When Mrs. Drummond-Burrell made the introductions and recommended Lady Adeline waltz with him, the chit smiled brightly. This would be even easier than Crispin had thought.

He was pleased with her obvious breeding. Her curtsey was graceful and she performed the waltz credibly well, with no blushing missishness. Unlike many of the young ladies around them, whose faces were red.

At first, he thought to entertain her with stories of his journey, but it soon became obvious that she was not interested in his Grand Tour. That more than surprised him. This plain little sparrow would take more convincing than he'd thought.

"Are you enjoying your Season?" After all, what else could one discuss with a lady just out?

Her wide, gray eyes met his and showed more interest. "So far it has been fine. As you know, it has just begun."

"But you must like London, particularly the shopping?" In his experience, all ladies loved shopping.

"Of course, but one can only purchase so many fripperies. Do you enjoy being in Town?"

It was better than being in the country. Yet he wanted to know if she liked the country as well. She'd be spending most of her time there, and posed his question to elicit the required answer. "I do enjoy it during the Season."

"Yes, I think that is how I shall feel. It has its place." He held her hands high as they turned.

"Do you like the country better?"

"At this point I do. However, as I said, the Season has just begun. Which county do you call home?"

"North Yorkshire, near the North Sea. My father is the Marquis of Normanby." That was an idiotic thing to say. She would have been made to study the peerage, and it made Crispin sound as if he was boasting.

"Indeed." She did not appear to be particularly impressed. But then, her father was also a peer. "It must be cold in the winter."

Ah, that was the problem. He couldn't blame her. Winter on the North Sea could be damnably icy. "When Yorkshire is too cold, we have an estate in Cornwall."

A smile curved her lips. "That must be a great deal warmer. I have heard plants from the tropics can grow there."

Never having been interested in agriculture, Crispin had absolutely no idea. "I believe you are correct. The weather is a good deal milder."

At the end of the set, he escorted her back to her circle, where her sister-in-law, Lady Wivenly, eyed him critically. He wondered if there was something amiss with his appearance, but that could not be possible. His valet would never have let him leave the house if he hadn't been perfectly turned out. It must be her way of inspecting all the gentlemen with whom Lady Adeline stood up.

He bowed over her hand. "I trust I shall see you soon, my lady."

"I look forward to it, my lord." She smiled as she curtseyed.

As he strolled away, Crispin kept his smirk to himself. After he'd corrected his misstep, their first meeting had gone exactly as he'd wished. He initially intended to find Sarah, but decided against it. He didn't wish to arouse suspicions by spending too much time in public with her. Instead, he went to a group of older matrons. If he was to continue to pursue Lady Adeline, he must first receive cards for other entertainments.

By early the next afternoon, Adeline was amazed at how many bouquets decorated the drawing room. Once she had got over her initial fear, Almack's had not been at all bad.

Although Lord Littleton had sent a lovely bouquet of pink roses with a card expressing a wish to dance with her again, she could have done without her dance with him in the first place. Not because he was boring, but because of the way he had hurt her friend. He had done nothing to dispel her notion he was a rake.

Adeline had greatly enjoyed her waltz with Lord Anglesey after he had ceased prosing on and on about his Grand Tour. And he was a better prospect. He was almost as handsome as Lord Littleton and not a rake. After all, Dorie told them all what a stickler Mrs. Drummond-Burrell was; therefore, it stood to reason that she would not recommend Adeline dance with a rake. He too had sent a nice posy of flowers. Lord Lancelot sent a poem, but as he'd spent most of his time staring at Augusta, Adeline did not think anything of it. He probably wrote them to all the ladies. Her brother had called him a wet-behind-the-ears puppy, and the other gentlemen in their group agreed. Still, she had flowers from several other gentlemen she had danced with as well, many of whom she would see again at Augusta's come out ball.

Eugénie strolled into the room, surveyed the blooms, and smiled. "As I knew it would be. You are a success."

Then she glanced at the clock. "But you must change. Today is your mother's at-home."

Oh, dear. Adeline had completely forgotten. Both she and her sister-in-law were expected to be there for the entire time, and she would be the one to serve tea. The at-homes in the country were rather dull, but she was interested in seeing which ladies would come today. "Tell her I shall be down directly."

Adeline arrived back in the front drawing room just as the butler opened the door to their first visitors. Henrietta and her sister, the Marchioness of Merton, were announced.

"Have you recovered from Almack's?" Henrietta took a seat on the sofa opposite Adeline.

"I feel as if I was nervous about nothing." She handed her friend and her ladyship cups of tea. They had spent enough time together that she knew how they took it.

"The first time is always the worst," Lady Merton commented. "At least, that is what I thought."

This was Adeline's opportunity to ask about Lord Anglesey. Her mother only remembered meeting him when he was a child. "Do you know anything about Lord Anglesey?"

Lady Merton set her cup in its saucer. "No. I asked Merton as well, but no one appears to know him. Apparently, he did not attend school."

"That is not at all unusual." Mama's lips twisted into a wry smile. "Many heirs do not. Wively only went because his tutors never remained long."

Eugénie chuckled. "That does not surprise me at all."

More ladies were announced, and the teapot was replenished several times. Adeline's other friends and their mothers or sisters—except Augusta, whose ball was that evening—visited, as well as other ladies, including Lady Jersey.

Adeline was impressed that none of the ladies, even their friends, remained for longer than fifteen minutes. Toward the end of the second hour, three other young ladies arrived with their mothers. Then the knocker was plied, and Lady Littleton and Lord Littleton were announced.

Adeline could not believe *he* had come. Glancing at the delicate chair that was the only place to sit, he grimaced, then propped himself up next to the fireplace while his mother took the chair near Mama.

Mama reached out and took Lady Littleton's hand. "Cristabel, I am so pleased to see you in Town."

Her ladyship squeezed Mama's hand. "My wardrobe needed refurbishing. We have a local modiste, but as good as she may be, no one can deny that the fashions in Town are more elegant."

"I heartily agree with you." Mama smiled. "I believe it has to do with the quality of the fabric."

"My lady, how do you and his lordship take your tea?" Adeline asked before her mother and Lady Littleton could settle in for a comfortable coze.

"We both like two sugars and a generous helping of milk." He straightened and came over to Adeline. She served his mother, but as she handed him a cup, their fingers brushed, and that strange awareness occurred again. It couldn't be an electrical shock. It was also odd that she did not feel it with the other gentlemen. "Thank you." He took a sip. "This is perfect."

"Annis," Lady Littleton said, "what is your blend? It is excellent."

Mama glanced at Adeline. "You must ask my daughter to write it down for you. It is one of her own making."

Adeline could not help but be pleased with the compliment. She had tried several different blends before settling on this one. "It is nothing complicated. I simply mix Ceylon with a lesser amount of Darjeeling and add a small bit of grated dried orange peel. I will be happy to send you a packet."

"Thank you. I will gladly accept the gift." Her ladyship took another sip.

The other ladies were standing to depart when Lord Littleton set down his empty cup. "Lady Adeline, if you are free, I would like to take you for a carriage ride this afternoon."

Miss Tice and Miss Martindale's jaws dropped, and Miss Emerson's eyes rounded.

Drat the man for posing his invitation now, in front of all these ladies. He knew Adeline could not refuse. She kept her tone even and polite when she would rather have boxed his ears. "That sounds lovely."

"I shall see you at five." He held his hand out to his mother as she rose. "Lady Watford, thank you. It was lovely. I agree with my mother that the tea was excellent." He gave a short bow to the others. "Ladies." And escorted his mother out of the room.

"He is soooo very handsome," Miss Martindale gushed. "I hope he comes to our at-home."

Miss Tice clasped her hands at her breast. "I wonder if he has an eligible friend who lives near his estate."

Adeline fought not to roll her eyes as their mothers smiled indulgently. The ladies should not be encouraged to behave thuswise.

Lady Emerson rose. "Lady Adeline, I agree with Lady Littleton about the tea. If you could see your way to sending me a packet, I would be grateful."

"Mrs. Tice and I would love a packet as well," Mrs. Martindale said.

"Of course." Adeline was thankful that the discussion about Lord Littleton had ended, and extremely pleased to find her tea so well received. "I will have the tea sent to you by the end of the day."

The at-home hours were finished; now the only thing she had to do was suffer through the carriage ride with Lord Littleton. If only she knew more about rakes. Having one for a brother was not much of a help. He never displayed his tendencies around her. But—she glanced at her sister-in-law—there was someone who could answer her questions, and Mama had already left the drawing room, so Eugénie was free to speak.

"Eugénie?" Adeline said before she could leave as well.

Her sister-in-law glanced at her. "*Oui?*"

She bit down on her lip. "I have some questions about men."

"Ah, *oui*. But you must know that I am not an expert on the subject. I only know who I should avoid." Eugénie sank down onto the sofa.

"You know more than I do," Adeline grumbled. "And you married Will."

"That is true." Her sister-in-law studied her long enough to make her want to fidget. "What is it that you wish to know?"

She clasped her hand in her lap. "How do I avoid a rake?"

Eugénie let out a low stream of light laughter. "*Ma petite*, if I knew the answer to that, I would not be married. *Oui?*"

Adeline frowned. "I do not understand."

"I had no interest at all in marriage when we met. I only wanted to save those who were enslaved and take them to freedom. I had no time for gentlemen. *Mais*, when a rake decides to wed one, it is very difficult to change his mind." Her sister-in-law's smile was a bit misty. "I set many tasks for your brother, but the greatest one was that he must love me and be faithful."

Tasks? That was the first time Adeline had heard about that. What kinds of tasks? "Why do I have the feeling that there was more to your courtship and marriage than we were told?"

A wicked grin dawned on Eugénie face. "Because there is. Much more."

"Is that the reason he is now involved in the work you do to free the slaves in St. Thomas?"

"*Oui*. In part." Her smile told her Adeline would learn nothing new.

Not that she was in danger of falling in love with a rake. But more information was always helpful, and she decided to acquire as much knowledge as she could. "He ran away from eligible young ladies for years. Why did he wish to wed you?"

"That is part of a much longer story." Eugénie raised a brow. "One I shall not tell you. But when he decided he wanted to marry me, he was very determined. I can only tell you that if a rake falls in love with you, you will know it. He will be impossible to avoid."

That was not much help. "But I do not wish to wed a gentleman like my brother. He is too difficult."

"Yes, Will can be a bit troublesome at times. Especially when he decides I should not do a thing I wish to do. But me, I like a challenge. *Toutefois*, they are not all the same. Huntley was a rake before he married, and you know how different he is from Will."

"I suppose you are correct." Even though he and her brother had been friends for years, they were like night and day. Adeline had not even thought about him being a rake. Yet her sister-in-law had given her an idea. Perhaps she should become more involved in Will and Eugénie's cause. It would give Adeline something to do other than worry about marriage.

Eugénie reached out and placed her hand over Adeline's. "Do not worry yet. *Moi*, I will keep a watch and send your brother after any man of whom I do not approve."

The only problem was that even her mother had no objection to Lord Littleton. Would Mama even care that he had hurt her friend? Whatever had occurred, no one was talking about it. In fact, his name was only mentioned as being the most eligible gentleman in Town. It would be up to her to discourage him. "Thank you."

"*C'est mon plaisir.*" Her sister-in-law rose. "I must go home. I will see you this evening."

"Until later." The conversation had not been as informative as she had wished. Yet she couldn't fault her sister-in-law for not having much information about gentlemen. Poor Eugénie had not even had a come out. By the time she had reached England, she was married and pregnant.

Adeline walked slowly to her bedchamber, trying to decide what to wear for her carriage ride. She had a very pretty new carriage gown. Not that she wanted to encourage Lord Littleton, but she might see Lord Anglesey. The next time she spoke with him, she would attempt to discover how much he actually liked the country. She wished he had visited today as well. Then she wondered if he had been invited to the Duchess of

Rothwell's ball, but decided he probably had not. The invitations had been sent out before the Season officially began, and Augusta's sister had no reason to know him or that he would be in England. Still, he was certain to be invited to other balls, and Adeline would see him at Almack's. Yet, just in case he was in the Park, she would wear her new gown.

Chapter Five

"So." They had just arrived home, and Frits's mother had turned for him to remove her mantle. "You are interested in Lady Adeline?"

Considering the spectacle he'd made of himself, he couldn't very well deny it. "I think I am. Or rather I am, but I must discover more about her." He took his mother's mantle and handed it to his butler, Creswell. "The problem is that she is a friend of Lady Dorie's."

"Ah. She is the one you mentioned." Mama frowned. "That *is* a difficulty."

"I am fortunate that I'm still received." Frits handed his hat and cane to Creswell as well.

"Oh, my dear boy." She lifted her skirts to climb the stairs. "Fortune had nothing to do with it. I received a letter mentioning you had left Town without notice. I immediately wrote back that there was an emergency at one or more of your estates in the north and you would be unlikely to return before the Season was finished." They reached the first floor. "I even wrote Lady Dorie's mother, and received a very nice missive in return, stating that she was glad to see you were such a diligent landlord. I must trust you will be more careful this Season. Decide what you want in a wife before you are swayed by a pretty face."

That was something he'd already discovered. Not that he wasn't being swayed by Adeline's lovely face. But he couldn't blame his mother for mentioning it. "I have been thinking. Whichever lady I settle on, would you be willing to plan a ball or some other entertainments, such as a theater party, or an outing to Vauxhall?"

"Naturally." Mama grinned. "I shall do all within my power to help you to the altar."

Frits wasn't fond of the way she had put it, but he did have to marry, and he was ready. And he needed help. "Thank you."

"That is what a mother is for." She reached up and patted his cheek. "Now, you must start dressing for your carriage ride, and I must rest."

He didn't know what she thought he should wear other than what he was already wearing. Instead of going to his bedchamber, he made his way to his study. He had a letter to write to Elizabeth Harrington concerning Lord Anglesey. Frits didn't know what he hoped to discover, but he didn't like the man sniffing around Lady Adeline. At first he thought it was that his lordship was such a puppy, much like Lord Lancelot. But now he believed it was more. There was an air of debauchery about Anglesey that bothered Frits. He wished there was something he could point to that would keep Wively from allowing the man near his sister.

Damn.

Frits groaned. There he went again. He had to make himself slow down until he knew that he and she wanted the same things out of life and marriage. Yet, when he'd looked into her eyes that day, he could have sworn he had finally found the right lady for him.

He gave himself a shake. With any luck at all, he'd know by the end of the day how she felt about several issues. In fact, he should discover as much as he could about her before he began finding ways around her barriers.

Frits took a piece of pressed paper from the stack on the corner of his desk, leaned back, and tapped his fingers on the arm of his chair, trying to decide if he should tell Elizabeth why he wanted to know about Anglesey, or if she would deduce the reason for his questions. Frits's father always told him never to put in writing anything that you did not want to be made public, and he certainly didn't want anyone else to know about his reasons for asking for the information.

Naturally, Elizabeth Harrington was discreet. She made a perfect diplomat's wife. But he'd always had the impression that her husband was not as restrained as she was, and he had no doubt she would show his letter to Harrington.

My dear Lady Harrington,

I hope this missive finds you and your family in good health. I trust that you have received a letter from Turley advising you that I would be writing, and that you are able to provide me the information I seek on Lord Anglesey, the heir to Lord Normanby. Turley said that he met him at an embassy event when he was last in Paris. As no one here seems to know anything about Anglesey, I am hoping you can tell me something about his character and trustworthiness. No one here seems to have even met the gentleman before.

Yr. servant,
Littleton

He sanded and sealed the letter, then called for his butler.

"My lord?"

"Please have this sent by the most expeditious manner to the British Embassy in Paris." Frits handed Creswell the letter.

"At once, my lord." He bowed.

"I shall want my curricle at ten minutes to five. Tell Lees I want the grays." Their color almost matched Lady Adeline's eyes.

"Yes, my lord."

Frits glanced at the clock. He still had over an hour before departing. Time enough to go through the correspondence his secretary had left for him. The first of which would be the estate reports. He was concerned about the effect the gales last month had had on the fruit trees.

By the time he was done reading and answering the letters, it was time to fetch Lady Adeline. Frits sent a prayer to whichever deity was listening that he wouldn't have to search for another lady.

Shortly before the appointed hour, he pulled up in front of Watford House in St James's Square and plied the knocker. The door was opened by a footman. Frits handed the man his card. "I have an appointment with Lady Adeline."

"I shall notify her you have arrived, my lord." After bowing, the footman sent a younger footman running for her ladyship. "Would you like refreshment while you wait?"

He hoped she wouldn't be that long. "Yes, please. Tea would be nice."

He was led into a front parlor that was decorated in soothing blues and greens. The door closed behind the footman, and Frits looked out the window with a view to the square. It wasn't long before tea arrived, and before he could take more than a sip or two—just enough to recognize the blend from earlier today—the door opened, and he could see Lady Adeline in the hall.

"I trust I did not keep you waiting too long, my lord." She had a polite smile, but was obviously not delighted to see him. Well, that was no more than he'd expected.

"Not at all. I was able to enjoy another taste of your excellent tea while I waited." He held out his arm, and stifled a smile at the adorable confusion on her face.

"You had tea?" She placed her hand on his arm and allowed him to lead her out to his carriage. "I thought gentlemen only drank tea when they had to."

"Er. I suppose some do." He assisted her into the curricle and put up the steps. "I am not a hydropot, but I rarely drink wine to excess, and I find few good reasons to drink strong spirits during the day. Occasionally, a glass of wine will not go amiss."

Her nicely shaped brows drew together, and he gave the horses their office. It surprised him that she had not mentioned either the beauty of his matched pair or his handsome curricle. Most ladies admired both.

"As I said earlier, I agree with my mother; your tea is wonderful." He looked forward to having her blend tea for him.

"Thank you. I had a package sent to her."

"I knew you would not forget." He smiled at her, and was pleased to see her gaze raised to his. But he could see her mind was still jumbled. Was she wondering what sort of gentleman she had met? "Do you use the same blend in the morning?"

"Oh, no. I always do what I say I will." Her words came

out slowly, then she gave her head an imperceptible shake. "No, my morning blend is much stronger."

"I would enjoy trying it sometime." Perhaps for the rest of his life. He bit his cheek. *Slow down!*

"Your horses are lovely. I adore grays." She had apparently decided to ignore his last remarks.

Ah, now they were getting somewhere. Or were they? "Thank you. My mother helped me select them. She is an excellent judge of good horseflesh."

"Your mother?" Lord Littleton must be making a May-game of her. "I have never heard of a gentleman taking his mother to help him look at horses."

"I didn't. She found them and suggested I take a look." He cast a fond eye at the grays. "One of our neighbors was going to take them to Tattersalls, but she saw them first."

Adeline only knew of one lady who had an absolute talent for selecting horses. It seemed Lady Littleton was another. What was interesting was that his lordship listened to his mother. And liked tea more than coffee. "I must commend you for taking her advice."

"That was something I learned early on. My father was adamant that she be kept happy."

They had reached the gate into the Park, causing Lord Littleton to have to pay more attention to the traffic, thus giving her an opportunity to consider what he'd said. It was yet another thing that did not fit her perception of rakes. Still, after what Dorie had said, Adeline could not be wrong about him, even if he did not drink to excess. What her sister-in-law said about different kinds of rakes made more sense.

They nodded to people they knew, and she noticed the utterly lascivious looks he received from some of the matrons and widows, but *he* did not seem to take note of their interest at all. In fact, when he looked at her, she had the same feeling she'd had before. As if she was the center of his attention.

Adeline had to think of something to say. Thus far, she was acting like she had more hair than wit. "Where is your estate?"

"My main estate is in Surrey, but I have several others throughout the country." They had slowed to a crawl, and he gave her a quizzical look. "One is in Cornwall. My gardener has convinced me to try to grow pineapples."

Perhaps he would know more about the area than Lord Anglesey had. "I heard that tropical plants can grow there."

"Yes, they can." He grinned. "But unless you wish to hear about sheltering berms and tree hedges and other such things, you will have to take my word for it that it can be done."

Against her will, Adeline was becoming interested in him. "Do you spend much time in Town?"

"Only the main Season." He had a rueful look on his handsome face. "I probably should not admit that I prefer the country. We are constantly making improvements, and I would rather be there when we try new ideas."

"Such as?" Lord help her. She should not encourage him. She should greet other people she knew and converse with him enough to be polite. But she liked farming and innovations.

"Well"—he seemed to settle back against the cushions, which were actually quite comfortable—"I have one herd of pigs that dine on chestnuts toward the end of the season."

That was odd. "I have never heard of such a thing. What does it matter what they eat?"

"It all started when one of my tenant's daughters

made a pet of a piglet. The main problem was, it wasn't their piglet. She had walked home from school with another tenant's daughter and the pig had given birth several days before." Lord Littleton's green eyes sparkled with mirth. "From all accounts, she held one of the piglets and began visiting it every day after school"— Adeline wanted to ask him about the school, but that would have to wait—"then one day the piglet followed her home."

"Oh, dear." Despite herself she felt her lips twitch.

"Indeed." He gave her a forlorn look. "Fortunately, the owner was more amused than upset. The problem came when it happened a second day. The girl was only seven, and she did not understand why the piglet couldn't be her pet." The put upon sigh he heaved made it harder not to smile. "There was apparently a great deal of crying and clinging to the animal, and I happened to be making visits and heard the contretemps." This time the lost look he had was one she had seen on both her father and brother's faces when their wives were weeping. "I bought the pig and gave it to the little girl with the provision that any of the piglet's progeny would belong to the estate. I also agreed to pay for feeding it and building a pen."

Adeline covered her mouth with her hand to hide her smile. "That was kind of you."

"It was the only thing I could think of." He moved the carriage along. "Not long after that, a friend returned from his Grand Tour and told me about a ham he'd had in Italy. What made it so special was that the pigs dined on chestnuts for a few months before they were slaughtered. I just happen to have a chestnut grove only a mile or so from the tenant's farm, so after her first fare was born, raised, and about ready, we let them loose in the grove." He beamed. "The results were amazing." He glanced at her and then frowned. "You probably didn't want to hear all that."

The problem was that she had wanted to hear it and wanted to know more. But what would happen if it got out that she enjoyed discussing farm animals? Would he tell other gentlemen? She could not risk telling him the truth. "It was a very enjoyable story."

"Thank you." His black brows came together.

"It is a pity that not all landowners can be so inventive." That was the truth, without telling him her secret about her love for farms and agriculture.

"That's what I think. So many peers and other gentlemen complain about not being able to wring more money out of their estates, but I believe that if you invest in them and try to be innovative, you will be rewarded."

"I think you are correct. My father says much the same thing." She found herself warming even more to Lord Littleton.

Adeline did not understand. It was a well-known fact that rakes engaged in brandy early in the day, gambled to excess—or until their fathers put an end to such foolishness, as her father had with her brother—and were dangerous to all ladies. But Lord Littleton was concerned about his holdings, land, and tenants; helped a little girl keep a pig; grew pineapples; and did not normally drink during the day.

And there was the school. She needed to hear more about it. Her mother had attempted to start a dame school, and it had met with little success. "You said you have a school for your tenants' children. How did that come about?"

"Not easily." She laughed at the face he pulled. "My

grandmother tried to start one in the last century and failed. Then my mother tried and heard the same objections about schooling not being any use for children. But I had the idea of paying every tenant who sent their children to school an amount sufficient to make it worthwhile for them to delay the children's chores.

"The distance is not far in country terms, but it is interesting the excuses that arise when a child has to get to the school on their own. So I started sending a wagon around to pick up the children each morning, and when the master's wagon arrives, a child gets in it."

"What an excellent idea." Adeline could not hold back her approval. And it would not have been fair for her to do so. "I shall tell my mother what you did."

"Lady Adeline." Lord Anglesey, sitting a bay horse, sidled the animal next to her and inclined his head. "How are you enjoying the Promenade?"

She had not even noticed the other people around them. "It has been lovely." She glanced at Lord Littleton, whose face had closed. Most gentlemen appeared to know one another, but either Littleton and Anglesey had never met or they did not like each other. "Do you know Lord Littleton?"

Lord Anglesey's smile tightened, as if he did not wish to know him. "No, I have not had the pleasure."

She pasted a happy smile on her face. "Allow me to introduce you. Lord Anglesey, this is Lord Littleton."

The men exchanged greetings, but their looks were tense. What could possibly be wrong?

Lord Littleton recovered first and smiled. "I hope you have a pleasant afternoon, Anglesey. The traffic is moving on and so must we."

Lord Anglesey backed up his horse. "My lady, it was delightful to see you. Littleton, please do not allow me to impede your progress."

Lord Littleton raised one brow. "Never fear, Anglesey. I do not intend to."

Adeline looked from one gentleman to the other. Something was going on. If only she knew what it was.

The carriage moved forward, and she was glad to see Henrietta with Lord Fotheringale. Lord Littleton drew up to them, and they all exchanged greetings and discussed the ball they would attend that evening.

As they drove off, he said, "If you have the supper dance free, I would be honored if you would allow me to stand up with you."

Unfortunately, Adeline had all the sets free. Although Will had said he'd dance with her when she did not have a partner. Earlier, before their carriage ride, she would have thought about making an excuse, but that would have been playing with fire. Even with her success at Almack's, she could not count on being asked for every dance at the ball. "I would like to dance with you."

His broad shoulders noticeably relaxed. He had been nervous. Now that was interesting. She was becoming less and less sure that he *was* a rake. He certainly did not act like her brother did. Perhaps it was time she found out exactly what *had* occurred between Lord Littleton and her friend. Because if he had set out to break Dorie's heart, Adeline could never have anything to do with him.

Chapter Six

Crispin was not happy to see Lady Adeline with another gentleman. Especially one as well regarded as Littleton. Even though they had not met before, he had an excellent reputation and was almost as wealthy as the Golden Ball. He'd probably even been invited to the Duchess of Rothwell's ball this evening, which Crispin had not. Although it would not be difficult to gain entry. It never was at the *ton*'s large balls.

He glanced at the other man's curricle and wondered if his father had a sporting carriage. It had not occurred to him that he would require one, but it appeared he did.

As he made his way slowly around the carriageway, he stopped to converse with people he had recently met and some he'd known from Paris. Earlier today, he had been informed that Lady Riverton was not at home. But she was here, riding in an open carriage with another matron.

He rode up to the landau, which had stopped due to the traffic. "My lady, good afternoon."

Holding her parasol against the weak sun, she inclined her head. "Good day to you, my lord." She glanced at the woman with her. "Lady Sutton, may I present Lord Anglesey? He has recently returned from Paris."

Lady Sutton held out one gloved hand, and a slight smile curved her lips. "A pleasure, my lord." She arched a brow at Sarah, who suddenly found her parasol more interesting than either him or her friend. "My lord, I am giving a small dinner tomorrow evening. I would adore it if you would agree to come."

He kept his gaze on her ladyship and refused to look at Sarah. The blasted woman was passing him off. He raised the hand still in his fingers and kissed the back of it. "Nothing would please me more."

Lady Sutton smiled like a cat let into the cream. "Shall I send an invitation to Normanby House?"

"Please do." He kept her hand for a few moments longer before returning it. If Sarah no longer wished for his company, he had no difficulty accepting her friend's attentions. "Ladies"—he bowed—"I shall see you later."

Still, being given his congé from Sarah in such a fashion churned in his gut. Crispin had never had a woman leave him before. He wondered who she would find to replace him, but he'd not go out of his way to discover the information. No doubt it would soon be clear enough. Nevertheless, he had a young lady to court and marry.

Damn Littleton. Crispin must trust that his greater rank and the promise of a marquessate would make him more acceptable, if not to her then to her parents. In the meantime, he would attend the ball this evening and dance with his chosen wife. Yet, the more he thought about it, the more he was certain he'd win her hand. That an eligible peer was interested in Lady Adeline would make his conquest all the sweeter.

After returning home and consulting with his father's stable master, Crispin was told there was a curricle he could use, as well as a pair of matched bays. By ten that evening—one would not wish to be early to a ball to which one had not been invited—he set out for Grosvenor Square, where he was told Rothwell House was located. However, when he arrived, there was no indication a ball was taking place. In fact, the house was mostly dark. There was an event farther down the square, and, after deciding he had the wrong residence, he went there, but that was not the right house either.

"Devil it." Had he been told the incorrect date?

Clenching his jaw, he went back home. He'd received several cards earlier today. All he could do was to go through them and try to work out which events Lady Adeline would attend.

Shortly after Frits returned home from his ride with Lady Adeline, he received a hand-delivered message from Rothwell House, informing him that due to an incident there, the ball had been moved to Worthington House in Berkeley Square. That was a huge undertaking. He hoped the Rothwells' home was still habitable.

Frits rang for tea, but before he could settle in to work on his correspondence, his mother ambled into the room and made herself comfortable on the small sofa next to the fireplace. Next, his butler appeared with a tea service including two cups.

Giving work up as a lost cause, he moved to a large chair across from her and waited for her to pour.

Once she had given him a cup and prepared her

own, she took a small sip. "How did your carriage ride with Lady Adeline fare?"

"It was nice." Mama frowned. "Thus far, we seem to have at least one thing in common." Actually, more than one thing.

Her brows inched up toward her lacy cap, and she took a long drink of tea. Perhaps he should offer her a glass of wine. He might need one as well. It had not occurred to him that his mother would decide to interrogate him about his ride with Lady Adeline.

She poured another cup. "And what would that *thing* be?"

"Farming." Frits felt a flush rise in his neck. Good Lord, not that. He wasn't fifteen or even seventeen and hadn't been for years. "We also discussed schools for the children on an estate."

She glanced at the sideboard. "I shall have a glass of wine."

Good. Despite what he'd said to Lady Adeline, this was one of those times when a glass of claret was required. Acceding to his mother's wishes, he poured two glasses and brought the decanter with him as well.

Mama drained half the goblet. "I realize that you love the estate, and farming, and the entirety that goes along with it. However, I really *do* think you could . . . *could* find it in yourself to make more elegant conversation with a young lady."

He supposed he could have talked about the weather or asked about her likes and dislikes. But he'd found out a great deal about her by discussing pineapples, and pigs, and farming techniques. Next time he would ask about her. He was interested in what Adeline thought and wanted. "But I needed to know what she thought of the area I like the best. I did not do that with Lady Dorie and look what happened."

"Yes, well." Mama refreshed her glass of wine. "I suppose you have a point. A happy marriage is mostly made up of shared goals. If she wants to be in Town hosting political parties and you want to be at Littleton or one of the other estates mired in as much muck, mud, and dirt as your tenants, that would not do." She focused her eyes on his. "Even though your behavior might make this Season more difficult, I do commend you for recognizing that you and Lady Dorie would not have been happy together. It is entirely too easy to think oneself in love with someone who is wholly wrong for one's happiness."

It was on the tip of Frits's tongue to ask who Mama was thinking of other than Dorie. That statement appeared to have its roots in a hard-won truth, but he decided not to. As far as he could tell, his parents had been extremely happy until Papa died a few years ago. If asked, Frits would have said they'd made a love match. Even if there had been someone else before they'd wed, it was long in the past and had not been destined to last. "Precisely my point. Aside from that, she enjoyed talking about farming. I could see it in her eyes." He took a drink. "I told her about the pigs."

His mother cast her eyes to the ceiling and groaned. "Then I suppose you must be correct about her. It is a sweet story, but many fashionable ladies would think it quite provincial at best and disgusting at worst."

He'd never thought of it that way. Perhaps that was the reason he'd never told Lady Dorie the story. Maybe that also was the reason he had never called or even thought of Lady Dorie by her name when he wanted to call Lady Adeline, Adeline. "I think you are right. The problem is that I feel as if she is holding herself back from me."

"Of couse she is. You did hurt her friend," his mother pointed out drily. "Any good friend would do the same."

He swirled his glass, watching the wine leave a clear coating on the side of the goblet. "What do I do about it? The only thing I can think of is to speak with Lady Dorie and explain why I left."

"At present, I cannot think that would work out well for you. Essentially, what you would be telling her was that she was not right for you, but you think Lady Adeline is, and could she please forgive you so that you can court her friend."

Put that way, it really didn't sound very good. "So what do I do?"

"Be patient. If Lady Adeline is the right lady, there will come a time when she must recognize you are the only one for her, and she will relent." Mama finished her goblet and rose. "In the meantime, be a consistent presence. I am going to take a nap before dinner."

"Don't forget, we are attending the Rothwell ball."

"I have not forgotten. I am not in my dotage yet." Mama gave him an exasperated smile and left the study.

He glanced at his wine and took a healthy swig. If he had to be too patient, he might start drinking more. He'd felt a physical pull to her as he never had with another woman. As if she was his lodestone. This evening he would waltz with her, and he already knew he wouldn't want to let her go. But how he was to convince her to pick him over her friend, Frits had no idea. That would not be easy.

And how was he to protect her from other men when he wasn't positive what he and Lady Adeline would be to each other? He only knew that he had an urge to do so that would not be denied. In fact, he'd start tonight. The only thing he could do to shelter her while he waited for Lady Adeline to decide he was the right gentleman for her was to keep other gentlemen away from her. Especially Anglesey. The man was up to no good. Frits could feel it in his bones.

He finished his glass and poured another. With any luck at all, he'd hear from Elizabeth Harrington soon. Still, Anglesey wasn't the only man who'd be interested in Adeline. There were quite a few gentlemen this year who were seeking wives. If only he could do what the first Baron Littleton had done and make off with the lady, marry her, and keep her hidden until she was clearly with child. That thought made him consider what he'd do to make sure she was his. His shaft hardened, and now that he'd thought about it, he could not unthink it.

He didn't nap, but a cold bath wouldn't go amiss. This afternoon he'd avoided looking at her plush form, the way her spencer hugged her breasts and hid them from view. Tonight, she'd be in an evening gown and the gentle swell of her bosom would be on display. The problem was, it would be on display for all the other gentlemen to see as well. Frits tossed off his wine. This was going to be a blasted difficult night, and he hadn't even seen her yet.

He was going to start praying he wouldn't have to be patient for too long. His fortitude had never been tested before, and suddenly his long-dead Norman ancestors were clamoring for a fight.

Blast it all. He was doing it again! Yet how in the hell did he make himself slow down?

* * *

Adeline was thrilled with her ball gown, the very first one she had ever owned. It was cream silk and embroidered all over with flowers and vines. The bodice had pearls and brilliants in it so that when she moved, it sparkled under the candlelight. Stepping back from the mirror, she saw that the skirts caught the light as well. "I have never had anything so beautiful!"

"I have to say, that Madame Lisette did a wonderful job." Fendall handed Adeline her reticule and fan.

"I am so glad Eugénie's friend recommended her." Adeline couldn't resist one last look in the mirror.

Her maid draped a spangled shawl over her shoulders. "You'd better go or you'll be late."

"Yes." She was looking forward to her friend's ball. Her own ball was not for another three weeks. By the time her mother had thought about it, it was too late to hold it earlier. If she ever had a daughter, Adeline would plan her come out ball months in advance. Nevertheless, this evening would give her an opportunity to see how everything was supposed to be done. When she arrived in the hall, her family was already waiting. Even Mama and Papa were attending.

Taking Mama's hand, Papa led them out the door. "I'm hoping I can talk to Worthington, Rothwell, and some of the others about the bill I'm sponsoring."

"It is Augusta's ball," Adeline muttered. "They might have other things to do."

"Nonsense." He helped her into the coach. "They'll find time."

She caught Eugénie's eye and gave a disgusted shake of her head. Surely every gentleman did not live and breathe politics. Lord Littleton had not mentioned the subject at all. Then again, he was not an ideal example.

Before long they were in the line of coaches letting guests off at the front of Worthington House. "I thought the ball was at Rothwell House."

"It was," Mama said. The coach drew up and the door opened. "But there was some sort of problem in the ballroom and the venue was changed."

It must have been a great deal of work to change the location. As soon as she reached Augusta in the receiving line, Adeline took her friend's hands. "Are you all right?"

"Yes." Augusta pulled a face. "The central chandelier in my sister's ballroom crashed and damaged the floor. Not only must the chandelier and the pulleys be replaced, but the entire floor will have to be refurbished."

Goodness. There must have been crystal shards everywhere. "Was anyone hurt?"

"Thankfully, no. It occurred after it had been cleaned and the servants had left the room." Augusta squeezed Adeline's hands, and she went on to the duke and duchess.

When she and her family reached the series of rooms that had been made to resemble a ballroom, she quickly found Georgie and the others. Gentlemen were crowding around them, and the instant Adeline arrived, she was besieged for dances. This was not at all what she had expected.

She glanced around, taking in the decorations, and from across the room, Lord Littleton lifted a glass of champagne to her in a salute. A stab of guilt pierced Adeline as she slid a look at Dorie. Should Adeline have agreed to dance with him at all? Not that she could have known it ahead of time, but she had enough offers, she could have danced each set twice. If she'd had any idea, she would not have accepted Lord Littleton's request for a set. His bright-green eyes captured hers, and she swallowed, hoping that her friend would forgive her for standing up with him.

Then Adeline remembered she'd given him the supper dance, and all her friends had just agreed they would spend supper together. Well, drat! Now what was she supposed to do?

The orchestra was still tuning their instruments when she caught Henrietta by the arm and pulled her aside. "You are closer to Dorie than I am. Do you know exactly what happened between her and Lord Littleton?"

"No." Henrietta bit down on her lip. "She will not speak of it."

"It must have been truly dreadful." Adeline flicked a look across the room. He was still there. He had been so nice to her. Perhaps it was his way of drawing a lady in.

"That's the only thing I can think," Henrietta agreed. "Has he asked you to dance again?"

"Yes." Adeline closed her eyes. The admission felt like it was being pulled from her. She'd rather keep it her secret. That though was impossible when they were all here, and everyone would see her standing up with him.

"There is really nothing you can do." Henrietta's prosaic tone had a soothing affect. "After all, we are at the mercy of gentlemen to ask us to dance."

"Very true. I feel as if I am betraying her." Just the admission made Adeline feel better.

"I am sure she will understand." The corner of Henrietta's lip quirked up, giving her a rueful look. "Until ladies can ask gentlemen to dance, we are all in the same position."

That was something to salve the conscience. Adeline

would simply refuse to enjoy dancing with Lord Littleton. The violins began to play the prelude to the first dance. "Come, our partners will be here soon."

They took the few steps back to their circle, and Lord Bottomley bowed to her. "My lady." He held out his arm.

"My lord." After curtseying, she placed her hand on his sleeve and could not help but notice that it was not as firm as Lord Littleton's.

The first dance was the cotillion, and she sent a silent thank-you to Will for practicing the steps with her. Despite her complaints about him, he had been fantastic about making sure she would not embarrass herself on the dance floor. Of course, he phrased it as not embarrassing *him*. With their parents present, he was finally able to dance with Eugénie, and he winked at Adeline when he looked at her from down the line.

"Why is Wively winking at you?" Lord Bottomley glanced at her.

"It is just his way of teasing." When he did not respond, she added, "When I was a child he taught me to wink."

His lordship looked aghast. "I shouldn't think winking was something I would wish my sister to learn."

Adeline smiled politely when she would rather have rolled her eyes.

Fortunately for him, the dance was beginning, otherwise she would have given him a set-down. It was one thing for her to criticize her brother. It was quite another for someone outside of the family to do so. She responded politely to his brief attempts at conversation, but was glad when the dance finished.

Her next set was with Lord Belmont. He was not as starched up at Lord Bottomley, but neither was there anything about him to awaken her more tender feelings. On the other hand, she did not have to worry about making conversation. Lord Belmont was more than happy to talk about himself, and his life was not nearly as interesting as Lord Anglesey's had been.

By the end of her third dance, Adeline had decided meeting the right gentleman for her was going to be just as difficult as she had originally thought. Yet, the next dance was with Lord Littleton, and try as she might, she could not but look forward to it. At least he knew how to make interesting conversation.

Chapter Seven

Frits gazed at Lady Adeline—who was inconveniently standing across the ballroom from him with Lady Dorie and the rest of her friends—and swallowed. Every time she turned, she sparkled, as if the stars had chosen to take up residence with her. Her only jewelry was the pearl necklace and eardrops she'd worn at Almack's. If he had his way, she'd wear rubies mixed with the pearls, or even with diamonds.

Turley snatched two glasses of champagne from a footman. "Don't you have some lady with whom you should be standing up?"

"Not yet." Not until the supper dance, if Frits had his way. Not another woman at the ball interested him. "I could ask you the same question."

"My answer is the same as yours." His friend raised his glass in a salute. "I suppose at some point we shall be recruited to stand up with ladies who have no partners."

He'd purposely avoided glancing around. Lady Worthington, Lady Augusta's sister-in-law, or her mother, Lady Wolverton, were no doubt on the hunt for stray gentlemen with nothing to do but dance to their tune.

"There are palms to hide behind." Frits would have to crouch down, but it would be worth it.

Turley looked at Frits as if he'd gone mad. "It's not as desperate as all that. As a gentleman who is a guest, I do not like being commandeered, but as a brother, I was glad of the practice when Elizabeth was first out."

Frits rested his eyes on Lady Adeline again and could not stop a scowl forming when Bottomley led her out to dance. Then something in her expression changed, and he knew his lordship had not found favor with her.

"You're staring at her." There was no need to explain who *her* was. Turley lifted a brow. "You've met her two times?"

"Four." If one wished to be precise, and it seemed important that one was.

"I assume you have spoken to her this evening. When was the third time?"

If one was required to speak to a lady in order to have met her, then it was three times. "I took her riding today."

Turley gave Frits a long, steady look. "And how did it go?"

He thought back to their conversation and felt his lips inch up. "She likes pigs and farming."

Turley, in the middle of taking a sip of wine, choked. He covered his mouth with his hand, then his shoulders started to shake, and he turned his back to the room. After a series of coughs and almost silent laughter, he turned back around. "Pigs?" And set himself off again.

"It was a pet." One look at Turley and Frits decided there was no point in explaining what would not have been understood. "The important part is that I now know she likes the country more than Town."

"You *think* she likes the country more." His friend took a long draw from his glass. "She can't have been here more than a week or two. That could very well change as the Season goes on. Most ladies find Town fascinating."

He hadn't thought of that. Not even his mother had mentioned the possibility. "But it might not."

"Still, to be sure, it will take most of the Season," Turley pointed out.

Hell. Frits downed his wine and took another glass from a footman. Why could these things not be simple? "I do not even wish to think about that. Isn't it enough that I must contend with her having Lady Dorie as a friend?"

"That is the reason this will take so long. You could find another lady." Turley's tone was hopeful.

"What do you have against Lady Adeline?" He barely even knew her.

"Nothing at all. She appears to be a nice young lady. I merely attempted to point out that if you chose another lady, one who was not a friend of Lady Dorie's, it would make your life easier."

Frits turned to glare at Turley and found him gazing at one of the young ladies who had been in the group at the Park with Ladies Adeline and Dorie. What was her name? Miss Featherton. That was it. If that was the way Turley was headed, he'd better take her family's influence into consideration. "Have you asked her to dance yet?"

"No," he responded, still staring at the lady. "I have not had an opportunity."

It was not good luck to stand alone. It made it easier to be snagged to dance with someone, but Frits was willing to sacrifice himself for the greater good. He wasn't the only one who needed a wife. It was time his friend set up his nursery as well. "I shall hold down this area, if you wish to brave rejection."

"Ye of little faith." His friend handed his champagne glass to him. "I will not be turned down."

Frits lifted the wine goblet. Had Turley not seen the mob of men that had been around the ladies when they'd arrived? "Good luck."

By the time Turley made it to where the ladies' chaperones were standing, the music stopped. The lady's partner took himself off, and he made his bow and spoke to the lady. His body stiffened. It was not good news. Then he seemed to relax, raised the lady's hand, and brought it to his lips. The interchange was interrupted by another gentleman, who then took Miss Featherton to the dance floor.

On the way back around the ballroom, Turley grabbed another glass of champagne, so Frits finished his glass and drank the one Turley had left with him and waited.

His friend ambled up and grinned. "The supper dance."

"That's a stroke of luck. I have the supper dance with Lady Adeline." Then again, it was a bit strange that particular dance had been available. "It is surprising that she only had that set free."

"What does it matter?" Turley shrugged. "I decided I wished to dance with her and now I will."

"I suppose you're right." Still, Frits had been on the receiving end of enough cunning ladies to know that something was afoot. He kept his grin to himself, but looked forward to seeing how this would play out. Featherton ladies had a reputation for getting what they wanted.

As Frits had suspected would happen, Lady Worthington approached them from the side, and they didn't see her until she was upon them. "Good evening, gentlemen. I realize you would prefer to hide on the side of the room, but I must impose upon you to dance with two young ladies."

"Being able to attend your ball is worth sacrificing ourselves." Frits had no choice but to give her a charming smile.

"I thought as much." She took his arm. "Please do not use that look on either Miss Tice or Miss Martindale. You will not be happy with the results."

Blast it. He hadn't even realized he was using it.

Turley smirked, and her ladyship turned to him. "You had best be careful as well."

"Yes, ma'am." He strolled on her other side.

Tice and Martindale. The names sounded very familiar. "Have they not been out for several Seasons?"

"You are thinking of their older sisters." Lady Worthington grinned. "I must tell you, they are exact copies."

Now Frits remembered. They were at Lady Watford's at-home. There were three young ladies, and for the life of him, he could not remember which was which. Not that it mattered.

"Perhaps behind the palm would have been a better place to hide," Turley grumbled.

"I still would have found you." They reached the young ladies, and Lady Worthington introduced them.

Frits made sure his smile was polite, but refrained from looking Miss Tice in the eye for more than a second, making sure he did not give her that look. Turley assumed an aloof, but polite demeanor. Still, when the set had ended, they were both relieved.

Making their way back to the place they'd claimed, Turley asked, "Do you think we're safe now?"

"I believe so. Lady Worthington is not the type of female to impose." Frits could not help but compare

Miss Tice with Lady Adeline, and Miss Tice did not measure up. She tittered a great deal and had little conversation. It might have been better if her mother had waited another year to bring her out. Yet one thing puzzled him. "Did Miss Martindale ask if your main estate was close to mine?"

"She did." Turley procured them two more glasses of champagne. "I thought she was just making conversation." He handed a goblet to Frits. "Come to think of it," Turley said slowly, as if remembering something from a long time ago, "I recall Elizabeth mentioning that the sisters were looking for gentlemen who held land close together."

That must have been what Lady Worthington meant when she said the sisters were "copies."

"You did tell her we did not?" That's what he'd done. Although they each had significant estates whose borders marched together. One might even call them favored estates, even though they were not their main ones.

"Of course. It is the truth." Turley wiped his brow. "That was a close escape."

They still had one more set before the supper dance, and Frits scanned the room. His gaze passed a young matron, then went back to her. "Who is the lady down three sofas from us in the dark blue gown with a feather in her hair?"

"Lady Riverton." Turley's response was prompt. "Her husband was Lord Broadhurst's heir. I met her in Paris."

Frits had seen Anglesey with her at Almack's. Thankfully, the man wasn't here this evening. "What do you know of her?"

"From what Elizabeth said, she had an unhappy

marriage. Her two boys live with Broadhurst, but she chooses not to."

Broadhurst was known to be a high stickler, and his son, the Earl of Riverton, had been even worse. He'd also kept a mistress. "I can't say that I blame her. She must have met Anglesey in Paris."

Frits wondered exactly how well she had known the man, and if he could learn more from her.

The music stopped, and Turley glanced toward the other side of the ballroom. "It is time for us to claim our ladies." Turley took a step, stopped, and glanced at Frits. "I do not mean that literally."

"Stubble it." He'd been chastised to take his time enough for one day. He was trying to go slowly, but the more he discovered about Adeline, the more he wanted her. Seeing her waltzing in the arms of other men had awakened a beast inside him that had obviously not felt it had needed to make its presence known before. Now it was roaring to be let out.

He needed goals for this evening. First, they would waltz. Just the thought of having her in his arms for a whole thirty minutes without interruption had his senses clamoring. Then, at supper, he would discover all her favorite foods. After that, he'd ask her to ride with him again, and try to coax a set for the next entertainment. Frits knew he would need to make sure that he asked for the set when there were other people around. That way she could not refuse him. But perhaps she would agree even if no one else heard. She had done it today. No, it was better to be safe than sorry. A twinge of guilt poked at him for trapping her into having to accept his company. But if it wasn't for her friendship with Lady Dorie, he wouldn't have to be so wily beguily about a perfectly normal request for dancing and riding.

Frits got to her just as she was returned to the group surrounding her parents. As soon as her partner turned away, he stepped in and purposefully turned the full force of "the look" on her. "My lady."

Chapter Eight

Lord Littleton's green eyes sparkled and warmed. That was a lethal combination. Was that what he had done with Dorie? Adeline curtseyed. "My lord. Have you enjoyed the dancing?"

"What I have done of it." A footman came by with lemonade, and he took two glasses. "Do you have need of refreshment?"

"Thank you." This time she was careful not to let his fingers touch hers in case the same thing happened as had the other times. "I am rather parched." Earlier, ices had come around, but her mother told her they had champagne in them, so Adeline had refrained. Now she wished she had not.

Her brother and sister-in-law came over, and they all chatted about people she did not know. Thankfully, Lord Littleton maintained a murmured running explanation of who the people were. He glanced down at her, a conciliatory look in his eyes. "You will soon come to know everyone."

"I suppose I must." Finally, the strains of the violins announced the next set, and she placed her fingers on his arm, steeling herself against the strange feelings she felt when they touched.

He laughed. "It is inevitable."

Inevitable? For a moment, Adeline thought he meant those feelings and almost gasped. Then she realized he was talking about meeting and getting to know the people she did not. "Of course."

She had thought, or rather hoped, dancing the waltz with him would be no different than it had been with the other gentlemen. She could not have been more wrong. The perfunctory turning and hopping had turned into something else. Something far more fascinating. He led her so expertly through the movements, she did not even have to think as her feet seemed to float on air. Then he smiled down at her, and all her breath left her.

My God! Those eyes!

"Do you like dogs?" The question came in the middle of a turn.

"Yes." Adeline loved her father's hunting dogs and had been accused of spoiling them. "When one of our hunting dogs had a litter, I tried to bring one of the puppies into the house, but my mother made me take her back."

"How old was she?" His brows had come together with concern. About the dog?

"Old enough. The puppy was weaned, and some of her littermates had been sold." The ensuing argument still stung. "My mother does not allow dogs in the house." When Adeline had her own house, dogs would be allowed.

"I'm glad my mother does not have an objection." His brow had cleared, and one corner of his mouth tilted up. "We have always had dogs in the house. The only rule is that we must keep them clean."

"Lady Augusta has two Great Danes." Adeline could

not stop a sigh from coming out. "They are beautiful and so well behaved."

"I know." He lifted her arms and turned her. "I have one of the puppies. Well, he's not a puppy any longer. He is about ready to turn three."

"I would love to meet him." The moment the words were out of her mouth, she knew she had made a mistake. Yet she could not take it back. She really did want to see the dog. "What is his name?"

"Maximus, but I call him Max." Lord Littleton grinned, making it clear how much he liked his dog.

"I like Maximus better than Max. It is more regal." And Great Danes were nothing if not kingly. Except when they were being funny.

"Perhaps you would like to go walking with us sometime." There was nothing in either his tone or his countenance that indicated the query was more than a friendly offer.

And Adeline would. She really, really would like to walk the dog. Keeping a smile pasted on her face, she broke her own heart. "Maybe someday."

He looked at her for a second, then said, "I shall try to find an opportunity. My time in Town is very busy, with the Lords, and events, and the like."

"The Lords." Adeline wanted to moan. "I completely understand that it is important for running the country. And that it takes laws to make changes for the good. But I do not understand how some people can devote their lives to politics." She took a breath. "There must be a way to be involved in politics and have time for other important things." Such as one's family.

"I absolutely agree." His voice was firm and unequivocal.

"You do?" She had not been looking at him for most of her diatribe, but his statement made her glance up.

"Yes." He met her gaze. Good heavens, looking at him was a mistake. It was as if he could see right through her. "I have friends who spend most of the year running to Town every time Parliament is called into session. I think it must take a toll on their families. My father was of the same opinion. It was his view that there was time to be in Town and time to be at home, and if it was a choice between his family or the Lords, his family was more important. I do not see a reason to believe any differently."

"I wish my father and mother thought that. Then again, some votes are important." She loved her parents, but since she had come to Town, she was feeling abandoned. Then again, she always felt that way.

"They are." Lord Littleton nodded. "But one can give another Member their proxy."

She had not known about that. "Interesting."

To her surprise, the dance came to an end. How had the time gone so quickly? Still, she would have supper to discuss ideas with Lord Littleton . . . or not. Augusta had arranged that they—the ladies—would all sit together and, naturally, that included Dorie.

Called back to her duty to her friend, Adeline assumed a polite mien and wondered what would happen next. She should sit next to Lord Littleton. They had danced together. It seemed that was the polite thing to do. But she could not hurt Dorie's feelings. The arrangements occupied her until they reached her circle.

Augusta, escorted by Lord Phineas, led the way to the supper room. Three tables large enough to fit all of them had been placed together. Once the ladies were seated, the gentlemen went to select the delicacies from the two tables that had been set up.

Dorie took the seat to one side of Adeline. "I feel as

if I must warn you about Lord Littleton. He is not to be trusted." Dorie's lips flattened.

"I am so sorry." Adeline wondered if her friend would say more, but after a few moments, she prompted, "What did he do?"

"I really do not wish to discuss it further." Dorie lifted her chin. "I am determined to put it behind me."

Although Adeline wished her friend would tell her exactly what had happened, her heart hurt for Dorie. "Yes, of course." Had she fallen in love with him? That must be it. Why else would she be so adamant about his lordship. "I will endeavor to avoid him."

"Unfortunately, you will not be able to." She gave a sad smile. "The rules of Polite Society are against you." She took Adeline's hand and squeezed it. "Protect your heart. Find a gentleman worthy of it. That is what I intend to do."

"That is good advice. Thank you for telling me to beware of him."

"I could not allow you to experience what happened to me." Dorie moved down the table when the gentlemen joined them.

Adeline steeled herself against Lord Littleton. She would enjoy his company and not fall in love with him. That was the only thing she could do, unless she suddenly had a full dance schedule. She wondered if Lord Anglesey would ask her to stand up with him the next time they were at the same event. Perhaps she should focus more on him. He seemed interested in her.

When Frits returned with the other gentlemen to the table, Adeline's demeanor was much chillier than it had been at the end of their dance. Lady Dorie cast him a surreptitious glare, and he pretended not to notice. She must have had a word with Adeline. In fact, he was positive the lady had done him as much damage as she could.

Bloody hellhounds!

The instant he thought he was making progress with Adeline, something happened to interfere. At least he was still sitting next to her.

He motioned for the footman to set down the plates. "I hope I chose well."

The smile on her lovely pink lips didn't reach her clouded gray eyes. "I am sure you did."

She cut into the lobster patty with her fork and ate. He devoured two of the things before he caught her with her mouth empty. "Are you attending Lady Brownly's musical evening?"

"Yes." Adeline's eyes brightened, but then the mask fell over them. "I have heard the singer, Mrs. Fodor, is excellent."

"I can attest to that." He had a feeling his next question was a forlorn hope. "Will you sit with me?"

"I cannot. I am already committed to sit with my friends." A line formed between her brows. "Perhaps another time."

He couldn't tell if she was truly sorry or merely being polite. Yet that spark in her eyes when he'd mentioned the musical evening had been real. Although Frits had always considered himself to be a patient man, it occurred to him that when it came to Adeline, he was not nearly as patient as he thought. Then again, he'd never had to be. Whatever he wanted was usually within easy reach, be it success in school, sports, or with women. Especially the latter. On the other hand, the women he'd been with had all been experienced and were looking for the same thing he was. Having to coax the attentions of an innocent young lady with a deep sense of loyalty to a friend who actively disliked him was proving to be much more difficult.

Frits restrained himself from quaffing his wine. "Perhaps you have a waltz free at Lady Elliott's ball?"

He was almost glad to see the brief look of panic in her eyes as she slid them toward his nemesis. "I–I do have a waltz free."

Ah, she couldn't lie either. That was good information to know. "The supper dance again?"

Adeline swallowed hard. "Yes, if you wish."

He wished for all her sets, but that was going to take time and finding a way around her concerns.

"Thank you." Frits wanted to ask her to ride with him tomorrow. But two days in a row would cause the *ton* to take notice, and it was too soon for that. "Perhaps you are free to ride with me the day after tomorrow?"

For the first time since the dance, she gazed directly at him. Her gray eyes had turned silver, and her lips had formed a line. "You are fortunate, my lord. I am free to ride with you."

"You honor me, my lady." He infused his words with as much sincerity as he could. He was grateful that she had accepted even though she hadn't wanted to. She was glancing around, as if looking for someone to save her from him. He needed to do something to entertain her. "I am thinking of having a new curricle made."

Her gaze landed on him again. "Why? Your carriage is very nice and well-made."

"I saw Merton riding with his cat. Maximus"—he decided to use the name she preferred—"has tried to climb into my curricle, but there's not enough room for him. After seeing Merton I thought if I just made the carriage a little larger, I could make a place for Maximus behind me."

Her eyes widened and she blinked, then she got that contemplative look in her eyes again. "That is an interesting idea. Are you truly considering doing it?"

"It started out as a fancy, but the Dane does like to go with me, so the answer is yes. I shall make time to visit my carriage maker within the next few days." Frits wanted to ask her to go with him, but he was very sure that was not the kind of outing in which a young lady would be allowed to engage.

"I look forward to seeing it and your dog." The last was said on a wistful note.

"I am sure he would like to meet you." Frits grinned. Was his Great Dane the way to her heart? "He loves people who are disposed to like him."

"Perhaps someday." Adeline toyed with the last of the food on her plate.

He was losing her attention again. "What is your home county?"

Her short, straight nose wrinkled adorably. "My father's main estate is in Herefordshire."

"You don't like it?" Frits had visited friends there. It was a beautiful county.

"It is not that as much as I do not like being left there all the time." She pierced a piece of cheese with her fork, but left it on the plate. "My parents are gone much of the time. My other brothers are at school or away, and Wively and his wife have the baby. So my younger sister and I do not get to travel farther than our market town."

That was completely opposite to how Frits had been raised. His parents had almost always been around. "When you put it that way, it does sound a bit dismal." Yet there was no reason she could not see as much of

London as she wanted. "Did you not tell me that you wished to visit the sights while you were here?"

Adeline tilted her head, as if trying to remember mentioning the subject. "I might have done so. I would like to visit the British Museum and the Tower of London. My brother mentioned taking his wife to Vauxhall."

"Those are excellent choices." And he would help bring them about.

"Lady Adeline?" Lady Worthington came up to them. "I am sorry to interrupt. Your family is leaving."

Adeline placed her serviette on the table. "I shall come directly." She turned to him. "I did have a pleasant time, my lord."

He rose when she did and, bowing, took her hand. "I did as well. I wish you a good night."

When Adeline curtseyed to Frits, he sensed her reaction to him as his hand engulfed her much smaller one. "Thank you, I shall."

He watched her join her family and went to find his mother, who was also ready to leave. Once they had bid adieu to Lady Worthington and were in the coach, he mentioned his plans. "I wish to get up a theater party that includes Lady Adeline. I also need your advice on the best way to escort her to the museum and the Tower of London."

"Let us take first things first. Tomorrow is my at-home. I am sure Lady Watford will bring her daughter and daughter-in-law with her when she comes. I will mention the theater to her, and we shall arrange a date."

That sounded easy enough. The at-home gave him another idea. "Would you mind if Max makes an appearance? Lady Adeline expressed an interest in meeting him." Even in the poor coach lighting, he could see his mother give him her surely-you-jest look. "It would be totally by accident, of course."

Mama let out a resigned huff. "Very well, but make certain it appears to be a mishap. You know I love him, but I do not wish to gain a reputation for allowing guests to be subjected to an overly affectionate beast."

An image popped into Frits's mind of the Dane sitting with his hindquarters on one of the sofas leaning against a horrified lady. "I'll make sure of it."

Lady Adeline, on the other hand, would be thrilled.

Chapter Nine

The following afternoon, Adeline followed her mother and sister-in-law to her mother's landau as they began morning visits. Their third stop was in Grosvenor Square. It was not until they were in the drawing room that she realized they were at Littleton House.

"I do not know why I'm surprised," she muttered to herself. Their mothers were old friends. Still, she'd most likely not even see him. They had not seen any other gentlemen during their morning calls. Yet he had come to her mother's at-home. Would he make a point of being there in the event she visited? Adeline hoped he would not.

A group of older ladies were in the process of departing, causing everyone to greet her mother. Once the matrons left, they were escorted to a drawing room and announced. Tea was served, and she had the pleasure of discovering it was the tea she had sent to Lady Littleton.

Adeline was nibbling on a lemon biscuit when a shout came from the direction of the hall and the door was nudged open by a large head. The dog grinned and, tail wagging, pranced straight to Lady Littleton.

She raised her hand, holding out her palm in a stopping gesture. "Maximus, halt."

And he did, even though the dog clearly did not wish to.

A dog! This was too good to be true. Adeline set her cup on a low table between the sofas. "My lady, may I stroke him?"

"Of course you may, my dear. Do so on his back so he can get to know you."

"Adeline"—her mother's tone was one of long suffering—"take off your gloves first."

"Oh, yes." She did as she was asked, then stood and walked to the dog. As soon as she was a step away he turned his head to her and waited. "You are such a good boy."

Suddenly, he turned around to the door, where Lord Littleton stood. "There you are." He gave his mother a contrite look. "I'll take him. He got away from the footman."

"I was going to stroke him." Her words were out before she thought about them.

"It will be better if you do it in the corridor," his mother said. "He has a tendency to shed."

"I'll leave the door open," Lord Littleton offered as he slapped his leg, bringing the dog to heel.

Adeline followed him out of the room. "I have seen Lady Worthington's Great Danes, but I have never had an opportunity to stroke one before."

She gently ran her hand along the dog's spine. His fur was soft, and the more she stroked him, the closer he got to her, until he was leaning a large portion of his weight against her. "You are such an excellent gentleman." He gazed up at her with soft brown eyes, and she rubbed his ears. "I wish I had a dog like you." A clock chimed and she stepped back, shaking out her skirt. She did not want to leave, but her mother would be upset if she remained too long. She bent down and planted a kiss on Maximus's head. "I had better go back."

"As should I." Lord Littleton smiled down at his dog. "I have some letters to write to my estate managers, answering questions about the spring planting, before Maximus's afternoon walk."

"How many times a day do you take him out?" It must be difficult to keep such a large dog exercised while in Town.

"Two long walks—one in the morning and the second in the afternoon—and one short one before he goes to bed. They are really rather lazy animals."

Lord Littleton was still standing there patiently when it occurred to her that he was waiting for her to go back into the drawing room. "Until the next time."

"Until then." He smiled, and she avoided looking at his eyes. They were the most dangerous part about him.

By the time she joined the ladies, it was time for them to leave.

"You have dog hair all over your skirt." Her mother shook her head. "She has been fascinated with the beasts since she first saw them."

"I cannot blame her for that." Lady Littleton smiled at Adeline. "I have long loved dogs. If you would like, and if your mother does not object, I can have Humphries, the footman who takes Maximus in the mornings, come by your house, and you may join them for their walk."

"Oh, I would love that." She gave her mother a

pleading look. "I frequently take a brisk stroll in the mornings."

"Very well." Her mother focused a stern gaze on Adeline. "I warn you that you are not to think about acquiring one."

"I understand." Unless she married a man who loved dogs as much as she did. Adeline would have to ensure that was on her list.

Once they were in the carriage, her mother said, "Lady Littleton and I have decided an evening at the theater would be entertaining. Neither of you have had an opportunity to attend."

The theater! Adeline did her best not to clap her hands. "I think that is a delightful idea. May we see a comedy?"

"Yes," Eugénie agreed. "I would enjoy that as well."

"I shall discover what is playing." Mama sat back against the plush swabs. "I do enjoy a good comedy."

That evening they all attended Mrs. Brownly's musical evening. Glancing around, Adeline found her friends and walked over to join them. From the corner of her eye, she saw Lord Littleton standing with Lord Turley.

The moment she reached Dorie and Henrietta, she was told they needed to think of ladies for Lord Exeter.

"But which gentleman is he?" Even though Adeline had heard a great deal about his lordship, she had no idea what he looked like.

"The tall man speaking with Lord Huntingdon near the stairs," Henrietta said.

She followed the line of her friend's gaze. The gentleman in question was tall and broad shouldered, with dark brown hair. "He's quite exceptional-looking. Dorie, are you sure you are not interested?"

"Positive." She focused on Adeline. "Are you interested in him?"

"Er, no." Just the thought of taking on so much responsibility put her off. She wanted something simple. "I am not ready to act as a mother to almost grown children."

The others joined them and inspected Lord Exeter as well; then they settled down to seriously consider ladies who might suit him. When the rest of the guests started making their way to the drawing room, Adeline watched with some appreciation his skill as Lord Exeter adroitly managed to sit with Dorie during the first performance. Yet she was not nearly as pleased when Lord Littleton joined her and her friends. The next time, she would not be the last one into the row of seats.

Yet instead of trying to engage only her in conversation, he addressed his remarks to all the ladies. "I was privileged to attend the opera in which she sang last year. It was truly amazing. Grown men were weeping."

"My sister said the exact same thing," Henrietta commented. "I am looking forward to her performance."

Lady Brownly stood in front of the small stage, and everyone quieted as she introduced Mrs. Fodor. The music started, and she began to sing.

By the time the piece was done, Adeline understood why the singer was so popular.

A short time after the first song had finished and Lord Littleton had left, Dorie joined them. "Please do not leave me alone with Exeter."

"You will have to be first to find your chair the next time," Henrietta said.

They made their way to the supper room, and Adeline was surprised to see Lords Littleton and Turley, who had been in conversation with her brother and his friends, join them. She and the other ladies quickly formed a group at one end of the table, making sure that one or the other of their brothers was between them and the interlopers. Then Dorie's mother entered the supper room, accompanied by Lord Exeter. That was interesting. Did it mean that Lady Huntingdon thought he would be a suitable match for her daughter?

Next to her, Georgie said, "I know she does not wish to be with Lord Exeter, and I feel as if I am a disloyal friend, but I have the sense that Dorie and Lord Exeter would make a good match."

Adeline had wondered about that very same thing. "Why is that?"

"My brother was talking about him, and everything he mentioned seemed to march well with what Dorie wants in a husband. I think she is afraid to trust her heart because of what happened with Lord Littleton last year."

Perhaps this was Adeline's opportunity to discover more about that particular story. "I heard that he was close to offering for her, then left Town."

"According to what I heard, there were several problems on his estates, and he had to leave to attend to them." Georgie frowned. "That, however, does not explain why he did not renew his attentions afterward. Although, from what I have heard about him, I do not think it would have been a good match."

Clearly, Adeline was not going to learn the truth until one or the other of them said something more to the point. That something had happened was clear. It was also plain that neither Georgie, Henrietta, nor Adeline had the full story. She glanced at Dorie and said a prayer that she would find her perfect gentleman. Thinking of gentlemen, she had not seen Lord Anglesey this evening. Did he not like musical evenings?

Once supper had ended, they all went back into the drawing room to listen to Mrs. Fodor again. This time, Dorie and Adeline were the first to enter the row of chairs. She felt a little cowardly about her behavior, but avoiding Lord Littleton was the best course. She liked his conversation too much. And his dog. She could happily have spent the rest of the day with Maximus.

Frits leaned against the back wall, considering his conversation with Exeter about Lady Dorie when Turley joined him.

"You don't look as if you're having a good time." He propped himself up against the wall as well.

"The music is excellent." Frits couldn't stop himself from glancing to where Adeline sat with her friends and not him. "The company is another matter."

"Am I being insulted?" His friend folded his arms across his chest.

"Not you. I had hoped to make more progress with Lady Adeline this evening." There was no harm in telling Turley what Exeter had said. "However, the problem of Lady Dorie might soon be resolved. Exeter is interested in marrying her. He thinks she is trying to avoid him, but he doesn't understand the reason. He wanted to know what happened between us, and I told him."

"Encouraging a new romance, thus drawing her ire

from you?" Turley seemed doubtful. "I am not at all certain that ladies overcome what they perceive as slights that easily."

That was not at all what Frits wanted to hear. "You would be much more of a help if you did not keep shooting down my ideas, or came up with some of your own." He tried to attend to the singing, but as excellent as Mrs. Fodor was, he could not get his mind off his courting problems. At least his friend hadn't reminded him to go slowly. "Would you like to attend the theater? My mother is making up a party."

Turley looked in the same direction Frits had been gazing. "Do you think she would invite Miss Featherton?"

Frits felt a slow smile form on his face. That was the reason his friend had stopped nagging him. "I think that can be arranged."

"A comedy?" Turley raised a hopeful brow.

"Indubitably. I see enough tragedies in real life." The song ended, and everyone began to applaud, even the servants.

"In that case, I would be delighted." Turley heaved a sigh. "My life and that of my sister would have been so much easier if our mother hadn't died when we were young."

"I don't say it often enough, but I'm very glad I still have mine." Especially now, when Frits was having so much trouble with Adeline. "You do know she would be more than happy to help you?"

"At the moment, she has her hands full with you," Turley scoffed.

Frits couldn't deny that. He saw Exeter speaking with Lord Huntingdon, Lady Dorie's father, and considered including Exeter in the theater party, but he'd want

Lady Dorie to be invited and that would defeat Frits's purpose for the outing.

"Speaking of tragedies," Turley said, clearly still thinking about the play, "there are a number of us planning to introduce a bill to repeal the Corn Laws. I'd like you to join our group."

Frits would dearly like to see the law repealed. All the damn thing did was create misery for the populace who could not afford any more strife. "Send me the proposal and I'll read it."

"We're meeting tomorrow morning before the session."

Turley sounded so hopeful that Frits hated to disappoint him, but that was a slippery slope. Not to mention that Adeline didn't care to be part of a political set any more than he did. "You know I do not discuss politics. If I have any ideas that would improve the bill, I shall make notations." When his friend didn't respond, he said, "My father always said—"

"Yes, yes, I know." Turley, of course, had heard it the last time he tried to cozen Frits into a political conversation. "That discussing these things leads to an inevitable loss of time with one's family and a possible loss of friends. But the only family member present is your mother, and all of your friends are supporting this bill."

"My mother who"—Frits held up his finger—"has agreed to assist me in my pursuit of Lady Adeline. And, once one starts, it is hard to stop."

"I can't argue with that," Turley grumbled. "However, politics is an invigorating activity."

Frits knew an attempt to tempt him when he heard it. "I must fetch my mother. I shall tell her about Miss Featherton."

Turley pushed away from the wall. "Good luck. I still think you are going too fast."

"I thank you, despite your doubts. I wish you the same." Frits did wonder what problem Turley could have with Miss Featherton. It wasn't as if *he* was involved in any perceived misdeeds.

The next morning, Frits—fully aware that his mother had not mentioned anything to Adeline about *him* accompanying the footman—and Humphries presented themselves at Watford House. The butler answered the door. "I am sorry, my lord, but Lady Adeline did wait as long as she could."

It was only ten o'clock. "Can you tell me what time she left?"

"Close to an hour ago." The butler eyed Maximus, who was happily wagging his tail. "She will be at least another half hour, but if you would like to wait?"

"No, thank you. We must be on our way." Why the devil hadn't Frits or someone asked her when she went for a walk?

As they made their way back to the pavement, Humphries looked at him from under bushy brows and opined, "You have to get up early to catch the worm."

Frits sighed. "I do not think Lady Adeline would appreciate being likened to a worm."

"A bird?" the footman said, as if trying to guess the answer.

"No. The bird catches the worm."

"There. I knew I had it right," Humphries responded, sounding satisfied.

The only time Frits slept in past six was when he was in Town. It was his present to himself for attending the Season. He'd have to start rising earlier. So much for scoffing at Exeter going riding early to catch Lady Dorie.

Something or someone must be making May-games of Frits, Exeter, and Turley. None of them had ever had problems with women before, and now three young ladies were tying them in knots. Did the women even know what they were doing? Or did it come naturally?

Now that was a frightening thought.

Chapter Ten

Crispin had spent a disappointing evening with Lady Sutton and left as soon as he'd been able. Unfortunately, her small dinner party had been small indeed. Only he had been invited, and the lady had expectations. Not that he wasn't happy to comply, but he found her to be rather demanding, and that was not to his taste. He liked to be in control of his liaisons.

He'd spent a restless night and woken early. When he was unable to go back to sleep, he decided to go for a ride. As luck would have it, Lady Adeline was strolling in the direction of Upper Brook Street with a footman following behind when he came upon her. "My lady. Good morning."

"It is indeed a lovely morning, my lord." Smiling, she curtseyed. "I did not know you were an early riser."

"I enjoy the early morning air when I have the opportunity," he lied. He detested rising before noon, and she was much too cheerful for the time of day it was. Then again, he didn't like it, but his mother would. "I'd be delighted to dance with you again at Lady—" He gave her a rueful look, hoping to discover which ball she'd attend next and make sure he had received an invitation.

She laughed lightly. "Lady Elliott's ball, if that is the one you mean?"

"Yes, of course. I completely forgot her name. I wish I had spent time on the Town before I was sent on my Grand Tour." Any time on the Town might have been helpful, but Crispin had enjoyed life on the Continent so much he hadn't wanted to return. "If I had, I would know more people and remember their names." Thinking about it, Crispin was sure he had not received a card for the lady's entertainment. But unless the location changed, he would be there.

"That is the next ball I shall be attending." Lady Adeline's smile became warmer. He was finally getting somewhere.

"Can you offer me the supper dance?" The more time he spent with her, the easier it would be to convince her to marry him, quickly.

"I am sorry"—a frown formed on her lips—"but that set is taken. I am free for the first waltz."

"The first waltz it is." He bowed. "I look forward to it."

"I as well, my lord." Her smile deepened.

As she rose from her curtsey, he saw a large dog accompanying Littleton and a footman. "Some people need to leave their cattle on their estates." In an instant, the smile left Lady Adeline's face, her formerly soft, gray eyes narrowed at him, and Crispin knew he'd just made a grave error. She obviously had a fondness for large beasts. "Not that I have anything against dogs. I simply believe they have their place."

"Many think the same. My parents, for instance." She turned a delightful smile on Littleton, who must have quickened his step to reach them so rapidly. "Good morning, my lord and Maximus."

The beast strained at his lead to get to her. Crispin

had made a serious mistake indeed and resolved to recover from it. "What a handsome gentleman you have, Littleton."

He inclined his head as the dog placed himself between her ladyship and Crispin's horse. "Does he not trust horses?"

"Not at all." The man smirked. "He gets on extremely well with horses. Some people, however . . ."

By this time Lady Adeline was stroking the animal. Crispin attempted to get her attention away from the Great Dane and back on him. "I should be on my way."

"Yes, of course. Please do not allow me to keep you, my lord. I shall see you at Lady Elliott's ball." She hadn't even looked up at him. He'd see that she didn't do that again.

"I will count the hours." Despite being miffed with her, Crispin did not at all like leaving her with his lordship. Unfortunately, he didn't have much choice. If he stayed, he would not compare well to either the dog or the man. He should have kept his damned mouth shut until he knew how Lady Adeline felt about animals. Perdition. He must be more disgruntled about last night than he'd thought to have made such a slip.

"Good day to you, Anglesey." Littleton's countenance could not have been smugger. He obviously knew he'd won this round. Crispin had not a doubt the man would do everything he could to cut him out when it came to Lady Adeline.

Once Lord Anglesey had taken his leave, Adeline turned her narrowed eyes at Frits, and he rapidly adjusted his features to show a suitably bland mien. "I was under the impression that Humphries walked Max in the mornings."

"Normally, he does." Devil it. Frits had not expected her to mention that. "But I happened to be awake and decided to take some exercise." Behind him, Humphries scoffed lightly, and Frits added, "I do go out with him in the mornings when I'm at home."

"Indeed." Adeline didn't sound convinced. She rubbed both of the Dane's ears, and he leaned his head into her stomach, wanting the attention to continue. Lucky beast. "I hope to see you later," she said to the Great Dane. Glancing at Frits, she bobbed a curtsey. "I will see you this evening, my lord."

He gave her his most charming smile. The one that usually had a woman ready to fall into his arms. "I am looking forward to our dance."

"As am I." Again, not convincing. If he'd not been watching her so intently, he would have missed the mistrust her polite expression and words it had masked.

That she truly did not trust him was a surprise. Frits had thought she was merely being loyal to her friend. He'd been certain he could eventually talk her around. But a lack of trust was another matter entirely, and he hadn't helped his cause at all by appearing with Humphries and Maximus. Somehow, Frits had to find a way to win her trust if he was to have any hope at all of attaching her affections.

Frits, Max, and Humphries continued on their way to the Park and Lady Adeline walked in the opposite direction. The only good that had come from this encounter was that he'd got rid of Anglesey.

"She's a downy one, she is," Humphries commented with more than a hint of approval.

"She certainly is." It dawned on Frits that Lady Adeline was not a typical young lady or indeed a typical lady. It would take a great deal of work on his part to earn her confidence. The trouble was how to go about accomplishing that task. He'd never had a lady distrust him before. He supposed the first thing he should do was stop attempting to trick her. "I will not be joining you in the mornings again."

At least not until she asked him to.

"As you wish, my lord."

Humphries had such relief in his voice that Frits glanced sharply at the man. "Keep it up and you'll be back in the stables."

His old servant's eyes sparkled with hope. "Can I keep walking Max?"

"No." His mother had decreed that livery must be worn while taking the dog out. That was what had led to Humphries's temporary elevation. Not that he saw it that way. Frits had heard him use the term "damned fart-catcher" more than once. "You know what her ladyship said."

His shoulders slumped; then he remembered to straighten them, and Frits took pity on the man. "I'll leave you to it. Take some extra time if you'd like."

"Thank you, my lord." Humphries lengthened his stride.

While Max—Maximus; he needed to remember to use the version of the name Adeline liked—and his footman continued on to the Park, Frits turned back toward home, applying himself to the task of making a certain lady understand he was serious about getting to know her better, and that he could be trusted.

He wasn't happy that Anglesey was going to be dancing with her this evening, but Frits would be taking her for a carriage ride the next day, and he had the supper dance that evening. No matter what happened, he would not be relegated to the end of the table at supper again. That might take some maneuvering. He'd probably do well to arrange it so that they went down to the supper room with her brother and sister-in-law instead of allowing her to follow her friends. But, considering what he now knew, would it be better to let her take the lead? That might make her start to trust him.

In the meantime, he'd see about having his new curricle designed. He'd told her he was going to do it and he would. With Anglesey chasing after Adeline, Frits couldn't continue to count on her being available to join him during the Grand Strut. But with Maximus as a lure, Frits had a better chance of coaxing her to ride with him. As long as he got the carriage built in time.

He entered his house and went straight to the breakfast room, where he found his mother reading the *Morning Post.*

"Good morning." He took a plate and began to fill it from dishes on the sideboard.

She set the paper on the table. "You are up early."

"I tried to get up in time to go for a walk with Maximus." Considering the dog didn't get up until eight, that shouldn't have been too difficult. But Frits never seemed to be able to wake up early in Town.

"Um-hm." She went back to reading the newssheet.

"What's that supposed to mean?" Taking his seat, he fixed a cup of tea.

Mama peeked over the top of the paper. "How did Lady Adeline react to seeing you?"

"Not particularly well." He sounded like he had as a boy, when a splendid idea turned out not to be. "I have decided not to do it again unless she agrees to see me."

"A wise decision." Several moments later, she turned the page. "I have found a date for the theater, but it is not for another ten days. Lady Adeline is committed to several balls and other entertainments between now and then."

He was disappointed, but he should have expected

as much. At least two of her friends were having their come out balls, and she'd have one as well. "Thank you for arranging it. Is Miss Featherton coming?"

"Yes, that was another reason for the delay. We do not have the time either." His mother started raising the paper to her face again. "I suggest flowers."

"I already sent a bouquet." He dug into a baked egg.

His mother sighed. "Send more. She is not one of those ladies who fawn all over you. You are going to have to exert yourself this time."

That was an excellent point, one he'd already discovered. "I'll go out after I break my fast." Mama finished raising the paper. "Is there anything else I should do?"

"Stay away from Lady Holloway. She was quite taken with you."

Lady Holloway? Who the hell was . . . "Is she a friend of Lady Wall's?"

"I believe so." Frits wished his mother would stop reading the blasted newssheet long enough to have a conversation with him. "I heard the rumor from Sally Jersey."

In that case, everyone in Town and their dog would have heard it. "Thank you. I had no idea."

"No." His mother sighed again. This time in exasperation. "You usually do not."

Frits thought that was a bit unfair, but let it pass. He would, however, make a point of looking at the betting book at Brooks's. If the rumor was rife, someone was bound to have wagered on it.

He finished eating. "I shall see you at dinner."

Without putting down her paper, his mother wiggled her fingers at him. And ladies complained about men reading during breakfast. No gentleman had anything on his mother's absorption in the news. He wondered if Lady Adeline read at the breakfast table. He hoped not. He liked to have a conversation during breakfast.

Taking one of his footmen with him, Frits went to Covent Garden and purchased flowers, then gave the servant instructions to deliver them to Lady Adeline. With that done, he drove to the carriage maker his family used on Long Acre. Mr. Hatchett, the owner, also made vehicles for two of the royal dukes, Gloucester and Cumberland, and Frits had to assume, having seen some of the other carriages, that the man was used to unusual requests. They spent several minutes discussing the design, and Mr. Hatchett promised to have a drawing sent to Frits in a few days.

Shortly past noon, he'd finished with the carriage maker and made his way to Brooks's, instructing his groom to take the horses. He would walk back home.

Frits flipped through the newest wagers and, not finding anything concerning himself, glanced into the dining room. Turley was in deep conversation with Lord Stanstead, and Frits decided not to interrupt them. There was no doubt at all that they were discussing politics. He'd have luncheon at his desk while he worked. Then Turley waved to him, and Frits had no choice but to join the gentlemen.

"We're discussing our next attempt to repeal the Corn Laws," Stanstead said.

The more liberal side of the Whigs had been trying to do that ever since the blasted laws had been passed. "You have to make it worth the Tories' while. They think of nothing but their own gain."

"They are convinced"—Stanstead's tone was as dry as dust—"that the laws will keep them from losing their heads like the French."

"When, in fact, the opposite is likely to be true." One

of the reasons Frits eschewed politics most of the time was because of the number of true idiots in the Lords.

"Exactly," Turley said. "We must find a way to convince them they are in more danger if the law is not repealed."

Frits ordered a beefsteak and listened to their ideas. Before long, the group grew and the discussion became louder, to the point that it was difficult to keep track of who was saying and agreeing to which idea.

He'd had enough. This was one of the reasons he didn't like political discussions. Not only that, but there were now several bottles of claret on the table. He'd had one glass, but had refused to partake of any more. How could they even think after drinking so much?

He placed his serviette on the table and inclined his head. "Gentlemen, please excuse me. I have several pressing matters to attend to."

Only a few of the men acknowledged him. That didn't surprise Frits—being so engrossed in the arguments as they were. When he reached the pavement, he was amazed at how early it still was. It had seemed to him that he'd been in Brooks's for more hours than he had.

When Frits arrived home, he went directly to his office, but no matter how busy he tried to make himself, he couldn't avoid glancing at the clock every few minutes. At one point he even went over to see if anyone had wound it recently. The hours had never passed so slowly. Letters from his estates normally held his full attention, but today they did not. Frits dropped his pen on the blotter and leaned back in the chair. Perhaps he'd just think of what he'd say to Lady Adeline to make up for his mistake that morning. Then he knew what had gone wrong.

Blast me for a fool.

It was as if the proverbial scales had fallen from his eyes. He'd known from the first she was different from any other lady he'd ever met. That was what had drawn him to her. Why then was he trying to attract her as he would any other lady? He'd never actually thought he'd been overindulged by female attention. In fact, he considered young ladies an irritation. But he must have got spoilt. He'd definitely become arrogant when it came to the female sex. He had to stop thinking about how to get her into his bed and instead find a path to convincing her she wanted to be in his life.

He also had to get rid of Anglesey.

Frits glanced at the clock. Damnation! It was almost five o'clock. How the hell had that happened? He tugged on the bellpull, and a footman appeared. "Tell Lees I want my curricle brought around as soon as he can get it ready."

"Yes, my lord."

Frits would start his new campaign this afternoon.

Chapter Eleven

Adeline had arrived home annoyed. She had not liked that Lord Littleton had attempted to trick her. Fortunately, her day had been filled with activities that required her attention, including an at-home at Lady Jersey's house.

Adeline, her mother, and Eugénie arrived at the same time as two other ladies, Lady Wall and Lady Holloway, a beautiful woman with rich, dark brown hair and blue eyes. After the women had been introduced, Lady Holloway gave Adeline an odd look that she did not understand. Particularly since she had just met the woman.

However, as soon as tea had been served, her ladyship addressed Adeline, "I find Lord Littleton an extremely compelling gentleman. What can you tell me about him?"

He is a rake.

Yet she could not say that, and that might be what the lady was looking for. "He is an excellent dancer."

"I imagine he must be. Most superior horsemen are also exceptional dancers." When had her ladyship seen Lord Littleton on horseback? "But come, Lady

Adeline, I have seen you riding in his carriage. Surely you must know more about him."

Adeline did not like to be pumped for information about his lordship. And she was certainly not going to tell her ladyship about his love of his dog or the pigs. "We discuss the most commonplace of things." She struggled for something else to add. "His mother is delightful."

Lady Holloway raised her perfectly arched brows, as if she was incredulous at this piece of information. "His mother?"

Yes, most people have them.

Adeline did not understand why it was so difficult to understand that he would have a lovely mother. She struggled to keep her polite countenance. "She is here this Season and living at Littleton House."

"Indeed." Her ladyship's lips formed a moue, as if her plans had been ruined.

Thankfully, she turned to Lady Jersey and began to talk about people Adeline did not know or know well. She was glad when her mother stood and they bade Lady Jersey adieu.

"Good heavens," Mama said as soon as they had settled themselves in her coach. "What did that woman say to you?"

"Lady Holloway?" Mama nodded. "She asked about Lord Littleton. I told her there was not much to tell her except that his mother was in Town."

Smiling, she leaned back against the velvet swabs. "Very wise."

Adeline did not understand that remark either. Sometimes she felt much greener than she wanted to be. As if there was a whole part of life that was being hidden from her because she was an unmarried lady. It was not fair, and it made her feel ignorant and, more importantly, vulnerable. She might want to have a few discussions with Henrietta or Georgie. They were much more up to snuff.

As her mother's coach made its slow way to the next morning visit, Eugénie turned to her favorite subject after her husband and child. Before Will had married her and brought her to England, she had been part of a group helping to rescue slaves in the Danish West Indies, where she had lived. She and Will were still funding the project—Adeline gave a portion of her pin money to the cause as well—but her sister-in-law was no longer personally involved in rescues, as she had been before. Eugénie was influential in trying to get more legislation passed concerning the current slaves. "When will Papa-in-law introduce the bill ending the slave trade in the British West Indies?"

"Soon, I believe," Mama replied. "It has a good deal of support, but unfortunately, there have been vociferous objections by those who still own slaves in the West Indies and other places. They wish to be compensated for what they perceive as loss of property."

"It is a shame that we cannot chain them in a ship and take them to work in the sugarcane and indigo fields." Eugénie's normally lyrical voice was colder than ice. "I wonder how long it would take for them to change their minds."

Adeline thought that was an excellent idea, even if it would be impossible to actually do. "Not long at all, I suspect."

"Hmmm." Her sister-in-law leaned back against the swabs.

Mama sighed. "I feel that I must point out that abductions, especially of peers, are against the law."

One of Eugénie's brows rose, but she said nothing, leaving Adeline to wonder if the seed would actually sprout, and if it did, how to stop it from bearing fruit. Neither her mother nor father would appreciate the scandal.

The carriage stopped, and they were ushered into Lady Bellamny's house, where Adeline found Georgie and Augusta as well as Miss Hanson, a young lady with a wealth of rich chestnut hair but a perpetually pinched look on her face, and her friend, Miss Archibald, who agreed with Miss Hanson in all things. They were neighbors in the country and had grown up together.

Georgie and Augusta made room for Adeline on one of the small chaises.

"How long have you been here?" she asked her friends.

"Just a few minutes." Georgie cut her eyes to Miss Hanson, and lowered her voice. "She has been asking about Lords Turley and Littleton."

"Lord Littleton is quite the topic of conversation." Adeline could not help keep the sarcasm from her tone.

"Despite how Dorie feels about him," Georgie said, "you must admit he is the most handsome gentleman in Town this Season and, my mother tells me, the most eligible."

"He is." Adeline did not like to admit the fact, but it was true. Exeter might have a superior rank, but he was being hampered by his mother's behavior. Gentlemen like Lord Anglesey had the promise of inheriting wealth and greater titles, but they were still under their fathers' thumbs and dependent upon them for their allowances.

The talk turned to fashions, Paris, and the news that the new Duchess of Wharton, a duchess in her own right, had been located and had recently arrived in Town.

"Where was she?" Georgie asked.

"In Tortola." Lady Bellamny fastened her eyes on Eugénie. "Lady Wivenly, you might know of her family, the Calders."

A line formed between Eugénie's fine brows, but she shook her head. "We did not often travel to Tortola. The islands appear close on a map, but it is not a short journey from one to the other." She took a sip of tea. "However, I shall make a point of meeting her."

During the exchange, all the other ladies had leaned forward, obviously hoping to hear something more about the duchess, and after a collective discontent went back to discussing other things.

"This Season is definitely becoming more fascinating." Georgie smiled brightly. "It will be exciting to see who she chooses for her husband."

"I suppose so." But as far as Adeline was concerned, the Season was interminable, and she would be just as happy to return home. The only gentleman who held any promise at all was Lord Anglesey.

As expected, her friend's remark set off speculation on who the duchess would choose to wed.

"I wonder if she will have to wait to be asked, or if the fact that she is a duchess enables her to propose to the gentleman," Miss Hanson said.

Lady Bellamny quickly put an end to that speculation. "The only lady allowed to propose to a gentleman is a queen or a princess."

An hour or so after arriving home, Adeline was making her way to the hall and had just finished pulling on her gloves when Abney greeted Lord Littleton.

His lordship stood straight and tall, with shoulders broader than any man had a right to. A slight smile was on his well-formed lips as he watched her descend the stairs. It must have been all the talk this afternoon, because he looked even more handsome than usual. She had never noticed how thick and long his black lashes were. They made his eyes appear even greener. And even though a streak of guilt speared her, Adeline could not help but be glad it was him she was riding with. At least he would not want her to gossip about other people. Still, she must address his behavior this morning. That could not be allowed to occur again.

He'd barely climbed into the seat beside her when he got a sheepish look on his face. "I have to ask your forgiveness for this morning. I have told Humphries that from now on he will walk Maximus without my interference."

"Thank you." Well, that took the wind out of her sails. Still, she was not going to let him get away that easily. "You are forgiven, but I was not at all pleased that you tried to jape me."

"You're not the only one," he grumbled to himself, and Adeline had to keep from smiling. "From now on, Maximus will visit with you accompanied only by his footman." Drat the man! She had been ready to ring a peal over his head, but he turned his sorrowful green eyes to her, and she could not do it. "I promise I will never attempt to deceive you about anything again."

She did not want to believe him, but his look was so sincere and open, she did not have a choice. He was telling her the truth. "Thank you."

"No. Thank you for allowing me to make my apology. I should not have done it." He threaded the ribbons through his fingers and gave the pair their office.

"I do look forward to walking with Maximus." The kennel master at home had taught her about walking the dogs. Of course, none of them were anywhere near the Great Dane's size. It would be more like walking a horse. Adeline still wanted a dog of her own. "It is a shame that the Worthingtons' dogs are not going to have another litter anytime soon."

"It might be sooner than you think," Frits said as he feathered a corner. "Worthington said something about this autumn."

Autumn. If luck was with her, she would be married by then and be able to get one of the puppies. Whoever she married must like dogs and want them in the house. She was not going to spend the rest of her life deprived of a housedog. Lord Anglesey's reaction to seeing Maximus had been disappointing. Then again, it might have been because Lord Littleton was there.

They entered the Park and began making their way behind the other carriages.

"Lord Littleton." Adeline's teeth clenched at the breathy female voice. She glanced to her side, but his size blocked her view, and she could not see who had spoken.

"Miss Tice." His bored drawl made her look past him to the lady in a high-perched phaeton accompanied by her friend, Miss Martindale.

Adeline pasted a polite smile on her face. "Good afternoon."

For a bare moment, a sour look appeared on Miss Tice's face, only to be quickly replaced by a slight smile. "Lady Adeline, I did not see you."

Adeline used her sweetest voice as she said, "That is not at all surprising. From that side I am sure it is difficult to see past his lordship."

"How very true." Miss Martindale tittered. "I was just saying how very large Lord Littleton is."

Miss Tice picked up her ribbons. "I hope we shall see you at Lady Elliott's ball?"

"Yes, indeed," Adeline responded. She was not sure who exactly the lady had addressed, but the tic in Lord Littleton's jaw assured her that he would not have answered.

"Ladies." He inclined his head and moved the carriage forward.

Having been caught wool-gathering, Adeline kept an eye out for the ladies who must be acknowledged and for a glimpse of her friends; she had not paid much attention to the other ladies since the first time she had driven with Lord Littleton. Now she saw Lady Sutton look him over as one would a particularly tasty treat, and Lady Holloway eye him speculatively. And although another lady wiggled her fingers at him, he did not appear to notice her; instead, he turned his attention to Adeline. Despite being a rake, he had impeccable manners.

"I ordered a new curricle with a place for Maximus." His boyish grin softened the strong, angular lines of his lean face.

"He will love being able to ride with you." From what she had seen of Augusta's dogs, they loved being with people.

"That's what I think." Lord Littleton nodded thoughtfully.

"When will it be completed?"

"In a few weeks. Perhaps less." In fact, Frits had agreed to a much higher price for the carriage so it would be constructed quickly. "I impressed upon them that I wanted it as soon as possible."

Another one of his former lovers tried to get his attention. This was becoming a damned nuisance. "Will you accompany us on its maiden drive?"

"With Maximus?" Her gray eyes turned silver, and

Frits hoped that meant Lady Adeline was delighted. "I would love to."

That was the first time she had been so happy when she'd accepted an invitation from him. He hadn't even had to ask her when she could not refuse. His chest puffed out until it occurred to him her happiness was probably because of the dog. "Excellent."

"Oh, look. There is Dorie and Lord Exeter."

Frits glanced in the direction she was pointing. "So it is." He sincerely hoped that his friend would capture Lady Dorie's hand soon. Perhaps once she had formed an attachment to another gentleman, Lady Adeline would not think so harshly of him. In the meantime, he felt as if he was treading water when he really wanted to swim to shore. "When is your come out ball?"

Her eyes widened, as if the question shocked her. Surely her mother planned a ball for her. Then her fine brows pulled together. "Not for another week or so. I think." She gave a decisive nod. "Yes, I think it's in two weeks. Mama is waiting for my godmother to arrive in Town, and she lives in the Lake District."

"Is it too early to ask you for the supper dance?" He prayed it was a waltz. He never got tired of waltzing with Lady Adeline. She was the most graceful lady with whom he had ever stood up.

She hesitated for a second, then her lips curved up. "Not at all."

"Thank you." They had completed one circuit and he would have asked her if she wanted to go around again, but the number of carriages had grown, and it would take them at least another hour before he could take her home. Well, nothing ventured, nothing gained. "Would you care to continue on?"

She glanced at the traffic, opened her watch brooch, and shook her head. "I should go home."

At least she didn't look happy with her decision. "I thought that might be your answer. I wouldn't want your mother to think I'd made off with you."

Raising her brows, she chuckled. "I am sure she knows you would do no such thing. Speaking of that, our mothers have just entered the fray."

He looked around and, sure enough, both of them were in Lady Watford's landau. Unfortunately, coming through the gate was Anglesey, and Frits could not avoid passing the man.

Making himself politely incline his head, he greeted his lordship. "Anglesey, well-met."

"Littleton," Anglesey said stiffly. When he glanced at Adeline, his smile reminded Frits of a trickster's. "Lady Adeline, a pleasure to see you again. I am truly honored to come across you twice in one day."

Frits was going to be ill on the spot.

"My lord." She gave Anglesey her hand, and Frits wished he could see her expression. "It is nice to see you."

At least she wasn't "delighted." "We must be going."

"Until this evening, fair lady." The rapscallion rode off.

"You do not like him, do you?" Adeline's head was tilted to one side, and she wore her considering look.

"Not particularly." Frits started the curricle again.

"Why?"

He pulled to a stop. If she was going to ask questions like that, he needed to pay attention to what he was saying and not his horses. "I can't really say." Other than that the man was much too interested in Adeline, and he didn't like it. No. It was more than that. Frits didn't trust the lordling. Why else would he have written to Elizabeth Harrington? "It is just a feeling." He wished he could tell her to stay away from his lordship. But he had no right, nor did he have any evidence against Anglesey. "That is all it is, a feeling."

"Hmmm. I noticed Maximus did not care for him." She stared straight past Frits, her eyes unfocused.

"I'd trust Maximus's reading of the man. Great Danes are very discerning." Perhaps if she couldn't trust Frits, she'd trust his dog.

Adeline gave a slight shrug. "You might be correct."

Sensing the conversation was over, he gave his horses their office. He'd like to be in a position to overtly protect her. But he wasn't, so he would simply have to do it by other means.

She gave a little snort. "Do you mean to tell me that you are not going to agree that you could be right?"

That made him smile. "Now that you mention it, I will."

He was rewarded by a light peal of laughter. "I thought you might."

Her cheeks were the same color pink as the flowers he'd sent that morning. It was odd that she had not mentioned them. "Did you like the bouquet I sent you?"

Her eyes rounded and she shook her head. "I haven't seen them."

"No?" He didn't think the arrangement had been so small as to be overlooked.

"I was out of the house all day and arrived home just in time to change for our ride. I shall look for them when I get home."

They were approaching Upper Brook Street when he had a thought. "Would you like to go to Gunter's for an ice?"

"Oh, I would love to!" She clasped her hands together at her breast, plumping them together, and he had to make himself look at her face. "I have not been there yet."

"Then it is time you visited." That was a much better idea than remaining in the Park had been. He'd be able to spend more time with her and not be interrupted by others passing by. Perhaps he'd even find a way past the barrier she had erected between them.

Chapter Twelve

Mmm. The Muscadine ice was divine. Adeline was absolutely certain she had never tasted anything so sumptuous in her entire life. "Thank you for suggesting this." She slowly sucked the last little bit from the spoon and thought she heard Lord Littleton groan. "Are you well? I have heard that eating ices too quickly can cause a headache."

"I'm fine." His tone was brusque as he turned abruptly and hailed a waiter. "I'm glad you are enjoying yourself."

"I am." This was better than all the balls she had attended put together. There was still a sheen of the ice in the dish, but the only way to get to it would be to lick it out. Stifling a sigh, she handed him the bowl. "Thank you."

His lips twitched as his grass-green eyes twinkled. "You may have another if you wish."

"No, thank you. I need a reason to return." As often as she could.

Adeline could not help but notice his lips as he smiled. The bottom lip was a little fuller than the top, but what was fascinating was the way the ends tipped up even when he was not smiling. How had she not noticed that before?

"Shall we make it a traditional end to a carriage ride?"

Well, that might be a problem. Adeline kept telling herself that she should not accept his offers of carriage rides, but for some reason she always did. Although, to be fair, he always asked when she could not politely decline. Except for today, when he had asked if she would like to go out with him and Maximus in the new carriage. Nevertheless, when they *were* riding together, and even though Henrietta said she thought Dorie would understand, Adeline hoped and prayed Dorie would not be there to see her.

This, though, was different. It seemed like more of a commitment. How bad could a promise to eat ices be? Especially when Adeline liked them so much.

She refocused her eyes and found him staring at her and prayed that if her friend found out, she would not hate her. Surely anyone who had tasted the Muscadine ices could not argue that they must be enjoyed at every opportunity. "I think that is an excellent idea."

"Thank you." Lord Littleton's chest appeared to grow broader, if that was even possible. "I should take you home. I'm sure your mother will expect you to be there when she returns."

"She probably will." Adeline hadn't even considered that her mother would not have seen them leave the Park.

When they pulled up in front of her house, he jumped down and beat the footman—who had come running out—to her side. She caught a breath as his large hands almost encircled her waist. Warmth spread from where his hands burned through the silk twill of her carriage gown through her body. She couldn't even breathe as he lifted her down, carefully placing her feet on the pavement. Not even her brother was as strong as Lord Littleton. Adeline had never thought of herself as petite, but he made her feel that way. As soon as he dropped his hands, she sucked in as much air as she could and gingerly placed her fingers on his arm.

After he escorted her to the door, he raised her hand, and Adeline could focus on nothing but his lips as he placed a kiss on the back of her glove. "Thank you for your company."

Staring at her glove, she would have forgotten to curtsey if she had not practiced the movement since she had been old enough to walk. "I had a very nice time."

"Until this evening." He stepped back and made his way down the short walk to his carriage.

"Yes." Although by now, he couldn't hear her.

The door opened, and she strolled into the hall only to see a large bouquet of pink roses standing on the ormolu table.

Abney bowed. "Those are for you, my lady. Her ladyship said you may read the note."

She did not require a note to tell her they were from Lord Littleton. After what he had said, she would have been shocked if they were not. "Thank you." Picking up the opened missive, she noted his strong hand. Fortunately, instead of writing a poem or an extravagant message the way some of the other gentlemen did, he simply wished that she would enjoy the blooms.

"Would you like them taken to your chambers?"

No! She almost shouted the word. She did not need his flowers in her bedchamber. They were too beautiful to be relegated to the drawing room, but she did not

wish to think about him more than she already did.
"Please put them in the morning room."

"As you wish, my lady."

She pulled out the hatpin from her bonnet but did
not remove it. She wasn't going to be stuck inside on
such a lovely day. "I shall be in the garden, reading."

And trying to forget about her waltz with Lord
Littleton that evening.

She must begin focusing more on Lord Anglesey. It
appeared as if he might be interested in her. Yet, despite his golden good looks, he didn't affect her the
way Lord Littleton did. And that was a problem she did
not need. On the other hand, she had spent much
more time with Lord Littleton. She would simply have
to do the same with Lord Anglesey.

"Did you see them?" Annis Watford said to her
friend and ally, Cristabel Littleton. As children, their
families' estates had shared a border, and the houses
stood near the boundary. Their mothers had been
great friends, and they had grown up together. Their
mothers had attempted to arrange a match between
Annis's older brother and Cristabel, but they could not
be in each other's company without insulting each
other and the idea died.

"Yes. If he has any sense at all, he'll take her to
Gunter's. I meant to suggest it to him earlier, but I
forgot." Cristabel glanced at Annis. "You did tell me
she has not been there yet?"

"She has not even had ice cream in years. I am not
sure she would remember eating one. We never think
about making them." Annis focused on the carriages
around them. It would not do to be behind in greeting

people. "I do hope they will make a match of it. I do not remember the process being so hard when I was young."

"Our parents arranged our matches," Cristabel reminded her drily.

"They did, but you must give them credit. They looked to see which men attracted us and were attracted to us." Annis still sighed when she thought of the first time she had seen William.

"You have a point." Cristabel brought a lace-trimmed handkerchief to her eyes and dabbed. "I knew Edmund was for me the moment I saw him staring at me."

Reaching over, Annis squeezed her friend's hand. "I know you miss him."

"I do." Cristabel blew her nose. "But now it is time to see Frits married, and I agree. I think he and Adeline are perfect for each other. If only it was not for Dorie Calthorp."

Annis waved to Lady Bellamny before asking, "What does she have to do with anything?"

Cristabel looked taken aback. "You really do not know what occurred?"

Annis shook her head. "When we're in Town we usually only attend the political events. This is the first year I've been to anything but those. Even so, I have been relying a great deal on my son and daughter-in-law to chaperone Adeline."

"Frits raised her expectations last Season, then realized at the last moment the match would not work. To make a long story short, he went home."

"Cristabel!" For a moment, Annis was too shocked to speak. "How could he have done such a thing? Surely he knew better."

Her friend's lips formed a moue and she sighed.

"It was not well done of him. Yet, in his defense, his attentions were not so particular that he raised the interest of the *ton*. Dorie is just like her mother, and it took him longer than it should have to realize that they were not meant for each other."

"Ah, I believe I understand. The difficulty now is that Adeline met Dorie almost immediately upon arriving in Town, and they are friends." That did make things more difficult. "My daughter is extremely loyal, but if we arrange things so that they are together more often, perhaps the attraction will become too strong for her to ignore. I do think she is, despite everything, interested in him." Annis smiled. "The dog helps too."

Cristabel chuckled. "Our thinking aligns. Oh"—she patted Annis's arm—"I also spoke with Sally Huntingdon. She has always liked Frederick but never thought he was the right gentleman for Dorie. She is of the opinion that Exeter would make a much better husband for her daughter. They have more in common."

"Now that you mention it, I can see that." Annis grimaced. "I live in daily dread that Adeline will insist on going back to the country."

"I am positive the only thing keeping Frits in Town is your daughter." Shaking her head, Cristabel shrugged. "He can go years without showing his face here for more than a week or so."

"Yet another reason we should see them wed before the Season is over. They can both return to the country and the animals." If only Annis could find a way to convince her daughter to set aside her loyalty to her friend. That, though, would not be easy to do. She and Cristabel would have to have a meeting with Sally Huntingdon. Annis had the feeling it would take the combined efforts of all the mothers to bring off this match.

* * *

Later that evening, after the second set had ended, Adeline noticed Georgie glancing down at her gown. "Is something wrong?"

"The bottom flounce is coming loose. I think one of the gentlemen caught it." She shook her skirt and, sure enough, there was a tear. "Will you come to the retiring room with me?"

"Of course." Early on in the Season, Adeline and her friends had decided they would go nowhere alone, especially at a ball.

She told her sister-in-law, and she and Georgie set off to find the retiring room. Once there, they glanced around. Two rooms had been put together, and there were several screens set up for more privacy.

"This is a good idea." Adeline led her friend behind one of the screens, where they found a chair, a table with pins and other items, and the expected chamber pot. "Stand here and I will pin it together." She sat in the chair and began to repair the skirt.

The door opened, and two ladies came in talking. After they left, all was quiet for a few moments; then a lady said, "He is quite the most handsome gentleman in Town and my mother said he is as rich as the Golden Ball and old enough to marry without his guardian's permission. Which the Golden Ball is not."

Adeline stopped what she was doing and whispered to Georgie, "That's Miss Hanson."

Georgie nodded, and placed her mouth next to Adeline's ear. "But who is the gentleman?"

Another lady tittered. That had to be Miss Archibald. "How are you going to get Lord Littleton's attention? He only dances with a few ladies."

"I am not going to *dance* with him." There was a pause. Adeline and Georgie exchanged a glance. "After we are betrothed I will have all his sets. I am going to write him a note. Actually, I have already written it. When we leave here I shall give it to a footman to deliver. That is when I shall need your help. Once he leaves the ballroom, you must tell my mother that you think something is wrong and bring her to the shrubbery on the right side of the terrace."

"But how do you know he will be there?" Miss Archibald asked.

Adeline realized she was holding her breath, then as silently as possible, let it out. "I have seen the way some of the matrons look at him," Miss Hanson said archly. "If he thinks there is a possibility of a liaison, he'll come."

Skirts rustled, and the door opened and closed. Adeline rose on her tip-toes to look through the carved design in the screen. The other ladies had left. She had wondered what those looks meant. She still did not know all of it, but it had something to do with being alone with a gentleman. Nevertheless, even a rake did not deserve to be trapped into marriage. "What a horrible thing to do. I have heard of ladies attempting to coerce gentlemen into marriage, but I thought it never really happened." To be honest, she believed her brother had been exaggerating. "I have to warn him."

"I agree." Georgie's brows rose as she glanced at her skirt. "After you finish pinning the ruffle."

"Yes, of course."

Two pins later, Adeline left the room with her friend.

Once they had reached the ballroom, she searched over the heads of most of the guests. Fortunately, Lord Littleton was one of the taller gentlemen. Still, it took a bit of time before she located him speaking with Lord Turley.

"I found him." She did not have much time before the next set, and her party was on the opposite side of the ballroom from Lord Littleton. She and Georgie skirted the side of the room, not stopping to talk to anyone.

Finally, they reached the gentlemen. "Lord Littleton."

A smile formed on his lips, and she dragged her gaze from it. "There is a lady trying to trap you into marriage. If you receive a note, do not follow its directions." The sounds of the quartet interrupted her. "I must go back. Promise me you will remain in the ballroom."

Confusion clouded his green eyes. "I shall."

Georgie plucked at Adeline's sleeve. "We will be late."

They made it back to their circle just as their partners for the next dance arrived. Adeline smiled brightly and curtseyed. "Lord Ailesbury."

"My lady."

Even though Adeline loved to dance, the next three sets were interminable. All she wanted to do was to explain everything to Lord Littleton, and she could not do that until the supper dance. She almost snapped at poor Lord Bottomley, who stepped on her toes as he was trying to look at Augusta. Mooning over her would not do him a bit of good. But he did not know that. And Adeline was very tempted to leave Lord Gray alone on the dance floor when he tried to switch places in a country dance to be closer to Lady Letitia. Granted she was pretty, and her lineage was excellent, but why he was interested in such a vain and superficial female, Adeline had no idea.

Lord Anglesey had been extremely attentive, even explaining his reaction to Maximus: "My dear Lady Adeline, I did not mean to upset you this morning. I adore dogs. I believe I was simply shocked to see such a large one." He smiled shyly. "My mother had pugs, and my father had hunting dogs, but they are both much smaller than a Great Dane."

She supposed that could happen. And he was being very contrite about his behavior. "I understand. They are quite large."

"Indeed they are." He gave her a charming smile. "They are also quite majestic. Do you not agree?"

"I do." Maximus was magnificent. "They are very sweet."

"Perhaps I should think of adding one to my household." His blue eyes warmed as he gazed into hers. "But only if my future wife would like such a grand animal."

Heat flooded her cheeks. Was he truly considering her? "Of course, the lady must be consulted."

"You are not only lovely, but clever." He drew her a little closer. "Have you been presented yet? My father is arranging for me to attend the Prince Regent's levee."

Due to her mother's fears about the queen's health, she had been rushed to Town to be presented in February. "I have, but my understanding is that it is much less complicated than a lady being presented."

He inclined his head. "Everything appears to be more complicated for ladies." That was the truth. "I do not wish to bore you about Paris, but do you know if there are salons here?"

Thank goodness Augusta had discussed her visit to a salon and told Adeline and the others about it. "Lady Thornhill holds salons that have been compared to the ones in Paris by those who have attended both."

"Excellent." His smile broadened. "Perhaps you will be allowed to attend and we may meet there."

Her mother had not mentioned it, but there was no harm in asking. "Perhaps we might."

The music ended, and Adeline curtseyed. "Thank you for the dance, my lord."

"My lady, I do not believe I have ever enjoyed a set more." Her cheeks heated again with the compliment. "Would you ride out with me tomorrow during the Promenade?"

"Oh, dear." She raised her hand to her mouth. Was tomorrow free? She could not remember. "I must ask my mother. She might have something planned."

He took her arm and began to amble back to where her circle was. "I shall send an invitation around, if that would suit?"

"Yes, thank you." He was so very nice. She would enjoy spending more time with him.

"It is my pleasure." His blue eyes sparkled appreciatively.

Adeline would have loved to spend more time with his lordship, but she had to get back to speak to Lord Littleton about the threat he faced, and Lord Anglesey was walking as if they had all the time in the world. Any other evening she would have been pleased that he wished to spend more time with her. Unfortunately, now was not the time. She hastened her steps.

Chapter Thirteen

Lord Anglesey remained with her, and Adeline was enjoying his company a great deal, but Lord Littleton would be here soon, and neither man behaved well around the other.

Unfortunately, his lordship had not yet taken his leave when Lord Littleton appeared before her and bowed. "Lady Adeline."

Lord Anglesey stiffened and his face became a mask. "Littleton, good evening."

"A good evening to you." He glanced around. "Should you not find your next dance partner?"

Oh, dear. Not this again. She held out her hand to Lord Anglesey. "I very much enjoyed our dance."

"My lady." He bowed. "I shall see you soon." Before she could respond, he stalked off.

Well, drat. Still, he could not very well remain when she had to speak with Lord Littleton. She glanced up at his lordship. "I have to tell you—" Perhaps she could take him off to the side and talk with him before the set began.

"But not quite yet." His voice was gentle as he placed

her hand on his arm as if nothing of note was happening. "As long as I am in the ballroom, I am safe, am I not?"

"Yes." That much was true. Her heart was beating a tattoo, stealing her breath.

She wanted to ask him if he had received the missive, but she realized there were too many people around them. He had been right to stop her from talking. In fact, this ball was much too crowded.

"In that case, we shall dance." He placed his hands on her waist, and she set hers on his shoulders.

She gave a tight nod. "Yes."

The whole incident had offended her sense of justice, and the few times she saw Miss Hanson, it was all Adeline could do not to berate the female. Yet it was easier than she had thought it would be to allow herself to relax and follow Lord Littleton's lead. He was quite the best dancer she had been with all evening. Sadly, even Lord Anglesey was not as graceful. Adeline never feared he would step on her feet, or allow his attention to be distracted by another lady. By the end of the set, she had calmed down considerably.

He tucked her hand in the crook of his arm as they strolled off the dance floor to an alcove with a bust of Diana, the goddess of the hunt, in it. The rest of the guests were making their way to the supper room, thus they were unlikely to be overheard.

He stopped a footman and procured two glasses of champagne. "Take a sip of this and tell me exactly what occurred."

"Thank you for the champagne." Adeline did not know how he could be so calm. She would not have been. Then again, she had never seen him become upset. This incident had certainly angered her. But perhaps this type of thing had happened to him before.

According to her mother, he was the most eligible gentleman in Town. What did not make sense to her was why Miss Hanson was trying to trap him into marriage. She was a beautiful young lady. Far more beautiful than Adeline, and, if gossip was to be believed, she was wealthy. Not only that, but her mother was very well connected. Perhaps the lady wished the distinction of marrying a gentleman so many other ladies seemed to want. Nevertheless, it was a dastardly way to go about it.

She took another sip of wine. "I do not know how you can be so calm."

"I have found that allowing myself to be overwrought doesn't do anyone any good, particularly me."

As Frits had wanted her to do, Adeline smiled.

Before their dance, he could see that she was becoming more and more agitated. He didn't think anyone else noticed, but he was coming to know her, and not much upset her calm good nature.

Except him, of course.

He hoped that was because she was starting to like him and did not want to because of what he'd done last Season. But then there was Anglesey, and she was smiling much too much when she was with the man.

"Tell me what exactly happened," he prompted.

He drank in the sight of her, the way her brow puckered. The way her slender throat moved with the motion of swallowing. He wished he could press his lips to her throat and feel her pulse. He wanted to see what color her nipples were as he—

This had to stop.

The next thing he knew, he'd be throwing her over his shoulder and striding out with her. Frits was sure one of his ancestors had done just that. He also remembered that his forefather had received a black eye from the lady for his presumption. It had still been bruised when they wed. Or so the story went. Whichever great-grandsire he was had succeeded faster than Frits was.

Holding the glass, she twisted it in her hands. "I was helping Miss Featherton pin one of her flounces. It had torn. We were behind a screen, and two ladies entered the room . . ."

When she mentioned the name of the lady attempting to trap him, a Miss Hanson, Frits could not place her. He wondered if he'd even met her. "What does she look like?"

"Very pretty, with rich chestnut hair and creamy skin. She has blue eyes." Adeline must have realized that he didn't know who she was talking about and added, "She is wearing a pale blue gown with silver netting."

Still nothing. He shook his head. He did not even remember seeing her this evening. "I am positive I have never been introduced to her."

Adeline's nicely rounded jaw firmed and her silver eyes sparked with anger. "What a fiend she is. It is bad enough to attempt to compromise a gentleman one knows, but I cannot think of a word contemptible enough for a female who would do so to a man she has not even met."

He could think of a few appropriate words, but they were not for a lady's ears. Especially Adeline's. He liked hearing her defend him, but now she was waiting for him to answer. To be as outraged as she was. "Yes, well."

She took another sip of wine. A larger one this time. "Did you receive the note?"

"I did." Frits promptly took it out of the pocket in

his waistcoat, unfolded it, and handed it to her. "It is singularly uninformative. It merely directs me to meet the writer near the bushes to the right of the terrace."

She perused the missive. "That is what she said she had written. She brought it with her." Adeline glanced around the room. "Do you have the time?"

Did that mean the lady knew he'd be here, or would any gentleman have done? There was no name on the message. He opened his pocket watch. "Five past the hour."

"The meeting is not for another twenty-five minutes." She looked up from the paper, and he was surprised to see a challenging, almost militant look in her eyes. She was ferociously furious on his behalf. Just the thought of her wishing to protect him warmed his heart, but, again, that made him want to sweep her off her feet and to his coach. "We could both go and confront her."

It was a good thing he'd not yet taken a drink; otherwise, he'd be choking. Frits might not know Miss Hanson, but he knew her type. He'd been plagued by them for years. And it would *not* be a good idea for her to know Adeline had ruined her plan. "I would prefer that we join the others for supper. Then, when you see her, you can tell me which lady she is."

Her finely arched brows furrowed, causing a line between them. Frits kept his elbows firmly against his sides. He was very close to drawing her into his arms. After several moments, she let out a huff of air. "I suppose that would be better than creating a scene."

"Much." Thank God she was being reasonable. Then again, she was usually sensible. He held out his arm, and she took it. "Not nearly as satisfying, but much better." Not only that, but tonight at supper, he'd make sure he was able to sit next to her.

When they reached the supper room, he was pleased to see that her family had held two chairs for them.

"What took you so long?" her sister-in-law asked.

Adeline glanced at him, and he nodded. "There was a lady who wished to compromise Lord Littleton, and I was helping him."

Her brother Wively patted her on her back. "Well done." He glanced at Frits. "It never ceases to amaze me how many ladies think that is a sure way to the altar." He slipped his arm about his wife, gazing at her besottedly. "Thank God I found Eugénie."

Frits had known the man for years. He found it interesting—almost comical—that after dodging marriage-minded ladies and their mamas since he'd come down from Oxford, Wively had left England to avoid marriage only to return with a wife. "I am eternally grateful that Lady Adeline sought to help me."

Her cheeks and the tops of her breasts were awash with a lovely deep pink. *Look at her eyes.* "I think I should eat something. All this intrigue has made me hungry."

"We have plates for you," Lady Wively said, indicating the table.

Frits held the chair for Adeline, and took the place next to her. It was the first supper where her friends had not surrounded her, relegating him to the end of the table with Exeter. In fact—he glanced around— all the young ladies were sitting with their families and the gentlemen who had stood up with them for the supper dance.

He dipped his spoon into the white soup. "Did we miss anything?"

"You might say that." Wively grinned. "Exeter defended his sisters, and the ladies decided that anyone who speaks badly about the girls will not be invited to any of their entertainments."

Something about that didn't quite make sense. "His sisters aren't out yet."

"And will not be for years," Adeline added. "This must have something to do with his mother's behavior."

"It did," Lady Wively said. "Lady Letitia was not at all happy about being introduced to Exeter; then she started saying that there must be something wrong with his younger sister, as neither of his older sisters had taken them in after their mother left. She could not see we were sitting here, but her voice carried, and he went straight over and told the lady and her mother that he would not stand for their slander."

"I never thought she was so cruel. I will certainly have nothing more to do with her." Adeline lifted her glass of wine. "I wish we had been here to see it."

"It was *très impressionnant*," her sister-in-law said.

For Exeter's sake, Frits hoped Lady Dorie thought the same. He desperately wanted her to decide to marry the man. "That was well done of him. It never does to allow false rumors to start."

Lord and Lady Watford had joined a political discussion with Lord and Lady Huntingdon and Exeter and Lady Dorie, leaving Frits, Adeline, and her brother and sister-in-law to talk about other subjects. Frits had been stunned and impressed to discover Lady Wively had actually been physically involved in saving slaves on St. Thomas in the Danish West Indies, and was still actively supporting the cause. What was even more interesting was the extent to which the venture captured Adeline's attention.

"Did I tell you that Eugénie has formed a charity that pays shipowners for helping free the slaves?"

Adeline asked. "Some of them are rescued at sea when the ships carrying slaves are stopped."

He knew British naval ships were tasked with the job, but he had not known private ships were involved as well. "I suppose our navy cannot find all the slave traders."

"Especially when some of the countries who sign laws ending the slave trade continue it," Adeline commented drily.

Another thing of which he had not been aware. "Who in particular?"

"Denmark and Norway." Pushing away the soup, she helped herself to two lobster patties. He'd have to remember how much she liked them.

"One of my friends is heir to a shipping company," Wively said. "He assists us."

That gave Frits an idea. One that would kill two birds as it were, save people, and improve Adeline's opinion of him. "Do you need more ships?"

"We always need more ships," Adeline responded. "And money. I give what I am allowed to from my pin money."

"I have a shipping company." He grinned when Adeline's jaw as well as her brother's and sister-in-law's jaws dropped. "My family long ago decided that the health of the barony would be better served by having a wide range of investments. I don't personally manage it, but I can put the ships at your disposal when required."

"*Merci.*" Lady Wively smiled gratefully. "We shall accept your kind offer."

When they had finished eating, Frits decided to escort Adeline to the hall while their coaches were being brought around. He was perplexed to find the rest of their group joining them. Then he remembered that for some reason, all the ladies in her circle departed after supper. Come to think of it, that was probably the reason she rose so early.

As they left the room, she squeezed his arm. "Do you see the two ladies in the corner next to the tree with the red flowers?"

He cut his eyes quickly in that direction. "Yes."

"Miss Hanson is the one in the blue gown." Adeline had tipped up her head, and her breath caressed his jaw, creating an almost overwhelming urge to dip his head and kiss her.

"I shall make sure to stay out of her way." And avoid an introduction. Although that had not deterred the female. Just then, Miss Hanson raised her eyes, and he quickly lowered his to Adeline, making sure that anyone—but particularly Miss Hanson—knew where his interests lay.

Adeline began strolling again. "Do you often receive unsigned notes?"

Where the devil had that question come from? "No." And that was all he was going to say on the matter. He did not want Adeline to think any worse of him than she already did, especially as he was going to wait until her mother was nearby to ask her to accompany him tomorrow. He'd told himself he wouldn't do that again, but he couldn't take the chance she would refuse him.

They reached her parents' coach and he waited while her mother and sister-in-law were handed up. "Can I tempt you into another carriage ride tomorrow?"

"What a lovely idea," her mother interpolated before she could reply, and he almost groaned with frustration. He didn't need *that* much help.

Adeline's lips pressed together. "Thank you for the kind invitation. I shall see you tomorrow."

He handed her into the carriage. "Until then." When he'd torture himself watching her lick the final bit of ice cream from her spoon.

Chapter Fourteen

Crispin fought to keep his polite mask in place as Lady Adeline joined the set with Lord Littleton.

Damn Littleton! How did he always end up with the supper dance?

Well, he wouldn't get it for tomorrow's ball. Crispin would write to Lady Adeline this evening, when he returned home, requesting the set, and have the invitation delivered first thing in the morning. Unless his lordship had already secured the dance. If so, there was nothing he could do about it but ask for the supper dance at the next ball. Yes. That was exactly what he'd do. He would also ask for the opportunity to take her for a carriage ride.

This was turning into much more work than Crispin had originally planned when he chose Lady Adeline. Leaning against a column, he surveyed the room. He could choose another one. There were enough ladies out, and some of them met his qualifications. But he'd already made up his mind to wed Lady Adeline, and there was no good reason to steer away from his course. From what he had heard, she was upset with Littleton because of something he'd done last Season. That should work in Crispin's favor. He'd simply have to be more persistent in pursuing her. By her reactions to him this evening, it would not be long before he could propose.

He caught a lady he'd been introduced to by the name of Miss Hanson giving him a speculative look. She was clearly on the hunt for a title. The lady was much more beautiful than Lady Adeline, but although her mother's birth was respectable, her father was a Cit, and that wouldn't do for him at all.

The Earl of Lytton approached Miss Hanson, bowed, and led her to the dance floor. Was he in need of funds? That was the only reason Crispin could see for his lordship to be interested in her. He was too high in the instep to pay attention to her otherwise.

"I am finding this ball vastly boring." Lady Holloway opened her fan, covering lips that owed more to cosmetics than nature. Her bodice revealed a large expanse of snow-white skin and plump breasts. It was a pity it was not nearly as low as what the ladies in Paris wore, but this was England.

Crispin had to agree. He'd met her ladyship the other evening at a card party and was pleased by his perspicacity in deciding to arrange to lease a small town house. His father's house was not nearly private enough for all Crispin's doings. Not only that, but few ladies wanted to engage in trysts at their own homes. Even the widows were cautious. "Can I interest you in another activity?"

She blinked slowly, her dark, thick lashes fanning out against her cheeks. Her tongue peeked out and licked her bottom lip, causing his cock to harden. Ever since Sarah had stopped allowing his visits, he'd been as randy as a goat.

She glanced at his breeches, and, unsurprisingly, his erection became more noticeable. At least he was wearing breeches and not pantaloons. "That rather depends on what type of entertainment you are offering."

He lifted his gaze from her bosom and caught her eyes. "Come with me and find out. I am sure you'll enjoy yourself."

"Hmmm." The witch dropped her eyes again, and he could almost feel her mouth on him. "Yes. I believe I will. Meet me outside. I have the red town coach. You can enter on the opposite side from the door."

How was it that Crispin had never noticed how dictative Englishwomen could be on their home territory? It was not like that in France. Here discretion ruled their lives. No wonder so many gentlemen frequented brothels or kept at least one mistress. "Are you not worried your coachman will talk?"

"I pay him well." She raised one brow. "If he wishes to keep his position, he will keep where I go to himself." Lady Holloway trailed her closed fan along his arm and left.

This night would not be a loss after all.

In anticipation of finding an amorous partner, he'd sent his carriage home. He didn't want any of his father's servants to know about the house he'd hired. Crispin waited for a while before making his way into the hall and out onto the pavement. The door closed on a small red town coach. He strolled to the other side and opened the door. "Do you want to give the address or shall I?"

She settled her skirts, taking time in answering him. "I will." Crispin gave her an address on Savile Row, and she knocked on the roof of the carriage and gave it to her coachman. Once the coach started forward, she said, "I do not think I have ever been there."

"The street is filled with a great many military men and their families, as well as some shops." She smoothed her skirts again, confusing him. She had appeared so confident before. "You do not have to worry about being seen. We can go in through the back if you wish."

"Thank you." Lady Holloway chuckled lightly. "I suppose I should admit that I have never done this before. I am recently out of mourning for my husband and have decided to live my life to please myself instead of my husband or family."

That was a story he'd heard many times before. "Will you remarry?"

She flashed him what might have been a grin. Or a grimace. It was too dark to tell. "If I do, it will not be anytime soon. I want to enjoy myself for a while."

"As do I." He took her hand and raised it to his lips. "Tonight, we will take it slowly and learn what the other likes." Many ladies in her position were surprisingly ignorant of the finer points of amorous congress, and he'd be more than happy to teach her. He liked watching their faces as they discovered bliss for the first time. He liked having myriad lovers, and despite his duty to sire an heir, he had absolutely no desire to tie himself down to one woman. As he did with his lovers, Crispin would make sure his wife enjoyed their time in bed, but she wouldn't be his only bedmate.

The clock struck two as he rolled off Lady Holloway and slipped his arm around her. Her heart still pounded a sharp tattoo, and her body glistened with their exertions. She had not been totally untutored, but her husband had never taught her how many ways there were to pleasure a woman.

No matter their intimacies, she still had not even told him her first name. Crispin supposed it was her way to maintain a distance, but he didn't like it. Using a bored drawl, he said, "I trust you enjoyed yourself, my lady."

Her blue eyes searched his. "You know I did."

"Yet, you will not allow me to know your name." He cupped one generous breast, molding it as he feathered his thumb over her nipple. He'd soon be ready again.

A shiver ran through her and her nipple drew into a tight bud. "I do not use yours either."

"But I have told you to call me Crispin." He drew the bud into his mouth, reveling in the way she pressed against him. He'd been lucky to find a widow so starved for a man. He stroked her already heated skin. "I believe I shall have to withhold my attentions until you give me yours."

"Jean," she gasped as he covered her and her legs wrapped around him. "It's Jean."

She moaned with pleasure as he plunged into her. God, he loved women.

Adeline rolled over and turned her pillow—for the thousandth time. Ever since supper last evening, the blasted man kept intruding on her thoughts. To make it worse, it was the wrong gentleman. That night she dreamed of Littleton's sharply molded lips and the dimple that came out when he smiled. She also remembered the strained expression on his face just before he hailed the waiter at Gunter's. That did not make sense to her.

Her dreams revolved around baby pigs and little girls. The girls had curling black hair and green eyes, and he was giving each of them a piglet. The strange thing was that in her dream, she had been there as well, encouraging them to give the piglets names. Then ladies were popping out of bushes and from behind sofas, trying to get his attention.

Adeline made herself stay in bed until her maid opened the bed hangings and curtains.

"Good morning, my lady," Fendall said, ruthlessly pulling the bed hangings back. "Your great beastie will be here soon." She stepped over to the toilet table. "I ordered tea and some toast to tide you over until breakfast."

Tossing back the covers, Adeline threw her legs over the side of the bed, then went to make her morning ablutions. "Thank you."

She hurried through the tea and toast. It was one thing to keep a gentleman waiting. That was almost required, although she never did. But it was quite another to keep a servant—especially one who was doing one a favor—waiting. That was rude.

She gazed out the window as she sipped her tea. It was clear, and a soft breeze wafted in from the window. "It looks like it will be a nice day."

"That's what Mr. Abney says, my lady."

The clock struck the hour and she rushed downstairs.

When Humphries arrived with Maximus, she was almost, but not quite, surprised not to see Lord Littleton. Yet he had said he would not come. Apparently, in some things he was a man of his word.

"Mornin' to ye, my lady." Humphries reached up, as if he would pull on a cap, then remembered to bow.

"Good morning, Humphries." Maximus leaned against Adeline's legs as he tried to wrap himself around her. "And good morning to you, Maximus." The footman shoved the lead at her. She wanted to take it, but

Maximus was big; well, huge might be a better word. "Are you sure I can handle him?"

"Nothin' to," Humphries assured her. "Jes' tell him ta heel, and he'll stay right by yer side."

"Maximus, heel." Much to her surprise and pleasure, the dog straightened and stood by her side just as he was supposed to. "What a good boy you are."

By the time they reached the Park, Adeline had got used to having the Great Dane next to her. What would it be like to have one with her all the time? That reminded her of the carriage his owner was having built. "Will you like to ride in a curricle?"

The footman barked a rough laugh. "There's no swither he'll like being with his lordship. The question is, what'll happen when he sees somethin' he wants." Humphries looked around. "Ye might want me to take him, my lady. There's plenty of squirrels hereabouts, and he'll fair pull ye off yer feet if he decides to take off after one."

It didn't take her long to work out why Maximus was so interested in the squirrels. Humphries whispered something in the dog's ear, and his head perked up. As soon as a squirrel ran across the lawn, the footman dropped the lead, and the dog bounded after it.

The smaller animal darted toward the nearest tree and dashed up it, stopping to chatter down at Maximus when he reached the first branch. "What will he do if he catches it?"

"Ain't no way he's goin' to catch that squirrel, or any other. He just likes to chase 'em." Humphries rubbed his chin. "If he did catch one, he'd probably try to lick it."

"Because he would want to taste the squirrel?" She did not wish to see the poor little thing eaten alive.

"Nah. To make sure it was all right. Ain't no dog as gentle as him. He's nothin' more than a big baby."

Tail wagging, Maximus pranced back to them, looking like he was grinning and clearly expecting praise.

"Did you make a good job of it?" Adeline stroked his head, as he wanted her to do. Then another squirrel appeared, and he was off again. "What do you do if there are small children around?"

Humphries raised his hand to his head, seemed to realize that he wore a hat and a wig, then dropped the appendage. "Normally, we're out too early for 'em. But if it did happen, I'd have to take him away. He'd try to lick the little ones, and the nursemaid'd go off screaming that the dog was tryin' to eat her charge." He shook his head dolefully. "Causes a lot o' trouble, it does."

Adeline had never seen a footman act as Humphries did. "You're not really a footman, are you?"

"Me? Nah. I'm a groom." He glanced down at his livery in disgust. "Problem is that none of these fine London footmen can handle Maximus. He plays his tricks on them and gets away. Thinks it a good joke to keep them running after him. It's a game for him, ye see. I call it chase me, chase, ye fool, ye fool." He sighed. "But her ladyship says that whoever walks him has to be in livery. So, here I am."

"I'm surprised that Lord Littleton doesn't countermand her." Humphries narrowed one eye, and she realized that he might not know the word. "That he does not tell her he is in charge."

The servant brightened with comprehension. "Not a chance. Littleton men are smarter than that, my lady. Unlike some I could tell ye about," Humphries said darkly, and Adeline wondered to whom he was referring. "They know keepin' their women happy is what keeps a man happy. That's what the old lord used to say. 'Course ye've got ta marry the right woman in the first place."

That was a very forward way of thinking. "His lordship's father?"

"Nah, my lady. His grandsire. Me da says it's been said as long as the Littletons have been around."

Maximus came back again, and Humphries decreed it was time to return to their respective homes. Once again, she was handed the lead.

Having warmed to the subject of the family, his tongue ran on fiddlesticks. "Take last year. We went home real fast-like after his lordship almost made a terrible wilsomeness about a lady"—she'd never heard of the word, but imagined it meant a mistake where he was from—"Nothin' against her. I saw her a few times. Right pretty she was, and a real high lady"—he glanced at Adeline—"not that you ain't. Yer just as fine as she was. Maybe even better."

"No offense taken," she assured him, wanting Humphries to continue.

He looked at her again, as if to assure himself that he hadn't insulted her and nodded. "She weren't the right one for a Littleton man. I coulda told him that. But a man's got ta find out on his own."

Adeline's pulse quickened. Was she about to learn the whole story about what had happened between Lord Littleton and Dorie from his lordship's point of view? "Why was that?"

Humphries looked pointedly at the dog. "Well, for one thing, she was never interested in Max, here. And every time his lordship started telling her about the estate, she'd talk about somethin' happening in the Lords." That sounded exactly like Dorie. "She made sure he knew she liked it here in London, a lot. Talked about how her da and ma spent most a their time in Town, and she wanted that too. Always tryin' ta get him to those parties where they talk politics, and askin' him what happened at the Lords that day. Not that his lordship knew." Humphries tapped his nose. "I heard it all sitting on the back of the curricle, so's if she wanted to get down and walk, his lordship didn't have ta worry about the horses." They rounded the corner into the square. "If you ask me, he shoulda paid more mind to what she was saying early on. Took him too long to make out that she weren't the right lid for his pot."

Adeline held back her laughter. What a way to put it. "Thank you, Humphries."

Again, he reached up for his cap before remembering to bow. Poor man. "Will we see ye tomorrow, my lady?"

"You will. I had an excellent time walking with you and Maximus." Until then, Adeline had a great deal of thinking to do. Fortunately, she was going shopping with her friends today. Perhaps she could discover more about Littleton and Dorie's ill-fated courtship. Adeline wanted to feel at least a little better about liking him. Not that he could ever be anything more than an acquaintance. But maybe what he had done was not all that bad. If Dorie had not been in love with him . . . Adeline stifled a sigh and wished he was not as charming as he was handsome.

Chapter Fifteen

A few days later, Frits lounged in a chair and stared at his wine. He'd only ordered it because it was too early for brandy, and one did not drink ale at Brooks's. He was certain that Max would bring her closer to him, but that plan had failed. Not only that, she was spending too much time with Anglesey. She had even danced the supper set with him last night. Frits needed to decide how to proceed with Adeline.

When Humphries had returned from the walk the first day, he'd told Frits how well she'd handled Maximus this morning. He wished he'd been there to see her. Unfortunately, he didn't see how her walking his dog, and going for carriage rides with him, or even standing up with her for one, and only one, set at every ball was helping her form an attachment to *him*.

"Mind if I join you?" Exeter asked.

Frits pushed out a chair with his foot. "Not at all."

Exeter hailed a waiter and pointed to the bottle of claret on the table. "I wasn't sure. You look to be in a brown study."

"I'm trying to figure out how to get a lady to trust me." Yet again, Frits considered how different Adeline was from the other ladies he'd known. She was special, and she affected him in ways no woman ever before had. He knew deep in his bones that he needed her in his life. The problem, the only problem as far as he could see, was that he had made a mull of it with Lady Dorie last year.

"I know the feeling." Exeter poured a glass of claret from the open bottle. "Sometimes I feel as if I'm treading water and I've forgotten how to swim to shore."

Sitting up, Frits looked at his friend. "It is exactly like that. In fact, I've had almost the exact same thought." He took a drink from his as-yet-untouched glass. "The question is what to do about it."

His friend had been drumming his fingers on the table, but stopped. "If there was some daring deed I could perform to prove to her I care about her . . ."

"I'm afraid the days of knights rescuing damsels in distress are just about over." As were the days of riding into castles and carrying ladies away. Although Adeline probably wouldn't like that anymore than his several-times-over great-grandmother had. Frits had to stop thinking about that. He tossed off the rest of the glass and poured another. Remembering that Carter-Woods had saved Lady Augusta from that idiot Lord Lancelot, and she'd still left for Europe. Frits grinned. "Sometimes it doesn't work even when one does save a lady."

"Pity." Exeter poured another glass as well. Fortunately, the next bottle had arrived. "I wanted ale, but when I went to The Bunch of Grapes the barmaids started to flirt, so I left."

Frits cracked a laugh. "I did the same thing. I hope someone takes them up on their offers. I don't want them to feel bad."

"It's strange"—Exeter gazed into the goblet—"how when you only want one woman, no one else will do."

"I knew it would happen eventually. I actually thought I was prepared." Frits drank more of the wine. "But I wasn't."

"I don't know how any man could be," Exeter mused. "I wouldn't have believed it if I'd been told." Glancing up, he frowned. "How did you know?"

"My father and grandfather both told me. Littleton men don't go down easily. It goes back centuries." Frits couldn't stop a sigh from escaping. He was glad only his friend was there to hear it. "After learning how all their struggles to avoid falling in love had failed, I decided to just fall on my sword."

"I take it that plan didn't work?"

"No. I let"—he was about to say "lust," but considering Exeter was trying to court Lady Dorie, he probably wouldn't take that very well—"attraction get in the way of good sense."

"She is beautiful, isn't she?" The man had a moon-struck look on his face.

"She is, but what is more important is that you want the same things in life." Exeter glanced at Frits as if he did not understand. "You want to be involved in politics, and she wants to be a political hostess. And your political views are the same. That sort of thing."

Exeter smiled proudly, as if the lady was already his. "I could see her having Whig parties even if I had not decided to switch parties."

"That would have been interesting," Frits muttered to himself. "Fortunately, you have no need to worry about it."

"I thought all of Lady Dorie's friends were interested in being politically involved."

He shook his head. "Not Lady Adeline." And thank

the Lord for that piece of luck. The way he was starting to feel about her, he didn't think she would be nearly as easy to give up as Lady Dorie had been. And he had no intention of running away from her. "She prefers the country." And liked stories about pigs and walking his dog. "If only I—never mind." He'd drive himself mad if he continued to focus on his mistakes. What he needed was a plan. One that was actually feasible. "What are you going to do about Lady Dorie?"

Exeter leaned forward. "There is a matter with which she can help me, and I am going to use that time to . . . well, not seduce her, as we will be in her family's house and chaperoned, but make her more aware of me."

"In other words, spend more time with her, but not in the Park, where most of the *ton* is." Exeter nodded, and Frits was reminded that he needed to ask his mother to plan an outing at Vauxhall. "An excellent idea."

"I did try to convince her father to arrange a match, but he refused."

Frits covered his mouth so that his laughter wouldn't be heard all over the club. "I cannot imagine what would happen if anyone attempted to force Lady Dorie into a marriage she did not want. I'm quite sure for all Lady Adeline's gentle ways, she would be as stubborn as a goat about it." He drained his glass. "By the way, when is Dursley due back?"

Exeter was helping Miss Chatham avoid Lytton until the gentleman she wanted to marry, Lord Dursley, returned to England. Exeter scowled. "Not soon enough, which is making my problem with Lady Dorie all the more difficult."

"Perhaps not." Frits recalled how he'd helped Elizabeth Harrington and her husband before they married.

"Sometimes it takes another person's interest to spark a flame that was banked."

"I hope you're right." They stood at the same time. "I have a carriage ride for which to prepare."

"As do I." And another visit to Gunter's. Maybe ices were the path to Adeline's heart.

Then what Exeter had said struck Frits. So far, he had been lucky that he and Adeline, except for one time, had not been in the Park when Lady Dorie was there. "What time are you going?"

"Five o'clock. Why"—Exeter glanced at his pocket watch—"Damn. I can't be late. You know how she is about punctuality."

"I'll try to think of something." Ices before the ride might work. Yet the best thing was to take her somewhere else.

"Good luck," Exeter said in a heartfelt tone as they reached Piccadilly to proceed in separate directions.

"Thank you," Frits answered. "I just need to think." Although, he hadn't had much success with that.

By the time he reached his house, he'd come up with an idea. He'd received the plan for his new curricle several days ago, and he was overdue for a trip to the carriage maker. Perhaps Adeline would like to come with him. But first he'd ask his mother if there was anything improper with his scheme.

"Creswell." Frits handed his hat, cane, and gloves to his butler. "Is her ladyship in?"

"She returned a few minutes ago, my lord. I believe she is in the morning room."

Frits headed to the back of the house. His mother was seated at a small cherrywood table, writing. "Mama?"

"Give me a moment." She sanded the paper and sealed it. "What can I do for you?"

"First, tell me if there is any impropriety in my

taking Lady Adeline to the carriage maker in Long Acre instead of the Park, and second, tell me if you can arrange a party to Vauxhall."

She pursed her lips in thought, then shook her head. "I cannot think of anything wrong with a trip to Long Acre, provided she agrees to go. As for Vauxhall, I believe that would be a splendid idea. I shall look into booking a box early next week."

"Before her come out ball?"

"Yes. Her mother thinks she is nervous about it. This and the theater will be just what is needed to take her mind off the ball."

Frits didn't like the sound of that. He did not want her to be worried about anything. "I didn't know Lady Adeline was concerned about it."

Mama lifted one shoulder. "It is probably only normal apprehension. Still, the theater and Vauxhall will be pleasant diversions."

He hoped that was all it was. "What sorts of things could disquiet her?"

"Oh." She blinked, as if surprised by the question. "Any number of things. Who will lead her out for her first dance, for example."

"Who would normally lead her out?" He didn't think she would accept his offer to do it. Aside from that, he wanted the supper dance. That would give him more time with her.

"Most likely her father or brother."

If that was what usually occurred, he didn't understand why Lady Adeline should be concerned about it. Then again, it was only his mother's speculation. He'd ask her this afternoon, if all went well. "Thank you for your help."

"Anytime, dear."

All he had to do now was find the right way to ask

her if she would like to see how his new curricle was progressing. And pray. He'd been doing a lot of that lately.

Adeline rode with Georgie in her family's town coach to meet Augusta, Henrietta, and Dorie at Hatchards. That was their favorite starting place for a shopping trip. The carriages would wait until they had selected their books, take the tomes to their respective houses, and meet them at Pantheon Bazaar.

She had started to greet her friends when Dorie said to Henrietta, "I would like it if I could walk with you and Augusta today, but I am committed to drive with Exeter."

The blood rushed to Adeline's feet, and she wished she had not agreed to go for a carriage ride with Littleton. Was there another place they could go? Perhaps he would agree to a ride in Green Park. Unfortunately, she did not even know if one did ride in Green Park. The only thing she knew about the place was that they had cows and one could purchase cups of fresh milk there.

Georgie linked arms with Adeline, tugging her into the store. Her mind had gone almost totally blank, and she had forgotten she was standing on the pavement. If she had not already ordered the books she wanted, she was certain she would not have remembered which ones she wanted.

"I gather you are promised to ride with Lord Littleton today?" Georgie whispered.

"Yes." Adeline's throat was so tight, she could barely get the word out.

"It is not the end of the world."

"Can one go for a carriage ride in Green Park?" She kept her tone low so that no one else could hear them.

"I do not believe so. It would disturb the people strolling in the park."

Well, drat. "I could become ill."

"Then you would not be able to attend Henrietta's come out ball this evening."

"That's tonight?" How could Adeline have forgotten? Raising her brows, Georgie nodded.

"I shall have to think of something else." If only Anglesey had asked her for a carriage ride today before Littleton did. But he seemed to have become more beforehand in his invitations. Or perhaps Lord Anglesey was tardy in his requests.

"I am sure all will be well." Georgie smiled. "Come; my sister-in-law asked if I could find a book on roses for her. I think they are upstairs in the back."

Adeline joined her friend and after several minutes— they kept getting distracted by other books—they found the section they wanted. But they were not alone. She held up her hand to cup the side of her mouth and whispered, "Do you hear that?"

"I wonder if we have come upon a tryst." Georgie said. "I have been told it sometimes happens."

They exchanged a glance before daring to peek around the corner of a bookshelf, then ducked back, hiding themselves again.

"It is only Miss Tice and Miss Martindale." Adeline wondered what they could be doing.

Georgie's brows drew together. "If only they didn't have more hair than wit. I think we should listen."

Adeline wanted to object, but she could not think of a good reason to do so. If anyone was bound to think of a bad idea, it was those two ladies. She nodded.

The whispers became louder, and one of the ladies

said, "I am positive that Lord Littleton has an estate that marches along Lord Turner's property. All you have to do is get his attention. Then we shall be able to live near each other."

"But how?" the lady practically wailed. "The only lady he pays any attention to is Lady Adeline."

Adeline glanced at Georgie, who cast her eyes to the ceiling. Surely this was not happening again!

"She is an earl's daughter," one of the ladies said. "I am certain her family will want her to look higher than a baron."

"Not one as wealthy and well-connected as he is," the other one said despairingly.

"Let me think." The two were silent, and Adeline could hear muffled conversations filtering up from below. Finally, the lady said, "We will arrange for you to be found alone with him. Then he will have to marry you."

Adeline dropped her head into her hands and muttered, "I had no idea that was such a popular idea."

"It happened only once to my brother," Georgie said. "But his reputation was so pristine, no one believed it."

Sounds of Miss Tice and Miss Martindale leaving made Adeline and Georgie move silently toward the wall. The two ladies, however, were not paying any attention to anything but their conversation.

"We do not even know when or where it will occur, or which lady will attempt to ensnare him." Adeline was disgusted by the whole thing.

"I am sure they will be at the ball this evening," Georgie said. "We shall watch and see which one of them Lord Turner favors. Then you can warn Lord Littleton."

"Bother." Adeline was starting to feel as if she was

going to spend her whole Season alternately trying to avoid him and protect him from scheming young ladies. Not that it was actually possible to elude the man. He knew Wivenly and his friends.

"I found it." Georgie held up a book. "Are you ready to go?"

"More than ready." He should go back to the country. Then Adeline could get on with her Season and possibly marry Lord Anglesey.

"My grandmother Featherton always says things work out the way they are meant to."

"I wish I could have as much faith." When they reached the counter, the others were paying for their purchases.

As they left Hatchards, Adeline strolled next to Dorie. "You and Lord Exeter looked as if you were having an interesting conversation last evening."

She appeared taken aback. "We were, rather. He has much to do to learn his new position, but he is coming along. Whatever do you discuss with Lord Littleton? I confess I never found his conversation that interesting."

Adeline did not know if that was true or said out of pique. Still, she might as well test it. "Pigs. He had a very sweet story about pigs."

"Pigs?" Dorie's brows rose. "What on earth could be interesting or sweet about swine?"

"It was the way he told it." Adeline tried not to sound defensive. After all, she had enjoyed the tale.

Fortunately, they had reached the milliner's, and the conversation ended as they walked into the shop. But at least she had found out what she had wished to know. Humphries was right: Dorie and Lord Littleton had not been at all suited. Not that the knowledge relieved Adeline of her loyalty to a friend. Still, it was something. Even if she wasn't quite sure what.

As the day progressed, she bought a bonnet and several other items she did not need. In fact, she required very little other than more stockings. One or two evenings' dancing and they must be replaced. She spent much of the time trying to discover alternate places to make a carriage drive. Yet by the time Littleton arrived, she still had no idea where they should go.

Chapter Sixteen

When Lord Littleton lifted Adeline into the curricle, she wished she could convince herself she was getting used to the feeling of his hands heating her even through her twill carriage gown, but she could not. Her breath caught and her heart raced, and she had to take a few gulps of air for her body to return to normal.

As she could not think of where they should go, she decided to place the burden on his much broader shoulders, and hope he did not mind finding somewhere new. "Must we go to the Park today?"

He glanced at her, his green eyes sharper than they had ever been before. "No. As a matter of fact, I hoped you might agree to accompany me to see how my new curricle is coming along."

That sounded interesting. She'd never seen a carriage being built. "The one for Maximus?"

Littleton grinned and chuckled. "The very same."

Her shoulders felt as if a load of stones had been removed. "Yes, I would like that immensely." He started the horses. "It is far?"

"Not particularly. It will probably take us the same

amount of time to go there, look at the curricle, and return as it would to get most of the way around the Park."

"Excellent." She smiled in relief. "It will be fun to do something different."

When Adeline grinned at Frits, the slightly hazy day became much brighter. Thank the Lord she had suggested they not go to the Park. "How did you spend your day?"

"Shopping." Her face scrunched up adorably. "I suppose I should tell you that there is another scheme afoot to compromise you into marriage. The only problem is that I do not know which of the two ladies it is. I should be able to ascertain that this evening."

Frits forced himself to frown instead of smiling. It was about time Fate decided to be kind to him. If Adeline was going to spend her time protecting him, he could not be even the slightest bit upset. Still, he made a point of heaving a huge sigh. "I do not understand why this happens. Or what I can do to stop it."

"Well, I am not sure there is anything you can do to make them cease. In this case, it is occurring because you apparently share a boundary with Lord Turner."

"We do. Our families have been friends for generations." Frits didn't understand. "What does that have to do with anything?"

"Have you met Miss Tice and Miss Martindale?"

"Yes, I have met both of the ladies, and Turner made me known to Miss Martindale again." He glanced at Adeline. "He is very taken with her."

"That is our answer. They are almost inseparable. And they wish to wed gentlemen whose holdings are close together." So much for trying to avoid the ladies. They had turned on to Piccadilly and he had to thread the carriage through a narrow space between two wagons that had stopped on either side of the street. "That was well done," she said approvingly. "Therefore, as Miss Martindale and Lord Turner appear to be forming a connection, she is looking for a gentleman for her friend."

"I have no words." Or he had plenty of them, but none he could say with Adeline present.

"Is there another gentleman you can think of who would meet the requirements?" Adeline glanced at him hopefully. "If we can find another prospect, she might leave you alone."

We.

She had used the word "we."

The word struck him so forcefully, he had to think about the rest of what she'd said. "Let me ponder it when I'm not distracted by traffic."

She looked around. "And to think I thought the Park was crowded. There are so many different types of vehicles."

London streets were always busy. He took them for granted, but it was interesting seeing them from her point of view. Despite the traffic, it wasn't long before they reached the carriage maker. She was staring at the large building and the various vehicles when he surprised her by lifting her down. He smiled to himself when she sucked in a breath. For all her curves, her waist was small enough that he could put his hands almost all the way around it. He held her so that they were face-to-face, becoming lost in the way her silvery eyes looked at him. They reminded him of the sun glinting off a sword.

"You really should put me down." Her voice was breathy and dry at the same time. He must be having an effect on her. One he hoped Anglesey wasn't having.

"Of course." Frits lowered her gently, wishing he had

an excuse to bring her close enough that their bodies touched on the slow slide down. He could imagine her arms around his neck and their lips touching. If only she was wearing short stays, he could feel more of her well-rounded body. Thinking of that. When had she changed from short stays?

"My lord." The sharpness in Adeline's tone made him drop his hands and offer his arm.

"Let's find the owner." He led her into the massive front doors.

"I've never seen so many different types of carriages." This time her voice was filled with wonder. "How much fun it would be to design one's own coach."

A clerk came up to them. "May I help you?"

"Yes. I am Lord Littleton. I'd like to know if Mr. Hatchett is available."

"He's out at the moment, my lord. I am his son. I will be happy to show you the work that's been done on your carriage."

"Thank you. That's the reason I came."

The man glanced at Adeline. "I'm afraid it's not very clean. The lady might want to have a cup of tea in the office."

"I am sure I shall be fine." She gave the clerk a polite smile. "I am extremely interested in seeing the vehicle. I have only seen finished ones."

"If you're sure"—Hatchett the Younger's tone indicated he thought she'd be unhappy with her decision— "then follow me." He led them into the back, and the man hadn't been exaggerating. Workers were in the process of building various carriages, and at one point they had to walk through sawdust. He stopped at the side of the curricle. The body had been completed, and the bench for the driver attached, but two men were frowning over the box that had been installed behind the bench. "Here you are, my lord."

"Is there a problem?" Frits asked the workers.

"I think we need to know more about the dog what's goin' inside the box," the older man with lightly graying hair said.

He put his hand on the top part of his hip. "His back is to here."

The younger man's jaw dropped. "That's a big 'un."

Adeline strolled around the carriage. "How are you going to get him up and into the box?"

The older man scratched his head. "That's a good question, miss."

And one Frits had not thought through. He had told Mr. Hatchett that Maximus was a Great Dane, but had not told him how large the dog was.

She pointed at the side of the box. "Could you make one of the sides a door and have steps going up to it?"

That was something Frits should have thought of. He glanced at the older worker. "I can't see a problem with that suggestion. Can you?"

"No, my lord." The man shook his head consideringly. "I think that'll work fine."

Frits bowed to her. "My thanks for solving the problem."

"It was my pleasure." Adeline smiled brightly.

"When do you think it'll be finished?" Now that he'd seen it, he couldn't wait to drive it.

"Another week should do it," the older man said. "We need to paint it before we add the leather."

"That will do. Thank you for your work."

Adeline seemed to have a skip in her step as they walked out of the building. "What color will you paint it?"

"A deep green. The leather will be medium brown."

He smiled. "My housekeeper is having a pillow made for the bottom of Maximus's box so that it can be washed."

"That is a good idea." Frits lifted her into the carriage and she scowled at him. "I am perfectly capable of getting in myself."

He knew she would object at some point and had his answer ready. "But that takes too much time. One must let the steps down and put them back up again."

She opened her lovely, deep pink lips and closed them again, shook her head, and gave him a skeptical look. All the while he maintained what he hoped to be an innocent expression. "If you would like, one day we can test my theory."

Adeline smiled sweetly, and he knew that what was going to come out of her mouth was not going to be at all sweet. "I think that is an excellent idea, my lord. Perhaps when you take me home we can time it."

"Perhaps. First, we must make our traditional stop at Gunter's." He climbed into the carriage and started the pair. "What flavor will you choose today?"

"I do not know." She tilted her head to one side. "What do you recommend?"

"The lavender is nice and light. You might like it. My favorite is chocolate."

"I think my favorite one will be Muscadine, but I must sample the others first." The sun decided to make a stronger showing, and she opened her parasol.

If he looked closely, he could see very faint freckles on her face. She was most likely trying to avoid them darkening. It wouldn't bother him if they were more noticeable. He liked freckles.

He avoided Oxford Street on their way back to Mayfair, thus missing much of the traffic. Soon, he pulled up outside of Gunter's.

A waiter ran up to them. "What may I bring you?"

"What flavors do you have today?" He'd forgotten to mention to Adeline that the flavors changed.

"Today I can offer you bergamot and punch, royal cream, chocolate, burnt filbert, parmesan, lavender, violet, orange flower, and vanilla bean."

"By punch I assume you mean the strong drink from the West Indies," Frits clarified.

"Yes, sir."

He glanced at Adeline. "Have you made a choice?"

"I shall try the parmesan."

That was a daring selection. He preferred the sweeter ices. "I shall have the vanilla bean." The waiter ran back into the shop. "If you like, you can try mine."

"Thank you." Sitting with her back against the bench, she had a satisfied look on her face. "I like coming here."

So did he . . . with her. He had a vision of them at Littleton coming up with ideas for ices. What else could he find that she liked?

The ices were delivered, and after Frits finished his, leaving a spoonful or so for Adeline, he watched as she licked the last of the parmesan ice from her spoon. This was torture.

The parmesan was very good, but Adeline liked the Muscadine better. Lord Littleton held out his bowl, and she dipped her spoon into the vanilla bean, then tasted it. "I like this as much as the Muscadine."

"Wait until you try the chocolate." His tone was low and gruff. "That should be last."

He did not look angry or in pain. What could be making him so different? "Are you so sure I will like it the best?"

"I am, but if you do not, it is no matter." His dimple popped out. Now he was back to normal. "We can't like all the same things."

That stopped her. Did they have a preference for so many of the same things? She had been so involved in not wanting to like him, she had not even noticed what they had in common. She wanted to playfully ask him which things he meant, but she was afraid to know the answer.

Coward.

Maybe she was. That did not make her feel better. As much as she had been enjoying her time with Lord Anglesey, it occurred to her that they did not talk about likes and dislikes very much. "I do not think it is possible for two people to enjoy all the same things."

"You are probably right." He signaled for the waiter and handed him their bowls. "We should leave before the rest of the *ton* joins us."

"I agree." She definitely did not want Dorie seeing her with Littleton at Gunter's. That would be awkward.

He gathered the ribbons and started threading them through his fingers, then stopped. "I did ask you for the supper dance this evening, did I not?"

She could not remember. Lord Anglesey had had the last two. Yet, had Lord Littleton asked for this one the night before last? He always did ask for the supper dance, so he must have. Adeline was certain she had not given it to anyone else. She would have remembered if Lord Anglesey had requested it. "You did."

"Oh, good. I've never attended so many balls before. I'm getting confused." The carriage moved forward. "How is the planning for your come out ball going?"

"Well." At least she *thought* it was. "There is a great deal to do. My mother is more worried than am I."

He looked relieved, but why would he be concerned at all? "Who is standing up with you for your first dance?"

"My father." At least she thought that was who was

leading her out. "Or my brother. They have been going round and round about it. I understand it is usually a family member."

"I would be honored to dance the supper dance with you." He had such a boyishly hopeful look on his face, she laughed.

"And I shall accept." She had missed standing up with him. He always made interesting conversation, and he listened to her. A tinge of guilt struck her, dampening her good mood. Anglesey was a much better match, and he was not a rake. She should be thinking more about him. Not only that, but she was beginning to doubt her first impression of Lord Littleton. He was not acting much like a rake. She must decide soon what to do if Lord Anglesey asked for her hand. "Have you been able to think of anyone whose land marches with Lord Turner's?"

"It's something I should know without thinking about it, but for some reason, the knowledge has gone straight out of my head. I'll look at a map when I am home. If there is an eligible gentleman attached to any of the properties, and he is not in Town, I'll go drag him here."

Poor Littleton looked so put upon, she had to laugh. He gave her a wounded look, and she struggled to bring herself under control and not go off into whoops. "I *am* sorry. It is not funny and I should not act as if it is."

"I depend upon you to watch out for me."

Good Lord. He was serious.

"Just make sure you are always with either me or one of your friends and you will be safe until we can find a solution."

"Don't forget that other lady is probably still planning to compromise me."

Good heavens. Adeline had forgotten all about Miss Hanson. "The same advice holds true. Do not go anywhere by yourself."

"I shall do exactly as you say." He feathered the corner on to Upper Brook Street. "When I marry, I wish to wed a lady who wants me for more than my title and my wealth."

"I cannot fault you." That is what she wanted as well, to be loved for herself and not her bloodlines or dowry. Fortunately, no one was attempting to compromise her into marriage. "Let me know tonight if you have found a gentleman for Miss Tice." And while he was doing that, Adeline would think of a plan to foil Miss Hanson. "I hope that they are the only two ladies who feel free to trap you into marriage."

"So do I." His words sounded heartfelt. He pulled up in front of her house, and was at her side, lifting her down, before she remembered they were to perform their little test. Again, his touch sent a pleasurable thrill through her. If only she knew how to stop reacting to him.

She took his arm and he walked her to the door. "I shall see you this evening."

Taking her hand, he bowed over and kissed her gloved fingers. "I look forward to it."

Goodness, her hand felt singed.

This has got to stop.

Chapter Seventeen

Abney bowed as Adeline walked into the hall.

"You have a note from Lord Anglesey, my lady. It arrived this morning, but her ladyship had it brought down after you departed."

"Thank you, Abney." She picked up the card and turned it over.

My Dear Lady Adeline,
    Would you do me the great honor of standing up with me for the supper dance?
    I shall impatiently await your reply.
                    Yr. devoted servant,
                    Anglesey

She hoped he was not too impatient. If so, he'd had a long day waiting for her answer. "I shall pen a reply directly. Please have a footman ready to take it."

"As you wish, my lady."

She went to the morning room, removed her gloves, and pulled out a sheet of pressed paper. She did not like having to give his lordship bad news, and remembered that she had another set free. Resolving to offer that dance to him, she wrote:

Dear Lord Anglesey,
    *Unfortunately, I did not receive your kind
invitation until after I was already committed for the
supper dance. However, you may have the first
country dance, if you wish.*
                Regards,
                A. Wivenly

Adeline frowned at the note. It was not very elegant,
but she could think of nothing else to write.

After she had sealed the letter, she took it to the hall,
where a footman was waiting. "This must go to Lord
Anglesey at Normanby House."

"At once, my lady."

Now, if she could just come up with a plan to stop
Miss Hanson and the others from attempting to sink
their fangs into poor Littleton.

Lord Littleton.

Adeline should not be so informal with him.

Crispin was in the study of his father's house attempting to answer a letter from his mother, demanding
to know what progress he was making regarding choos-
ing a bride, when the butler brought in a note on a
silver salver. "For you, my lord. A footman from Watford House brought it."

Finally. He was glad he hadn't waited there all day
for a reply. "Thank you."

He tore open the seal, read the missive, and cursed.

It must be Littleton. How in hell had the man
stolen the march on him? Crispin threw the missive
onto the desk.

"Will there be anything else, my lord?"

He was surprised to see the servant still there. "No,

that is all." He had to answer Lady Adeline if he had any hope of standing up with her this evening. "Wait for a moment. I must send an answer."

He penned a short acceptance and handed it to the footman.

There must be a faster way to secure the lady. As soon as they were wed and she was breeding, he could go back to Paris. This evening he'd ask for the supper dance for the next ball—that must be what Littleton had done—and to take her for another carriage ride. In the meantime, Crispin had hours before the entertainment. He wondered if Jean was up for another tryst. His cock hardened at the thought of her.

Shoving the letter to his mother aside, he dashed off a note to his lover.

> *My darling,*
> *Meet me.*
> *A.*

Crispin sealed the note and tugged the bellpull. A different footman opened the door. "Take this to Twelve Green Street and wait for a reply. Do not tell anyone where you are going."

"Yes, my lord."

Not ten minutes later, the servant returned. "The answer is yes, my lord."

"Very good. Have my curricle brought around, and tell Cook I shall want a picnic basket with two bottles of champagne." It was a good thing he'd planned to eat at his club that evening, so that the cook had not planned on him dining at home. Angering that particular servant was never a good idea, and his mother would be certain to hear about it.

Crispin arrived at the small town house before Jean did, leaving it to his groom to take his carriage back.

He'd hired a maid of all work, and now he gave her the basket. "Set this up in the dining room. After you're done, you may have the rest of the night off."

The girl bobbed a curtsey, "Yes, my lord."

A few minutes later, his lover arrived. "Jean." He pulled her through the door and kissed her. "I am immensely glad you could join me."

"As am I." She rubbed her hand down his cock. "My, how hard you are, my lord."

Almost hard enough to spill right there. "I brought a picnic, but I thought we might like to retire to the bedroom first."

"An excellent idea." She removed her gloves one finger at a time, and when she reached up to remove her bonnet, the fabric of her gown stretched across her breasts.

He couldn't wait until he was inside her. "I want you."

By the time they had reached the first floor, her bodice was undone. Jean laughed. "You are very good at that."

"It's a specialty of mine." He gave her a playful grin.

In seconds, they were naked on the bed and he was licking and sucking his way down her body. When he got to her cunny, he stood and positioned her so that the tops of her thighs were at the end of the bed.

As he buried his nose in her sex, he saw it. "What is this?" Not that he didn't know what it was. A string to a sponge. "And how did you know about it?"

Jean sat up, startled. "One of the other widows told me it would stop me from getting pregnant. I thought I would try it."

He was tempted to pull it out, but then she'd probably leave. "You didn't give your husband any children."

"Neither did his first two wives." The chill in her voice had his erection softening. "I do not know what you have against it. Surely you do not want a bastard."

"I was merely surprised." He shrugged. "It is normally considered a whore's trick."

"Perhaps I should leave." She started to roll off the bed, but he stopped her.

"No, stay." He cupped her breasts, feeling them furl beneath his touch. "Forgive me. I should not have reacted as I did."

"I noticed you did not say you would marry me if . . ." The words were sharp, but the tone was anything but.

She did not wish to wed him, but she wanted reassurance. He was good at giving that. "You know what my father wants, and you do not wish to marry again so soon." He took one nipple into his mouth as he rolled the other. "I do not like the feel of the string, but I will grow accustomed."

"The same friend told me when it is safe without the sponge." Jean's eyes glazed and her voice turned sultry.

"Until then, I'll make do." He kissed his way down her body until she was writhing with lust, then pulled her to him and plunged into her. Women were made to give pleasure to a man.

Sometime later, they made their way to the dining room, dressed only in robes he insisted remain untied so he could admire her breasts and the dark hair between her legs. There was freedom in not having servants around. He never got tired of the way a woman looked.

Jean wasn't as comfortable as he was. "You are sure the maid is gone?"

"I gave her the night off." Leaning over, he whispered in her ear. "In case I want to take you on the table. Have you ever had amorous congress on a table?"

She swallowed. "You must be the most decadent gentleman I know."

"Your husband didn't know how to pleasure you." They'd reached the bottom of the stairs, and he slid his hand between her legs. "Next time, you will know better."

She leaned back against him and rubbed. "At this rate, we won't get to the dining room."

"Hold the back of that chair and bend over."

Later, she was pulling apart a piece of cold chicken when she asked, "I am surprised you have not made more progress with the lady."

He might, if he could get Lady Adeline alone. He poured Jean more champagne. "I have some thoughts as to how to move the wedding along, but I shall require some assistance." Reaching out, he fondled her breast. "Would you be willing to help me?"

Her eyelid dropped and her breathing shortened. "What did you have in mind?"

Crispin lifted her from the chair and kissed her. "You could find us alone. I have been told the fountain at the garden party we will soon be attending is secluded." He had her against the wall and lifted her, sliding into her as he did. Jean's legs wrapped around him. "If you are willing."

"Yes." Her back arched. "God, yes."

"I don't know what to say, but thank you." Had a more generous lady ever existed? "You are a queen among women." Crispin wondered if she'd agree to go to France with him.

A blush rose from her breasts, up her neck, and into her cheeks. "It is my pleasure."

He sent her home in a hackney and walked to Normanby House, arriving with very little time to dress for the ball. He had one dance with Lady Adeline, and he intended to make the most of it. If he could get her alone, he might be able to steal a kiss, and a bit more. Once she got a taste of what he could give her, she would be easily convinced that being his wife would have its benefits. For as long as he was there.

St James's Square, where Normanby House was located, was not all that far, and Crispin chose to walk there. Unfortunately, that turned out to be a mistake. He had not arrived before the music had begun for the country dance Lady Adeline had offered him. Then it occurred to him that if she did not see him, she might give the set to another gentleman.

Damn. He couldn't afford that.

He made his way around the room, looking for her or any of the members of her circle, but it wasn't until he had traversed most of the ballroom that he found her. "My lady. Please tell me that I still have the country dance."

She looked over his shoulder before meeting his gaze. "I am sorry, my lord. When I did not see you, I accepted Lord Quartus for the set."

"It is my loss." Crispin's back teeth hurt, but he loosened his jaw. "May I stroll with you between the sets?"

"No." Lord Wively stood behind his sister. "You may chat with us, but my sister does not stroll between sets."

"Thank you, my lord." Hell! Crispin had no idea she was being watched so closely. "I will be happy to engage in a coze with your circle."

The man's smile had too many teeth. "You are most welcome."

So much for trying to get her alone. He'd have to be patient until the garden party. "I shall see you after the dance."

"Until then." She curtseyed.

Crispin damn well wasn't going to stand here waiting for her. He began to stroll the edges of the room. There must be some way he could occupy himself until the set was finished. He had made it over halfway around the ballroom when he saw Jean and thought of a perfect way to spend his time until he had an opportunity to speak with Lady Adeline again.

Completely unbidden, a low growl emitted from Frits as he watched Anglesey walk away from Adeline. The only good part was that the man appeared disgruntled.

Turley chuckled. "You can't keep every gentleman away from her."

"I don't want to keep *every* other man away from her." That was a lie. If Frits had his way, he'd be the only gentleman she danced and spent time with. "I want to keep *him* from her."

"I grant you, I don't particularly care for him either." Turley raised his quizzing glass and focused it on Anglesey. "And like you, I cannot articulate the reason."

The puppy approached Lady Holloway. "Have you noticed that the only people with whom he appears to associate are widows and matrons?"

"Now that you mention it, it is odd." Turley lowered his quizzer. "He did the same in Paris." He glanced at Frits. "To the best of my knowledge, he does not frequent any of the clubs either."

If he dared leave London, he would go to France to see what he could discover about Anglesey. But Frits would not leave Adeline alone. "I'm going to join Lady Adeline's circle. Do you wish to join me?"

"Not this time. I think I'll see who is in the card room." Shaking his head, Turley looked at Frits. "I still think you are moving too quickly." Then something or someone caught his eye. "I will join you after all."

"I cannot seem to stop myself." She was Frits's lodestone. He could not think of another lady in his arms for a waltz, or one who smiled so joyfully when seeing Max or going for a carriage ride. Yet, at the same time, she did not bother hiding her intelligence and strength. With her, he'd never have to guess what was bothering her or where he stood. Even now when he, admittedly, did not know her as well as he wished he did, he could see when she disapproved of something he had done. Fortunately, she did not remain upset for long, and she was quick to forgive his transgressions. Both were excellent qualities in a wife.

Chapter Eighteen

Adeline could not stop staring at her brother in something akin to shock. "Thank you. I had no idea you have been taking your chaperonage of me so seriously."

"My darling little sister." He placed his hand on her shoulder. "I have been watching you like a hawk, and when I haven't been able to do so, my friends have been helping. There is not a set you have danced in which someone has not made sure a gentleman did not attempt to make off with you."

Perhaps "stunned" was a better word. She didn't know what to say. "I–I thank you."

He swept her a courtly bow. "It is my pleasure. One day Eugénie and I will have a daughter." He glanced at Eugénie and smiled. "And I will depend upon you to help her during her come out."

Adeline glanced from her brother to her sister-in-law. They were so devoted to each other. How could she have missed the depth of their love? Tears pricked Adeline's eyes, but she could not resist teasing her brother. "I knew you wanted something from me."

He grinned. "I want you to find the love I have."

Adeline waved her hand in front of her face to ward

off the tears. "William Wively, you are not to make me cry."

His eyes flew wide in panic. "What did I say?"

Eugénie held out a handkerchief. "Something sweet, I am certain, *mon amour*, but ladies cry at sweet words."

"Is anything wrong?" Lord Quartus had to appear at the exact moment Adeline did not wish anyone to see her.

"Nothing, I assure you." She gave him a bright smile. "Shall we?"

"You are sure? I am a very easy fellow to talk to." His face was full of concern that she did not understand. They had just met.

"My sister-in-law was correct. My brother said something lovely to me. It was as unexpected as it was welcome."

"I understand." Lord Quartus bowed as they took their places in the set. "They are happy tears. My sisters get them as well."

"Yes." She was relieved when the dance began. Still, what Will had said made her feel much more secure. For the first time in a long while, she was glad he was her brother. Maybe rakes were not as horrible as she thought. Perhaps Will could explain more about them. "I do not remember seeing you before. Have you just arrived in Town?"

"Actually, yes. I was assisting one of my brothers, and Hawksworth, my eldest brother, invited me to visit him for a while."

"He is married to Meg Featherton, is he not? Her sister is my very close friend."

"Indeed he is. I have to say, I think the Feathertons are an excellent family."

Adeline did not know much about the rest of the

family, but Georgie and her parents were wonderful people. Then Adeline remembered what her friend had said about her sister helping her husband's family.

When Lord Quartus returned Adeline to her circle, Littleton was there, and for some unknown reason, her heart beat faster.

"Lady Adeline." He smiled and bowed. "I hope you are having a delightful evening."

"I am." He was up to something. She knew it in her bones. As much as she enjoyed his company, she could not bring herself to trust him. "What are you doing here? Our dance is not for more than another hour."

"I saw Miss Hanson and Miss Tice, and I decided I was safer in your company." She half-expected he was joking, but the dimple did not appear in the strong, lean planes of his face, and his eyes were not twinkling.

"I see." She let him take her hand and kiss it. His lips touched the thin kid of her gloves, and she could have sworn they burned through to her skin. Why did he affect her like this? "Were you able to find another gentleman for Miss Tice?"

The dimple came out as the corners of his lips rose. "I did. I found two. One to the north of Turner's estate and one to the west. But only Mr. Fitzwalter is in Town. He is the heir to Lord Fitzwalter."

Adeline had never heard of the man, but that did not mean much. "Is he here this evening?"

"At this ball?" Lord Littleton shook his head and appeared regretful. "No. Although I have it on good authority that he will be at Lady Wall's entertainment."

"Let us hope he and Miss Tice take a liking to each other." Then Adeline would only have to worry about Miss Hanson.

"I'm not at all sure it matters to Miss Tice who she

weds." His voice was drier than dust. "As long she resides close to her friend."

"I believe you are correct." Adeline felt her nose wrinkling and rubbed it. "Still, one can be optimistic about the matter. After all, she will have to live with whoever she marries and not Miss Martindale."

"Well said," Lord Littleton drawled. "If only he'd done something horrible to me, I wouldn't feel bad at all about sacrificing him. But needs must, and it will not hurt him to attend a few"—he seemed at a loss for words—"more sedate entertainments."

"Now we just have to find someone for Miss Hanson." Adeline thought back, trying to remember with whom the lady had recently danced. One gentleman stood out, but she did not think she could recommend him even to a lady as coldhearted as Miss Hanson. Oh, well. Nothing ventured, nothing gained. "What do you think of Lord Lytton?"

"Not much." The distain on Littleton's face took her aback. "Aside from that, he'd never marry the daughter of a Cit."

"Are you certain?" Many gentlemen felt the same, but it did not make sense. "He has danced with her more than once." Unlike ladies, gentlemen did not *have* to dance with a lady.

He shook his head. "I don't know why he has, but he is too puffed up in his own consequence to marry her."

"Well, bother." Adeline scanned the room for other likely prospects. "We will have to think of someone else."

"I have no doubt her father wants to buy her a title. From what I understand, he was surprised that when he married so far above his station it did not provide him the entrance into Polite Society he wanted."

"I do not understand why he thought it would."
That was it. Adeline was going to stop trying to make
sense of what people did. "Was she ostracized?" That is
what usually happened when the daughter of a peer
married out of her social class.

"No. Her father didn't have a feather to fly with, and
she did not take during her two Seasons, as her family
wished. I don't know exactly how the marriage was
arranged, but I believe it had something to do with a
friend of the earl's who knew Hanson. To make a long
story short, they wed, and her family benefited greatly.
Lady Cornelia's younger sisters were able to marry
well, and esteemed her for their good fortune. Despite
everything, the marriage turned out well. Miss Hanson
is a considerable heiress as well, having a large dowry."

That explained why the lady was accepted by Polite
Society. Not for her money, of course, but her family
connections. But what a font of information Littleton
was. "How do you know all this?"

His eyes twinkled and he grinned. "My mother."

"How very helpful." He placed Adeline's hand on his
arm and moved her a little away from her circle . . .
actually, *their* circle. He knew and was accepted by all
the gentlemen. "My mother could recite the history of
a bill being presented to the Lords, but has no real interest in other matters." Such as marital prospects.
Though Mama would discover all she needed to know
if anyone asked for Adeline's hand.

"It is satisfying to be able to have one's questions
answered." He'd moved closer to her, and warmth ra-
diated from his large body. "My interest in bloodlines
and other matters tend to be limited to animal husbandry."

"I find the subject of"—the pulse at the base of
Adeline's throat beat a rapid tattoo, and a charming

blush rose in her cheeks—"things to do with plants and animals interesting."

He'd ask her to take a stroll with him, but Turley had heard what her brother said to Anglesey. Still, what Frits was about to do would get him in even more trouble if he was discovered. "I probably shouldn't mention it to you, but I've had an offer to breed my Holsteins with a bull from a breed called Friesland out of the Netherlands. The man wants to see if they will produce more milk."

Adeline's neck was long and graceful, and he loved watching it move as she swallowed. "I have not . . . not been encouraged to learn about breeding"—her chest and face became bright rose—"er . . . animals."

Or anything else, he'd wager.

"What the deuce are you discussing?" Wively sounded as if he'd like to strangle Frits.

"Cows." He and Adeline answered immediately and at the same time.

"Just cows." Her tone was soft as she peeked up at him from beneath thick brown lashes.

Wively had a totally incredulous look on his face as he addressed his sister. "Cows?"

She nodded.

He fixed his quizzer on Frits. "Cows?"

"Yes." Frits knew his innocent look, which got him out of so much trouble, would not work on her brother, so he tried to look businesslike. "Holsteins and a breed called Friesland."

Wively narrowed his eyes, much like his sister did, but it looked odd through the quizzing glass. "I do not understand why that would make my sister blush like a red rose."

"Oh, that had nothing to do with the cows." Adeline coughed for good measure. "I–I had something caught in my throat, and had trouble catching my breath." She was a terrible liar.

Wively lowered his quizzer and his brows. "Find something else to discuss." Then went back to his wife.

"Oh, dear." She started to laugh and quickly covered her mouth. "Perhaps we should move on to pigs."

Frits couldn't help it. He barked a laugh so loud that the people near them turned to stare. "Now I've done it."

Adeline's shoulders were shaking, her hand was still firmly over her mouth, and she gazed at him, her eyes bright with tears and laughter.

He strove to bring himself under control, but tears started in his eyes as well. "I don't doubt my mother will hear about it with her morning tea."

She sucked in a large breath and hiccupped. "I cannot stop laughing."

"Adeline." Lady Wively cupped Adeline's elbow. "I believe we should go outside for a few moments. The fresh air will be good for you."

Wively stood behind his wife. "Cows again?"

"N-n-n-ooo." Adeline shook her head. "P-p-pigs."

"I'd no idea you had such a strange sense of humor." He turned to his wife. "See if you can calm her down. Her next dance partner will be here soon."

Frits turned to follow her and her sister-in-law, but Wively latched onto Frits's arm. "*You* remain here." Her brother closed his eyes as if he were in pain. "I suppose you expect me to believe you were merely discussing farm animals."

He was not about to betray Adeline's trust. "We both like animals."

"I think the two of you have lost your minds." Fortunately, the words were not forcefully said. "She hasn't laughed like that since she arrived in Town."

Neither had he, and it felt good. "I shall strive to keep farm talk out of the ballroom." From the corner of his eye, he saw his hostess in full sail, heading straight at him. "Please tell Lady Adeline that I'll be back soon."

Frits glanced around and found Turley standing nearby, talking to a young lady. "Excuse me." Frits took his friend's arm. "I must speak with Turley. I'll return him when I'm done."

"What the devil are you doing?" Turley said in a harsh whisper. "I was just making some progress."

"Miss Tice is trying to have me dance with her. I need to hide."

"Oh, now I understand." He looked confused. "Where shall we go?"

"Here." Frits ducked behind a door and almost ran into a footman, and held out a hand to steady the man. "Excuse me. Is there a parlor that leads off this corridor?"

"Three doors down."

Dragging Turley with him, Frits followed the servant's directions. Once they were in the room with the door closed, he said, "Both Miss Tice and Miss Hanson are attempting to force me to marry them. So far, I have been successful in not being presented to Miss Hanson and avoiding a hostess asking me to dance with Miss Tice."

Turley clutched his belly and laughed.

"I do not see what is so funny about any of this." Frits glanced around the room for a decanter of wine or brandy and found nothing. "And stop laughing so loudly. Someone will hear you and come in."

"No need to worry." Turley smirked. "Like a knight of old, I shall protect you."

"Stubble it." The situation was not at all amusing. Frits wanted to wed Adeline, not some other lady.

"If you do not require my assistance, I'll go." His friend turned toward the door.

"No!" Frits grabbed Turley's arm again. "I have to find a way to go back into the ballroom to be with Adeline."

"Adeline?" His eyes widened as his brows inched up his forehead.

"Lady Adeline." Damn, Frits had known he'd slip up sooner or later. At least he hadn't done it when her brother was around. That would have been disastrous. "I can't help thinking of her like that. It's a pretty name." And he felt closer to her when he used it. And that was the lamest excuse he'd ever made.

Turley rolled his eyes. "I suppose you can't just run home like you've done before?"

"Not this time. I have to avoid those ladies and hope there are no others." Aside from that, this time was different. It was still aggravating and dangerous, but Adeline was spending more time with him. He'd even made her happy this evening. "I wish Exeter would hurry up and secure Lady Dorie."

"What does that have to do with anything? Hasn't he started to court Miss Chatham?" Turley opened a sideboard and took out two glasses and a decanter of something. Leave it to him to find something suitable to drink.

"No. Miss Chatham is waiting for the gentleman she wants to marry to return to England. He's helping her to avoid Lytton until that happens."

Turley handed Frits a glass. "It's truly amazing the things you're able to discover."

"After what happened last year, I feel responsible for Lady Dorie, so I asked him." Frits drank down half of the glass before he recognized the drink as ratafia. "God, that's horrible stuff."

"Beggars can't be choosers, and I definitely feel like a beggar. I'll look to see if there's anything more palatable." He turned back to the sideboard. "How long do you plan to hide in here?"

"Until the next set begins." Frits held his breath and drained the goblet. "I should be safe after that. Did you find anything else?"

Turley pulled the stopper out of another bottle and sniffed. "Claret."

"Much better." Frits held out his glass. "While we're stuck in here, help me think of a way to convince Lady Adeline that she can ignore Lady Dorie's feelings about me."

His friend shook his head. "I have not a clue how you go about doing that." Turley sipped the wine. "And I'm not sure you would want a lady who would betray a friend."

"You have a point." Frits plopped down on a sofa. "I could be waiting for her for a very long time." He glanced around the parlor and saw a set of French windows. "They might lead to the terrace."

Turley strolled over and pulled back the curtains. "They do. We might do well to reenter the ballroom from there."

That was what Frits had been thinking. "We shouldn't have to wait much longer."

Turley opened the window the slightest bit. "Nothing yet." He closed it again.

Frits had not heard any music either. As long as they were here, he might as well see if his friend had any ideas. "I need to find a gentleman to dangle in front of Miss Hanson. He should have a title."

"Nothing like sacrificing your fellow man," Turley said with feeling.

"We must know someone who is at a standstill and needs a rich wife." How hard could that be? "Her father may be a Cit, but her mother is a lady and well-connected."

"Why don't you ask your mother?" Turley finished his wine and set the glass on the sideboard. "She always knows everything."

"I will, but I wish to cast a wider net." Frits strained to hear whether the music had begun again.

"Let me ask some discreet questions when I'm at my club or at the Lords." Turley gave him a long look. "At least you're consistent."

Now what was Turley about? "What's that supposed to mean?"

"You go after a lady with the same single-mindedness as you ran away from one. I must admit that although you danced attendance on Lady Dorie last Season, you did not pursue her as you have Lady Adeline."

"Thank you." Frits heard the faint sound of music. "I think the next set has begun." Maybe this time he could remain with Adeline the rest of the evening.

Chapter Nineteen

When Adeline came back into the ballroom, she glanced around for Littleton and did not see him. Surely he had not gone off by himself. He might be a rake, but that did not mean he was stupid. "Where did Lord Littleton go?"

Her brother lifted his quizzing glass to his eye, seemed to change his mind, and dropped it. "He grabbed Turley and left. Something about not wanting to meet Miss Tice."

"Oh, that's good, then." Adeline let out the breath she was holding. She was glad he had taken a friend with him.

Her brother fixed her with a hard stare. "Adeline, what exactly is going on?"

She debated telling Will. If anyone had knowledge of what Littleton should do, he would. Before tonight, she would not have thought to confide in him, but that had changed. "There are two ladies attempting to make him marry them. Do you have any advice you can give him?"

"I wish I did. I left England, but that won't work for most gentlemen." Her brother heaved a heart-felt sigh. "I'll tell you, young ladies can be the very dev—persistent."

"So I have noticed." The prelude for the next set began, and her dance partner approached and bowed.

When she returned to her family after the dance, she was pleased to see Littleton was present; unfortunately, so was Lord Anglesey. Adeline hoped they would not snipe at each other again.

"Lady Adeline." He swept her a bow. "I am here to request the supper dance at tomorrow evening's ball."

"Sorry, Anglesey," Littleton said. "She has promised that set to me."

Adeline ground her back teeth. She was going to murder Littleton. Smiling warmly at Lord Anglesey, she said, "Perhaps the quadrille, my lord."

"I would be honored." He glared at Littleton. "My lady, are you free for a ride in the Park?"

"Not tomorrow. I have plans." That was the truth. She was walking with Georgie and the others.

"The next day?" Lord Anglesey's eyes narrowed at Littleton.

She was glad she did not have to accept Littleton's request for a ride, yet she could not like the way his lordship was making this a contest. "Yes, I am available."

"Thank you." He bowed again and took himself off.

For Littleton's part, he scowled at Lord Anglesey's back. What *was* between the two of them?

"I don't like him," Littleton said, as if he could read her mind.

"Do you know of anything against him?" Adeline held her breath. Surely there was nothing wrong with Lord Anglesey. He was younger than some of the other gentlemen and had not been on the Town very long, but that must be to his benefit. He would have been less likely to engage in bad behavior than the gentleman standing before her had. In fact, he was perfectly charming, and he was so very handsome, with his Byronic looks and golden hair.

Littleton shook his head. "No."

"Well, then." Adeline stifled her sigh of relief. She had been correct. There was no reason she should not look to Lord Anglesey as a possible mate. "I have no excuse not to stand up with him or ride with him."

He inclined his head, as if to acknowledge the truth of her statement. "I've asked Lord Turley to help me find a husband for Miss Hanson."

Will glanced sharply at Littleton. "Well done. That was one thing I never thought to do."

The longer this went on, the more sympathy Adeline had for her brother. "I agree. That is an excellent idea. What traits did you tell him to look for?" He explained what he and Lord Turley had discussed. "Do not limit it only to gentlemen looking for a wealthy wife. One of the reasons she is interested in you is that you are so well set up."

"I'll keep an ear out as well," her brother volunteered, surprising her yet again.

"Thank you." For years, even after Will had married, she'd believed he was a rogue. Not that she thought he was unfaithful to his wife, but she had the idea that he was a here and therian. To be wrong not only pleased her, but made her wonder if she was mistaken about another gentleman. After all, if Adeline had misjudged her own brother—whom she had known all her life—could not a lady with less knowledge of a gentleman be mistaken as well? What would be the best way to discover the truth of the matter? No one discussed the things gentlemen got up to with unmarried young ladies. She slid a glance at her brother. If she asked, would he tell her?

Yet, if Littleton was not a rake, he had still treated

her friend badly. Granted, she knew what Humphries thought had occurred. And she knew what Dorie had said. Still, Adeline had the feeling that the truth was somewhere in the middle.

It was time for the supper dance, and Lord Exeter led out Miss Chatham.

"A penny for your thoughts." Littleton was waiting for Adeline to take his arm.

"I had hoped that Lady Dorie and Lord Exeter would make a match. I cannot see her with Lord Fotheringale."

"Concerning Exeter's intentions, things are not what they seem." Littleton's eyes were like soft green leaves. "However, it is not my story to tell."

Adeline nodded. "There appear to be a great many things that are not as they appear in Town."

"That's the truth." His arm encircled her waist. "It makes tenant squabbles and the like seem so much simpler."

"Perhaps that is because they are. For the most part, everyone is honest about what they want." That was probably because here, it involved looking for a husband or wife.

"For the most part." He gazed down at her, but his smile was so wistful, she wished she could ask him what it was he wanted. Yet another thing that could not be spoken. "Whereas here, there are a great many things people will not discuss."

"Yes." Adeline wished she could give all her friends what they wanted—Dorie danced by with Fotheringale— yet perhaps not everything they wanted was the right thing for them. Not everyone, of course. But there seemed to be a lot of miscalculations about what might make one happy. And at least one situation that was not what it appeared to be. When had life become so complicated?

Adeline was in a brown study, and while Frits had her to himself, he wanted her attention on him. "Have I told you about Sebastian?"

"No." She appeared puzzled. "Who is Sebastian?"

He grinned to himself and started telling the story. "Well, he started out as a barn cat, but he quickly turned into a kitchen cat. Now he fancies himself a family cat." Frits heaved a dramatic sigh. "The next thing I know, he'll run away to London."

"To see the king." She was laughing again, and his heart swelled. "Does he really exist?"

He gave her an affronted look. "Naturally he exists. I do not make up stories."

She had relaxed into his arms again. "What does he look like?"

"He's a red-and-cream tabby cat and very spoiled." Frits wished he could have brought the cat to Town, but that would have presented all sorts of problems, especially if he wanted to go outside. "He and Maximus are great friends."

"I have seen how well Great Danes and cats do together." Adeline appeared wistful again, and he vowed that once they married, she would have pets.

"Great Danes get on with most animals." He smiled at her. "Cows, horses, goats—although the goat isn't always happy at first—chickens also have to be convinced." She had started to chuckle lightly. If he kept it up, he'd have her laughing again. "They are very friendly dogs."

"Except for squirrels," she pointed out.

"That is a cultural problem." He schooled his

countenance so that he presented a serious mien. "Squirrels run when they're afraid. Dogs run to play."

"Ah." Her silver eyes shone with mirth. "A definite difference in cultures. That explains it." She shook her head thoughtfully. "I do not know how that problem can be resolved."

"There you have it." Frits wanted to hold her closer, but with her brother looking after her, he didn't dare. "All would be well if we could only explain to the squirrel that the dog simply wants to play."

Adeline smiled up at him, and his world tilted. He'd been right all along. She was the perfect lady for him. "That is something I'd like to see."

She was happy, and that was how he wanted her to be. Yet every time she saw Lady Dorie, Adeline pulled away from him. Somehow, he had to find a way around the problem.

Something caught the corner of Frits's eye. Anglesey was standing next to a young widow, Lady Holloway, who was shaking out her skirts. Normally, that wouldn't mean much. The man seemed to spend a great deal of time with widows, and ladies shook out their skirts. Still, there was something about the two of them. The way his body leaned next to hers and hers to his. The movement of the waltz caused him to lose sight of the pair.

"Is anything wrong?" Concern infused Adeline's soft voice.

"Nothing." He turned his attention to her. "Something caught my eye and I was attempting to discover what it was that appeared odd."

"As far as I am concerned, there are a great many things that are odd." Her disgusted tone made him smile.

"Indeed." He led her into a twirl.

"What do you think of Lord Belmont for Miss Hanson?" Rotating around, he glanced in the direction Adeline was looking. "He seems to meet her requirements."

"He's not as rich as Croesus, but he is wealthy enough." His family was good. He was well liked, and women thought he was handsome.

"And she seems to be enjoying his company." Adeline glanced at Frits. "I think she stood up with him because she wished to and not because she had to."

She was correct. The smile on the lady's face was not merely polite. "What an astute observation."

"That might mean we just have to worry about Miss Tice." That lady was dancing with Lord Bottomley, and her smile was definitely not one of joy.

"Will you bring the other gentleman with you tomorrow?" Adeline's thoughtful look was on her face.

Frits was not at all certain he could easily convince Fitzwalter to come. It might take drastic measures. Still, even if the lady was not as beautiful as Adeline, Miss Tice was pretty. He wondered why she had not taken better; then he remembered that she was only interested in gentlemen who lived near her friend's potential new home. "If I have to tie him up and cart him there."

Adeline's laugh was like the tinkling of small bells, and it warmed his heart and other parts of his body as well. He caught sight of Anglesey and the lady again, and Frits realized what it was he saw. If they weren't having an affair, he was still a green lad. It was all there: the lips close to an ear, the man's slow perusal of the lady's bosom, and the way Lady Holloway dropped her gaze. He knew if he followed either of them after the ball, he'd find them together. And to think the curst rum touch had the gall to keep bothering Adeline when he had a lover.

"What are you looking at?" Adeline appeared perplexed.

"I solved what had puzzled me earlier, and it is nothing." Nothing he'd tell her, in any event.

"That is good." She grinned. "It has occurred to me that if Miss Hanson has found her match, and Miss Tice can be as easily dealt with, you will not have to remain with me at balls and other entertainments."

Frits just kept his jaw from dropping to the floor. Devil it! He'd not even considered the consequences of having no lady attempting to trap him. Of course, Adeline thought he was staying with her because of the threats to himself. What was he to do when he didn't have the excuse?

"Er, I suppose so." He damned sure wasn't going to agree with her. "I do like your company."

A polite mask dropped over her mien. "I wonder if they will have lobster patties this evening."

Hell and perdition.

He was going to have to think of something soon. "If they do, I will ensure you have several."

The edges of her lips wanted to tip up. They were trembling, and he silently cheered them on. But they lost the battle. "Thank you."

Frits turned his mind to supper. If Lady Dorie was with Fotheringale, she would not be helping Adeline avoid him. He'd have to be sure to secure his chair before going to get their food. Frits was tired of being relegated to the other end of the table. He'd had too much fun talking with her and her family the other night. The set ended, and he slowly escorted her back to her brother and sister-in-law, all the while thinking of ways to achieve his immediate goal.

When they reached her family, her sister-in-law took Adeline aside. What was that about?

A moment later, a broad smile appeared on her face, and she came back to him. "I have been told that Gunter's has supplied the ices for this evening."

Frits's lips curled up as well. "Would you like one of each flavor?"

"Do you think I could?" Her expression was almost childlike in its wonder. Then her eyes dimmed a bit. "Without appearing to be too greedy?"

"If we share them, no one will think you are gluttonous. They will think I am."

"We do not need to taste the ices we already have." Ah, she was becoming interested in how to do this and not garner attention.

"Indeed. I shall only choose the ones you have not sampled."

Her eyes were shining again. "Yes. That will work."

All he had to do was try to sit as far away from Lady Dorie and Fotheringale as possible. Just then, his mother, Lady Watford, and Lady Huntingdon joined the group. "I thought my mother was at a dinner this evening."

"I thought mine was as well." Adeline's fine brows drew together. "I wonder what they are doing here."

His mother and Lady Watford began talking with Lord and Lady Wively, while Lady Watford joined her son, his wife, Lady Dorie, and Fotheringale. Shortly thereafter, they headed toward the supper room.

It was only once they were well away that Mama said, "We should go down now."

Something was going on. But as long as it kept Frits with Adeline, he didn't care what the ladies were up to.

His mother gave him a knowing look and indicated

that they should take a table across the room from where Lady Dorie was sitting.

He quickly complied. "Will this one do?"

"Yes, indeed, my dear. An excellent choice." Mama turned to Adeline. "I hear you have taken to Maximus, and he to you."

"Yes. He is a handsome boy." Frits pulled out a chair, and she gracefully lowered herself onto it. "I very much enjoyed walking him this morning."

Wively came up to Frits. "Shall we? I wish to make sure we have our choice of the ices. My wife is fond of them."

He wanted to say Adeline was as well, but as far as he knew, their visits to Gunter's were between them.

As they strolled to the long table where the delicacies where laid out, he caught more than one lady looking at him in a calculating way. Perhaps he'd found the answer to his problem. Adeline didn't have to be the only one who overheard plans to compromise him.

Chapter Twenty

The next afternoon, Cristabel poured tea for Annis Watford and Sally Huntingdon. The three of them were in Cristabel's parlor, and she had left instructions that unless the house was burning down or someone was seriously injured, they were not to be disturbed.

She handed her friends their cups. "We must take a hand in our children's affairs."

"I have a plan to turn Dorie from Fotheringale." Sally's satisfied expression made Cristabel focus her attention. "I have arranged it so that Naomi Fotheringale had to invite us to dinner."

Annis's eyes widened slightly. "I am impressed. Not that I would *want* to dine with her."

"Well, who does?" Sally said. "The whole point is to make my daughter realize how unsuitable a match her son would be."

"Speaking of matches for Dorie"—Cristabel decided to approach the problem directly—"I understand she is still angry with Frederick."

"That would have been a disastrous match." Sally pressed her lips together. "But you have to admit he did not handle it well. And I do not blame her for being furious about his behavior, and for being hurt."

"I agree. He should have at least told her he was leaving Town. I do not fault her at all. The onus is completely on him." As Cristabel had told him in no uncertain terms. "However, Frederick must marry. Both Annis and I believe Adeline is the perfect wife for him. We are doing everything we can to promote the match. The problem is that Dorie has warned Adeline against him, and that is presenting a problem."

Annis nodded. "The girls have become such good friends that Adeline feels guilty for enjoying his company. And she will not come to know him better until she feels as if she is not betraying her friend." She glanced at the ceiling and sighed. "Although first he must convince her that he is not a rake."

"Frederick is not a rake!" Two pairs of eyes under raised brows stared at Cristabel. "Well, not any more than Wively or Huntley were."

"But they are now married," Sally pointed out.

"Only after they left England." Really, that term was thrown about too frequently these days. When Cristabel was young, a gentleman was meant to gain experience. "Before that, they did the same things Frederick has done."

"But he has the reputation because he only associated with widows and women of questionable virtue," Annis objected.

"As did Wively." Cristabel sniffed. "One cannot blame a gentleman if he takes advantage of invitations by widows and unhappy wives." She speared the other ladies with a hard look. "I did not hear you complaining about your sons' behavior."

"I suppose you are correct." Annis grimaced. "Wively was most likely worse. I have a feeling from things that have been said that he did not initially act as he should have with Eugénie." She smiled happily. "But all is well now. I must feel differently because I have Adeline to worry about this Season."

"I hate to say it, my dear, but Frederick is too handsome," Sally said. "He looks like what every lady imagines her prince will." She gazed down at her tea. "I firmly believe that is the reason Dorie thought she was in love with him." Shaking her head disgustedly, she continued, "That, and everyone said what a beautiful couple they made. Enough of those types of comments and even someone like Dorie can have her head turned."

"Well," Cristabel used her driest tone, "there is nothing I can do about that. He looks just like his grandfather Littleton."

Annis held out her cup for more tea. "The question is, what will it take for Dorie to relent?"

Based on what Annis had told Cristabel, Adeline was loyal to her friends. "I would like to know that as well. He is trying to think of ways to make her want to marry him, and you *know* the sorts of ideas young men consider excellent."

The other two ladies rolled their eyes.

"Only too well," Annis remarked.

Sally held out her cup as well. "I would love to be able to tell you that I shall instruct Dorie to tell Adeline that Frederick is a good man, but telling her to do anything has always been fraught with problems. What I can do is to start planting seeds. Some of them will be about how ill-suited she and Frederick were, others about how it is not fair to keep a friend from the gentleman for whom she *is* suited."

"Yes." Annis nodded. "She must see the whole affair as a lucky escape for her."

"And not as her being wronged," Cristabel added.

"Those are both important points." Sally took a sip.

"Now, do we know of any specific thing he thinks is extremely important that Adeline likes as well?"

"Pigs," Annis and Cristabel said at the same time, then glanced at each other and laughed.

"They discuss farm animals?" Sally looked aghast.

"According to Wivenly," Annis said, "Frederick and Adeline were laughing so hard over them, she had to be taken outside to calm down."

A sly smile formed on Sally's lips. "I can guarantee you that Dorie would not understand what could be humorous about pigs."

"I daresay not many of us could." But that was exactly the type of thing that made Adeline perfect for Frits.

The previous evening, Frits had accompanied his mother, Adeline, and her mother to the theater. The play was amusing, and they all enjoyed it, but, as far as he could see, it had not helped him get closer to her at all.

He'd spent most of today hunting down Fitzwalter, only to discover he had begun much too early. By the time Frits finally thought to try the man's rooms, it was almost three in the afternoon.

Using his cane, he rapped on the door and waited. As he was about to knock again, it was opened by a servant he could only assume was a valet. He handed the servant his card. "I wish to see Fitzwalter."

"I am terribly sorry, my lord, but he has not yet left his bedchamber."

That scobberlotcher. Frits was ready to ring the idler's neck for all the trouble he had caused him. One way or the other, Fitzwalter would shortly be awakened. "In that case, it is high time he was up. Make some tea or coffee—"

The valet cleared his throat. "My lord, he drinks ale in the morning."

"Not this morning he won't. Bring coffee, and make it strong." That should get the man going. "And bring whatever remedy you have for pot verdugo as well as food."

"Yes, my lord." The valet hurried off to wherever the kitchen was.

He stepped inside the small hall with a fireplace, and immediately found the parlor, off of which lay the bedroom. The rooms were not much different from the ones he'd had at the Albany. He slammed open the door to the bedroom, and it bounced against the wall with a satisfying crash.

"What the bloody devil is going on?" Fitzwalter poked his head out from between the bed hangings.

"Good morning." Frits used a cheerful tone, but practically shouted the words, as if he was speaking to his great-great aunt, who was deaf. The noise made the other man wince. "Or, I should say, good afternoon."

"Littleton." Fitzwalter groaned as he fell back behind the hangings. "What the devil are you doing here?"

Knowing it was a sunny day, Frits opened the curtains before opening the bed hangings. "Bringing you back to the land of the living. I require help, and you are the only one in Town who can assist me."

Fitzwalter slammed a pillow over his head. "If you want my help, you should be kinder. I've a devil of a head."

"Of that, I have no doubt." Frits remembered those days all too well. "Your man is bringing coffee." He ripped off the pillow and tossed it across the room.

Fitzwalter rolled over and glared. "I prefer ale."

"Ah, yes. The hair of the dog. I need you sober."

He eyed the younger man consideringly. "Do you require aid rising?"

"No, blast it all, I do not." Fitzwalter sat up and blenched. For a moment, Frits thought the man would cast up his accounts.

But he had no time to coddle the idiot. Instead, he asked sweetly, "Are you sure you do not require help?"

"No." Fitzwalter attempted to stand and fell back to the bed. This was worse than Frits had thought. He hovered over Fitzwalter, but was waved back. "Blast it all. I'm never going to drink again."

"You aren't the only one who's made that vow."

"Damn you, Littleton." He managed to lurch up and disappeared behind a screen. By the time he had finished minimal ablations, the valet was back with coffee, a glass holding some vile brown-looking stuff, and toast.

Taking out his quizzer, Frits focused it on the toast.

"Just to make sure he holds it down," the valet said. "Once I know that, I'll bring up some rare beef directly."

"Good man."

As Frits lounged in a chair, Fitzwalter grimaced at the glass, but tossed it off and poured a cup of coffee, adding three large lumps of sugar. "I've never known you to be so cruel. What is this all about?"

"Turner is getting married." The other man's jaw dropped and seemed to be stuck in that position. Frits waited until the shock passed. "The lady to whom he is betrothed has a friend who wishes to wed a gentleman—"

"Now wait just a moment—"

He held up his hand, quieting Fitzwalter. "A gentleman who lives close to Turner. You and I are the only two in Town, and I already have a lady in mind. The only thing I want from you is to meet her, ask for a few dances, and take her walking or in a carriage around the Park. I am not asking you to offer for the lady."

Fitzwalter swallowed a gulp of coffee. "Set her cap at you, has she?"

"In a manner of speaking." Frits had decided not to betray the knowledge that she planned to trap him.

"That's all I must do?" The light flooding the room made the dissipation on the other man's face clear. Any guilt Frits had had left him. It really was time someone stopped Fitzwalter's excesses.

Frits nodded. With any luck, they'd make a match of it. Lord knew Fitzwalter needed a steadying influence in his life. A wife would do it.

Fitzwalter reached for the pot to pour another cup of coffee, but took a piece of toast instead. "For how long?"

"Just until I am betrothed. Probably two or three weeks." If it took any longer than that, Frits was liable to do something drastic. As it was, his other scheme was chancy at best.

"Very well." Fitzwalter leaned back in his chair. "I'll do it, but you will owe me."

He was clearly thinking of something, but Frits couldn't make out what it could be. There was a lot he'd give to have Adeline. "What do you want?"

"Gertrude." The man acted as if he was asking for the most important thing Frits owned. He almost laughed. Not that he didn't have affection for the heifer, but . . .

"You do know how many times we've sold her to your father and had to give him his money back because she wouldn't stay?" The blasted cow always managed to get out of the barn or the pasture and crossed miles of Turner's property to get home.

A militant light entered Fitzwalter's eyes. "I told my father that I could convince her to stay. He didn't believe me, but I want to show him I know what I'm talking about."

Frits had no idea what his friend would do, but he had to stop the threat from Miss Tice. "I agree. If you manage to keep Miss Tice entertained and away from me, you may have Gertrude. Unless she finds her way home again. And you must vow not to mistreat her."

"I do vow it." Fitzwalter actually looked insulted. "I'd never hurt a cow, no matter how hardheaded she is."

Frits stood. "You will dine at my house at eight. Be dressed for a ball."

Rising, the man started to bow, then thought better of it. "I shall be there."

He inclined his head. "I'll see you, then."

As he strolled out of Jermyn Street on to Piccadilly, he tried not to think of Adeline in Anglesey's carriage this afternoon, but that was a lost cause. The only thing Frits could do was take his curricle so he could be there and make sure she was safe with the runagate. He did not truly think the man would attempt anything he should not with Adeline, but he could hope. That would give him an excuse to rearrange the worthless fribble's face. She was the first woman to raise all his primitive warrior instincts, and he was looking for an excuse to drive his fist into the other man's nose.

As pleasant a vision as that was, he still had over an hour before he could go to the Park, and headed to Hatchards. His mother had ordered some books, and it would give him a chance to see if there were any new volumes that interested him. He stopped first at the clerk's desk, ascertained that some of the books his mother had ordered were in, and asked that they be delivered to Littleton House. Then he made his way upstairs to see if there were any new tomes on agriculture or animal husbandry.

He was almost to the back of the store when he heard whispering. But before he could investigate, a hand reached out and clutched his sleeve. "What the— Adeline? Wh—"

Reaching up, she slapped her hand over his mouth. "Shhh."

He followed her between the bookshelves, and found Miss Featherton was present as well. A man couldn't have everything. Adeline placed one finger against her lips before she and her friend turned their ears to the books.

"Every time I try to have him presented to dance with me, he disappears." Whoever was speaking was clearly distraught.

"I shall arrange to have Turner do it. He and Lord Littleton have been friends for years." Good God! No wonder Adeline had made him be quiet. That was Miss Tice and her friend, Miss Martindale. "Do not despair. We will manage."

He had to hide. Or perhaps he could sneak out if he did it quietly. There were sounds of chairs moving. It was too late to leave. Adeline took his arm and guided him farther along the shelves. A few moments later, steps could be heard on the stairs. He wanted to wrap his arms around her for saving him.

"I wonder how often they have their discussions here?" Miss Featherton mused.

"I do not know, but they obviously think it is the best place to have them," Adeline responded. "It makes no sense to me." She turned to him. "What brings you here?"

"Books." The answer came out more as a question. He must still be stunned. "My mother ordered some, and I wanted to see if there was anything new."

"Now that they are gone, you will have this area to yourself." She and her friend were getting ready to leave.

"I finally found Fitzwalter," he said, in an attempt to make her stay. Still, it was close to four o'clock. He did not know how long it took her to prepare for a carriage ride, but he wanted to spend more time with her.

Her eyes lit up as if the sun was shining off silver. "Will he agree to meet Miss Tice?"

"Yes, but I had to agree to give him Gertrude." For some reason, it was important that he tell Adeline that. Not that she knew the significance.

Her forehead wrinkled in confusion. "Who is Gertrude?"

"A heifer. His father has purchased her several times, but she always comes home."

A muffled chuckle emitted from Miss Featherton, which he ignored.

"I do not understand." Adeline's well-shaped brows came together. "If she does not wish to leave her home, why would you continue to sell her to Lord Fitzwalter?"

"I didn't. My father did." He left it at that, trusting she would not be satisfied with the answer.

She gave him a look that clearly stated she did not understand. "Please explain."

"Later." Miss Featherton linked her arm with Adeline's. "I must go home if I am to be ready when Lord Turley arrives." She smiled at him. "My lord, I am positive this is a fascinating tale that Lady Adeline would love to hear, but can it wait until this evening?"

Frits and Adeline exchanged looks, and for the first time, he knew they had something stronger than a mere connection. "I suppose it must. I cannot in good conscience do anything to make you late. Although keeping Turley waiting might do him some good."

A trill of light laughter burst forth from Adeline.

"Be that as it may," Miss Featherton said, "we must go."

Adeline gazed longingly at the books. "I hope you find what you are looking for."

"Thank you." Little did she know that Frits had already found exactly what he was looking for.

Chapter Twenty-One

"Don't you wish to stay a little longer?" Crispin lay on the bed, watching Jean don her chemise.

"If I do, you shall be late for your appointment with Lady Adeline, and that will not help your case with her." Sitting on the chair, Jean rolled her stocking up her leg.

"I suppose you're right." He stretched before throwing his legs off the edge of the bed. "I must think of something to talk about with her. I haven't told her about Paris yet."

She stopped in the middle of fastening a garter. "Does she want to travel?"

"I have no idea." He pulled his shirt over his head. "We have never touched on the subject. Once she marries me, she won't be going anywhere."

"In that event, I would not mention it to her. Have you asked her other questions about her likes and dislikes?"

The socks he'd picked up fell to the floor. Jean probably had a good point. He did not want Adeline dreaming about Paris. "No. Should I?"

Jean looked down her nose at him. "Yes, of course.

All ladies like to be asked about the things they enjoy. I am surprised you did not think of it before. After all, you ask me."

Well, put like that . . . "What do you suggest I do?"

"As I said. Ask her about herself, what she likes." She donned her stays, lacing them in the front. "Discover what she dislikes. She will be more interested in you if you show some interest in her. Have you approached her father?"

"I sent him a letter, but that was over a week ago, and I have heard nothing from him." Instead of compromising her, that would be the easiest way to bring about securing the lady. Unfortunately, it did not seem as if Lord Watford was interested in the match.

"It would help your cause if the lady at least liked you. This is only her first Season. Her parents might not care if she makes a match this year." Jean placed a bonnet on her head and drew on her gloves.

He pulled on his boots, then sauntered over to her and kissed her neck. "I shall do as you say."

Turning to face him, she smiled. "I look forward to hearing what happens."

"You shall. Tonight at the ball. I am sure we can find somewhere to have a private conversation." Being able to slip away with her had been the only interesting thing about the blasted balls.

"Ummm." She pressed her body against his. "This time you must be more careful of my gown."

"I think I can manage that." By the time he'd got her alone, he'd been desperate. This evening, he wouldn't let himself lose control.

"Come, my lord. You must bathe before you meet the young Lady Adeline."

He doubted the lady would know what she was smelling, but he had to admit he needed a bath.

Adeline was looking forward to her carriage ride with Lord Anglesey, but she was more than pleasantly surprised when he asked how she was and waited for a reply.

"I am quite well, thank you." He handed her into his carriage. "And you?"

He smiled, and it appeared genuine. "I have had an excellent day, which only promises to get better."

Once his lordship had his ribbons adjusted, he gave his horses their office. "What do you do during the day?"

"Oh, the usual. I take care of some business and visit my club. The same things most gentlemen do." He turned the corner onto Orchard Street, and for the first time she noticed that he was not as skilled as Littleton. "What did you do today?"

What had changed that he was deepening their conversations? Was he considering actually courting her? "I went for an early walk, assisted my mother with some household duties, then did a little shopping with friends."

"Do you find London to your taste?" He slid her a quick glance.

This was her opportunity to get to know him better as well. Whatever had caused the change, Adeline decided she had nothing to lose by answering honestly. "The Season has been interesting, but I prefer the country. One is too confined in London."

"I must agree with you. There are too many rules." He sounded disgruntled.

She did not know how he could complain. Gentlemen

could do almost anything they wished. Perhaps he missed the country. "Do you like the country as well?"

"My family's estate is beautiful. I look forward to seeing it again." Hmmm. That was evasive. "I intend to spend most of the summer there."

"Where will you go during the times you are not at home?"

The corner of his mouth tilted. "Probably to one or more of the other estates."

Adeline was pleased to hear he did not wish to return to Town.

They reached the Park and joined the throng on the carriageway. Several people greeted them, and Georgie and Lord Turley came up beside them so that she could say good day to Adeline.

Littleton joined them. He was riding the black gelding he'd ridden when they first met. She would like to go riding more often, but her mother did not approve of anything faster than a sedate trot in Town. "He is a handsome lad. What is his name?"

"Thank you." He stroked the horse's neck. "This is Apollo. His mother is one of our mares."

"Good afternoon, Littleton." Lord Anglesey's tone conveyed his irritation. "We must not hold up traffic."

"I completely agree." Littleton smiled pleasantly as he kept pace with the carriage. "Holding up any of the older matrons is certain to draw a rebuke."

"Don't you have somewhere else to be?" Lord Anglesey's jaw tightened.

"Not at all," Littleton responded, as if the other man had not just tried to hint him away. "I'm happy to keep you company."

He was incorrigible, but Adeline had a hard time not laughing and kept her mouth tightly closed. As he kept up a stream of small talk, Lord Anglesey became sulky. For the first time, she wondered how old he was. He certainly did not have the address of Littleton or indeed any of his friends. How had she not noticed that before?

They had arrived at the gate when Littleton executed a bow. "My lady, until this evening. Anglesey, it's been a pleasure."

Anglesey mumbled something she was sure would have made her ears burn.

She met Littleton's gaze, and his green eyes brimmed with laughter. "I shall see you later, my lord."

"He must be the thickest-headed man I have ever met," Lord Anglesey muttered as he drove out of the Park. "Why did he not leave?"

That was actually a very good question. Why had Littleton remained with them? Adeline knew the men did not like each other and, even though she enjoyed Littleton's company, it was clear Lord Anglesey did not. And Littleton knew it. Had it simply been to irritate the man, or was it something else entirely? Perhaps she would ask him this evening.

"I am sorry our ride was ruined," Lord Anglesey said. "Is it possible that you have a dance available this evening?"

She did feel sorry for Anglesey. He had been making an effort to engage her attention, and she had the feeling he had made up his mind to get to know her better. She was glad about that. "Yes, I have the second country dance."

"Thank you." He flashed her a smile. "I believe you were telling me why you enjoy the country more than Town before we were interrupted."

Only if one could call entering the Park an interruption. But perhaps she was being too harsh. "As I said, there are more restrictions here. When I am at home, I can walk and ride by myself. Here I must have a footman or a groom accompany me. Even when I go shopping with my friends, footmen must be in attendance." Although, she had to admit, they were sometimes helpful. "Therefore, one must plan everything in advance."

Anglesey's brow furrowed. "I would have thought you'd be accompanied by a maid instead of a footman."

She had seen maids accompanying other ladies. "I do not know why it is, but my parents and those of my friends all insist on footmen. I cannot imagine any of the maids would have time to attend me. They have too much to do."

He nodded. "Now that I consider it, the maids do seem always to be busy."

Something in the way he spoke made her think that he never considered such things. But why would he, when he had been traveling so much? "What do you like best about the country?"

"The beauty of nature and the fresh air. One need never be concerned about the smoke."

That was true. Still, she felt as if he was repeating what someone else had said. "What do you do while at home?"

"I have not been there since I began my Grand Tour." He pulled his curricle to a stop in front of Watford House, quickly hopped down, and came to her side of the carriage. Instead of putting down the carriage steps and assisting her to the pavement, he waited for the footman to do it. Only then did he escort her to the door.

She had been on several carriage rides this Season, and this was the first time the gentleman had waited for a footman. Adeline gave herself an inner shake. Perhaps he was raised more formally than the other gentlemen she had met.

Taking her hand, Anglesey bowed. "Thank you for your delightful company, my lady."

"Thank you for yours, my lord." Adeline curtseyed.

"I look forward to our dance this evening."

"Yes indeed." She entered the house feeling as if something was missing; then she knew exactly what it was. They had not gone to Gunter's. She hoped there were ices this evening. Littleton had her supper set, and if there were any, he would see to them.

Adeline halted on the stairs. It was strange how Littleton crept into her thoughts. She continued up toward her room. In fact, he spent too much time occupying her mind. Every time she thought she had banished him, he came back. Of course, it did not help that he seemed to physically insert himself into her life as well.

What *had* he thought to accomplish today?

Frits was rather pleased with the way he'd stuck a spoke into Anglesey's wheel. Once he had arrived, the man had not had an opportunity to speak with Adeline at all. And she seemed perfectly ready to converse with him. He could almost feel sorry for the here and therian.

Almost, but not quite.

He had no respect for a gentleman who would attempt to court a lady while carrying on an affair with another woman. Especially when that lady was Adeline, and he planned to marry her.

Glancing around, he spied Turner with Miss Martindale and rode over. "Good day, Miss Martindale, Turner."

"Good afternoon, my lord." She caught Turner's eye and raised one brow.

The man cleared this throat. "Littleton, well-met. I haven't seen much of you this Season."

They'd been at almost all the same entertainments, but Turner had apparently been so focused on Miss Martindale, he hadn't noticed anyone else. "Speaking of seeing people, I just had an interesting conversation with Fitzwalter."

"Huh." Turner seemed surprised. "I didn't even know he was in Town."

"Who is Mr. Fitzwalter?" Miss Martindale's voice rose in a question when she said "mister."

Turner replied, "His father, Lord Fitzwalter, owns the estate to my west."

"Oh." As Frits hoped, Miss Martindale definitely looked interested.

"He's coming to dinner this evening and accompanying me to the ball." He'd baited the hook, now it was time to see if the fish would bite. "I'd appreciate it if you could spend some time with him. If you knew a lady who would stand up with him, that is even better."

The corners of Miss Martindale's lips curved up. "I do know a lady to whom I can present him."

"Thank you. I look forward to seeing you this evening." He inclined his head, and rode around a bit more.

This matchmaking was almost enjoyable. Across the carriageway, Belmont was driving with a lady, and Frits made his way close enough to ascertain that it was Miss Hanson. It seemed as if neither of the ladies would be his problem much longer. Yet, other than the fear that one of them might succeed, he could not complain too much. Their schemes had given him an opportunity to remain close to Adeline, something he fully intended to continue to do.

That evening, after the third set, Frits saw his plan with Fitzwalter come to fruition in a more fruitful manner than he'd expected.

Frits was standing with Adeline and her family when the man strode up to him, grabbed his hand, and shook it. "You never told me how beautiful Miss Tice is. To think I would have missed out on meeting her if you hadn't dragged me out of bed this morning."

He repressed his glee. "I take it your meeting went well?"

"By God, yes," Fitzwalter said with feeling. "She is not only beautiful, but delightful as well."

"Does this mean you don't want Gertrude?" Frits actually wanted to see what the man had in mind to keep the cow with him.

"No." Fitzwalter laughed. "A deal is a deal, and I need to show my father I know what I'm about." He shook Frits's hand again. "Have a good evening."

"That was interesting." Adeline tilted her head. "I still do not understand why he wants a cow that runs away."

"Cows again? I don't understand either of you. One would think you could find more interesting topics of conversation." Wively narrowed his eyes at them. "Unless this is some sort of code."

Adeline gaped at her brother. "Why on earth would you think we had a code?"

"Never mind. Do not leave this spot. I must speak with Eugénie." He stepped over to his wife.

"*What* was that about?" Adeline gazed after her brother.

Equally confused, Frits shook his head. "He obviously has a much more devious mind than we do."

She lifted one shoulder. "Well then, back to Gertrude."

"None of us are quite sure why she won't stay," Littleton said. "Obviously, Fitzwalter has something to prove. He promised he will not mistreat her. I'll be interested to see what he has in mind."

But that did not answer Adeline's primary question. "But why sell her at all?"

"My father did it because she refuses to breed." A stricken look appeared on his handsome face. "I apologize—"

"No, no." Fighting her blush, she held up one hand. "I asked, and there really is not a more delicate way to put it." Heaven help her. No matter how interested she was in the cow, she had to change the discussion. If not, her brother would be over here, wanting to know what was being said. Littleton grabbed a glass of champagne and handed it to her. "Thank you."

"My pleasure." He glanced toward the French windows at the end of the room, and she followed his gaze. "I would take you for a stroll, but I don't think your brother would allow it."

As hot as it was, she wished they could go outside. Lord Turner and Miss Martindale stepped through the French windows. Adeline was certain they would make a match of it, and Miss Tice was taken care of, at least for now. "You are free to spend your evenings elsewhere, if you please."

Littleton frowned at her. "What do you mean?"

"You do not have any other ladies attempting to compromise you into marriage."

"We cannot be sure about that." He glanced around like a fox being chased by a pack of hounds. "We only know that you have not *heard* of anyone else." He pointed at Lady Riverton. "I believe she has a mind to coerce me into marriage."

Adeline almost rolled her eyes. Caro Huntley had mentioned the lady's aversion to the married state. "I happen to know for a fact that Lady Riverton does not wish to wed again."

"There is sure to be someone else," Littleton insisted. "It happens every Season. That's the reason I never remain in Town long."

Chapter Twenty-Two

Adeline was not at all sure what to make of Littleton. He had seemed almost panicked. Of course, she remembered hearing that her brother had once climbed a tree to get away from avaricious young ladies. She supposed Will must have been terrified to have done that, in his new boots no less. "Very well; we may go on as we have been."

"Thank you." Littleton let out a breath. "That makes me feel much better."

An awkward silence fell, and she felt as if she must fill it. "When will your new carriage be completed?"

"It is being delivered tomorrow." His usual ready smile returned, and the dimple made an appearance. "Would you like to take a ride in it?"

"I would." Adeline was looking forward to see how her suggestions looked. "Will you take Maximus?"

"I think I shall." The green of his eyes deepened. "We can see how he likes being able to go out for a ride in Town."

He was the sweetest of dogs. Adeline had fallen in love with the big beast. "I think he just wants to be with people." She saw her next dance partner approaching. "Here is Lord Anglesey."

Littleton's jaw set and his lips formed a thin line. He looked as if he wanted to make a derogatory comment, but instead said, "I hope he doesn't step on your toes."

"Thank you." Good Lord, not this again. She would have to have a discussion with Littleton about his animosity toward his lordship, but Lord Anglesey was upon them.

During their dance, his lordship continued his tack of asking her questions about herself. Earlier, she had hoped that he was forming an attraction to her, but was he? She was not a beauty or an heiress, and he did not know her that well. Although he was attempting to change that. She had been flattered by his attention to her, but now she was not sure. Why her over some other lady? Was it to win in a nonexistent contest for her with Littleton? If so, she wanted nothing to do with him, and it was not something she could ask the man.

Adeline caught sight of Littleton glaring at them from his post beside her brother and sister-in-law. What on earth did he think could happen to her on the dance floor? She could only suppose he had decided to look after her because she was helping him.

By the time the set ended, she still did not have a clue what Lord Anglesey was about and was glad to have the relatively undemanding company of Lord Bottomley for the next dance. He was happy to discuss the weather and other innocuous subjects. Then she made up her mind. She was no pawn in a gentlemen's game. She would ask Lord Anglesey about his intentions toward her.

Adeline was with Littleton for the supper dance. Not for the first time, indeed not even for the second time, she had to admit that he was a much better dancer than her other partners.

At supper, the talk turned, as always, to politics. She

and he were the only ones who did not actively take part in the discussion, and she almost wished they were sitting together. He would find a different topic of conversation. Yet, her friends had reverted to their usual habit, protectively surrounding her and Dorie, while Lord Exeter and Littleton were relegated to the other end of the table. It seemed unfair and a little bit mean. Yes, it was true that Dorie did not wish to be anywhere near Littleton, but that did not mean Adeline should do the same when she had stood up with him for the supper dance. It did not seem polite. The next time he had that set, she would sit with him, but far enough away from Dorie to keep her from becoming upset.

The next afternoon, Adeline eagerly awaited Littleton's carriage and could not stop herself from peering out her bedroom window for a glimpse of it. "Here it comes!"

"Come away from there," her mother commanded. "You know better than that."

"But I want to see what it looks like from above," Adeline objected. "I am better able to see how it turned out."

"How what turned out?" Ignoring her own advice, Mama joined Adeline at the window.

"Lord Littleton's carriage, with room for his dog." She turned back to the view outside just as the carriage came to a stop. "Do you see how the box for Maximus is made? That was my idea."

"Oh, dear Lord." Her mother closed her eyes. "You had better marry someone who loves animals as much as you do."

That was probably a good idea. "I must go." She

bussed her mother's cheek and reached the top of the stairs at the same time Littleton was ushered into the hall.

He grinned boyishly. "Are you ready?"

"I am." She placed her hand on his arm. "Did you have any trouble getting Maximus in the box?"

"He was a bit hesitant at first, but when he understood that he'd be able to come with me, he got right into it."

Adeline held her breath as Littleton lifted her into the carriage and the tingling warmth accompanied his touch.

Maximus immediately put his chin on her shoulder, wanting attention. She stroked his silky ears. "You are such a good boy."

When Littleton took his place on the bench, the dog licked the side of his face. "I'm glad you're happy. Lie down again."

Maximus did as he was told, and they drove out of the square to the Park. "I wonder if people will comment or maintain well-bred countenances."

"By pretending everyone drives around with a huge beast in their carriage?" Littleton grinned. "I hear Poodle Byng was extremely put out when he saw Merton's cat in his curricle."

Adeline believed it. She had never met a young man so puffed up in his own conceit. She would love to see his expression. "Maybe he'll be there today."

Not ten minutes after they arrived, she got her wish. However, it was not the man but his dog that took exception. The poodle, obviously not used to seeing other dogs in the Park, began to bark madly.

Maximus placed his paws on the edge of the box, she grabbed his lead, and Littleton quietly commanded, "Maximus, stay."

The tension left the lead, but when the other dog continued to yap, he let out a deep bark loud enough to startle the poodle and most of the people around them into silence.

"That did it." Littleton raised a brow at Byng. "You might want to spend more time training your dog not to make so much noise."

Polite laughter broke out around them, and Littleton slid her a look brimming with hilarity. "I think you have your answer, my lady."

It was all Adeline could do to stop from going into whoops. "I believe I do."

"When we go to Gunther's, shall we let him have a vanilla ice?"

She did not know anyone else who would treat an animal to ice cream. "I think that is an excellent idea." She turned to stroke the dog and found his nose in her face, and he licked her. "You realize that this will be all over Town by this evening."

"Yes." Littleton looked extraordinarily pleased. "I believe it will."

If only he had not hurt her friend so badly, Adeline could come to like him very well. But, unfortunately, the past could not be changed.

The next morning, Frits dropped the letter from Elizabeth Harrington on his desk. According to her, there was nothing out of the ordinary about Anglesey.

Blast it all!

Frits could have sworn there was something smoky about the man. Other than Anglesey shagging other women while pretending to be interested in Adeline. Something Frits could tell her that would give him permission to watch over her. Still, he was sure the rogue was up to something devious. Last night at the ball, he'd almost, almost, followed the man to expose his behavior. But that would, unfortunately, have ruined the lady's reputation, and he hadn't wanted to do that.

Maximus ambled into the room, his tongue lolling to the side of his mouth. "Well, boy, we'll just have to protect Adeline without her permission."

The dog leaned against Frits's leg to be stroked before going to his pillow for his morning nap. Frits glanced at the clock and sighed. It was too damned early. But ever since Adeline had begun going on walks with his dog, he'd been unable to sleep until his usual time. He might as well be back in the country if he was going to get up before a decent time. Still, he had a lot to do before Lady Potter's party this afternoon. It was most likely the only entertainment to which he could bring Maximus. Something Frits was sure Adeline would love. The Great Dane was as close as she was going to get to having her own dog until she married him. Unfortunately, he didn't think she even knew he wished to wed her. And she was still holding him at arm's length. That was likely to go on as long as Dorie held her grudge. He wished he'd never come to Town last year. That was what came of not following tradition. He was the first Littleton man to voluntarily look for a wife. And what had happened? He'd made the wrong choice. With Adeline, it was as if his feelings for her had just been there, waiting to reveal themselves.

Frits was in his bedchamber putting the finishing touches to his cravat when a sharp rapping sounded on the outside door.

"My lord." Creswell sounded as if he'd run up the stairs. "An urgent message from the Foreign Office came for you."

The only person who'd send Frits a message through there was Elizabeth Harrington. Had she discovered something? "Come."

His butler entered, holding out a missive with his name written in Lady Harrington's neat hand. Ayles held up his jacket, and Frits shook his head. "I'll read this before we finish."

Popping open the seal, he shook out the letter.

My Dear Littleton,

The very next day after I wrote to tell you there was nothing important about Anglesey, Paris became abuzz with the news that the Spanish Duke of la Algaba arrived in the city with his wife, daughter, and the daughter's one-year-old baby boy. She (the daughter) is being introduced as the Countess of Anglesey! You may imagine my shock.

Apparently, she and Anglesey were married in Madrid, and he left shortly thereafter, promising to return within a month or so. Obviously he intended to abandon the poor lady. Not only that, but she was quite young when they wed. She has just last week turned seventeen. I can tell you that many in Paris, including Harrington and I, were completely deceived by Anglesey. He said not a word about being married, and indeed presented himself as a single gentleman.

Naturally, the moment I learned the facts, I knew I must write to you immediately. No doubt, many others in Town and elsewhere in England will shortly know of his treachery. However, I pride myself that you will be the first to hear the wretched truth about his lordship. Even Harrington said I must send you word at once.

> *Yr. friend,*
> *E. Harrington*

*PS I believe that Lady Anglesey and her family will
arrive in Town within the next two weeks. The duke
said they will stay with the Duke of San Carlos,
Spain's ambassador to Britain, until they see their
daughter settled.*

*PPS Please write to me and tell me everything that
happens. And please try to ensure that everyone treats
poor Lady Anglesey well. She puts on a brave front,
but I am concerned that that is all it is.*

Frits felt a slow smile stretch his lips as he reread the
missive. This afternoon's entertainment was going to
be much more interesting than anyone expected. As
to the young Lady Anglesey, he'd have a word with his
mother. She would be able to ease the young lady's way
into Polite Society.

He glanced at the letter again and did a quick calcu-
lation. Devil it. She had been just fifteen when that
scum had seduced her.

"Is there something wrong, my lord?" Ayles asked as
he lifted the jacket again.

"No, Ayles." Frits held out his arms, allowing his
valet to ease on the jacket. "It is very good news."

"Excellent, sir." Ayles smoothed the back of the
jacket.

Excellent indeed. For everyone but Anglesey. "Please
tell Humphries to get Maximus ready, and inform him
that he will ride with me, and send word to the stable that
the horses will need to be walked for a bit. I must speak
to her ladyship before we depart."

Fifteen minutes later, Mama's jaw snapped shut for
the third time. "The *blackguard*! There are not words
strong enough for what I am feeling. If I was a man, I
would run him through with a sword, or shoot him

where it would count the most. And to think of the way he has been carrying on. I had it from Annis Watford, who heard it from her daughter-in-law, that he had asked Lady Riverton to marry him. If it was not for his poor wife, I would make sure he is no longer accepted by the *ton*." His mother sat down at her writing table. "You are correct, of course. We cannot take out our ire on Lady Anglesey. I shall dash off a note to his mother, informing her that she should repair to Town as soon as possible." Mama took out a piece of pressed paper. "I do not know what she will think of him marrying a Spaniard, even though her father is a duke. She and Normanby—well, mostly Lady Normanby—made Anglesey return to England so that he could wed an English lady." Mama dipped her pen into the standish. "At least there is an heir. That ought to make them happier about the marriage."

This was going to be the scandal of the Season, but why she needed to be involved he didn't know. "I think it is very likely that someone will have written her from Paris."

"Yes, but whoever informs her of her new daughter-in-law and grandson might not know they plan to arrive in England so soon."

Frits couldn't argue with that. He did want to get to Lady Potter's house without delay. The bounder needed to be kept away from Adeline. "Do you wish me to wait for you?"

"No, no." Mama waved one hand as the other took up her pen. "You go. I shall meet you there."

He kissed her on the cheek. "You are the best of mothers."

She glanced at him, her eyes appearing a little moist. "I could not have asked for a better son. I am certain you will handle this disclosure properly."

"I'll do my best. But I'll be hard pressed not to plant Anglesey a facer."

"He deserves that and more," she muttered as she turned back to her writing table. "Oh, and be careful. I hope you are taking Humphries with you in the event Maximus sees something interesting."

"I am." When Frits had conceived the idea of having his dog ride around with him, he had not thought of Maximus's reaction to other animals, such as squirrels. He'd been very good about other dogs, but squirrels seemed to drive him mad. After one particular incident, he and the groom had fashioned a harness that could be attached to the carriage. "He can no longer jump out of the curricle."

"Thank heavens for that. Now go." His mother made a shooing motion. "I want to send this off."

Chapter Twenty-Three

It had been several days since Maximus's first ride in the carriage, and except for the dog's brief attempt to greet a herd of cows—what he thought he had in common with bovines, Frits did not understand—the hour's drive to the garden party was uneventful.

When he arrived at the house, the drive was crowded with carriages. Frits jumped to the ground and let down the steps, then waited for Humphries to let the dog out of his box.

"We'll be a few hours at least," Frits said to the groom. "If you'd like, you may go into town and find a tavern."

Humphries glanced around. "It looks like there's some tables set up near the stables. I'll just stay here. You never know when Max will be ready to leave."

"He'll be fine. Lady Adeline is here, or will be shortly."

"Ah, in that case, all is well." Humphries scrambled onto the front bench and started the pair.

"Sarcasm does not become you," Frits grumbled, knowing the servant hadn't heard him and might not even understand the word. Still, the sentiment was correct. The dog was now better behaved for Adeline than he was for him. "Come along. Let's find your lady love."

Frits found her by instinct and the slight pulling on the lead as they made their way through the crowd of guests. The only problem was that she was strolling with Anglesey toward one of the wide woodland walks. Lengthening his stride, Frits fought to catch up with them, but every few seconds someone stopped him to comment on the dog. Fortunately, Maximus had seen Adeline and also wanted to find her.

He came up with the only excuse he could think of to get away from people. "Please excuse us. Maximus needs some privacy."

Finally, they broke through to the paths, and Frits let the Dane lead. The trail curved around until he could hear water bubbling. Adeline and Anglesey were alone, but probably not for long. Still, she could not possibly have understood that he met to take her to such an isolated place. If they were discovered . . .

Hell!

Frits dropped the lead.

Adeline had been interested to see the fountain Lord Anglesey told her about, but she had not realized it was quite so far away from the lawn. "I think we should return."

"It is just here." He smiled down at her. "Just a few more steps. I'm sure we will not be the only ones there. I understand it was created in Italy of pink marble."

A few more steps should not matter. The fountain did sound beautiful.

"See. There it is," Lord Anglesey announced.

"Oh, my." It was huge, with life-sized figures and water splashing. Adeline had never seen anything like it. She started to stroll around it when he stopped her, placing his hands on her waist. "My dear Lady Adeline."

Heat lurked in his summer-blue eyes, and she knew he was about to kiss her. She tried to step back, but he held her so tightly, she couldn't move. "We must go back."

"We will, but first—"

Relief flooded Adeline as Maximus pushed himself between her and his lordship. The dog's whole body wagged with joy as he leaned against Adeline, forcing her away from his lordship.

"Good afternoon, my lady." Lord Littleton bowed. "Anglesey."

"Littleton." Lord Anglesey gazed over Adeline's shoulder, and she turned her head. There was a second path on the other side of the fountain. "We are having a private conversation."

Was he waiting for someone to join them? A trickle of fear ran down her spine. What was going on?

"Indeed." Littleton raised his quizzing glass. "I cannot imagine what you could have to talk to her about in such a location."

Anglesey's eyes hardened. "That, my lord, is my business."

Frits indicated Adeline. "I believe it also affects Lady Adeline."

Frowning, she glanced from Anglesey to Frits. "What affects me?" She really should not have allowed herself to come here. "We should go back to the rest of the guests."

"I was going to propose," Anglesey ground out.

That is the reason he wanted to be alone with her, and Littleton had ruined it. Then another thought occurred to her. Why here and not at her home? "Have you spoken to my father?"

"I tried." Anglesey clipped the words. "He did not answer me."

"If you have not even spoken with my father"—Adeline took deep breaths as her anger increased. How could he have imagined—"What, my lord, makes you think I would accept without my parent's approval? What sort of lady do you take me for?"

Anglesey's gaze again strayed toward the other path. He *was* waiting for someone. But to what purpose?

Littleton's fingers curled to form fists, and the sound of people talking reached her. "I believe, my lady, that if you refused his lordship, he intended to compromise you into marriage."

For a moment, she couldn't comprehend what he had said. "*Compromise me?*" He nodded. Lord Anglesey had said he had not heard from her father, but was that a lie? "Did my father refuse you?"

"No." A tic had developed in his jaw as Lady Riverton and Lady Holloway emerged from the second path and reached the other side of the fountain.

In a few moments, they'd be able to hear everything. Littleton was right. Lord Anglesey had planned to compromise Adeline.

Littleton put his quizzer to his eye and focused it on his lordship. "That, my lady, unfortunately, I cannot tell you." Raising his voice, he drawled, "Especially considering he already has a wife."

"A wife!" Lady Riverton's outraged tones pierced the air. "You are married?"

Lady Holloway's mouth hung open before she was able to compose herself. Then she cut a sharp look at the other lady. "You blackguard. You scoundrel."

As the women were making their way toward Lord

Anglesey, Maximus began herding Adeline away from the others. Stepping forward, Lord Littleton took her arm, coaxing her from between the combatants.

She glanced at him. "How do you know he is married?"

"I received a letter from Lady Harrington in Paris. It seems that Lady Anglesey, her son, and her parents, the Duke and Duchess of la Algaba, arrived in that city searching for her husband."

"It's not legal," Lord Anglesey spat out. "The marriage is not legal."

"Indeed?" Lord Littleton raised a brow. "The duke and duchess say you and she were wed in Madrid."

"It was a papist ceremony." Lord Anglesey's eyes jumped from the other ladies to Littleton and Adeline. He shook his head, trying to convince them he was telling the truth. "It won't be recognized here." He focused on the two ladies. "If it had been legal, I would not have left Spain."

Adeline could not believe what she was hearing. Neither Lady Riverton nor Lady Holloway appeared to soften toward the scoundrel, and Adeline's rage grew. The worthless, contemptible, despicable blackguard.

Lady Riverton's eyes narrowed to slits. "You got a gently bred lady with child."

"A very young lady at that." Littleton said casually. "She has just turned seventeen."

"Seventeen, and she already has a child?" Adeline had never in her life been so shocked. The scoundrel tried to deny not only his wife, but his child as well. He should not be allowed to get away with such wickedness. But before she could lash out, Lord Littleton again calmly raised his quizzing glass and inspected Lord Anglesey as if he was a disgusting insect. "As well traveled as you are, I am amazed that you do not know that any marriage meeting the legal requirements of the country in which it is performed is legal in England."

The blood left Lord Anglesey's face, and for a moment Adeline thought he would faint. If he fell backward, he would hit his head on the rim of the large fountain and, strangely, that did not bother her at all. He *should* feel as much pain as he had caused his wife. Then she remembered what Littleton had said earlier, about the blackguard's scheme to compromise her, and she focused on the two ladies. "My ladies, did anything particular make you decide to come out here?"

Lady Riverton lifted one shoulder. "Lady Holloway told me that Anglesey suggested we might like to view the fountain."

Lady Holloway turned a bright shade of red. Adeline was certain she had known.

Adeline drew in a deep breath. Littleton had been right. The cur had intended to compromise her. And if the news of Anglesey's wife and child had not reached England, she could have been made to marry him. Then what would have become of her?

Her fingers curled into fists. She had never wanted to strike anyone so badly in her life. Actually, there was no reason she should not. Making sure her thumb was on the outside of her fist, as her brother had shown her, Adeline lunged forward and struck. Something made a crunching sound, and blood spurted from Anglesey's nose.

"Excellent flush hit." Littleton nodded approvingly. "And you didn't even get any blood on your glove. Very well done indeed."

He placed the palm of his hand on her waist, and she put her fingers on his arm. "I wish to go back."

"Certainly." His large hand covered hers, and his

warmth seeped into her. Until then, she had not realized how cold her fingers were. They also hurt a little, but it was worth it. "Ladies." He bowed. "We shall leave his lordship to your tender mercies."

He escorted Adeline back the way she had come. "I must thank you for saving me. I . . . I do not wish to think about what could have happened. I should never have gone off with him, but he made me think he was actually interested in . . . Suffice it to say, I know better now."

Lord Littleton grinned. "Maximus and I would never allow any harm to come to you."

She glanced down. The Great Dane was at her side, and she ran a hand along his back. "Then I must thank both of you." They had reached the turn before the path opened to the lawn when he stopped. "Is something wrong?"

With one long finger he traced her jaw, causing butterflies to lodge in her chest. His lips brushed against hers once, twice, then settled briefly as his fingers stroked her cheek. "I never kissed Lady Dorie."

Adeline had not asked the question. She was not even sure she had thought about it, but if she had, she would have assumed that he had kissed her friend. Was that not what rakes did? "You didn't?"

One corner of his mouth tilted and brought out the dimple. "No."

"You should not kiss me either." Yet her words were not nearly as firm as she wanted them to be. Suddenly, she didn't know what to think. Her mind was so focused on the feeling in her lips, she couldn't think. What was wrong with her?

"No?" He grinned like a child who had got away with stealing sweets. "I will take you back to your mother."

Adeline tried to summon anger for what he had

done. For the kiss. But her stupid mind liked it. "Yes, that would be for the best."

She was trying to decide the best way to forget about it when they emerged from the wood along the edge of the river and saw Lord Exeter rowing straight at the boat Dorie and Lord Fotheringale were in. "Is he mad?"

"No." Lord Littleton pointed to another punt headed directly toward Dorie's boat. "He's trying to avoid a collision."

Lord Exeter's boat hit the bow of Dorie's skiff and turned the boat just before the punt sailed by. "That was well done of him."

"I agree. But I might need to help Turley stop Exeter from murdering Fotheringale."

"What do you . . ." The boats had reached the shore, and Lord Turley was making his way toward Exeter, who was handing Dorie out of her rowboat. His lordship looked as if he really might commit murder. "I shall go to Dorie."

Lord Littleton squeezed her hand. When had he taken it? "I didn't tell her about the piglets either."

So, it was not that Dorie had forgotten. Adeline smiled to herself. For some reason, that admission pleased her more than the kiss. "I know."

He released her hand and strode off toward the crowd around Exeter. She exchanged a glance with Georgie, then they both hurried to Dorie. Yet Adeline could not help but look at Lord Littleton. Her lips still tingled. What was it he wanted from her?

She couldn't think about it now.

* * *

After literally stopping Exeter from maiming or killing Fotheringale, Frits saw the two ladies from the fountain, but not Anglesey. If the man had any sense of self-preservation at all, he would leave Town as soon as possible.

Frits would rather have spent more time with Adeline, but after consoling Lady Dorie, Adeline had gone off with her other friend, and there was no way he was going to be able to get close to her again today.

Still, he'd kissed her. It was no more than a whisper of a kiss, but it had affected him like no other kiss ever had. And it had satisfied none of his constant lust for her. Still, it was a kiss. Adeline's first kiss.

And Frits wanted more. And the only way to get more was to marry her.

After Adeline and Georgie had seen to Dorie and ensured she had suffered no ill effects—other than being in a temper with Fotheringale—from the boating incident, they strolled over to a table laden with food.

"I think any idea Dorie has of a match with Lord Fotheringale has ended," Georgie said as she selected bread and thin slices of ham from a platter.

"I agree. Apparently, he did not listen to her warnings at all." Adeline decided against the ham and put equally thin slices of beef on her plate, as well as some cheese.

"I shall put that on my list of requirements." Georgie added salad and a strawberry tart to her plate, and Adeline followed suit.

"I as well." Her lips still tingled from Littleton's kiss. "A gentleman should listen to a lady he wishes to wed."

They picked up glasses of lemonade and found a bench, then Georgie said, "How did you come to be strolling with Lord Littleton?"

Adeline debated not telling her friend everything, but she had to tell someone, and she could not tell her mother or her sister-in-law. Will would be bound to discover what had occurred, and he would either challenge Anglesey to a duel or kill him outright. "He saved me from Anglesey."

Georgie's eyes rounded. "Indeed?"

"Anglesey meant to compromise me into marrying him." Adeline took a sip of lemonade and swallowed. "But he is already married." Unfortunately, Georgie had just taken a drink, and the lemonade spewed out of her mouth. "Oh, dear." Adeline took out her handkerchief and started mopping her friend's gown. "I should have paid more attention to what you were doing before I told you."

"No, no. It is quite all right. The gown is yellow." Georgie took another swallow of the drink. "He is despicable. Tell me the rest."

Adeline related that his lordship had married a very young, gently bred lady, got her with child, and left her, thinking the marriage was not legal in England.

"What a . . . a . . . Oh, bother, I cannot think of a word horrible enough for him and his behavior. Thank God Lord Littleton found you."

"He has never liked Lord Anglesey, but could not say why." He must be a very good judge of character to have known there was something wrong with the scoundrel. "In any event, Lord Littleton saw Lord Anglesey take me into the woods, and got to us shortly after we arrived at a fountain—that, by the way, is beautiful—and

Maximus put himself between Lord Anglesey and me. Then Lady Riverton and Lady Holloway came from another path. I think Lady Holloway knew what Anglesey was going to do. Lord Littleton told everyone what he had discovered from Lady Harrington in Paris, and I hit Lord Anglesey."

Georgie tilted her head and stared at Adeline. "You slapped him?"

Pressing her lips together, Adeline shook her head. "No. I punched him in the nose. I think it is broken."

Her friend held the handkerchief to her mouth and went into silent whoops. "W-w-well d-d-done!"

"Thank you." She *was* proud of herself for taking that particular matter into her own hands. After everything that had happened, it made her feel powerful. "My hand hurts, and it is probably bruised, but it was worth it."

"I should say so. What did Lord Littleton say?"

Now that she thought about it, his reaction had been gratifying. "He said it was well done."

And a little later he'd kissed her. But that was something Adeline would keep to herself.

Chapter Twenty-Four

When Frits arrived home from the garden party, he immediately sent a letter to Lord Watford requesting a meeting. Then waited, and waited, and waited, and waited.

Blast the man.

On the fourth day, Frits strode into his secretary's office. "What is going on in the Lords today?"

Roberts stared at Frits as if he had transformed into someone or something unrecognizable. "The Lords?"

He would've thought the man was making a May-game of him, but for the fact that his secretary's mouth gaped open. "I'd like an answer sometime this century."

The mouth snapped shut. "Right away, my lord." He shuffled through some papers and pulled one out. "There is a vote this afternoon at three o'clock."

That most likely meant there would be meetings before the vote. "If anyone needs me, I'll be at White-hall."

"Yes, my lord." Roberts's disbelieving tone followed Frits out of the office.

He chuckled to himself. There was no way his secretary could keep this a secret. Soon, most of his senior staff would be wondering if their world had tilted upside down.

Not wishing to wait in the house for his carriage to be readied, he walked out the back door, across the lawn to the stables, and barked, "Have my town coach readied."

In much less time than it would have taken to have sent the order, he was on his way to Whitehall. However, once there, he had a devil of a time hunting down Lord Watford. Frits finally caught up to his lordship in close conversation with another gentleman as they strode down a corridor.

"Lord Watford."

His hopefully soon-to-be-father-in-law glanced at Frits and blinked. "Littleton, are you here for the vote? We could use you."

"I actually need a few moments of your time." His lordship turned back to the other man, about to dismiss Frits. "But I'm happy to vote for anything you want as long as I can speak with you."

"I'll join you in a moment," Watford said to the other gentleman. He looked at Frits. "Come with me." They entered a small closet. "What can I do for you?"

Frits let out a breath. "I sent you a letter asking for an appointment. I wish to marry Lady Adeline."

"Talk to me after the vote." Watford strode out of the room.

Bollocks!

That was one way to ensure Frits stayed for the vote. He pulled out his pocket watch. Over an hour to go, and he didn't even know what to do until then.

"Littleton, what are you doing here?" Turley clapped Frits on the back.

He glanced around, but didn't see anyone in the corridor. "I came to ask Lord Watford for permission to marry Lady Adeline, but he wants me to vote on something before he will give me an answer."

His friend's laugh started deep in his stomach. "I wondered what it would take to get you here."

"What is the bill?" If he was going to support something or not, he should know what he was doing.

"The government is attempting to indemnify the actions of ministers concerning anything they might have done regarding the West Indies. We are opposed, based on the theory that if they did what they were supposed to do, they don't need indemnification. The issue has been ongoing for a few months. You will be expected to vote against the bill."

That sounded fair. "I don't have a problem with that."

"Good man. What are you doing now?" A door opened, and several peers entered the corridor.

"I have absolutely no idea. The last time I was here was when I took my seat."

"You might as well stay with me." Turley shrugged. "I can show you where to sit."

That sounded like a good idea. "Very well."

Frits followed his friend around, doing relatively nothing that he could see, until it was time to enter the chambers. Then, at the last minute, the vote was canceled. "Does this happen often?"

"Yes." Turley nodded. "If the government doesn't think they have enough votes to pass the bill, they'll cancel it."

Frits glanced around. "I must find Lord Watford. I wrote to him four days ago."

"I'd be surprised if he's even had time to read your letter." Turley looked around. "I'll help you find him."

But when they finally discovered where the man was, he looked harried and begged off. "I don't have time now, but if you can come by Watford House early tomorrow morning before I leave, I shall make time for you."

Frits didn't know what to think. Did his lordship not care if his daughter married? He also did not want Adeline to know he was speaking to her father, and early morning was problematic. That was when she walked Maximus. "Would it be possible for you to stop by Littleton House on your way here?"

"Yes. I can do that." Lord Watford waved to another peer, who was waiting for him. "I'll be by at half past nine."

Frits took a step back and bowed. "Thank you, my lord."

As his lordship strode off, Turley asked, "Would you like to stay and see how things work?"

As far as Frits was concerned, this place was a madhouse. Cats in heat were easier to manage and made more sense. "No, thank you. I must be going. I left my coachman walking the horses almost two hours ago."

"All right. I'll see you tomorrow evening, if not before."

Tomorrow evening was Adeline's come out ball. He hoped to have an answer from her father before then.

The next morning, not knowing what Lord Watford liked, Frits had coffee and tea ready, as well as the makings of a substantial breakfast. His lordship was punctual and was shown into the breakfast room.

He waved the man to a chair. "Coffee or tea?"

"Coffee, please." Lord Watford surveyed the room, which was one of the reasons Frits had met him here. It was one of the most pleasant rooms in the house. He handed his lordship the cup of coffee. "Thank you."

Frits poured a cup of tea for himself. "Would you like anything to eat?"

"No, thank you. I've already broken my fast." He pointed at the coffee. "My wife won't allow coffee in the house. She says it makes everything smell."

Frits didn't care one way or the other. Adeline could do as she wished after she took over the household. "I hope you enjoy it." He waited for his lordship to begin the conversation, but after a few seconds, decided the man was waiting for him. "I would like to ask your permission to marry Lady Adeline. I believe we have a great deal in common." Including their lack of interest in politics and Town. "And I think I could give her the life she wants and deserves."

Watford poured another cup of coffee. "Do you love her?"

Frits wanted brandy. That was the last question he'd expected to receive, and he had managed to avoid thinking about that particular emotion. Then he remembered the kiss, and how it had changed everything he knew about kissing. "If I am not already in love with her, I am very close."

"An honest answer." Lord Watford regarded Frits. "That is refreshing. My wife, who has spent much more time thinking about this issue than have I, thinks the match would be a good one for both of you. I shall bow to her expertise. But the person you must convince is my daughter." His lordship finished his coffee and rose. "I wish you good luck. I must be off."

Frits walked his lordship to the door. He should be relieved and happy that he had permission to convince Adeline. But he still had the sword of Damocles in the form of Lady Dorie hanging over his efforts to wed his lady. On the other hand, Exeter's plan for Lady Dorie this evening might be just what Frits needed to move his own courtship along.

* * *

Four days after the disastrous garden party, Crispin was still suffering from the broken nose Lady Adeline had given him. Thankfully, Jean and Sarah had said they would not discuss what had occurred; to do so would only harm Lady Adeline. Yet, Sarah had warned him that if she saw him without his wife, she would give him the cut direct. In other words, even if he hadn't had a broken nose, he could not show his face in Polite Society.

Perdition!

It still seemed impossible that he had a wife and a son. Crispin wasn't sure he wanted either of them. What the devil was he going to do with her when she did arrive? Her French had been excellent, but her English was almost nonexistent. He didn't even know if he'd recognize her.

His father's butler knocked on Crispin's bed-chamber door. "My lord, her ladyship has arrived. She expects to see you in her parlor in an hour."

"Thank you." He'd been putting off writing his father about the discovery that he had a wife. And an heir. Now he'd have to explain how it came about to his mother, who had always been much sterner than his father.

An uncomfortable prickling sensation slithered down his spine. As if spiders were attacking him.

Dear God, she knew.

But how could she know, and how had she arrived so quickly?

He shook himself to get rid of the feeling, but it clung to him and wouldn't let go. He needed time to organize his thoughts, and an hour was not nearly long enough. Then again, she had never believed the stories he'd crafted to get himself out of trouble. His mother had always seen right through them, as if she'd witnessed him doing whatever it was he'd tried to deny.

"My lord." His valet held the door open as footmen rolled in a bathtub. "I think the dark blue jacket and breeches."

She must be furious. "How bad is it?"

"According to her maid, she is in rare form. They barely stopped to rest on the way here."

When he knocked on the door of his mother's parlor, her companion opened the door, inclining her head as he entered. His mother was seated behind an elegant, curved burl desk.

"Mama." He bowed. "I see you are in good health."

He sauntered forward, and as he reached one of the two delicate chairs and began to sit, she raised one blond brow. "Remain standing, Anglesey. You will not be here long."

This was going to be every bit as unpleasant as Crispin had feared.

"You have disgraced this family. Unfortunately, I am not in the least surprised." He winced and braced himself for the rest. "Over the years, I have argued to no avail against the lack of discipline your father allowed. He was certain you would grow out of your fecklessness. Although how he could have thought that when no one was allowed to say you nay, I have never understood." Her gaze met his. "I see someone took issue with your behavior." He bit his lip and resisted touching his nose. "Good for them. You have two choices." She held up one finger. "You can go with me to meet your wife and son in Dover, and attempt to be the husband, the man, you should be. If she will have you, that is. From there, we will travel immediately to Normanby, where you will be examined by our doctor to ensure you have not contracted the pox." For the first time he felt a surge of anger, but forced himself to remain outwardly calm. She held up a second finger. "Or you may return to the Continent." He was about to pounce on that choice when her eyes hardened. "You will be provided an allowance that is sufficient for your needs until you come into the title. But do not think you will be allowed to run amuck once you are in Normanby. You will have a trustee who will approve all your expenditures."

That could not be possible. "For how long?"

"For the rest of your life." Rising, she went to the door. "You have until tomorrow morning to make your decision. If you wish to return to the Continent, you will depart immediately."

For a few moments, Crispin couldn't move, and when he turned he found himself alone. Alone to make the choice that would set the course for the rest of his life.

He walked slowly back to his chamber. Neither option was one he ever thought he would have to choose. One path would allow him all the freedom he wanted, but even though he'd eventually come into the title, it would be hollow. And he had seen what happened to gentlemen who had "funds sufficient" for their needs. It was never enough. The other path was a life he'd never thought to have or to want. But remaining and taking up his duties was the only way to . . . what? Be reconciled with his family, claim his rightful place? Could he do it? Did he want to do that?

The day before Adeline's come out ball, Georgie was announced. She strode into Adeline's parlor.

"Lady Normanby has arrived in Town to try to control the scandal her son created."

"I wish she would take him back to the country." Adeline still shivered over the close escape she'd had. If it had not been for Littleton—Lord Littleton. Lately every time she thought about him, which was far too often, she forgot to use his title—she would have been ruined. "Better yet, a dungeon."

"You might want to know that it is being put about that he fell and hit his face on the fountain." Adeline was glad she had told Georgie everything that day. Well, almost everything. She had much more access to gossip than Adeline. "No one knows you were present, and because of the boat incident, no one remembers you being with Lord Littleton, or not being with the main group."

"That is helpful." Adeline had still debated telling her mother what had occurred, but could not take the chance. Wivenly had been furious that Lord Anglesey even danced with her. Her brother had also been angry with himself that he had not seen Lord Anglesey for the bounder he was. Not that she didn't want the scoundrel punished, but she did not want her name associated with his at all. And there was Littleton. She had not seen him since the party. What was she to make of his kiss?

"Speaking of Lord Littleton," Georgie said. "Have you decided whether he interests you?"

"I think he must. I have been unable to think of much else other than him." And not for lack of trying. A footman had brought lemonade and biscuits. She took a long drink. "But I am not sure I can trust him, and I do not wish to betray Dorie."

"Both of those are valid concerns." Georgie ate a biscuit and took several sips of lemonade before saying,

"I believe you must speak with Dorie. She cannot tell you to trust him. Lord knows she does not. But perhaps you can get a sense of how she would feel if you and he acted on this attraction you have."

That would be one fence cleared. "You are right. I must have more information before I can decide what I want to do."

"Excellent." Georgie stood. "Now it's time for us to go shopping."

Shopping? Adeline had completely forgotten. She wondered if she would run into Littleton again. "Give me a few minutes to change."

Chapter Twenty-Five

The next day, Adeline arrived at Huntingdon House as early as was polite. After what had occurred the other day, she was almost sure her feelings toward Littleton had increased. She might even be close to falling in love with him. Yet she had to know from Dorie's point of view what had happened between the two of them. Then, depending on what Adeline heard from her friend, she would ask him for his side of the story. Hearing it from Humphries was not good enough. At least not for her.

She was welcomed, bowed to, and led into what looked to be a morning room.

"My lady, would you care for some tea?" the Huntingdon butler asked.

"Yes, please." Tea was helpful for all sorts of things, including passing the time when one wanted to just get on with it.

Fortunately, the tea tray arrived just before Dorie did.

"Adeline." Her friend held out her hands. "Please do not tell me that we made plans and I have forgotten."

That was a fair question. Other than for a ball, she had never been here before. "Not at all. There is something

I must discuss with you, and I do not wish to do it with our other friends present."

Dorie sat next to Adeline on the sofa and poured the tea. "What do you wish to discuss?"

She took a sip of tea, then set the cup down. "Lord Littleton." She waited for the expression of shock to pass from Dorie's face. "I have . . . rather, I am developing feelings for him, and I know he has affection for me. What I do not know is whether I can trust him with my . . . my, er, feelings."

Dorie rubbed the bridge of her nose. "I do not know if I can give you that particular answer. What I can tell you is that, after much thought, I have decided he and I would not have made each other happy."

That had been clear to Adeline for weeks now. But it did not answer her questions. "What did he do to attach your affections?"

Dorie smiled a little. "He paid attention to me. We danced and went on carriage rides. He would occasionally send flowers." Adeline always had fresh flowers from him. Was that simply his way of getting a lady to notice him? "He was so handsome and charming that I was very taken with him." Dorie stared down at her hands, which were twisted together. "I thought I was in love. Yet lately, I have realized what I felt was infatuation."

"What did you discuss?" Adeline and Littleton always found things in common to talk about.

"Not pigs!" Dorie smiled. "We did not discuss much at all. Thinking back on it, I did most of the talking. At the time, I thought it was charming that he wanted to listen to what I had to say. Now, I have the idea that he did not speak much because what I was discussing was not what interested him." She picked up her cup and took a sip. "Then one day he was gone. A few days later, my mother received a letter from his mother saying there was an urgent problem at one of the estates. Naturally, I could not write to him, nor could he write to me. And for a while I thought he would return to Town, but he did not. Not even for the autumn Season." She glanced at Adeline. "That was when I was certain he had not left Town, he had left me, and it hurt."

That had not been well done of Littleton. "He was a coward."

"I suppose one could say that. I recently mentioned it to my brother, and he said he would have acted in the same manner. Of course, you see, my expectations had been raised. Still, we all know how miserable Kitty Pakenham was for accepting Wellington when he proposed only because he had raised her expectations and not because he cared for her. Truthfully, I would not have believed or accepted it if he had told me he thought marrying me would be a mistake. I can see that now." She shrugged. "He did not even kiss me. For which, I suppose, I should be grateful. Although it made me sad at the time."

Adeline slowly let out the breath she had been holding. He had been telling the truth. "If it means anything, I do not think you would have been happy together."

"No. It is the whole thing about pigs." Dorie took Adeline's hands and squeezed them. "I do think that you and he might be perfect for each other. I have also recently learned that one should not ignore one's feelings about a gentleman. Your heart is your true guide. Trust it."

That was what she needed to hear. Not only to trust

her heart, but that Dorie no longer thought Littleton had deliberately hurt her. "Thank you."

Tears filled Dorie's eyes. "One of us should be happy. I believe I have missed my chance."

Adeline wanted to tell Dorie that things between Miss Chatham and Lord Exeter were not as they appeared, but Adeline did not know the details and could not raise her friend's hopes to have them crushed again. "I have heard it said that things work out the way they are supposed to."

"Yes. I have heard that as well." Dorie's tone held a sorrow that tugged at Adeline's heart.

She wished she could help, but did not know how. Perhaps Littleton would have an idea. If not, Georgie was sure to have something sage to say. She always did. "I shall see you this afternoon."

"I am looking forward to shopping. It always makes me feel better." Dorie and Adeline rose and made their way to the hall.

"You will be at my ball this evening?" Adeline asked.

"Of course. I would not miss it for the world." Dorie bade her adieu, and Adeline collected her footman.

She looked forward to seeing Littleton again. She had been right to wait until she'd spoken with her friend, but now it was time to move ahead to whatever the future brought. Yet, with his reputation, she still needed to be careful. She would not allow him to break her heart.

Later that evening, as Adeline sat before the mirror, a sense of excitement infused her. She was dressed for her come out ball. She had not expected to be enthusiastic about the event. And she had expected the pale, peach-colored gown to look insipid. Instead, it made her skin glow. The necklace and earrings her mother had given her—delicate, figured gold with drops of turquoise—provided a vivid contrast. "I actually look pretty."

Fendall cast her gaze to the ceiling. "That's because you *are* pretty, my lady. And your type of looks won't fade when you get older." She placed a spangled shawl on Adeline's shoulders. "It's time for you to go down."

Rising from the bench, she donned her gloves and picked up her reticule. The worst part would be the receiving line. After that, she could forget it was her ball and enjoy herself. Once again, Littleton had the supper dance. She would spend the time assessing him as a potential husband.

She joined her parents, brother, and sister-in-law in the drawing room for a glass of champagne before they took their places in the receiving line.

Papa kissed her cheek. "You look lovely."

She returned the kiss. "Thank you. I feel as if I look well."

Mama was next to the windows, speaking with Will and Eugénie. They turned to greet her.

"I do not know what it is about this evening," Eugénie said. "But there is something in the air."

"It's hot." Her brother's bored drawl had her shaking her head.

"*Non.* It is more than that." She lifted her head, as if she had caught a scent. "But you are correct. I very much enjoy the heat. It feels like St. Thomas in summer."

Abney entered the parlor. "My lord, my lady, the first carriage has arrived."

"Come along," Mama urged them out of the room. "We must take our places."

Even though this was the first time Adeline had stood in a receiving line, it all went as she expected it would. After all, she had been through enough of them on the other side. The greetings and responses were exactly the same as they always were. Then Littleton's head rose above the others in front of him, and he caught her eye and smiled. As he drew closer, she could admire his beautifully tied cravat and the emerald pin nestled in the folds. His black jacket molded his shoulders, which seemed even broader than before. One lock of ink-black hair fell across his forehead, making her want to wrap the curl around her finger. As his smile grew, the dimple deepened, giving the strong planes of his lean face a gentler look. Even as he greeted her family, he seemed to keep her in his gaze. Perhaps Eugénie was right and there *was* something in the air.

"Good evening, my lord."

As Frits went through the receiving line, his jaw almost dropped when he saw Adeline. She was always beautiful, but tonight, she glowed. When he got a better look at her gown, his mouth began to water, and his cock stiffened. If it wasn't for the blond lace at her neckline, and the way her bodice winked in the candlelight, he would have sworn she was half naked. The gown was almost the same color as her luminous skin, albeit embroidered with small flowers and vines. Whose idea was it to let her out like this? He gave himself an inner shake and blinked.

Not naked—although he could envision her thusly—but extraordinarily enticing. That gown was made for slowly peeling off her.

It was all he could do not to stop himself from taking her arm and carrying her out of the house. He did have her father's permission to marry her. "Lady Adeline." Frits bowed over her hand, barely touching his lips to her fingers, yet he could feel her reaction to him. He pitched his voice in a low whisper. "I cannot wait until our dance."

Gazing up at him, she searched his eyes, as if looking for understanding. "I look forward to it as well."

Something sharp poked him in the side. "Move along, Littleton." Lady Bellamny held her cane. "You are holding up the line."

The silver flecks in Adeline's eyes sparked as she chuckled.

So much for that. "Yes, my lady."

He reached the ballroom and saw Turner, who'd joined Fitzwalter and Frits for dinner, and had taken Fitzwalter with him to the ball. Next to them were Miss Martindale and Miss Tice. Frits hoped the meeting Fitzwalter was to have with her father before the ball had gone well. Avoiding the other guests, he made his way along the side of the ballroom and joined Turley.

"Littleton, good evening." He lifted his hand, and a footman appeared with champagne.

"Good evening to you." Frits took a glass.

Exeter joined them. "Can I ask both of you to stand up with Miss Chatham again this evening?"

"Of course," Turley replied.

Frits nodded his agreement. "When do you expect Dursley back?"

"He'll be here tonight. Not a word to anyone. It's to be a surprise for Miss Chatham."

"And Lytton as well, I imagine," Turley muttered.

Exeter grinned. "A very unwelcome surprise for his lordship."

"Something tells me this will be a momentous ball." Frits followed Adeline's progress down the stairs into the room. Thank God this farce would end tonight. "I'm going to join Lady Adeline and her family. Do you wish to join me?"

Turley shook his head. "I'm waiting for someone to arrive."

"Very well. I shall see you later." Frits threaded his way through the crowded room to where Miss Chatham stood and asked her for a set, then made his way to Adeline. As soon as Exeter had made his feelings known to Lady Dorie, Frits intended to ask Adeline to allow him to court her. Mentioning marriage would only scare her. But first, she had to see that her friend was making a much better match than she would have with him. As his mother had pointed out, and he concurred, it was growing increasingly clear that Lady Dorie was as much in love with Exeter as he was with her. After she was settled, perhaps, Adeline would forgive Frits for hurting her friend and allow herself to know him even better. Frits already knew exactly how and in which ways he wanted to better know Adeline. She was temptation personified.

"My lady." He bowed and, after kissing her fingers, placed her hand on his arm.

"My lord." She raised one brow. "Are you still hiding from some lady or another?"

Every single one of them except for her. "One can never be too careful."

The orchestra finished tuning their instruments, and Wrively stepped over to them. "Adeline, my dance, I believe?"

She grinned. "Yes, it is."

She placed her hand on his arm, and Frits felt as if

he'd lost part of himself. If only events had fallen in line for Exeter to have secured Dorie sooner, so that Frits could have properly courted Adeline, been betrothed to her, and had all her dances.

He glanced around the room. Exeter stood next to Miss Chatham and her mother. Frits should have asked when exactly Dursley was going to present himself. Then again, maybe it was better if Frits didn't know.

He'd be watching the clock slowly mark the time. Adeline was the only other lady with whom he would dance this evening. Not that he usually stood up with other ladies. It was also growing increasingly difficult to see her go off with other gentlemen. If the Fates were kind, much of that would soon change.

Frits was leading Miss Chatham out for their set when Lady Dorie and Fotheringale strolled through the French doors, followed shortly thereafter by Exeter. There was only one reason Frits could think of for Fotheringale to want to go outside with her. The man was going to propose. Leave it to a dunderhead like that to make a mull of their plans. No wonder Exeter was making haste after them.

They still had not returned by the time the set ended, and Frits was back with Adeline. Fotheringale strode back into the ballroom in a dudgeon.

"What is Lord Fotheringale doing?" Adeline asked.

"It appears as if he is departing." That was promising.

"Without taking his leave of my mother?" Her brows slanted down into a frown.

Frits grinned. Fotheringale was going to hear about his behavior. "Apparently so."

"Well." Adeline had not thought the man could be so rude. He had almost made it to the stairs when she finally caught a glimpse of his face. "He looks angry."

Littleton continued to grin. "He does, doesn't he?"

Something was going on. "Do you know what is happening?"

"I think he was planning to propose to Lady Dorie and—"

Exeter and Dorie had entered from the terrace. Adeline held up her hand, silencing him. "What is Dorie doing?"

Littleton moved so that he was next to Adeline instead of facing her. "Do you remember I told you that all was not as it seemed with Exeter and Miss Chatham?"

"Yes." Adeline drew out the word, trying to make sense of everything as she answered. Dorie and Exeter stopped, and he searched the ballroom.

"You are about to find out the truth." Littleton motioned with his chin to the steps.

Standing on the stairs, surveying the room, was a tall gentleman with blond hair who Adeline had never seen before.

The man found who he wanted, reached the main floor, and headed toward Dorie's family. "Who is he?"

"That is Viscount Dursley. Apparently, he and Miss Chatham have an understanding." Littleton pointed to where Dorie's family stood, and Adeline saw Miss Chatham was next to them. "Watch."

Many of the guests had stilled. It was like being part of a play. Lord Dursley said something to Miss Chatham, who turned and leapt into his arms, and Dorie and Exeter gazed at each other, clearly in love. It was like a fairy tale come true. "Well. That is a satisfactory conclusion."

Littleton chuckled. "Shall we dare to leave your family's circle and wish them happy?"

"We shall." A deep sense of happiness welled in Adeline for her friend. Dorie had thought she'd lost Exeter. But now everything would end the way it should. "Even Wively cannot fault us for that."

They started strolling the short distance, and Littleton placed his hand over hers, engulfing it. "I'm glad he finally won her. They are perfect together."

They joined the throng just in time to hear Dorie say she would not entertain Exeter's offer until the morning, and the accompanying laughter.

Yet there was still one matter that remained unsettled before Adeline could move forward with her life.

Chapter Twenty-Six

Adeline tugged Littleton toward a pair of long windows. "I must know something." Or two somethings.

His gaze caught hers as he nodded. "Anything."

Would his story differ from what his groom had told her? "What happened between you and Dorie?"

He drew his hand down his face. "She was the Incomparable, and I was dazzled. By the time I realized we were ill-suited, it was almost too late." He glanced at Adeline's hand on his arm. "As you know, I never kissed her. Strangely enough, I never even thought about it. That should have given me a hint that she was not the right lady for me. Nor did I ask her father for permission to marry her. Still, I knew she expected both." He pulled a chagrined face. "I didn't see any way to explain how I felt. I still don't know what I could have said. So, I left Town and went on a tour of my estates." He twined his fingers with Adeline's. "Is that what you wanted to know?"

Everything he'd related comported with what she had heard from both Humphries and Dorie. But she needed to know more. "Almost."

His eyes bore into hers, more serious than she had ever seen them. "Go on."

Adeline took a breath. She was either going to be greatly embarrassed or extremely happy. "Have you found a lady that you are sure would suit you?"

"I have." His eyes were still on hers as he smiled. "I think you and I are well matched. So much so that I spoke to your father this morning."

Her heart began pounding so hard, she was surprised he did not hear it. "You did?"

"I did." He raised her hand to his lips. "I asked him if I could court you, and he said that was up to you." Turning her hand over, he pressed a kiss onto her palm. If he kept this up, her heart was going to fly out of her chest. He truly was a rake. "I shall warn you, I'll do almost anything to keep you next to me."

The look on his face when she had said that he no longer needed her finally made sense. "Even find imaginary ladies who wish to trick you into marriage?"

"Well, the ladies existed. Their intent toward me might not have been what I thought, but I still think I need you to protect me."

"Hmm." His gaze slipped to her lips, causing hers to tingle. Their one kiss had been a mere taste. "I suppose I could do that."

"Will you allow me to court you?" His voice was lower, more seductive. How much of himself had he been holding back?

Adeline was excited and terrified at the same time. She raised her eyes to his. "Yes, but only if you are certain."

"There are no mistakes this time." His green, green eyes held a promise in them. "When I return home, I want you by my side."

Adeline couldn't draw a breath. This sounded like a proposal instead of a request to court her. She wasn't ready for that.

"I'm moving too quickly." He gave her a sheepish smile. "Just allow me to court you. For now."

Now her voice left her, and she couldn't speak and had to nod. She had thought she'd known him, but did she truly?

His smile broadened. "I'd like you to call me Frits. That's what my family calls me."

She took a huge breath and let it out. "You may call me Adeline."

"Thank you, Adeline." For the first time since he . . . Frits had started to speak when she heard the music, and she glanced around him. "I thought I had a partner for this set."

"Whoever he was probably did not wish to interrupt." There was a definite smirk on his lips.

She really should not think about his lips if she was not certain she could marry him. She could not kiss him. It certainly didn't help that he was staring at her lips as if they were akin to Gunter's ices.

Adeline cleared her suddenly thick throat. "What does courting entail?"

"More of what we've been doing. You might consider allowing me to walk with you and Maximus in the mornings." This last part was said so innocently that no one listening to it would think he was asking permission to walk his own dog.

"I believe that can be arranged." She narrowed her eyes slightly. "If you can rise that early. Humphries told me you did not waken until later."

"Apparently"—Frits's tone was as dry as sand—"he doesn't know that ever since *you* started walking Maximus, *I* have not been able to sleep to my usual time."

She gave him an innocent look. "In that event, you will not have any difficulties."

"*Minx.*" The word was harsh, but the funning light in his eyes gave it a different meaning.

Adeline had the feeling she was entering into a different form of communication that she did not understand. "Is that good or bad?"

"Good." He trailed one finger lightly along her jaw, then dropped his hand as if he'd been burnt. "I want you to feel free to say whatever you wish to me, even if it is something I don't want to hear. Not," he added hurriedly, "that I think you were criticizing me. I recognize teasing when I hear it."

Yes, this was an entirely new form of discourse. One Adeline thought she would like.

After Frits had returned home that evening, he poured a brandy and reviewed his conversation with Adeline. He'd desperately wanted to touch her. But even the feel of her soft skin under his finger had his senses raging to go further. Take possession of her lovely mouth and plunder. Hold her so tightly that nothing could come between them.

He stared into the glass before taking a drink. Unfortunately, it was clear she wasn't prepared to be rushed. The look of alarm she had worn when he'd said he wanted her with him when he left Town made him realize he had to take this slowly. He, not she, had spent weeks waiting to be able to declare himself. In fact, for her it was entirely the opposite. Although friendly to him, she had been doing her best not to want him. He thanked the deities that she had actually agreed to allow him to court her, but unlike their friends, that was exactly what it would be. His chance to show her how much he loved her. Frits had no doubt that was what it was. He'd never reacted to any other woman the way his mind, heart, and body responded to her. If only there was a way to get Adeline to his main estate. She could meet the animals he'd told her about, and speak with his tenants, and see the life he had to offer her. But how to do that in the middle of the Season when they weren't even betrothed yet was the difficulty. He doubted even his mother could come up with a plan that would succeed.

Still, she had agreed that he could walk Maximus with her in the mornings. He would take her for carriage rides and to Gunter's in the afternoons, and now he could dance with her twice at every ball. Hopefully, there wouldn't be too many of them before she agreed to marry him. Perhaps their families could dine and attend other entertainments together as well. His mother would be happy to arrange that. Frits took a long drink, barely feeling the burn of the fine French brandy.

Courting might be harder than what had come before it.

The next morning, he was in the hall with Maximus before Humphries arrived.

The groom's eyes widened. "I don't think her ladyship is going to like you comin' along."

Frits didn't know what it said about him that he couldn't resist a smug smile. "Last night, Lady Adeline agreed to let me court her, and specifically gave me permission to walk the dog with her."

"All right, then. If she said so." The groom still walked to Upper Brook Street, and when Adeline strolled out the door, Humphries immediately said, "I told his lordship that if ye didn't want him, he couldn't stay."

Adeline laughed as Frits rolled his eyes. "He has my

permission to remain, Humphries. Thank you for being concerned."

The man handed her the lead. As he took Adeline's other arm, Humphries muttered, "It's about time."

Adeline blushed a very pretty rose, but it could only be because she was embarrassed. "I do not suppose you could keep your opinions to yourself?"

"Never have afore," the groom said as he took up his position behind them.

Her color was still high, but her lips twitched, making Frits feel better. She stroked Maximus as he leaned against her. "I suppose it is that way with all longtime personal servants."

He didn't even have to look to know the groom was smirking. "It certainly appears to be with mine. Shall we?"

"Yes. Maximus, come."

Frits led her down the shallow steps and onto the pavement. He was always impressed by how well-behaved the dog was with her. At one point, a squirrel darted out from a bush, and he was getting ready to grab the lead when Maximus looked at Adeline, who handed him a treat. "Good boy."

She might even get the damned cat to listen. "That was impressive."

"It is the treats. He is very happy to do as I ask as long as he receives a reward."

He was not going to let her dwarf her accomplishment. "It is not a small achievement. I insist on giving you the credit you deserve."

She blushed again. "Thank you." They didn't talk, but Frits did not think the silence between them was uncomfortable. When they reached the next crossing, she said, "Tell me about Littlewood."

"It is the most beautiful of my estates. I would even go so far as to say it's one of the most beautiful places in England. We have a river that flows through the property, an old wood, and meadows. The house is a comfortable walk from the market town of Littleton, but two villages are also included in the holdings, and several tenancies."

They had entered the Park, and Humphries took Maximus. Frits and Adeline sat on a bench. "That sounds lovely. What does the house look like?"

"The oldest part of the house is the hall. It dates to the twelfth century. Fortunately, the rest of the house is much newer." He glanced at her and grinned. "It is only three hundred years old."

Her brow wrinkled as she looked at him. "Has it been modernized at all?"

He sent thanks to his father and grandfather. "Yes. We have all the modern conveniences. There is even a way to bring hot water through pipes to the floor where the family's bedchambers are located."

"My father considers himself very modern, but even we do not have that luxury."

Frits hoped that meant she would learn to love his home as much as he did. "I think you will find it more than comfortable." He bit the inside of his cheek. He should have said "would," not "will."

"It sounds like it." She gazed across the open space. "I think Maximus has tired himself."

He followed the direction in which she was looking and saw the dog lying down. "Would you like to ride with me this afternoon?"

"Yes." Her eyes sparkled with enjoyment. "I would like that very much."

Frits arrived at five o'clock to collect her. As they headed out of South Audley Street, he asked, "If you do not mind, I would like to stop at Hatchards."

"I do not mind at all." She smiled up at him, and his

chest squeezed, making it hard to breathe. "I could go there every day."

He envisioned them together sitting at Littlewood next to the stream on a warm summer's day with his head on her lap, or the other way around, and one of them reading to the other.

He had just turned on to Piccadilly, when Adeline shouted, "Look!" She pointed to the side of the road.

What the devil did that cur think he was doing? Frits stopped the carriage. "Can you hold 'em?"

"Yes." She nodded. "Save him, please."

He jumped down and grabbed the hand of a man who was once again getting ready to strike a small boy. The child cowered in the gutter.

"This ain't none of your business," the ruffian growled, his face mottled red.

Adeline held her breath. The bounder was a big brute. Almost as big as Frits, but brawnier. Frits wrenched the whip handle out of the man's hand. Before the blackguard could retaliate, he drove his fist into the man's jaw, and followed it up with two punches to the stomach. As the brute folded over and dropped to his knees, Frits lifted the child, placing him on the bench next to her. Wrapping her arms around him, she held him close and watched as Frits turned back to the man.

"I don't know what you intended, but I will not stand by and watch a child abused." He glanced at the glossy phaeton next to the man. It clearly did not belong to the man. "I shall expect to hear from your employer." During the time he was talking, Frits had been gathering the whip. He raised one brow. "I'll take this with me unless you wish to feel its sting." The scoundrel remained on his knees, and Frits flung his card at the beast. "That is my direction."

"You'll hear from my master all right, but it won't be what you want." The scoundrel spit at Frits's boots and missed.

Frits stepped toward the cur and the man slunk back. "I wouldn't wager on that."

He climbed back into the curricle, and Adeline hugged the boy. "What is your name?"

"Peter." His brownish-green eyes were huge with fear when he glanced at Frits. "Please, mister, I better go with him."

"No." She'd never heard such a commanding tone from Frits before. The whole time he had been dealing with the ruffian, he'd used a bored drawl.

"His lordship is correct. You must not go with that man. He could have killed you." When the lad began to shake, she held him even closer. His hair brushed her chin, and that was when she knew for certain. He was a mulatto. His hair had the same texture as Eugénie's housekeeper's granddaughter. But what had happened to this boy? It wasn't that there were no Negroes or mulattos in England, or in London for that matter. Many of her sister-in-law's servants were former slaves. And Uncle Nathan, Eugénie's stepfather, had brought his servants from St. Thomas when he moved back to England. Some Negroes were even wealthy businessmen. What shocked Adeline was that this poor child was being treated just as she had been told many slaves were in the West Indies. "We need to go to my brother's house straightaway."

Frits looked at her and inclined his head. "As you wish."

She prayed Will and Eugénie were at home, but, in the meantime, Adeline needed to calm the little boy. "Everything will be fine. My sister-in-law is from St. Thomas. Do you know where that is?"

He nodded. "It's not too far from Tortola."

Adeline kept her tone calm. "Is that where you are from?"

The child nodded. "My mama and me."

Frits pulled up in front of the house on North Audley Street, and a footman ran to the horses' heads.

"Are my brother and sister-in-law at home?" she asked.

"Yes, my lady." The man nodded and smiled. "Both of them."

Peter stared at the servant, who was a shade or two darker than he was. "Is he a slave too?"

"No." Littleton lifted the child from her arms, then held out his arm to her. "There are no slaves in England. It is not allowed."

"That's right," the footman said, then turned to Adeline. "I take it there's a problem?"

"Yes." She struggled not to let the fury she'd been repressing take hold. That would not help the little boy. "Some man was trying to whip him."

"Her ladyship will help you get it sorted out." He lifted his chin to where Maximus sat. "Do you want him to come with you?"

The Great Dane was very well behaved. There was no reason he should not come inside. "Yes. Frits, if you let down the steps, I shall take Maximus."

Chapter Twenty-Seven

The door opened and Will's butler, Bates, a tall mulatto, opened the door and bowed. "My lady."

He looked at Frits.

"Good afternoon, Bates. This is Lord Littleton." She glanced at the child. "This is Peter. We need to speak with her ladyship."

"Follow me, my lady, my lord. They are in the morning room." He opened the door and stood back. "I shall bring a tea tray."

"*Oui, merci.*" Eugénie came forward to greet them.

"This is Peter." Adeline leaned forward and kissed her sister-in-law's cheeks. "We rescued him from a scoundrel who was whipping him."

"*Alors.*" Eugénie's eyes hardened. "We cannot have that. Come and have a seat while we wait for tea."

That was not a long wait at all. Bates had brought Peter a cup of milk, several biscuits, and a jam tart.

After Adeline told them what had occurred, she turned to Peter. "You said your mother was from Tortola as well, and she is here?"

The little boy nodded. "Miss Lettsome needed her to do her hair for her come out."

Eugénie's lips pressed together. "Did Miss Lettsome ask that you come as well?"

"I don't know." Peter shrugged. "All I know is that Mr. Lettsome is going to be very angry, and his lordship said he'd protect me."

Clearly, Frits's promise held a lot of weight.

"Indeed I shall," Frits confirmed. "As will Lord Wivenly and the ladies."

"What do we do next?" Adeline asked her sister-in-law.

"We must find out exactly what the situation is. The mother might not know that the moment she stepped on shore, she was no longer a slave." Eugénie glanced at Frits. "You said you gave the man your card."

"Yes." He pulled a face. "I suppose that means I had better go home. He might not waste any time calling."

"That would be best." She drained her cup and set it down. "*Toutefois*, I think it is better if Peter stays with us for a time."

"What are we going to do if his mother still believes she is a slave?" Adeline prompted.

"Rescue her." Will tugged the bellpull. "It won't be the first time. After we have the whole story, we can make plans."

Adeline supposed that was the only answer she would get until the child's "owner" spoke with Frits. She glanced at him. "What will you do when he arrives?"

"I don't know." His black brows slanted down. "I suppose I'll have to decide that based on what his story is."

"If your mother is home, I could come with you." The problem was that Frits would have to send a message to his house for the answer.

"*Non.*" Eugénie slowly shook her head. "We do not know these people. They are very *sournois*." She frowned.

"Devious. If they have brought the mother and son to England and have kept them captive. You are safer not meeting this man." She focused on Frits. "And you must not believe what he says. You must only discover where he lives. Then we will save the mother."

"Very well," Frits agreed. "I shall follow your directions."

Adeline walked him to the hall, where she took his hands. "Be careful. I cannot imagine what type of person wants to own other people, but he cannot be much better than his employee."

"I have no doubt you are correct." He raised her hands and placed a kiss on each palm before curling her fingers closed. "I will ensure my largest footmen are present when I meet with him."

She was glad he'd be protected. "I shall see you this evening."

His eyes caught hers, and for a moment she thought he would kiss her right here in her brother's hall, but instead, he placed warm kisses on her knuckles.

"I look forward to it."

Once Frits arrived back at his house, he didn't have to wait long for Mr. Lettsome to present himself.

"My lord," Creswell said stiffly, "I have placed the person for whom you have been waiting in the front parlor."

Leave it to servants to know the quality of anyone coming to visit. "Should I arm myself?"

"Certainly not, my lord." The butler's chin rose. "I would not allow a ruffian in the house. However, the person is not a gentleman."

"Interesting." Frits rose. "We shall not require tea."

"I did not think you would, my lord. Shall I announce you?"

His butler really was on his high ropes. "No. I need information from the man. It's better not to appear too high in the instep."

"Very good, my lord. I shall have two footmen standing outside the room."

What Frits was to make of that, he didn't know. Well, it couldn't hurt, and he had told Adeline he'd have footmen at the ready. "As you will."

He made his way up the corridor to the hall and entered a small parlor used only for people one did not wish to see for long. The man was fashionably dressed, but it was clear that neither Weston nor Hoby saw his custom. "Mr. Lettsome." He turned, and Frits was a little startled by a gaudy ruby-and-diamond pin, as well as several fobs. "I am Littleton." He motioned for Lettsome to take a seat. "I assume you are here about the child?"

"Of course I am." The man's belligerence took Frits aback. "You had no right to take my prop—the boy. His mother wants him returned immediately. She is extremely worried about him."

That was a lie based partially in truth. The problem was that he didn't know how much truth was involved. He could easily believe that Peter's mother was frantic with worry. On the other hand, he didn't think Lettsome cared about her feelings at all.

Lettsome continued to stand, as did Frits. He couldn't get the blackguard out of his house fast enough. "Did your employee not tell you that he was about to whip the lad?"

That knowledge did not appear to affect Lettsome. It was as if he didn't care. "It was merely a threat because he was misbehaving."

"It did not look like a threat to me." The man was just as much a scoundrel as his henchman. "I stopped him as he was about to turn a threat into a reality."

"Nevertheless, his mother wants his return. I shall take him now." Lettsome started toward the door, and Frits blocked his way.

Now he knew why Lady Wivenly had decided Peter should remain with her. If he had been here and heard the scoundrel, the mention of his mother would have made Peter want to go with Lettsome. "He is sleeping. If you give me your direction, I shall be happy to bring him to you."

Lettsome glanced at the door, clearly considering searching for the child himself. Then he seemed to reconsider, and bowed. "I am at Fifteen Fenchurch Street in the City."

Frits stepped to the door. "My butler will show you out."

As he left the room, Creswell entered. "My lord?"

"Please show Mr. Lettsome out." They might all require baths after having the slave owner in the house.

"Certainly, my lord."

Frits took one of the footmen aside. "Tell Creswell to make sure all the doors and windows are secured and a few footmen are posted to guard the most likely places a person might try to break in."

"Yes, my lord."

Once Lettsome left, Frits went back to his study and wrote a short note to Adeline's brother with the address. He was sanding it when he decided to go himself. One never knew if he could be of help.

When he arrived at North Audley Street, he was pleased to see Adeline was still there. He bowed to her and her sister-in-law. "The address is in the City. Now what do we do?"

"*We* don't do anything." Wivenly grinned and held

up a hand when Frits started to protest. "I know you want to be part of this, but you've been seen and would be recognized. Adeline said the woman was a lady's maid for the daughter. I'll send a few of my servants, and they'll be able to find out when and how best to convince her to go with them."

"You must understand how valuable slaves are to the owners in the West Indies," Lady Wively said. "The English are not allowed to purchase more, so they try to work with the Danish to smuggle them in. They are frequently caught."

Frits and Adeline exchanged glances. It was clear that neither of them had thought past saving the child from certain harm. The blackguards had his name and direction, but at least they didn't have hers. "In other words, he'll do almost anything to get the boy back."

"*Exactement.* They are convinced they will be bank-rupted without slaves." A line formed between her eyes. "Not only that, but by taking the child, you have threatened their lives. If it were to be known they were keeping slaves in England, he could be prosecuted and lose his status."

This was much more complicated than Frits had thought. Thank God Lettsome didn't know Adeline's name. "He'll expect the lad to be returned by tomor-row."

"My servants will go this afternoon," Wively assured Frits. "Just like Polite Society, wealthy merchants have their own Season for their daughters and sons."

"We have a ball this evening," Adeline added.

Frits would be happy to stay here until they found the mother. He wondered if Adeline would remain.

"Which we shall attend," Lady Wively said, killing his budding idea to spend time with Adeline and not the rest of Polite Society as well. "It is possible that someone will watch to see if you go out." Her ladyship's chin firmed, as if she expected an objection.

So much for that. "Would they have followed me here?"

Wively shook his head. "I doubt it. If you had been followed, someone on my staff would have alerted us. They are very aware of the dangers."

What he wanted would be tantamount to a proposal; still Frits glanced at Adeline. "May I have three dances this evening?"

Her beautiful smile made it hard to breathe, and he knew she held his heart in her hands. "You may, my lord."

How much longer would it be before he could propose and have all her sets? "Shall I take you home, or is it better that your brother sees to it?"

"My wife and I will make sure she arrives home safely," Wively stated.

"You may join us for dinner if you like." Taking Adeline home was something Will had insisted upon after Frits had gone. Her brother did not want them seen together before they could get Peter and his mother to safety. Frits being invited to dinner was the price Will had to pay.

Frits's smile warmed her and sent the butterflies in her stomach flitting around. He had been a perfect hero today. Her perfect hero. "I am honored. Let me dash a note off to inform my mother."

Her brother rang the bellpull. "I'll send a groom with the note. There's no reason for anyone to see my livery."

"In that case, have him take it to the stables." Frits

glanced down and frowned. "I'll have to return home to change before the ball."

Will stared at Frits and shook his head. "I wish I could say we are of a size, but you're larger than I. Ask to have your kit sent here. My valet will assist you."

When they were notified that Frits's clothing had arrived, they all went to dress. An hour later, they were back in the drawing room.

"What will happen when the mother is brought here?" Adeline was determined that she would not be pushed to the side when it came to the rest of the plan.

"That will depend upon the circumstances. There may be more family members than the boy and his mother." Eugénie gave Adeline a long, speculative look. "You wish to help, do you not?"

"No!" Leaning forward, Will had barked the word.

Her sister-in-law raised one imperious brow. "Adeline has earned the right, and we will be present to see that she does not come to harm."

He didn't look satisfied, but inclined his head sharply.

"I want to assist as well." Frits glanced back and forth from her sister-in-law to her brother. "I must see this through."

Even though Adeline never doubted he would continue on the course on which they had begun earlier, she was glad he had made his wishes known.

"At least you can protect yourself," Will grumbled.

That wasn't at all fair. "Do you not remember teaching me to defend myself?"

"That was a long time ago, and you've never actually had to do it," he said dismissively.

"Indeed." She raised one brow in the same manner as her mother. Adeline knew because she had spent hours practicing the expression. "How do you think Lord Anglesey got his broken nose?"

Suddenly, her brother looked as if he meant to commit murder.

Frits groaned and covered the bottom half of his face with one hand. "You weren't going to tell anyone about that."

That turned her brother's ire on him. "You were there?"

"I was." Obviously, Frits was not going to say anything else.

Well, blast. She should have kept her mouth shut. "He stopped his lordship from compromising me. But I was the one who hit the scoundrel."

"Who knows about this?" Eugénie poured wine for all of them.

"Lady Riverton, Lady Holloway, and us." Adeline pointed to Frits. "They were just as shocked as I to hear that Anglesey was already married."

"It's a good thing he's not here or I'd break more than his nose," Will growled.

"I think we should congratulate Adeline on hitting him." Eugénie smiled proudly at her and raised her glass. "To a job well done."

"Thank you." She grinned at her brother. "I had a thought that someone should plant him a facer, and I remembered that you had taught me how to do it, so I did."

Will drank down half of his wine. "Did you remember to put your thumb on the outside?"

"Yes." Frits's lips were twitching, and she knew it was only a matter of time before he burst out laughing. "Although, I have to admit it did hurt, and my knuckles were bruised." Her maid had put her hand in ice when she had returned home.

Fortunately, before the conversation could go further, her brother's butler announced dinner, and Eugénie steered the conversation to safer ground. "You asked what we will do next." She waited until Will held her chair and lowered herself gracefully into it. "If it is the two of them, and we do not have to worry about other family members Lettsome might be using as weapons, I shall write to a friend of mine who is from Tortola and is a member of our group." She placed her hand on Will's arm. "I have had an opportunity to speak with the Duchess of Wharton, and she has expressed an interest in our cause and might be able to assist us as well."

They were in the smaller family dining room, which had a round table. Will sat next to her and Frits next to Adeline. She sipped the chilled white wine that had been poured. "What will she do?"

"Aside from having a great deal of information and contacts on Tortola," her sister-in-law smiled, "she can also help to arrange for employment and sometimes training in a new profession."

"Isn't she also invested in a shipping company?" Frits asked.

Eugénie glanced at him sharply. "That is not at all well known."

He shrugged. "All ships must have repairs. It's the nature of the business. I own a shipyard."

Good Lord! What did he not own? Adeline could not help but hear how wealthy he was. Although, she'd had no idea of the details. "Why?"

"As I said, all ships require maintenance. Once we had the ships, it made more sense to my grandfather to buy a shipyard than to pay someone else."

It made sense to her as well. "And you work on other ships as well."

"Yes." He smiled. "It keeps us busy when our ships are out."

Dessert in the form of fruit and cheese had been set on the table when the butler came into the room. "My lady, our guest has arrived. Shall I fetch Peter?"

Eugénie held an orange in her hand. "Not yet. Has she eaten?"

"I do not know. I shall ask, and if she has not, shall we feed her first?"

"Yes, please. Then we shall meet her in the"—she furrowed her brow—"the small drawing room. It is more *confortable.*"

"Yes, my lady."

Adeline had taken some strawberries and cheese, but now was not hungry.

"You might as well finish," Frits said. "She probably didn't dine before coming here."

"Of course." She applied herself to eating what she had taken, and waiting.

Finally, her sister-in-law rose. "Do you gentlemen wish to remain here?"

Frits stood, and pulled out Adeline's chair. "I do not."

"You just don't want to miss anything." Will pushed back his chair. "We shall accompany you, my love."

They followed Will and Eugénie to a room next to the morning room, which Adeline had never seen before. It was decorated in light greens, blues, and creams. A flower-patterned silk covered the walls, and the same pattern was used for the curtains, that were closed. However, dozens of candles brightened the room. And, although it was not cold, a fire had been lit. It was cozy. Just the sort of place one could feel free to talk. Will poured four glasses of wine and handed one to Eugénie. Adeline had never noticed before how he always took care of his wife first.

Frits took two glasses and handed one to Adeline. "Now we wait."

Chapter Twenty-Eight

Adeline took the glass Frits proffered and swirled it before taking a sip. "I hope it is not too long." She had heard about the rescues and settling of former slaves, but she had never been a part of the planning before. "You mentioned Lettsome might have some hold over Peter's mother."

"I did," her sister-in-law said. "If that is the case, we will find a way to rescue them as well."

Frits's forehead creased. "Do you ever fail?"

"*Non.*" Eugénie's eyes met his. "We cannot afford to be unsuccessful. Fortunately, we have people living in the British West Indies who assist us."

"The duchess's family?" Adeline asked. She knew Anna Wharton's father had married a mulatto lady, and they had several grown children.

"Among others." Eugénie glanced at the clock. "I will wager she has seen Peter. My staff is very softhearted."

Just then, the door opened and the butler bowed. "My lord, my lady, Mrs. Rymer."

Mrs. Rymer was tall, with skin the same light brown color as her son's. Her hair was reddish-blond and curled loosely, framing her face. She wore a snowy white mobcap and a simple black gown. She was a beautiful woman. Although she returned Eugénie's smile, hers was tight, and her fear was palpable.

"My lady." Mrs. Rymer curtseyed.

They all rose, but only Eugénie went to meet the woman. "Welcome to our home. Have you seen your son?"

"Yes." The woman's smile loosened at bit. "He is having a wonderful time. He said there are children like him."

Children who looked like him, but were free. "Please"—Eugénie motioned to a comfortable chair—"sit and we will have tea."

As if the butler had just been waiting for the words to be said, he entered with the tea tray and set it down in front of Eugénie. Once everyone had a cup, there was no roundaboutation or small talk. "For whom are you afraid?"

The question startled Adeline. She would have been—oh—more subtle, she supposed. Still, she did not understand how her sister-in-law knew the right question to ask. Then again, Eugénie had a great deal of experience dating to before she had met and married Will.

"My husband. He is still on Tortola." Mrs. Rymer's hands shook as she set her cup down. "Before we left, I was told that if I tried to escape with Peter, he would no longer be allowed to work as a shipwright, but would be sent back to the fields."

She obviously knew that once she and her son reached England they were free and only that threat would keep her enslaved.

Eugénie's lips formed a moue. "What if we brought him here?"

The woman's amber eyes widened. "But can you do that without Mr. Lettsome discovering it?"

"Indeed we can." Eugénie took a sip of tea. "We have done it before."

Sitting next to Adeline, Frits had taken her hand in his as they resumed their seats and watched the discussion. He'd met people—mostly men—from different parts of the West Indies, but Mrs. Rymer's diction was so good, no one would think she was from anywhere but England. She reminded him of his mother's and sisters' ladies' maids.

He had been happy to be on the periphery of the conversation until she said that her husband was a shipwright. "If you can bring him here, I have a position for him."

Adeline squeezed his hand and smiled. He'd offer a dozen men jobs, more, to keep both her hand and her smile.

"But how?" Mrs. Rymer appeared fascinated and a bit doubtful.

"That is not too difficult," Lady Wively replied. "There are several ships in the Canary Islands that will be sailing soon for the West Indies. I shall send word that we need to free your husband."

Adeline gave a confused shake of her head. "But could Lettsome not do the same thing to imprison"— she frowned—"make matters worse for Mr. Rymer?"

"He would have to send a ship or a letter from here to either Tortola or to a ship leaving from here heading to the West Indies." Lady Wively's lips tilted into a sly smile. "I will use birds."

Frits didn't understand how that was possible. Yes, pigeons had been known to fly a little over one thousand miles on a journey, but the West Indies was three times that far at least. Still, Lady Wively was no fool, so he had to believe that if she said it was possible, it must be. "Can you explain how you do that?"

"As I said, we have a group. Our members live in," she raised one shoulder, "shall we say, various places. The bird I send will fly to one place, then another bird will be sent. Eventually, one will land in the Canary Islands, and my message will be taken to a ship."

Frits calculated the distance and factored in that the birds did not fly at night. "That would take about one week to arrive in the Canaries." And they would not have to worry about the wind being in the right quarter. "Whereas a ship leaving from London would take at least twice that long."

"*Exactement.*" Lady Wivenly smiled approvingly. "Once our ship reaches its first stop in the West Indies"—he noticed she was being very uninformative about exactly where the members of the group were located—"another bird will be sent to Tortola." She glanced at Mrs. Rymer, who appeared to be as engrossed in the plan as were he and Adeline. Probably more, considering it was her husband at risk.

Wivenly, lounging back against the sofa next to his wife, had obviously heard it before. "If your husband is working in the shipyard, I assume he earns a salary, most of which is paid to Lettsome?"

"Yes. He is allowed to keep about a quarter of what he earns. He is saving to buy our freedom."

From what Frits had heard, before England had outlawed new slaves being brought onto their islands, that was fairly common. It was less so now. Completely mistrusting the man, he wondered if Lettsome would ever allow the family to buy their freedom.

It would, though, be easy for a man to be called to a ship for repairs, and for the ship to depart before the man was taken ashore. "He knows you and your son are here. What is keeping him from making his way here?"

Mrs. Rymer had taken out a handkerchief and was wringing it. "They threatened to sell Peter to the Danes."

Adeline glanced at Frits. "They might be successful in putting him on a boat for St. Thomas here."

Considering the number of dishonest ships' captains he had come across, that didn't surprise him at all. He now realized why Lady Wively's group was so careful. "How do we protect Mrs. Rymer and Peter until Mr. Rymer arrives?"

Everyone looked at Lady Wively, but it was Wively who spoke, "We take them out of London and hide them until he is in England."

"My primary estate is in Surrey," Frits said. "It's not too far to keep an eye on them."

"But they know who you are," Adeline objected. "If I were them, that is the first place I would go."

"My sister is correct, however, you are right as well. We will use the smaller estate of a friend of ours." Wively grinned. "You might know of it. Broadmore."

Know of it? Frits's family had been trying to buy it for an age. "I know it quite well."

Adeline glanced from him to her brother. "Where is it?"

"It is on the east side of Littlewood." No doubt her brother knew how many offers he'd made on the property.

"Oh." Her smooth forehead wrinkled as she looked thoughtfully at Wively. "Is it wise to have them so close to Littlewood?"

"I don't see that we will have a problem. If they decided to search outside London, they won't think to look anywhere other than Littleton's estate. And there is nothing connecting us to the duchess's estate."

"It's a fortified manor house with a large curtilage,"

Frits added. "Peter will be able to play outside without fear of discovery."

"There are also other children there," Lady Wively said. Mrs. Rymer's mouth opened. "Not mulattos or blackamoors. That would bring too much attention to the estate, and we would no longer be able to use it."

She nodded.

"Mrs. Rymer." Adeline placed her empty cup on a small side table. "Will you allow us to help you and your family?"

Frits had not even thought to ask the question, but, of course, it was the woman's decision to make.

After gnawing on her bottom lip for a while, she finally nodded. "If you are sure you can get my husband away from Tortola, then yes."

Although the sound wasn't loud, they all breathed a sigh of relief. But there was still another problem to resolve. "Now that that's settled, what am I to tell Lettsome?"

Silence settled over the room until Adeline broke it. "Mrs. Rymer, did anyone know you left the Lettsome house?"

"The cook knows, but she is the only one." Mrs. Rymer glanced at them. "She knew—everyone knew—what was going on, and most of them did not approve. Yet, what could they do?" She picked up her cup, found it empty, and set it back down. "When your servant came to the door, she sent the scullery maids on an errand so they could truthfully say they did not see me leave."

Adeline poured the woman another cup of tea, then turned to Frits. "You can say that you were out for the rest of the day and evening, and when you returned, the child was not there." A cunning look entered her silver eyes. "You can even tell him that you thought Lettsome was responsible, and you are not at all happy about it."

"What an excellent idea," Lady Wivenly said approvingly.

"I wholeheartedly agree." He had no idea his love could be so devious, and admired her even more. "That might make him think I don't know anything about the lad's disappearance." At least he hoped it would.

"To further that story," Wivenly said, "my groom was instructed to tell your servants, if asked, to say that the child was no longer there."

With everyone saying the same thing, that should throw Lettsome off the proverbial scent.

The butler entered and bowed. "My lord, my lady, you will be overly late for the ball if you do not depart immediately. The coach is waiting." He turned to Mrs. Rymer. "If you please, madam, your clothing and Peter's have arrived. Mrs. Newton, our housekeeper, will show you to your rooms."

The ball was the best one Frits had ever attended and it was all due to his ability to dance with Adeline three times and remain with her for most of the evening. He also learned the value of a well-placed scowl directed toward gentlemen who thought to ask her to stand up with them.

All three of their dances were waltzes, and it was hard not to hold her closer to him than propriety dictated. They didn't dare discuss the boy and his mother, but there was nothing stopping him from telling her more about Littlewood. He suspected she would want to see the pair comfortably settled, which meant that *he* might be able to entice her to visit his home.

"You are in a very good mood this evening." They made the turn at the end of the dance floor.

"I'm always in a good mood," he lied, although it did take a lot to anger him. Such as seeing a man try to harm a child. "Still, it has been an excellent day."

They held their clasped hands over their heads and pranced around.

"It has been." Adeline had to glance away, hiding her smile the first time Frits frightened away a would-be dance partner. She was sure he did not realize that she knew, but the knowing look on her brother's face had given it away.

She was so impressed by him and the way he cared about a child he had never even seen before, it was as if all her questions and doubts had been resolved. And the way he had remained by her side, even when she was not giving him a reason to, spoke favorably for him. Early in the Season, she had vowed not to marry a rake—and when he'd asked if he could court her, she was still positive he must be one of the species—then something her mother had said about her father being a rake before they wed, and what happened when rakes fell in love, and how they wanted to protect their ladies, began to make sense. Now that she thought about it, that was definitely something her brother and his friends did, and she knew for a fact that they had all been rakes. Well, with the notable exception of Merton.

"I believe this is my set." Frits's breath lightly brushing her ear caused pleasurable frissons to scramble down her neck and over her shoulders.

"I think it is. Not that I have any other dance partners."
Tilting her head, she met his too-innocent gaze.

"I cannot be sorry about that." A smile played around
the corners of his mouth.

Was there a male equivalent of a minx? For that was
what he was.

They took their positions, and now that she allowed
herself to enjoy his company, Adeline could admit that
she loved the feel of his hand engulfing her fingers,
and the solidity of his palm on her waist. To be held in
Frits's arms as if she weighed nothing more than air was
thrilling. Unlike her thoughts about Lord Anglesey, she
did not wonder why Frits wanted her. There was something about his determination and certainty that convinced her he just wanted her. For herself and no other
reason.

He captured her eyes with his sparkling green ones,
and they did not even have to talk. Her thoughts me-
andered to the one kiss they had shared, and she wondered when he would kiss her again. On the other
hand, they were never in a place where he *could* kiss
her. Perhaps instead of riding in his carriage, they
would be better served by walking in the garden at Watford House. There was a small rose arbor in a secluded
corner of the garden that would give them sufficient
privacy.

"You are deep in thought." His low voice intruded
on her thoughts, and heat infused her face.

Adeline was absolutely not going to tell him what
she had been thinking. "I—I was thinking that I would
like to accompany the child and his mother to the
country."

"Is that what made you blush?" His slightly grave
tone sounded like he was ready to seduce her right

here in the ballroom. How was it possible that he could do that just using his voice?

"Umm, no." Fortunately, the music ended, saving her from the embarrassment of answering.

Unfortunately, he did not allow the conversation to end. "Hmm. If it was not the journey"—he tapped his perfectly sculpted lips, riveting her eyes to them—"what else could it be?"

Except when he had asked her to allow him to court her, Frits had behaved like a perfect gentleman. Yet now, now Adeline wondered if she would like to see more of the rake. No, she was *certain* she wanted to see that side of him.

As heat traveled up her neck into her face, she ducked her head. Goodness, she did not even have the excuse of another dance partner to leave him until she could regain her countenance.

Yet, as if he knew she needed a moment, he greeted Exeter. "Is the wedding set?"

"Yes." The man smiled broadly. "In ten days. Lady Huntingdon is sending out invitations for the wedding breakfast soon. I hope to see you there."

"I wouldn't miss it." Frits glanced at Adeline, and she thought he might mention them. Instead, he slapped Exeter on the back. "I can't tell you how happy I am for you and Lady Dorie."

"I as well." The look in her eyes when Dorie had told Adeline she thought she had missed her chance had been distressing. "I think you are very well suited." And very much in love.

Dorie joined them, took Exeter's arm, and glanced at Adeline and Frits. "I hope we are not the only ones who find their perfect mate this Season."

He drew Adeline closer, causing her skirts to brush the tops of his dress pumps. "I hope so as well."

Her friend's smile included Frits. At last, the contretemps was ended. Georgie strolled through the door to the terrace with Lord Turley, and Adeline motioned toward the couple with her chin. "I think this might be a productive Season."

The others looked in the direction she had indicated and nodded in agreement. It would be wonderful if all her friends wed this Season. Henrietta had mentioned that Lord Phineas had been seen traveling toward Dover, and Adeline wondered if he would be able to convince Augusta to marry him.

Dorie and Exeter, being an engaged couple, joined the next set because they could dance together as much as they wished. That raised the question of what Adeline needed to know about Frits to ensure he was the absolute right gentleman for her?

Or had she already decided and merely wished to kiss him again?

But how to manage it?

All through supper, she let the conversation float around her as she considered one plan and then another. Any kissing in the Park was plagued with problems. Even if they went off on a path, they could be discovered, even early in the morning. She could, she supposed, suggest they go to the terrace, but even now her brother might object. That would be embarrassing.

The rose arbor in her mother's garden was the best place for a kiss. But how should she encourage him to kiss her again? She might need time to make him understand what she wanted. But first, he had to come to her house. There was nothing for it. She must act with daring. "You should come to tea tomorrow."

"Tea?" His eyes roamed her face, as if searching for something. "I would be delighted."

But now that she had invited him, would she have the courage to take him to the arbor and kiss him?

Or would he be able to work out what she wanted and kiss her first?

Chapter Twenty-Nine

The next afternoon, Frits arrived promptly at three o'clock. When it came to Adeline, he was always either perfectly on time or early, because she was equally punctual. Of the many things they had in common, this was her most endearing trait. Well, that and her habit of looking at him as if she was actually interested in what he had to say and not his wealth or rank. Not to mention loving his dog. Now that he thought about it, he found most of her traits charming. Nevertheless, if he managed to bring Adeline up to scratch—and it appeared more and more likely he would—never again would he have to wait on some woman who thought requiring him to kick his heels would make him appreciate her more. Which it never did.

The butler answered the door and escorted him to a sun-filled room at the back of the house. That they would still have so much light at this time of day gave him pause. Then he noticed that not only the wall to the garden was filled with windows, but the side wall was as well.

As soon as he was announced, he bowed. "My ladies."

"Littleton"—Lady Watford rose to greet him, and Adeline followed—"I am delighted you could join us."

Her ladyship began organizing the tea tray that had just arrived, giving him time to greet his soon-to-be betrothed. Clasping Adeline's fingers, he was pleased to feel them curve around his. He raised her hands to his lips and gently pressed a kiss on each one. "Thank you for asking me to tea."

Her silver eyes widened, and a light blush bloomed in her cheeks. He'd never tire of her blushes. After they married, he'd have to think of ways to keep her blushing.

She lowered her eyes, and her long, thick lashes created fans on her cheeks. "I–I thought we should spend more time together. Without everyone else in the *ton* around."

"I quite agree."

Her mother cleared her throat. "Adeline, please come and pour."

The rose in her face deepened as she looked down at their hands. Reluctantly he let hers go, and placed her hand on his arm. "I like milk and two sugars in my tea."

"Thank you for telling me." He escorted her the short way to her mother, who had patted a place on the sofa.

Once Adeline had taken her seat, he took the chair nearest her.

As he had expected, she poured with confidence and grace. "Perhaps after we finish, we can stroll in the garden."

That was a surprise. "It looks lovely. I believe I see some roses I haven't seen before."

"I had no idea you were interested in roses," Lady Watford said, and launched into a discussion of the flowers, some of which had been brought back from Persia in the last century.

Frits made the appropriate answers, but couldn't wait until he had Adeline alone. It had to have been the longest cup of tea he had ever experienced.

Fortunately, once they had finished one cup, she rose and donned a bonnet that had been on a chair by the door. "Shall we?"

"Yes." He forced himself to slow when what he wanted to do was drag her outside where they could be somewhat alone. "Do you enjoy gardening?"

"I do." She smiled at him. "But unlike my mother, I rather enjoy getting my hands dirty." She gave him a wry look. "Unfortunately, our gardener does not appreciate my assistance."

He'd sack any gardener who made her feel unwelcome. "In that case, you need your own garden, where your gardener listens to you instead of to himself."

Her answering laughter was not the false titter frequently heard in Polite Society, but one from deep inside her. "That is exactly what I require. A place where I can plant what I wish."

Frits had just the spot for her at Littlewood, and a gardener who would be happy for her involvement. How soon could he take her there? "Exactly."

She led him down a winding path past a fountain of a woman pouring water from an urn, and another of a boy urinating. He stopped and stared.

"It's a replica of a famous fountain in Brussels." Adeline stopped with him. "My grandfather saw it on his Grand Tour and sketched it. When he came into the title, he had it built."

"Interesting." Frits might have to take Adeline to Brussels someday to see the original one, and try to understand why a lad pissing was so important.

She started walking again, and he went with her. Where was she taking him?

Finally, she stopped in front of a fragrant display of white and yellow climbing roses covering an arbor. "I want you to see the arbor roses. They were brought here from China."

"They are magnificent." He could easily see them at Littlewood. Would Adeline like to re-create this arbor there?

Next to him, she stilled. Then she breathed in and out again and stared up at him. "When you kissed me at the garden party, and I told you that you should not—"

Ah, this was where she was taking him. "And I said no, but made it a question."

Her fingers clutched his sleeve so tightly, his valet would never get the wrinkles out. "I thought"—she bit down nervously on her bottom lip—"well, I—"

This would take all day if he left it to her, and they might not even get where they both wanted to be. "Yes."

Gathering her in his arms, Frits lightly touched his lips to hers, adding pressure only when her mouth softened. God, the only other kiss he'd ever experienced that was so innocent and sweet was the last time he'd kissed her. Rising on her toes, she slid her arms over his shoulders, tangling her fingers in his hair. He held her tightly against his chest, so that she wouldn't fall. Or so he told himself. The feel of her lush breasts pressed against him almost brought him to his knees. When he stroked her back, and down over her bottom, she opened her lips on a sigh, and he deepened the kiss, sweeping his tongue into her mouth, asking her to join him, and she did. Slowly at first, tentatively as if she was learning a new dance, then with increasing urgency. Her arms tightened and his cock strained against his pantaloons and her lower belly. His body clamored to make her his. If he lifted her the slightest bit more, she'd be able to feel his erection on her mound. Just the thought had his heart beating harder.

The breaths they exchanged had become ragged. Somehow, her feet ended up on top of his, and he knew he had to stop this, stop them before he convinced himself that the rose bower was the perfect place to consummate their union.

He stroked her petal-soft cheek with his thumb and slowly broke the kiss. "Adeline. My sweetheart." Her silver gaze was filled with confusion and desire. "I love you."

Adeline had never thought a kiss could be so, so consuming. So wonderful. Being held by Frits was better than she had ever thought it could be. The tingling she had felt before when he touched her was nothing like the flames licking her skin and heating her blood. The part between her legs throbbed with desire. She had never experienced so many physical sensations at one time, and she wished it could continue. Then he was gazing at her with his warm, emerald eyes, and saying he loved her, and she was not ready for that. Yet if she did not tell him that she loved him too, especially after that kiss, he might give up on her. And she knew she absolutely did not want him to do that. He would think she was a wanton, kissing a gentleman she was not sure she loved or wished to wed. If only he had waited a few days more.

Still, what would it hurt to say the words? She was so close, so close to knowing her heart. She didn't even know what else she was waiting for to be sure. "I love you too."

He smiled and kissed her again. Slowly, gently, as if

he was determined not to allow the kiss to flame as it had before. He held her to him and sighed. "We should go back. Your mother will come looking for us if we don't."

"Of course." Adeline had forgotten all about her mother.

He caught her hand in his and twined their fingers together as they strolled back up the path. "I'd like you to visit Littlewood. It's not far from Town. Only a few hours."

"Yes. I would like that a great deal." A breeze ruffled her hair. Her hat. It must have fallen off. "I have forgotten my bonnet."

"I'll go back for it," he offered.

"I shall go. If my mother sees me, she will wonder why I removed it." She turned, but Frits went with her.

"I am *not* going to the house without you." He looked almost panicked.

He was right; that would be begging her mother to ask questions. "I suppose we can both fetch it." The hat was on the ground. Frits picked it up and brushed it off before handing it to her. "Thank you."

"It is my pleasure." His voice sounded more formal than it had before. Was something wrong?

She donned her hat, and once again they ambled toward the house. Perhaps it was her. Her temples started to throb, and Adeline resisted the urge to rub them. She did not want him to think he had given her a headache.

Mama met them as they entered the morning room with a bright smile on her face. "I trust you had a lovely walk?"

Refusing to meet her eyes, Adeline placed her bonnet on a hook on the wall.

"You have a beautiful garden," Frits said. "I was amused by the fountain of the boy. Adeline said her grandfather had it made."

That was all it took for her mother to relate the history of the fountain and why it was so beloved in Brussels, giving Adeline time to compose herself. Not from the kiss, but from the declarations they had both made. Why, oh why, hadn't she thought about the consequences of kissing him again?

Well, actually, for the first time. She had not returned the last kiss. If only she knew what to do. How to make entirely sure that she loved him. The only good thing was that he had not proposed immediately. But . . . why hadn't he? Surely that was what a gentleman did after he kissed a lady. The dull ache spread to her forehead, and she rubbed it. What if he never intended to wed her? No, that did not make sense. He had already spoken with her father.

She always seemed to be a step behind him, and she could not understand the reason.

"Adeline." Frits took her hand. "Are you feeling well?"

"No." She started to shake her head, but it hurt. "I think I need to rest for a while."

"I understand. It's quite warm outside." Raising her fingers to his lips, he kissed them. "I'll see you in the morning if you're feeling better."

"I am sure I will be." She never got headaches. This was what came from lying to him. It must be. There was no other reason for the sudden pain.

She pressed her knuckles into her forehead, and tears sprang to her eyes as her head pounded. Then she swayed.

Before she could catch herself, she was in Frits's arms. "Where shall I take her?"

"Follow me. I do not understand it. She is never ill."
Mama left the room and strode to the hall and up the
stairs.

Adeline pressed her head against Frits's hard chest.
What was wrong with her? Why couldn't she be as in
love as he was?

"I hope she has not caught the grippe. I have heard
it is going around," her mother muttered. "I'll have the
whole house down with it."

Frits placed her carefully down on her bed, while
Mama spoke with Fendall.

"Everything will be well." He stroked Adeline's head.
"Just give it time."

She was trying to decide what he meant when his
hand was replaced by a cool cloth. "My lady," Fendall
said, "as soon as everyone leaves I'll make you more
comfortable."

Sometime later, when she woke, her throat was
parched, and she was hot and her very bones hurt.

"Take some of this. It will help your fever." Fendall
lifted her up and touched a cup to Adeline's lips. She
was grateful for the liquid, but it was bitter. "It's willow
bark tea. Drink it down."

She heard a male voice talking, but it wasn't Frits.
"It is influenza. Watch her for the next day. If she gets
any worse, send for me."

Worse? How could anything be worse than this? It
was retribution for telling a falsehood. Every part of
her body ached.

Why had Frits left?

"Because your mother would not allow him to remain."

Who had said that? It sounded as if it had come
from inside her head. Yet, it made sense. Something

was making her face blessedly cool, but the rest of her body was hot. Too hot.

Adeline kicked her legs, trying to get the bed-covers off.

"Tsk, tsk, my lady," someone said. Adeline did not recognize the voice. "You've got to stay quiet. Doctor's orders."

This must be retribution for being untruthful.

I will never, never lie to Frits again.

Chapter Thirty

Bloody hellhounds!

He'd gone too fast, again.

Frits splashed brandy in a glass and sat behind his desk.

Coxcomb. You know better than to rush your fences.

If he'd kept his thoughts to himself, Adeline wouldn't have felt as if she had to lie to him. Why couldn't he have just given her a kiss and waited for the rest of it? He knew she was coming around. Albeit slowly. At least he hadn't magnified his mistake by dropping to one knee and proposing.

He'd actually blamed himself for her headache until he'd received the note from Lady Watford, telling him Adeline had the grippe. At least he couldn't be responsible for that. No one in his household was ill.

Frits took a long draw of the brandy. He still thought getting her to Littlewood was his best course of action. But until he could manage that, he'd concentrate on things that might make her feel better; fresh fruit and flowers from his estate, perhaps some lavender. He could go to Hatchards to see if there were any books she'd like someone to read to her—hopefully him, but that was probably no more than wishful thinking. No one was going to let him into her sickroom. Therefore, that was all he could—would be allowed—to do for now. He'd also find out when Peter and his mother were going to Surrey. When Adeline was well enough, he'd be able to give her the news.

Damnation.

Frits tossed off the brandy, poured another, pulled out an already cut piece of foolscap, and made a list. He still berated himself for a fool, but doing something made him feel better. He tugged the bellpull and shortly thereafter the door opened.

"My lord?" Creswell bowed.

"Take this and do whatever is required to see the tasks are accomplished. Tell Humphries that Lady Adeline is ill and will not be able to walk Maximus until she is feeling better."

"Yes, my lord." The butler took the sheet. "Her ladyship is quite fond of Maximus, is she not?"

"Yes." Fonder of the dog than she was of Frits. He glanced at his butler. "Why?"

"Well, perhaps when she is up to receiving visitors, she might like to see him."

"That's an excellent idea." He should have thought of it himself. "Thank you."

"It is my honor, my lord." Creswell left the study, closing the door behind him.

The last time Frits was ill, Maximus had remained in bed with him. He'd gladly take the dog to Watford House, but couldn't see Lady Watford allowing a dog in bed with Adeline. A pity that. It would make her feel better.

Broth, plasters, and possets.

Taking out another sheet of paper, he wrote the items down.

Frits wished his mother was home, but she had left

as he was returning. He tugged the bellpull again. This time a footman appeared. "Tell Mrs. Hubbold I wish to see her."

Several minutes later, his housekeeper knocked on the open door and entered, looking a bit puzzled. "Good afternoon, my lord."

"When my sister had influenza, what did you do for her?"

"We kept her nourished with beef tea, and when she had a rattle in her chest I made a mustard plaster to keep her from getting pneumonia. After she'd got over the worst, Cook made a nourishing oxtail broth." She thought for a few moments. "We placed lavender around her room to help freshen the air."

Lavender. He was glad he'd remembered that. "Good. I've already asked for lavender to be sent. Send the rest of that to Watford House for Lady Adeline. She has influenza."

"Yes, my lord." His housekeeper gave him a curious look, but dropped a curtsey and left the study.

Perhaps he was overdoing it a little, but better that than doing nothing. God, he felt helpless. Frits pushed the brandy aside and called for a tea tray. But once he'd finished his repast, he picked up the glass of brandy again. Her mother said she'd never been sick before. What did that mean? She must have had the normal childhood illnesses. Yet that would have been years ago. What if her body didn't know how to fight off the grippe? What if she died? People died all the time from influenza.

Whole villages perished!

He couldn't lose her when he'd just started to convince Adeline she belonged with him. Part of her had to know that. Why else would she have felt as if she had to lie to him?

Frits strode to the hall, donned his hat and coat, departed the house, and headed toward Upper Brook Street. He'd find out himself how she was doing.

Frits plied the knocker, and the Watford butler opened the door. "My lord?"

"I've come to discover how Lady Adeline is faring."

"About as well as can be expected, my lord. The doctor was here and left some powders for her. I fear it will be a difficult few days."

He wanted more information. "Is Lady Watford in?"

"No, my lord. She had an engagement this evening." How could the woman even think about going out, nevertheless doing it, when her daughter might be dying? If he could, he'd be with Adeline now, doing everything possible to keep her alive. The butler cleared his throat. "It is better this way, my lord. Tending the sick is not one of her ladyship's many talents. I assure you, Lady Adeline is being well cared for. Shall I tell Lady Watford you called?"

"Yes." Nursing the ill might not be a talent, but she should be here supervising Adeline's care. Well, if her mother wouldn't do it, Frits would. "You may also tell her that I have ordered several items that will be of benefit to Lady Adeline to be delivered tomorrow. I shall come by again in the morning." Or later this evening. It wasn't that late. After all, someone had to keep an eye on her.

"As you wish, my lord."

Frits stalked home. He'd have to ask his mother how far he could go in taking care of Adeline. But when he arrived at Littleton House, he discovered she had returned and departed again leaving a message that she would be out for the evening.

Damnation.

He called for Humphries.

The old groom entered Frits's study. "Yes, my lord?"

"We need to find a way to sneak Max into Lady Adeline's bedroom." Frits couldn't be with her, but his dog could, and it would make her feel better.

Cristabel and Annis grinned at each other as the Watford butler bowed and left the small drawing room.

"I think that went well." Annis poured two glasses of sherry and brought one to Cristabel.

"Yes indeed." She took a sip of the wine. "My housekeeper told me that Frits has ordered the broths and other remedies we use for influenza to be delivered here. He is also sending fresh fruit from Littlewood."

"I had better tell my housekeeper and cook to be prepared to receive them. I suppose I'll be soothing some ruffled feathers. Fortunately, Pierre will understand when I explain that Lord Littleton is a man in love."

"You were about to tell me what happened when Frederick came for tea." Cristabel could not wait for her son to be settled and start giving her grandchildren. Not that her two married daughters had been backward in that regard, but they lived far enough away that she was not able to see the children very much. Frits's children would be raised at Littlewood.

"Everything seemed to be going well between the two of them. Adeline even suggested that she show him the garden." Annis arched a brow. "The only reason I can see for that was so that they could have a private conversation. She even took him back to the rose arbor."

"The one you call the kissing arbor?" Cristabel started to get an inkling of what had gone wrong.

"The very one." Her friend sipped her sherry. "They were gone for a fair amount of time, but when they returned there was a great deal of tension between Adeline and Frederick. They barely looked at each other. She was coming around." Annis shook her head. "I know she was. Otherwise she would not have invited him to tea and gone out in the garden with him. I wish I knew what had happened."

So did Cristabel. "Then Adeline became ill."

"Yes. It came on so suddenly. Littleton caught her as she fell and insisted on carrying her to her bed-chamber." Annis smiled. "He would have remained if he could have. I practically had to drag him out."

"Hmm." Cristabel sipped her sherry. "I will wager my diamonds that Frederick did something for which she was not ready. Do you think he kissed her?"

"I am quite sure he did." Annis stared at the fire-place. "Then again, she *did* take him to the rose arbor, and she did not cry out or come running back."

"In that case, it must have been something he said rather than something he did." Cristabel applied her mind to what her son could have done. "Oh good Lord. I hope he did not propose."

Annis gave a frustrated sigh. "I can see it now. They kissed and he decided it meant she was ready to marry."

Feeling as if she had to defend her son, Cristabel said, "That is how it is usually done, but I do see your point. He should have waited a bit longer."

"If only Adeline was a bit more incautious."

"I must say, I rather like her prudence." It showed a maturity beyond her years, for which Cristabel was thankful. "Frederick will simply have to take a few steps back, and be more patient with her."

"That will probably be for the best," Annis agreed.

"I do hope they resolve all of this before the Season ends."

"She will most likely not be herself for a few weeks." Poor Adeline would not be up to attending any evening entertainments. The thought gave Cristabel an idea. "After Dorie's wedding to Exeter, we could all go to Littlewood. The fresh air will be much better for Adeline than staying in Town."

"What an excellent idea." Annis smiled approvingly. "It will also allow her to come to see how Frederick is at home."

"My thoughts exactly." From what Cristabel knew of Adeline, that should finally bring her up to scratch.

"What is that beast still doing in her bed?" Mama's sharp whisper woke Adeline.

"Hush. You'll wake her." Adeline didn't recognize that voice.

The door clicked shut.

She felt Maximus cuddled next to her, and she reached out, stroking him. "I thought I'd been dreaming, but you really are here. How did Frits manage it?" The dog stretched and started licking her hand. "You are right. I need to bathe." The bed hangings were open on one side, allowing the scent of lavender to reach her. She tried to sit up, but one long leg plopped across her body, pushing her back down. "I'm as weak as a kitten. How long have I been ill?" Maximus yawned and snuggled his large head against her shoulder. "Silly, expecting a dog to answer."

She did have to get up, though, and her throat was parched from even that little bit of talking to the dog. Reaching out, she picked up the mug on the bedside table, and drank. The liquid was tangy, like a lemon, but not nearly as tart. "What *is* this?"

Whatever it was, it was good.

"You're awake." Fendall strode into the room and pressed her palm on Adeline's forehead, nodded, then set about fluffing her pillow. "It's definitely gone. How are you feeling?"

"Worn out, but my head is clear. How long was I sick, and"—she held up the mug—"what is this?"

"Four days. Her ladyship was getting ready to send for another doctor. Thank the Lord your fever broke last night." Fendall took the mug. "That is orange juice." She sniffed and wrinkled her nose. "Lord Littleton had the fruit brought from his estate. I'll order you a bath."

His dog—he must have missed Maximus a great deal—and his oranges. What else had he done for her? The lavender. That must have been from him as well. Adeline did not remember it being used in a sickroom before. Frits must be the kindest man she knew. She must thank him . . . No, she must tell him how grateful she was for his care.

He was everything Adeline wanted in a husband.

A part of her was still the tiniest bit concerned that he was a rake. Then again, he was *her* rake, and he was not a bad rake. She wasn't making any sense. He loved her. What did it matter what he was before?

Adeline was not that hungry, but she must regain her strength if she wanted to see him. "Food." But when she turned her head, her maid had gone. Maximus snored softly. "I might as well sleep a little myself."

The splashing of water stirred her from sleep again. It would feel good to be clean. She swung her legs over the bed and sat, causing her head to swim, and collapsed back onto her pillows. "I must be even weaker than I thought."

"Here, my lady." Fendall rushed to the bed. "Let me help you." She slid her arm under Adeline's shoulders and slowly lifted her so that she was sitting up again. "Take a few breaths, and I'll walk with you to the bathtub."

It took longer than Adeline could have imagined it would, but she was finally lying in warm water while the upstairs maid changed her bed linens. She would have liked to have had her hair washed, but that would have to wait until she was stronger.

Maximus got down from the bed and, after looking at her, scratched on the door, and someone let him out. "I hope my mother allows him back in again."

"Her ladyship's gone out." Fendall picked up a bucket of clean water and frowned. "Let's see if you can stand while I rinse you."

Adeline nodded, and her maid helped her rise. She wobbled a bit, but managed not to fall. "I should eat something."

"Let's get you dry and back into bed." Once that was done, her maid tugged the bellpull and set about cleaning up the bath towels. "His lordship sent over what he called a pot liquor. His old footman swore it would have you strong again in no time."

She found herself looking forward to discovering what kind of broth it was. In fact, she wanted to know more about the Littleton household. "Has Lord Littleton been here often?"

"Every few hours, from what I've been told." Her maid went to the door. "He tried to sit in the corridor, but her ladyship chased him off."

Oh, my.

The knowledge did more than warm Adeline's heart.

It made that organ beat so fast, she thought it would take flight.

"I love you."

She loved him too. Really and truly loved him. Why she had not recognized it before she didn't know.

When the soup arrived, she was thrilled to discover it was thicker than she thought it would be and extremely tasty. Accompanying it was more orange juice and a bread so light it had to have been baked by Pierre. Regretfully, almost as soon as she finished the repast, Morpheus took her in his arms again.

For the next two days, all Adeline did was eat and sleep. Even her favorite books could not keep her awake long. No one came to take Maximus away, for which she was thankful. Nor did her mother demand that he be removed from her bedchamber or her bed. On the third day, the doctor visited and proclaimed she could get up, sit in a chair, and take the air as long as she did not tire herself.

"What you do not want to do, my lady, is to have a relapse," he said sternly. "No gadding about until you have regained your strength."

As soon as he left, she rang for Fendall. "I must wash my hair."

"The bathtub should be here"—she cocked her head—"now."

It was a warm day, and once Adeline's hair had dried, she was allowed to sit in the garden. If she was lucky, Frits would stop by. Almost the moment she was on the chaise that had been carried to the terrace, Henrietta and Georgie were announced.

"I am so glad you are finally well enough to get up." Georgie bussed Adeline's cheek. "We were not allowed to visit you at all."

Henrietta dropped a light kiss on Adeline's forehead.

"We offered to help nurse you, but we were told we could not take the risk of contracting the grippe."

Georgie rolled her eyes. "As if we cared."

Maximus, who had gone to sniff around the garden, came prancing back and took up a position on the ground next to Adeline.

Henrietta stroked him. "Whose dog is this?"

"Lord Littleton's." Two curious pairs of eyes focused on Adeline. "He thought Maximus would make me feel better. According to my maid, he kept me from thrashing around with the fever."

"I have always thought animals have a calming effect," Henrietta said sagely. "Their presence works on cranky babies as well."

Georgie smoothed her skirts. "Will you be well enough to attend Dorie's wedding?"

Goodness. Adeline had forgotten all about the wedding. "When is it?"

"In two days." Georgie's brows came together. "I know she will understand if you are not strong enough."

"No." There was no way Adeline was going to miss that ceremony. "I shall be there even if I have to be carried."

"Excellent," Henrietta said, grinning.

"My lady," Abney said, "Lord Littleton insists upon seeing you."

Georgie and Henrietta exchanged glances.

"We shall see you later," Georgie said rising, then curtseying. "My lord."

"My lord." Henrietta curtseyed as well. "Adeline, we will come by again tomorrow."

"I look forward to seeing you."

Frits stroked Maximus, who had got up to greet him, but his concerned gaze was on Adeline. As she searched his bright green eyes, she knew she had been right. She did love him.

She patted the chaise cushion. "Please, come sit with me."

Perching on the small space, he took her hand. "I cannot tell you how happy it makes me to see you up and looking well."

She curled her hand around his warm, strong, slightly callused fingers. "You are not wearing gloves." Well, that was a stupid thing to say. "I mean—"

"When word came that you were allowed out of your chamber, I came immediately and forgot them."

"I like the feel of your hands." Not that she had much with which to compare them. They were rougher than her father's. She placed her palm on his cheek. "I love you. I love that you care for me so much that you braved my mother and brought Maximus to me. You must have missed him exceedingly." His thumb brushed her face below her eye. "I am convinced no one could love me more than you do."

Chapter Thirty-One

"Because no one can." Frits's heart soared as he gently touched his lips to Adeline's. "Are you ready to hear a proposal, or shall I wait?"

Adeline was still too pale, but her eyes lit up, and her smile was all he could wish for. "I am ready."

For days she was so ill, he thought he was going to lose her. He had almost decided to wait until she was stronger, until they were at Littlewood. But when she'd declared her love for him this time, he knew it was the truth, and he couldn't wait. He couldn't lose this moment.

The speech he'd been planning for weeks went out of his head, and for a second, he couldn't even talk. That's when he knew he would just speak from his heart. "Adeline, when I look at you, I can see you with our child, our children. I can see you by my side in all I do." Frits raised their linked hands to his lips and kissed each of her knuckles. "I don't know what I would do without you. It almost killed me to know you were so ill, and I was not allowed to be with you. My life would be empty without you in it. Will you be my wife, the love of my life, and the mother to our children?

Will you stay by my side for the rest of our lives?" He took a breath. "And can we wed soon?"

Adeline laughed so hard she started to cough, and Frits swore to himself. Fortunately, Abney brought tea, and she was soon able to answer. "Yes and yes. I will be your wife and the mother to your children, and I want nothing more than to remain with you for the rest of my life."

"Do you mind if we marry at Littlewood?" Frits had thought long and hard about this. The plan was for her and her mother to visit as soon as she could travel. Once she was there, he didn't want her to leave.

"I would be happy to have the wedding there." He held the cup to her lips and she drank. "When do you wish to wed?"

"We cannot depart Town until after Exeter and Lady Dorie's wedding. If you are well enough, a day or two later, if that suits you."

"That sounds perfect." This time she reached up and kissed him, and it was all he could do not to take her into his arms. Yet, she was not well enough for even deep kisses. A wet tongue landed on his cheek, and Adeline laughed. "I think Maximus is feeling left out."

Frits rubbed the dog's ears. "He's going to have to get used to some changes." Such as not always being able to be with him or Adeline. "Do you want me to leave him with you?"

Her pearl-like teeth bit her bottom lip, and he almost groaned with need. "If you do not mind."

"Not at all." She gave him a dubious look. "I would rather he be here with you for the nonce. We will all be together before long." All he'd have to do was to get his mother to speak with Lady Huntingdon again.

"How did you get him into my room? I cannot believe Abney or Mama allowed you to bring him."

Frits grinned. "I came by so often that first day that your butler stopped manning the door. I was waiting for that to occur. After all, butlers have many more duties than that. Once I knew he was occupied elsewhere, Humphries came with me, and he got the footman to follow him out of the hall. Then I came in and snuck Max to your room. I think your maid was actually happy to have him there. She told me later that he made you much calmer, and when you did start to become restless, he would settle you." He wasn't going to tell her that when her mother found out about Maximus, her ladyship had tried to evict the dog. Adeline's lady's maid had argued against it, and he'd had to call his mother in to intervene.

"That must be the reason he was allowed to stay." She stroked the Great Dane's ears. "Thank you for thinking of it."

"It was my pleasure." He remembered the other thing he wanted to tell her. "Peter and his mother are safely out of Town, and Lady Wively sent the message to the West Indies."

"That means Mr. Rymer will be here by early autumn, if not before." Smiling, she gazed up at Frits. "Thank you for making sure I knew."

"I've been thinking about their situation. You will remember that I suggested he could work at my shipyard. I wrote the manager, and he agreed that Mr. Rymer would be an excellent addition. It seems his reputation has preceded him."

"Frits, that is wonderful." A little color came back into her cheeks. "They have no family here to help them. Perhaps we should find a house for them and set it up as well." A line formed over the bridge of her nose as she thought. "With Mrs. Rymer's participation, of course."

"I hadn't thought of that, but you are right. We should ensure that they have no immediate worries."

He heard the clicking of shoes on the terrace and glanced over his shoulder. "Good morning. We have an announcement to make."

His mother clasped her hands together. "You are getting married."

Before either he or Adeline could verify her statement, Lady Watford let out a loud huff. "Thank God. It's about time. I shall inform the rector of St George's."

Adeline grimaced and looked at him, then shook her head. "Mama, we wish to have the wedding at Littlewood as soon as it can be arranged."

"Aha!" His mother exclaimed as her mother scowled. "I do not know why you thought it would be otherwise, Annis. I should have accepted your wager." Mama smiled at Frits and Adeline. "Shall we invite the tenants and the neighbors?"

"Yes, please," Adeline said. "It will be a good opportunity to meet everyone."

"Annis, you may invite as many people as you wish." His mother apparently could not resist a triumphant smirk. It was a good thing they were longtime friends.

"I should have known." Lady Watford sighed. "Adeline, you require new clothing. I shall ask my modiste to attend me immediately. This is a horrible time of the Season to have anything made quickly, but I'll do my best."

"I have some ideas on how that can be achieved." Mama linked her arm with Lady Watford. "Let us leave the children alone, and we will discuss the arrangements."

Adeline dipped her head and tried to hide a yawn, but he'd seen it. "You need to sleep."

"That's all I've been doing," she complained.

"If you nap a little now, you might be able to join the family for dinner." He'd cajoled more than one recovering person with promises of treats.

"Will you be there?" He swooped her into his arms and started inside.

"As soon as I ask your mother." He had every expectation her ladyship would agree. They were going to be family soon.

By this time next week, Frits and Adeline could be married.

Owen Davies wiped his sweaty hands on his breeches before he knocked and entered Mr. Lettsome's study. "You wanted to see me, sir?"

The man looked up. The almost refined appearance he gave to all of London was replaced by stern lines and anger that Davies was afraid was directed at him. He'd been so irked with the lad, he'd forgotten where he was. "You've got to get the boy and his mother back. I cannot afford to lose the money Rymer brings in from his work in the shipyard. If we don't go back with them, he'll find a way to escape." The only hold they had on the slave was his family. "I also can't bear the cost of replacing them with paid servants, or the prices the Danes charge for new slaves." That Davies didn't believe. Lettsome was a pinchpenny. "But this time you've got to be smart about it. If you get caught, I can't help you."

What was unsaid was that Davies could lose his position if he didn't succeed. "I'm keeping an eye on his lordship's house."

"They are not there." Lettsome spat the words. "There

was no way the boys I hired could have missed a woman being brought into the house."

"I know it, but there was that woman who was with his lordship. I'll wager that she has 'em, or knows where they are." Women were soft. She was the one who made his lordship interfere. Davies started to fidget and stopped. "I'll find them, sir. I ain't never let a slave escape yet."

"See that you do."

That conversation had been almost two weeks ago, and each day he'd waited for word. Finally, one of the boys came up to him at the pub he'd started patronizing and slid onto the bench opposite him. "I found the mort."

"How?" It'd taken Davies too long to learn that *ladies* didn't go to gentlemen's houses.

"'E's been goin' to the same place every time I turned around for days now. It's got ta been her 'ouse."

"Have you seen her?"

"Na, but I 'eard she's been sick."

Davies slid the coin across the table and it disappeared into the lad's coat. "Tell me when you see her."

"You got it." The boy left as quickly as he'd arrived.

This time he'd find out where Rymer's wife and son were. Davies would do whatever he had to make her tell him where the slaves were. He drained his glass of ale. It wouldn't be long now.

That evening, Frits and his mother had come to dinner, and the next morning, Adeline went over designs and fabric with her mother's modiste. A few hours later, she had finally selected sufficient gowns and other garments to start her on married life.

"I'll do my best, my lady." The modiste stared at the list she'd written. "Most of it will have to be sent after you leave Town."

"Lady Littleton has several seamstresses coming up to Town to help. If you can get the clothing done enough, it can be finished in the country."

The woman nodded. "Normally, I like to see the final results myself, but I understand your haste."

"I appreciate you agreeing to take the time to attend my daughter. If it was up to her, she would probably not have a new wardrobe at all."

"I'll see that it does not come to that, my lady." The woman sounded properly horrified.

Adeline had almost fallen asleep on a daybed when her mother and the modiste had begun discussing how all the gowns would be finished. It really was not true that she'd forgo new gowns. Hadn't she been complaining all Season that she wanted more color in her garments? What she had not wanted was to be in Town waiting for the clothing to be completed.

A satisfied smile curved her lips. And now she would not have to.

The following day was Dorie and Exeter's wedding. Adeline and Georgie sat together in St George's Church and Henrietta attended Dorie. The ceremony was lovely, but Adeline was thankful that she would not be marrying in the large church. Not that she knew anything at all about the church at Littlewood, but it had to be smaller and more comfortable than this.

When she arrived at Huntingdon House for the wedding breakfast, Frits was waiting for her. "How are you feeling?"

"A little tired still." She did not want to put off their

journey to her new home, but she was afraid she might have to.

"Sweetheart, you look pale." Frits's lips pressed together for a moment. "We should wait a few more days before journeying to Littlewood."

"As much as I would like to disagree with you, I am afraid you are correct." He led her to a table and held the chair as she sat. "I dislike disappointing you."

"Disappoint me?" He looked surprised. "Never. It would take much more than you finishing your recovery to do that." He raised her hand and kissed it. "I believe there are ices to be had. I'll get some for you."

Georgie took one of the other chairs and propped her chin on her palm. "Well?"

Adeline couldn't stop the grin from growing on her face. "We are betrothed. Our families will be traveling to Littlewood as soon as I am able. How much notice will you need for the wedding?"

"I am so happy for you!" Her friend hugged her. "I shall leave as soon as I receive your invitation."

She scanned the room and saw Frits returning with the ices. He had brought one for Georgie as well. "Please do not say anything here. This is Dorie's day."

"I quite understand." Georgie accepted three glasses of champagne from a footman. "I will tell Henrietta after we depart."

Frits placed the ices on the table. "Ladies, I hope you like what I chose."

Adeline tasted hers. "Mmm. Muscadine."

"Mine is lemon." Henrietta looked at Frits. "Thank you. That was a good choice."

"My pleasure. I'm glad you like it." He glanced at Henrietta and Adeline. "Have you told her?"

"About our betrothal? Yes, but we agreed that it

would be better not to let it be widely known at the moment."

He nodded. "Prudent of you. I told Turley and Exeter yesterday. He and Lady"—Frits stopped for a second— "Exeter are traveling to their property in Kent first so that they can attend our wedding."

Adeline finished her ice and took a drink of champagne. "I am glad they will be there."

"As am I. It appears that the new Lady Exeter has decided to forgive me my transgressions."

"It's about time," Georgie muttered. "Nevertheless, all's well that ends well."

Adeline agreed.

Chapter Thirty-Two

Adeline was finally traveling to Littlewood today. She and her maid strolled out to the gated square in front of the house. The past week had been so busy, it was the first day since Dorie's wedding that Adeline had had the opportunity to do something not regarding the move, recovering her strength, and the wedding. Even now, her trunks were being loaded onto wagons bound for Littlewood. She and her family, along with Frits and his mother, would depart after luncheon.

As it was, they only had a few minutes before Frits arrived. Yet the square was in full bloom, and she wanted to see the flowers. "I suppose I should be sad to be leaving home, but I'm not. I have heard so much about Littlewood and the people, and animals, that I am excited to finally meet them."

"I must say I agree, my lady. It will be nice to be in the country again. I've had a chance to talk with Lady Littleton's maid, and she said she's never seen a more beautiful place." A small boy ran by, and Fendall reached out to steady Adeline. Her strength had only recently returned.

She smiled at the gesture. Even Maximus had taken

to walking slowly so she could lean on him, but he was back with Frits now. "Thank you, but I am no longer ill."

Her maid gave a tight nod, but said nothing.

"So, we meet again, my lady."

Adeline raised her chin as she looked at the man who'd tried to whip Peter. "What are you doing here?"

"Lookin' for you." The miscreant had a smug smile on his face. "I'm guessing you know where my master's property is."

"*Property.*" She speared him with a glare. How anyone could refer to a member of the human race as property was beyond her. "People are not goods." She wanted to argue the point with him, but it would not do any good. Instead she inclined her head. "Good day."

As she turned to leave, he grabbed her arm, his fingers digging painfully into her skin. "Not so fast. I want to know what you did with the woman and the boy. It'll go better for you if you just tell me."

Adeline stilled, as rage coursed through her. That would be the first and the last time he threatened her or anyone else. Without looking at the man, she tightened her arm, ready to use him as a brace to whirl around and punch him. But before she did that, she'd give him one more chance. "Release me."

"Not a chance. You're coming with me." Before she could swing her arm, he started dragging her toward the gate.

Fendall dashed past, screaming for help, and the scoundrel changed directions. Adeline dug her feet into the ground, made a fist, and swung, hitting him on his temple. His grip loosened just enough for her to pull away, and suddenly Maximus was there lunging and jumping on the man as he went down. Then there was the sound of wood cracking.

A strong arm came around, holding her firmly against Frits's solid chest. "I've got you."

Glancing to the side, she saw the villain on the ground, next to one of the small obelisks marking the paths of the square. Blood dripped from the pointed top of the stone, and a pool of blood was forming under his head. "Is he alive?"

"I doubt it." Frits's voice was grim. "We have company."

Fendall was approaching them with a constable and two footmen.

"Ah, Constable," Frits said in a well-bred drawl. "Excellent timing."

"I heard a scream." The officer looked at the scene, then crouched down and inspected the man before pointing at her maid. "I was told he attacked the lady."

"Yes, he did." Pulling back from Frits's embrace, Adeline placed her hand on his arm. She might very well have killed a man. It was time she spoke for herself. "He attempted to abduct me. I hit him, and then Maximus"—the dog was now standing firmly against her leg—"leapt upon him. He appears to have hit his head on the marker."

The officer had pulled out a pocketbook and a pencil. "Do you own the dog, my lady?"

"No, he belongs to Lord Littleton." It wasn't until then that she realized she'd been stroking him as she spoke.

The constable wrote something down. "He appears very attached to you."

"Lady Adeline and I are betrothed." Frits placed his hand over hers. "As you said, my dog has become quite fond of her."

"I see, I see. Thank you, my lord." Another constable joined them, and the first one said, "I'll need you to fill out a report describing what happened, if you don't mind."

Taking a breath, she asked again, "Is he alive?"

"No, my lady. He's not. We'll remove the body as soon as we can."

Frits smiled. "I shall be happy to give you a statement as soon as I return her ladyship home."

The officer looked a little sheepish. "I'll need statements from the lady, and her maid as well, my lord. Unless you were here to see the attack?"

"No." Frits's lips formed a thin line. "I arrived as the miscreant fell."

"Yes, of course," the constable said.

Poor Frits. He was probably blaming himself for not being there to protect her.

She would have to take the matter in hand. "Constable. Please come with me. We are preparing to leave Town. It will be better if you have the statements before we do."

"Yes, indeed, my lady. That would be the best thing to do."

After a brief conversation between the law enforcement officers, the second constable organized the removal of the body, aided by the Watford footmen.

She led the way to the front drawing room, tugged the bellpull, and asked the footman who responded for a tea tray. Then Adeline took a piece of foolscap and cut it into sheet-sized pieces. "These should be large enough. Fendall, would you like to write your statement first?"

"Yes, my lady." The maid sat at the writing table.

Once the tea arrived, she offered a cup to the constable while he waited for them to finish, and her mother sailed into the room.

Mama looked at the officer and frowned. "What has occurred?"

Adeline handed her mother a cup of tea. "I was assaulted in the park. The villain is dead."

Her maid rose and handed her statement to the constable. "If that's all, my lady, I'll finish preparing your last bag."

"Thank you, Fendall." Adeline smiled at her maid. "You did an excellent job sounding the alarm."

"I'm glad I was there to help." The maid bobbed a curtsey.

"I wish to thank you as well," Frits said. "I am glad you will be joining our household."

"You're welcome, my lord."

As she left the room, Lady Watford sat on the sofa against the back wall. She was obviously waiting until the officer left before speaking. Frits was only glad that his mother was not there. She wasn't nearly as cool as her ladyship.

Adeline sat to write her statement, and he watched her closely, wondering when she was going to start blaming herself for the death. As horrible as the scoundrel was, and as much as he thought the man deserved to die for even touching his beloved, she was bound to take it hard. Any lady would.

When she finished, she handed the constable her statement. "This is everything."

"Thank you, my lady."

"I believe I'm the only one left." Frits took his place in the chair, wrote his brief account of what he'd witnessed, and handed it to the officer. "You have the full account now."

The officer read what he'd written, and nodded his head twice. "Thank you very much, my lord. I believe this will make everything right." Bowing, he left with the butler.

Once the constable had gone, Adeline turned to him. "What did you put in your statement that made him so happy?"

"The truth. Although you punched the blackguard and he started to fall, if Maximus hadn't jumped on him, he wouldn't have gone down as heavily as he did." Frits took her hands in his. "Sweetheart, his death was not your fault."

"Oh." Adeline seemed stunned for a moment. "I am glad to know that I was not the actual cause of his death. Yet I cannot but feel that he will not be missed by many."

Eugénie entered the room a few moments later. "What is wrong? Abney said a constable was here."

As Adeline explained what had occurred, Lady Wively's expression became increasingly stony. "You may rest assured that the overseer deserved to die. Mrs. Rymer, she confided in some of my staff about the overseer. His name is Davies and he is responsible for several deaths."

"Why was he not prosecuted?" It was amazing to him how the man got away with it. "I know for a fact that at least one slave owner was charged and convicted of the death of a slave."

"That is true, but first one must have a witness who will speak up." Lady Wively explained. "Davies preys— preyed on young women and children, and he was careful that no one was nearby to see his actions. Do not be sorry for him."

Adeline's jaw had firmed. "I have never heard of such perfidy. The man was a monster."

Frits agreed. If Max hadn't seen to it, he would

have ensured the overseer never made it back to the West Indies alive.

Abney knocked on the door. "My ladies, my lord, luncheon is served."

"Thank you, Abney." Frits tucked her hand in the crook of his arm.

"I believe this has ended as he deserved." Eugénie rose.

Adeline glanced at him and her sister-in-law. "Thank you both for your help. I had not thought I needed to hear all you had to say, but I did."

"Before we go into luncheon," Lady Watford rose from the sofa, "Adeline, are you certain you are able to travel this afternoon?"

"Yes, of course."

"Very well, then. I shall see you in the small dining room."

Frits held his other arm out to Lady Wivenly, but she smiled and shook her head. "I shall go ahead."

He liked the way Adeline leaned on him a little as they made their way up the corridor to the small dining room. He pulled out a chair for her and sat beside her, making sure she had a sufficient amount to eat. After all, she was still recovering.

Her father had still not arrived by the time they had eaten luncheon. Lady Watford glanced at her pin watch. "We cannot wait for him any longer."

"Annis," his mother said, "If you and Adeline travel with us, you can leave your coach for your husband."

Frits stifled a groan. He had hoped that his mother would travel with the Watfords, leaving Adeline to ride in the carriage with him.

"That will settle the problem of how he gets there. Now I just have to resolve the difficulty of making sure he gets in the coach to go down."

"Will and I are traveling to you in the morning," Lady Wively said.

"I'll take care of that part," Wively offered. "I'll come by here and get him in the carriage, then instruct Joseph Coachman not to make any detours."

"That will be extremely helpful, my dear." Her mother nodded approvingly. "You might want to explain to him that he would not wish to miss the wedding."

Wively frowned. "When is the ceremony?"

"As soon as we finalize the arrangements." Adeline gazed lovingly at Frits, and he wanted to take her into his arms again. "All the instructions were sent to the staff at Littlewood, so it might be as quickly as two days."

It would be in no more than two days if Frits had anything to say about it. "I have the special license, and your sister has already sent messages to her friends, asking them to arrive tomorrow."

"Definitely no detours, then." Wively rubbed his chin. "Eugénie, we had better ride with him."

"As you wish."

It was going on two o'clock, and Frits was ready to go home. "While you are organizing that, the rest of us must depart."

A flurry of hugging ensued, but fifteen minutes later, they were headed west, out of London. His senior staff had departed for Littlewood with most of the baggage earlier that day, leaving the staff that usually remained in London to look after the town house. Once they arrived at Littlewood, his butler, Creswell, would set a watch and, upon Frits and Adeline's arrival, have the servants lined up to greet their new mistress-to-be. Frits was excited about introducing them to her.

The knowledge that once they stepped into the coach, he would never be without Adeline again warmed his heart like nothing had before. She was exactly the wife and helpmate he had been looking for.

"Adeline, dear," his mother said as they crossed the Thames. "I want you to know that even though I will not be living at Littlewood, I shall be nearby and will be available if you have any questions."

"Thank you." She smiled at his mother. "I am positive I will rely on you a great deal."

Frits couldn't believe what he had heard. "You are going to live with Grandmamma at the Dower House?"

His mother looked at him as if he'd lost his mind. His mother and grandmother only got on well if they were not sharing a household. "Before his death, your father and I agreed it would be better if I resided at the Lilacs if your grandmother was still living at the time of your marriage."

Frits mentally reviewed the properties the barony owned. "I don't recall that we had a property by that name."

"*You* do not," she said archly. "I do." She turned to Adeline. "It is a lovely little house between the village of Littleton and the house just beyond the Littlewood boundary."

If it was the house he was thinking of, it had at least ten bedrooms. Then again, it was much smaller than Littlewood.

The next two and a half hours passed quickly, and before he knew it, they were entering the gate to Littlewood. "We're here."

"Already?" Adeline asked, surprised. "That was a quick journey." She looked out the window. "The view is very pretty."

Frits thought so too. Lime trees lined the drive that curved gracefully up to the house. "The trees are over two hundred years old. After dinner I'll show you the gardens and lake."

Excitement lit up her eyes, making them shine like polished silver. "I cannot wait to see everything."

On the opposite bench, their mothers exchanged pleased, conspiratorial looks. His mother had told him what she had done. He wondered if he should tell Adeline about the part their mothers had played in trying to make this match and decided that if he did tell her, it would be much later. When their children asked how they met and married.

The coach swung around the curve and stopped. Before the footman had the stairs down, his household servants and employees had finished lining up. To him, it was an impressive sight. He hoped Adeline thought so as well. It was important that she love the land and people as much as he did.

Frits surveyed the front of the house as he waited for a footman to let down the coach steps. Normally, he would have jumped down, but this was a formal occasion for his staff, and he knew better than to behave casually about it. The wide, stone steps leading to the front door glistened under the sun. Even the casements had been scrubbed.

He handed down his mother and Lady Watford before Adeline stood in the open door. "Are you ready?"

"Yes." She beamed at him. "Never more so."

Chapter Thirty-Three

Joy bubbled over as Adeline stared at the house. As Frits had said, the old hall was the first thing one saw. Tall, circular towers built of light gray stone flanked the wide front door, and battlements connected the towers. As they had rounded the drive, she had been able to see the more modern part of the house, which was built from the same stone. Rather than looking like a jumble of different periods, as some houses did, it appeared as if the later additions had been the plan all along. "It's beautiful."

He had a wide smile as he handed her down and escorted her to the servants, who had lined up to greet her.

The butler bowed. "My lady, welcome home."

Tears of joy pricked the back of Adeline's eyes. "Thank you, Creswell."

"Allow me to present the staff."

Frits remained by her side as she met the servants and asked questions of each one, so she would remember them and their names more easily. When she had met everyone, including the boot boy, the housekeeper, Mrs. Hubbold, showed Adeline to her rooms.

The bedchamber was painted in a muted green and had a view to the north. An open door led to a parlor in the same colors. "Most of your clothing and other things are in the mistress's chambers. I hope you'll be happy with these rooms until the wedding."

"Thank you." Adeline took off her bonnet. "These will suit nicely."

"I'll inform Miss Fendall you have arrived." The housekeeper bobbed a curtsey and skirted Frits, who was lounging against the jamb of the doorway.

He peered inside the room. "You'll like the other apartments better. They face south. Do you still want to take a stroll around the grounds after tea?"

More than anything. Not only did she need to stretch her legs, she was curious about the rest of the property. "I do." She stripped off her gloves and walked to him. "Have you found out whether all is ready for our wedding?"

"It is set for the day after tomorrow." Bending his head, he drew her into his arms and kissed her. "After this evening, we won't have much time to ourselves for a few days."

Adeline stood on her toes and slid her arms around his neck. "I know."

"My lady," Fendall asked from behind Frits. He was so tall and his shoulders were so broad, Adeline could not see around him. "Do you wish to change?"

"Yes. Something comfortable. I am going to explore the gardens."

"And a little farther than the garden." Heat lurked in his eyes. "We have a stream you'll want to see."

She dropped her arms and stepped back. "How do I get to the room where tea will be served?"

"I'll come back for you. The house is not difficult to navigate, but you'll want a tour before you attempt to go about on your own."

"I can see that." He backed up and her maid entered. "A half hour?"

"I'll see you then." She watched him saunter toward the stairs. They must have put her as far away as possible from him.

Fendall held up a cotton-block print gown that Adeline had before she went to Town. "It's not new, but if you're going to be tromping about, it will work with your stout leather half boots."

"Especially if we are going to be near a stream." She splashed water on her face and washed her hands.

She was tying the ribbons of an older straw bonnet when Frits returned. "You look charming."

"Thank you." Taking his arm, he led her down the stairs to the back of the house and onto a long, wide terrace that ran the length of the wing. On one side was a formal garden placed between the two wings, and on the other was a large expanse of lawn leading to the woods. Spanning the length of the house were a series of gardens and fountains. "I do not think I have ever seen such a beautiful and clever design."

Frits beamed with pride. "If you look closely, you can see the path through the woods. The stream is through there."

"I cannot wait to see it." Adeline was very glad she wore her heavy boots. Their mothers hailed them from a seating area of chairs, small sofas, and tables that appeared to have been made for the terrace. "What do you do with the furniture when the weather is bad?"

"It is stored in the winter, but once it's brought out, we cover them with oilcloths at night and when it rains."

Adeline was so excited about her new life, she felt like bouncing on her toes. This house was perfect. Frits was perfect. Then she realized something or someone was missing. "Where is Maximus?"

Frits grimaced. "He decided he was not home until he rolled in cow and horse dung, so he's having a bath."

She had not thought about that aspect of the country and wrinkled her nose. "Eww."

"Come. Let us drink our tea." He laughed. "You'll learn to sniff before you let him lean against you."

Frits was glad Max had made himself unsuitable for Adeline's company today. He had plans for her that did not include the dog. This was the first time since they were betrothed that he'd be completely alone with her. And even though they'd be wed in less than two days, they would be the longest days of his life if he couldn't make her his.

Holding hands, they ambled along the path, and he pointed out a number of wild orchids and found, to his delight, she was familiar with all of them. Finally, they reached the stream and glade, dotted with wildflowers. At one end of the glade, a folly built like a cottage stood next to the stream.

"Oh, Frits." Adeline started forward, then glanced back at him. "This is the most beautiful place I have ever seen!"

They strolled along the water and watched fish darting around the rocks until they reached the folly. "My great-grandfather built this for my great-grandmother to have a place to escape from their twelve children."

He took out the key and opened the door to a small entry that opened up to one large room painted white and decorated with soft, chintz-covered furniture, including a wide daybed. French windows filled the wall overlooking the stream, and the folly was set just far enough back from the water for an excellent view. As he had instructed be done, the windows were open, and lacy curtains fluttered gently on the sides of the windows. The square table was set for two, and a picnic basket was set in the middle of the table.

Adeline went to the windows and stood. "She was a fortunate lady."

Coming up behind her, he slid his arms around her waist and nuzzled her hair, breathing in the spicy scent of lavender and lemons. "Most of the follies on the property were built for wives. If you wish for one of your own, you may have it."

He fluttered kisses along her jaw and felt her lips tilting up. "If they are all as well furnished as this one, I might not need my own." She turned slowly in his arms. "We should make a survey of them."

Frits liked her idea. He hadn't visited most of them for years. "An excellent idea."

He found her lips and she opened to him, meeting his tongue with hers. Adeline moaned, and his already erect cock hardened even more. "Be mine."

She slid her small, perfect fingers up over his shirt and under his loose shooting coat, pushing the garment off his shoulders. "Yes."

For the first time in the course of his plan, he wondered if she even knew what he meant. She had started on his simply tied cravat when he held her hands still. "Do you know what I am asking?"

Her cheeks flared red, but her eyes held only a little confusion. "I think I do. You wish to have marital relations, do you not?"

She was going to be the death of him. "Er, yes, but do you know what that entails?"

Her gaze cleared. "I know a little. Lady Merton and Eugénie were very helpful in that respect. But I have been assured that what I do not understand, you will teach me."

Yes, yes, he would. He'd teach her everything. "That will be my absolute pleasure."

She had managed to untie his cravat and threw it to the floor. "Kiss me again."

If his shaking fingers were any indication, his years of practice getting women out of their clothing had left him unprepared for the reality of Adeline. The process was made even slower by his inability to refrain from kissing each inch of skin that was revealed. When he arrived at her breast, he thought he'd died and gone to heaven. Her full, creamy mounds were topped by rosy nipples waiting for him to feast on them. Palming one breast, he licked the other before drawing a tightly furled bud into his mouth. She tasted like herself, with a bit of honey added. There should be an ice in her flavor.

Adeline moaned and wriggled against him, pressing her bosom against his mouth. Then she tugged at his shirt and, obeying her command, he drew it over his head. "Clothes off."

He pushed her garments over her hips and they fell to the floor with a soft whoosh. He pulled off his boots while she stepped out of her clothes and removed her half boots. She stared up at him, unsure of what to do next, and, he thought, a little nervous at being naked before him. He drank in the sight of her small waist and generous hips. Reaching out, he skimmed his hand over her body. It was softer than silk or rose petals. "You are beautiful."

She blushed again, and he reminded himself to take this first time slowly.

"So are you." Adeline could not take her eyes off Frits's chest. Soft black curls covered his broad, muscular chest. Tiny, dark-rose nipples peeked out from the curls, and she wanted to taste them as he had tasted hers. She had been nervous at first, and was glad she had been told this might happen before her wedding night. Actually, she was happy this was not their wedding night. This was much more natural.

She placed her hands on his firm chest and rubbed her thumb over his nipple. Her sister-in-law was correct. She should take this time to explore her soon-to-be husband.

Moving her hand down, she savored the texture of his stomach until she reached the band of his breeches and stopped. "May I?"

He stood perfectly still, as if he had been frozen in place. His Adam's apple moved as he swallowed. "Yes."

She unbuttoned the placket, and his member sprang out, almost into her hand. Carefully, she reached out and touched it. It was as soft and hard as she'd been told.

Frits tensed. "In bed." He voice was low and harsh. "Now."

Adeline grinned to herself as he picked her up and carried her to the daybed, then captured her lips again. She broke the kiss and pressed her lips down his throat. "I love that you think I am beautiful."

"There is no thinking about it. From the second I saw you, I knew you were the most beautiful woman in the world. You captured me with your eyes." He took the pins from her hair and watched it fall. "As I said, beautiful." Then he grabbed the reins again, pressing openmouthed kisses over her chest until he reached her breasts.

When he drew her nipple into his mouth, heat and need once again flooded her mons. She wanted more. She wanted him. Adeline's hips lifted, and she writhed against him, searching for surcease, and he placed the palm of his hand between her legs and rubbed.

The tension grew when he placed one finger in her sheath. "Let go, my love."

His mouth was on her breast again, and suddenly there were too many sensations. She gasped, sucking in air, and suddenly the tension broke, shattering her to the winds. Before the tremors stopped, he plunged into her. The pain was sharp as he stretched her, and she could not stop from crying out.

Frits ceased, his forehead resting against hers. "How painful is it?"

"It hurt, but it's better now." The feeling of being stretched started to fade. "Try moving again."

"Wrap your legs around me. That might help."

She did as he'd suggested and he moved slowly. Soon the tension was building again, and waves of pleasure crashed through and around her.

"Adeline!" he called her name as he plunged one last time before collapsing off to the side and bringing her with him. He pulled up the blanket from the end of the bed and covered them. "Are you well?"

"Yes." She was overcome with a sense of peace and belonging she had never felt before. Making love had been everything she had been told it would be and more. It was no wonder no one was able to capture the feelings in words. "I am better than well. I could spend the rest of my life here with you, making love."

"We shall never leave." He kissed her temple, and held her closer. "The vicar will have to come here to marry us."

Laughter burbled through her at the image. "That would be a sight."

"Our mothers and friends . . ." He laughed too. "I don't think my mother would mind nearly as much as your mother would."

"Oh, dear. Can you imagine her face?" She wondered if her mother and father had anticipated their vows. It seemed a great many betrothed couples had.

Frits went on with a list of people who would have to come to them for the ceremony and celebration. "Maximus, of course, and—"

"Not Humphries." Adeline was in whoops, and tears flooded her eyes. "I do not wish him to see me in bed."

"I don't wish any man other than me to see you in bed." Frits kissed her hard. "Are you hungry or thirsty? There is food and drink in the basket."

She was, rather. "Now that you mention it."

After making sure she was well covered against a chill, he padded to the table and brought the basket back. "Let's see what we have." He opened the lid. "Ham, the one I told you about, our estate cheese, roasted chicken, our cook's seed cake, bread, pickled vegetables, probably my grandmother's recipe, and wine."

"I think whoever packed the basket thought we would be here for a long time." She flashed Frits a grin. "I wonder if they are expecting us for dinner?"

"I can assure you that they are. My mother mentioned it to me." He glanced at the daybed and shook his head. "I think we're better off using the table."

Adeline agreed. "Hand me my chemise."

He'd rather that she remained naked, but he did as she asked. Eating while unclothed would come later. He took the basket back to the table, and they unpacked it.

He was elated when Adeline declared the ham and the cheese the best she'd ever tasted. "I understand why the ham is so prized. We make cheese as well, but it is not as sharp as this. It is excellent."

"I still need to decide if we should breed our cows with the Friesian." He'd put off making the decision while he was courting her.

Placing her elbows on the table, she linked her hands and put her chin in the middle. "You are concerned it will affect the milk for the cheese?"

"Yes. It's not only the cheese, but the butter and cream as well."

Raising her head, she drank some wine. "If only you could taste the milk and the products produced from it before making a decision."

"Holland isn't far." Frits let his words hang there. He was certain that she was as much of a homebody as he was. Still, a short trip across wouldn't be too much trouble.

"No," she said slowly. "It is not." He was right. Adeline was no more eager to make the journey than he. "Then again, it would be good for the barony to find out if the breeds are compatible. You might decide that they are not, but you want the milk on its own."

"In that case, we will go. I have cousins in Holland I haven't seen for years. Maybe we can visit them as well."

"That will be interesting. I thought Frits was German, but it is Dutch?"

"Yes. My grandmother—the one living in the Dower House—is from Holland." He smiled at her. "She will probably be at dinner this evening."

"I wonder what time it is." He'd seen Adeline glancing around. But there was no timepiece here. He hadn't even brought his pocket watch.

"I'll look." He rose from the table and walked out to the shallow terrace. "It's going on six."

"We must be going." She touched her head. "Help me find my hairpins."

"I like your hair down." She shot him a glare. "Very well. I'll find your pins." Frits started searching. It was amazing how far they could go. "They won't start dinner without us. My valet will tell them to set it back."

Adeline was on her hands and knees, looking under the bed. The view of her round bottom had him getting hard again, and he sighed.

"What time is dinner?" she asked.

"Today, it's at seven. Usually it is at six. You may change the time to suit yourself."

"Not tonight I can't," she grumbled, and Frits had a hard time holding in his laughter.

Chapter Thirty-Four

Early the next morning, Adeline accompanied Frits to meet Gertrude. He had told Adeline that the heifer was five years old, but she acted more like a much younger cow. That must be because she had not been bred. The head cow looked at poor Gertrude aghast as she frolicked with the calves. "When will Mr. Fitzwalter come for her?"

"We'll have to take her over. If we don't, she might not get there. She's very canny. But to answer your question, I am not sure. He is still in Town, hoping to wed Miss Tice."

"If Miss Tice and Miss Martindale do what their sisters did, they will have a double wedding." Meaning twice as many mothers involved in the decisions. Then again, their mothers had been through this before.

He shrugged. "I suppose I will hear from him when everything is settled."

By midmorning, her father had arrived with Will, Eugénie, and the baby. Papa grumbled that Will had refused to allow him to stop by Whitehall on the way out of London.

That afternoon, Henrietta and Georgie arrived with all the news of the past day. Adeline discovered that the rooms she was in were all connected to those of her friends, and they had been given a parlor as well. Yet the day was so nice, they gathered on the terrace for tea, and Frits joined them.

After exclaiming over the gardens and the house, they settled down for a comfortable coze. "The most important thing that happened," Georgie said, "is that Lord Turner and Mr. Fitzwalter refused to wait until the end of July to marry."

"That is, when St George's has a time available," Henrietta interpolated.

Georgie nodded. "Then Lord Fitzwalter became involved and demanded that the wedding be held at his estate."

"That sounds like him," Frits mumbled. "Did he actually go to Town, or did he write a letter?"

"He wrote a letter." Henrietta frowned, showing them what she thought of such cowardice.

"Well, naturally, the world was coming to an end," Georgie continued. "Mrs. Tice and Mrs. Martindale told everyone their girls were inconsolable. And I believe her. When I saw the ladies, they both had puffy eyes, as if they had been weeping."

"But Mr. Fitzwalter saved the plans." Henrietta picked up the story. "Apparently, there is a village that belongs partly to the Turners and partly to the Fitzwalters."

"There is a market town." Frits nodded thoughtfully. "Years ago, there was a boundary dispute and a line was drawn down the middle of the village. The church is on both sides of the properties, which has worked out to the church's benefit over the years. The situation has benefited the town as well, due to the ongoing competition between the families to ensure that their side of the town is the most prosperous."

"The weddings will be held there," Georgie said.

"Lady Turner, Lord Turner's mother, will host the ladies before the wedding, which will take place in three weeks."

"Is it one wedding or two, if they are marrying at the same time?" Frits mused.

"You have as much of an answer as I do," Adeline said and her friends shrugged and shook their heads. "What is important is that the problem was solved."

A few hours later, Exeter and Dorie arrived, and Adeline had never seen her friend happier.

"Oh, Adeline." Her friend reached the top of the steps and hugged her. "I am so glad we could be here. Married life is wonderful!" She turned to Frits, and Adeline held her breath. "Lord Littleton. I wish you happy. You and Adeline are perfect for each other."

"Thank you." He bowed. "I see you have found your perfect mate as well."

"Yes." Dorie gazed lovingly at Exeter. "I have."

That evening, after dinner, the gentlemen brought their brandy and port and joined the ladies on the terrace.

Frits's mother strolled out holding a paper. "I have heard from Lady Normanby. Anglesey left for the Continent. He is required to write their solicitor at least once a quarter to prove he is still alive. Other than that, they do not expect to see him again."

"I thought he was going to try to behave as he should?" Mama asked.

Sitting next to Adeline, Frits took her hand and squeezed it gently.

Lady Littleton shrugged. "She does not explain other than to say that Lady Holloway went with him."

Creswell stepped out onto the terrace. "Viscount Turley has arrived. He will be down shortly."

"Thank you, Creswell." Frits heaved a sigh of relief. "I wasn't sure he was going to make it."

Adeline was relieved as well. Turley was standing up with Frits. She had asked Georgie to attend her.

When Turley joined them, he explained that he'd stopped at an inn and eaten. "Littleton dines at such an ungodly early hour, I knew I'd miss dinner."

Frits raised his quizzing glass and aimed it at his friend. "However, knowing you were going to be late arriving, we dined at seven this evening."

A stricken look appeared on his face. "I am sorry. I should have asked."

From inside the house, the clock struck ten. Mama rose. "I'm for my bed. Adeline, you should come as well. Tomorrow will be a busy day."

All the other ladies agreed it was time to seek their couches as well.

"Gentlemen, do not be late," Lady Littleton admonished as she went into the house.

Adeline and her friends reconvened in the parlor, where they found two open bottles of wine and four glasses. She poured one for each of them.

"Where will the wedding be held?" Georgie asked as she helped pass the glasses around.

"Here in the chapel. It is not used much any longer, but it is easier for the tenants to get here than to the town. After the ceremony, there will be a wedding breakfast set out on the lawn. It is tradition that the lord and lady join in as well." She sipped her wine. "I had wanted to start meeting the tenants before the wedding, but there was not enough time."

"They will love you." Georgie grinned.

Dorie and Henrietta agreed.

Adeline yawned. "I do not know why I am tired. We

stayed up much later in Town. It must be the country air." She rose. "I shall see you in the morning."

Adeline woke early but pretended to sleep as her maid laid out the gown in which she would be married. When she had shown the modiste the tulle fabric with seed pearls Augusta had sent from Paris when she visited there before traveling on, the woman came up with a design to use the fine netting over a Pomona-green silk gown. The effect was as lovely as Adeline had hoped it would be. Knowing she would be outside for much of the day, she had eschewed slippers and had leather half boots dyed the same color as her gown.

"My lady, are you ready to rise?" There was no fooling Fendall. "Your bathwater will be here soon."

"I am." She left the bedroom again. When she came back, Adeline was out of bed. "Why are you running back and forth?"

"We moved everything yesterday, and one of the younger maids did not hear the instructions that the items in the clothespress was to remain in this dressing room. Everything I need is here now."

"What do my new apartments look like?" It occurred to her that every time she asked about them, the person she asked changed the conversation.

A knock came on the door and her maid opened it. Two footmen rolled in a bathtub, and others carried buckets.

Fendall picked up the towels from where they were warming on a screen placed in front of the fireplace. "I am told the place where they can obtain the hot water is closer to your new chamber."

Adeline was going to ask about her new rooms again, but decided it was no use. She would see them later.

She was still in her wrapper when Georgie, Henrietta, and Dorie entered the room.

"We have things for you." Dorie held out something wrapped in paper. "It is blue."

Adeline opened the package to find a pair of beautifully embroidered blue garters. "These are lovely. Where did you find them?"

"I had them made." Her friend beamed. "My sister-in-law showed me a pair she had."

"This is something borrowed," Henrietta said as she handed Adeline the two gold hair combs Dorie had worn when she married.

Georgie gave Adeline a reticule that matched her gown. "I knew you had not remembered to have one made."

Next, her mother entered the chamber carrying a square, velvet-covered box. "I have been keeping these for your wedding day." She put the box on the toilet table. "They were your great-great-grandmother's on my side."

Adeline opened the box and gasped. Inside lay a necklace with loops of pearls interspaced with emeralds and a pair of earrings. "Mama, these are magnificent."

"My lady, you have to dress," Fendall reminded Adeline.

Her mother gathered her friends. "I will see you in the chapel."

"I'll be downstairs, waiting with your father," Georgie said.

Fendall made short work of getting Adeline dressed. She met her father and Georgie in the hall. "Where is the chapel? I have not even seen it."

"There are inner and outer entrances," Georgie explained. "We are to use the outside entrance today. People are already lining up to see you." That was something Adeline had not expected. "That means you will have to walk down the aisle instead of coming in from the side, like Dorie did."

It would be strange to be part of a promenade where she was the sole focus, but . . . "If I must, I must. I will not keep Frits waiting."

She took one of her father's arms and her friend took the other. Creswell bowed. "If you will follow me."

Georgie had not been exaggerating. People lined the path from the front door around to what had been described as a small chapel, but was much larger than Adeline had expected. As she walked with her father and friend, she saw most of the pews were already full, but her focus was on Frits. He was splendid in a dark blue jacket and breeches, a waistcoat embroidered with silver thread, and a perfectly tied, snowy-white cravat with a large, square, emerald tiepin nestled in the folds.

He smiled broadly as he gazed at her and mouthed, *I love you.*

I love you too, she mouthed back, and Adeline could swear that most of the women and girls in the church sighed.

When she reached the vicar, the church, which had been a buzz of noise, became so quiet, one could hear oneself breathe. People leaned forward in their seats, and the vicar began the service. She and Frits spoke their vows in clear voices, and when he got to the part about worshipping her body, she could not stop her cheeks from heating, which caused light chuckles from several in the church. Frits slipped on her finger a ring of gold set with a large square emerald that matched his signet ring, and two square diamonds on either side of the emerald. Adeline was amazed that it fit so perfectly.

Finally, they were proclaimed man and wife, and the church broke into cheers.

"I have never seen a wedding like this one," Georgie Featherton said as they went to the side of the church to sign the register.

"Neither have I," Adeline admitted.

"Wait until you see the festivities." Frits handed his wife the pen. She would be the first to sign. "They will go on until late tonight."

Adeline signed the register and handed the pen back to him. "Are we required to remain until the end?"

"No, we'll slip away quietly." Frits signed his name and waited for Miss Featherton and Turley to do the same before placing Adeline's hand on his arm. "Are you ready to brave our well-wishers?"

She looked as excited as he felt. "Lead on, Husband."

"I like the sound of that, Wife." By that time the church had emptied, and their tenants, neighbors, and friends had lined up outside.

The second they stepped out, children started throwing flower petals on the path that wound around the house to the lawn outside of the ballroom, and the adults shouted congratulations.

Long tables had been set up with all sorts food, and two multitiered wedding cakes were set in the middle of each table. Cider and lemonade were on two other tables.

"Look at those cakes." Adeline's eyes rounded. "When did your cook have time to bake them?"

"He had help. Ladies and women in the area contributed layers. The wedding of a lord of Littleton really is a community celebration."

"I can see that." She glanced toward a woman handing out small bags. "What is that?"

"Wedding gifts from our family to our guests."

Abney approached with large glasses of champagne, and Frits handed one to Adeline. "To us and a long and fruitful marriage."

Tears blurred her eyes as she lifted her glass to him. "May we always be as happy and in love as we are now."

"You cannot cry." He was only partly teasing. He knew the tears were because she was happy, but he couldn't stand to see a female cry.

"I'm not going to." She sniffed. "This is so much better than it would have been if we'd wed in Town."

Men, women, and children started coming up to them, and Frits introduced them to Adeline. He was happy to see that, as she had with their servants, she asked each person questions. Then friends of his and his parents had to meet her. Everyone who was present approved of her. After all the guests had had a chance to wish them happy, they cut the cakes.

Frits held her hand and did his best to appear to amble around. But his target was a small door tucked into the side of the house. Before opening it, he glanced around, making sure no one saw them, then whisked her inside.

Laughing, Adeline reached up and kissed him. "That was well done, my lord."

"It was, wasn't it?" He drew her into a longer kiss. "I think it's time we found our chambers."

"That in itself will be a surprise." Her eyes sparkled. "No one would tell me what they looked like."

Frits hoped it wouldn't be too much of a shock. He led her up a set of secondary stairs normally used by the family to avoid having to go to the hall by the main staircase.

When they reached the second floor, she glanced around. "This is much different from the guest wing."

"There are not as many rooms, so everything is larger." Frits used his key to open the door.

"You keep it locked?"

"Only because of my friends, who might decide to play what they think of as a joke." As a younger man, he'd done his share of wedding pranks and other things to a wedding chamber. "One would hope we'd all grown out of it, but it's better to be safe than sorry." He swung the door open to the large bedchamber. "This is it. Your dressing room and parlor are through the door on the right, and mine are through the door on the left."

At first, Frits held his breath as she looked around the room, but she was taking too long. "What do you think?"

She turned around and smiled. "That I will have plenty of room for the things I like to keep in my bed-chamber. It really is set up for two."

"That's always how I've seen it. I have never been able to allow myself to spread, as it were, to the other side of the room. I knew that one day it would be my wife's."

"Hence the empty bookshelf." Her eyes brimmed with mirth. "And the bedside table, and wall." She seemed more curious than upset.

He was about to open the door to her sole area when she turned her back to him. "Will you unhook me while I take down my hair?"

"Gladly." The other parts of their apartments could wait.

Chapter Thirty-Five

Eight weeks later

Frits entered Adeline's parlor as she finished reading a letter from her sister-in-law. "I am going to ride over to Fitzwalter's to see how Gertrude is faring. I'd expected her back by now. Would you like to come with me?"

If her husband had not appeared so serious, Adeline would have laughed. For the past two days, he had been going to the stables every few hours to see if the heifer had arrived. "I would. Give me a few minutes to change."

"My love, shall we take the carriage?"

"I think that would be a good idea." She adored riding and had been indulging daily, but this morning Fendall and Mrs. Hubbold, the housekeeper, had felt they needed to tell Adeline that she was breeding. Not that she was completely astonished by the news. She simply hadn't thought of it. Her courses had never been regular. Yet, once the women pointed out that she had all the indications of being in a delicate condition, she realized that her body had been changing. Ergo, she had to give up riding her horse for the next several months.

He had a relieved smile on his face. Had even Frits realized they were going to have a baby?

Once they arrived at Highend Hall, the Fitzwalter estate, they called on Mr. Fitzwalter and his new wife. She and Frits had attended the wedding breakfast, and been part of a few local entertainments with the couple. Both Adeline and Frits had to admit that marriage had improved Miss Tice.

They were welcomed warmly and offered tea. While the former Miss Tice poured, Mr. Fitzwalter asked, "Are you here about Gertrude?"

"I am." Frits's forehead creased. "Truthfully, I'd expected her back by now."

Fitzwalter grinned. "Once we have finished our tea, I'll take you out to see her." He picked up a plate of seed cake. "You must try this. My wife brought the recipe with her and is the best I've ever tasted."

Mrs. Fitzwalter colored with pleasure.

Indeed the cake *was* one of the best seed cakes Adeline had ever had. "May I have the recipe?"

The lady pulled a face. "I wish I could share it with you, but it is a family secret. I only received it when I married."

"I understand." Not that *her* family had secret recipes. None of the ladies had been that domestic. "I will have to visit more often."

"Well, then." Fitzwalter rose. "If you are ready, we can visit Gertrude."

Frits stood and Adeline followed suit, as did Mrs. Fitzwalter. The walk to the field where the cows were kept took a good half hour, but the weather was fine. They reached a fenced-off portion, and Gertrude was there, next to a young bull. Both had their heads down, chewing grass.

Adeline watched as they stopped every so often and rubbed their heads together. "Good heavens."

"I've never seen such a docile bull," Frits remarked. "Where did you get him?"

"From a gentleman farmer," Fitzwalter replied. "The bull's mother died, and instead of putting him with another cow, his daughters started to hand-feed the calf. Soon, they were making daisy chains for him and leading him around like a dog. To make a long story short, he became too tame."

"When we saw him," his wife said, "and after what John told me about Gertrude, I suggested we buy him as company for her."

Fitzwalter nodded and put his arm around his wife. "It was an extremely clever idea. She made a chain of herbs and grasses to hang around both their necks, and they became fast friends. To our delight, last week, they decided to take things further. I expect we'll have a calf late next spring."

"I never would have believed it." Frits shook his head. "I suppose she's all yours now."

"You're not the only one." Fitzwalter laughed. "My father said we were full of nonsense, but he's had to admit he was wrong."

Having met Lord Fitzwalter, Adeline could imagine the older man's chagrin. Then she took a good look at the bull. "Is he a Friesian, by any chance?"

"You've a good eye, my lady," Fitzwalter said. "He is indeed."

"Could you give us the name and direction of the farmer? We have been discussing the breed." She would not say more than that.

"Of course."

She wrote it down in her pocketbook, and the four of them made their way back to the house.

"Speaking of clever ideas," Frits said after they'd left Highend. "Yours was ingenious."

"Thank you. We can try the milk from the Friesian without having to journey to Holland." Now that she knew she was carrying, Adeline did not wish to travel.

"Indeed." He nodded thoughtfully. "And next year we will be able to sample the milk from the cross between our cows and the Friesian."

"Still, the most important thing is that Gertrude is happy." Adeline had been almost as concerned as Frits about the heifer.

"Yes." He glanced at her and grinned. "I almost forgot. I received a letter this morning from my shipyard manager that Mrs. Rymer has settled in, and he and his wife will keep a close eye on her."

"That is excellent." Adeline and Frits had set up an account for the woman to draw upon, but decided staying away from her would be the best thing for her. One never knew if they were being watched. "Eugénie wrote to me, saying that Mr. Rymer is on his way to England."

"That's even better news." Frits's look was so happy and contented, Adeline felt as if her heart could not contain its joy.

She touched her stomach. Their life was turning out exactly the way they both wanted it to.

AUTHOR'S NOTES

I hope you enjoyed Littleton and Adeline's story.

If you read *Enticing Miss Eugénie Villaret*, book 5 in *The Marriage Game*, you will already have been introduced to Eugénie and Will Wively. England ended the slave trade in 1807 under the Slave Trade Act. In 1808, the British navy established the West Africa Squadron, whose job it was to stop the transportation of slaves. These efforts were hindered by other countries that had not yet stopped the trade. It was not until 1833, under the Slavery Abolition Act, that they forced the slave owners in their colonies to free the slaves by paying the former owners the equivalent of twenty million British pounds over a period of years. As I state in the book, if a slave left the British West Indies and went to England, Wales, or Scotland, they were automatically free. However, if they returned to the West Indies, they could be enslaved again. Interestingly, if a slave from another Caribbean island managed to make it to one of the British islands, they were considered free. The British West Indies were the only islands that did not require legal or court documents proving the person's freedom.

There really was a smuggling trade between the Danish islands and the British ones. No one knows how many slaves were actually smuggled in to the British West Indies, but if it was discovered that a slave had been, the person was automatically freed.

Slaves also had certain rights, among them to be treated well. In 1811, a slave owner was convicted and hanged for murdering one of his slaves.

It is true to this day that under English law, a marriage that is legal in the country in which it is performed, it is legal in England. The only exception is having multiple wives (or husbands).

All the extramarital activity in this book did occur in the upper and lower classes. The Regency has been described as the 1970s but far, far laxer. Except for well-bred young ladies, of course. The middle class was much more moral in its views and looked down upon adultery or extramarital sex.

Weddings were very different then than they are now. Betrothal rings did exist, but they were also used as wedding rings. Brides did not walk down the aisle, nor was there a large, invited presence for the wedding in church. Usually, only the bride and groom's parents or guardians and their witnesses attended. However, anyone could come in and watch. The wedding breakfast was the huge celebration. Additionally, the bride would wear a gown that could be worn again later.

As always, if you have any questions or comments, please feel free to contact me. If you enjoyed the book, I'd love it if you joined my Facebook group: The Worthingtons. If you are interested in all things Regency, I monitor a group called Regency Romance Fans.

All the links to my books and social media,
as well as my newsletter, can be found at
www.ellaquinnauthor.com.

Ella